VANESSA AND HER SISTER

ALSO BY PRIYA PARMAR

Exit the Actress

Vanessa

and

Her Sister

❧

PRIYA PARMAR

BLOOMSBURY CIRCUS
LONDON · NEW DELHI · NEW YORK · SYDNEY

First published in Great Britain 2015

Va̶̶̶̶̶̶̶̶̶̶̶̶̶̶̶̶ter is a work of historical fiction. Apart from the well-known
act̶̶̶ people, events, and locales that figure in the narrative, all names, characters,
̶̶̶̶̶̶̶̶ incidents are the products of the author's imagination or are used
f̶̶̶̶̶̶̶̶̶̶̶̶̶̶̶̶ resemblance to current events or locales, to living persons, is
̶̶̶̶̶̶̶̶̶̶̶̶̶̶̶ rely coincidental

̶̶̶̶̶̶̶̶̶̶̶̶̶̶ is a̶̶̶̶̶̶̶̶ of Bloomsbury Publishing Plc
̶̶̶̶̶̶̶̶̶̶̶̶̶̶̶ Square
London
www.bloomsbury.com

Coventry City Council	
TIL*	
3 8002 02209 527 9	
Askews & Holts	Feb-2015
	£12.99

Bloomsbury is a trademark of Bloomsbury Publishing Plc

Bloomsbury Publishing, London, New Delhi, New York and Sydney

A CIP catalogue record for this book is available from the British Library

Hardback ISBN 978 1 4088 5020 6
Trade paperback ISBN 978 1 4088 5021 3

10 9 8 7 6 5 4 3 2 1

Book design by Barbara M. Bachman
Typeset by Hewer Text UK Ltd, Edinburgh
Printed and bound in Great Britain by CPI Group (UK) Ltd, Croydon CR0 4YY

MIX
Paper from
responsible sources
FSC
www.fsc.org   FSC® C020471

for
Tina and Nicky
who made growing up fun

and

for
M and D
who gave us the moon

CAST OF CHARACTERS

(as of 1905)

STEPHEN FAMILY

SIR LESLIE STEPHEN — literary critic, biographer, died in 1904

JULIA DUCKWORTH STEPHEN — his second wife, philanthropist, died in 1895

VANESSA STEPHEN (THE DOLPHIN, NESSA) — Julia and Leslie Stephen's eldest child, painter

JULIAN THOBY STEPHEN (THOBY, THE GOTH) — second eldest sibling, Cambridge graduate, law student

VIRGINIA STEPHEN (THE GOAT, GINIA) — third eldest sibling, writer

ADRIAN STEPHEN — youngest sibling, Cambridge undergraduate

GEORGE DUCKWORTH — child of Julia's first marriage to Herbert Duckworth

LADY MARGARET DUCKWORTH — his wife

GERALD DUCKWORTH — child of Julia's first marriage

STELLA DUCKWORTH — child of Julia's first marriage, died in 1897

FRIENDS

CLIVE BELL — Cambridge graduate, art critic

RUPERT BROOKE — Cambridge undergraduate, poet

LADY ELEANOR CECIL (NELLY) — friend of Vanessa and Virginia

LORD ROBERT CECIL — her husband, Member of Parliament

THEODORE LLEWELYN DAVIES—friend of Thoby, and
cousin of J. M. Barrie's 'Lost Boys'

VIOLET DICKINSON—friend of Virginia's and family friend
of the Stephens

E. MORGAN FORSTER (THE MOLE)—Cambridge
graduate, novelist

ROGER FRY—Cambridge graduate, curator of the
Metropolitan Museum in New York City

HELEN FRY—his wife, artist

DUNCAN GRANT—cousin and lover of Lytton Strachey,
artist

SIR WALTER HEADLAM—childhood friend of the
Stephens, classicist

JOHN MAYNARD KEYNES—Cambridge undergraduate,
economist

HENRY LAMB—painter

WALTER LAMB—his brother, Cambridge graduate,
classicist

DESMOND MACCARTHY—Cambridge graduate, journalist

GEORGE MALLORY—Cambridge undergraduate,
mountaineer

LADY OTTOLINE MORRELL—socialite, literary hostess

IRENE NOEL—friend of Vanessa and Virginia,
descendant of Lord Byron

MARGERY SNOWDEN (SNOW)—friend of Vanessa's from
the Slade School of Art, artist

JAMES STRACHEY—younger brother of Lytton, Cambridge
graduate

LYTTON STRACHEY (STRACHE)—Cambridge graduate,
journalist

SAXON SYDNEY-TURNER (SAXE)—Cambridge graduate, a
member of the Treasury Office

LEONARD WOOLF—Cambridge graduate, cadet in the
Colonial Civil Service in Ceylon

HILTON YOUNG—childhood friend of the Stephen siblings,
Cambridge graduate

Virginia Woolf
Asheham House
Rodmell
Sussex

2 December 1912

Dearest Nessa,

She arrived in an inauspicious brown crate. Your painting is smaller and rougher than I expected. Mrs Virginia Woolf in a Deckchair—what a marvellously blunt title. Without it, I am not sure anyone would know it is me given the empty face, but Leonard says he recognised the set of the shoulders right away.

Where shall I put your beautiful canvas? Leonard thinks the upstairs hallway. Would you choose when you come down next week? You know how I like it when you decide these things. You are still coming down?

There is an unrushed calm about your Mrs Woolf. Is this how you see me, dearest? The woman in the painting looks whole and serene and loved. Am I still lovable? Or have I undone that now?

No, my summer Dolphin, it must not be. Someday you will love me and forgive and we will begin again.

Your
Virginia

PART ONE

VANESSA STEPHEN

..

1905–1906

'Your letter was such a blessing.
Did I write you a very silly letter?'

(VANESSA STEPHEN TO MARGERY SNOWDEN,
13 AUGUST 1905)

THE PARTY

Thursday 23 February 1905—46 Gordon Square, Bloomsbury,
London (early)

I opened the great sash window onto the morning pink of the square
and made a decision.

Yes. Today.

Last Thursday evening, I sat in the corner like a sprouted potato, but
this Thursday, I will speak up. I will speak out. Long ago Virginia
decreed, in the way that Virginia decrees, that I was the painter and she
the writer. 'You do not like words, Nessa,' she said. 'They are not your
creative nest.' Or maybe it was orb? Or *oeuf*? My sister always describes
me in rounded domestic hatching words. And invariably, I believe her.
So, not a writer, I have run away from words like a child escaping a dark-
ening wood, leaving my sharp burning sister in sole possession of the
enchanted forest. But Virginia should not always be listened to.

A list. Parties always begin with a list. Grocer. Butcher. Cheesemon-
ger. I wish Thoby had some idea of how many are coming tonight. I
suggested to Sophie that she make only sandwiches. She said it was bar-
baric and flatly refused.

Neither Thoby, nor Adrian, nor Virginia would ever think of anything so banal as sandwiches or napkins or teaspoons. Mother or Stella
was always there to do that for them. Now I do it. I will speak to Sloper.

I am sure we should order more whisky for Thoby and wine for Adrian. And for the guests? Does Mr Bell drink whisky or wine? I can imagine him drinking either. I have no idea what Saxon drinks, but we have cocoa for Lytton, and I am sure that Desmond will drink anything we put in front of him and declare it to be his favourite. Virginia of course will drink nothing.

Later (eight-thirty a.m.)

The morning's heavy quiet was split in two.

'Nessa!'

Virginia was shrieking downstairs.

'Nessa!'

I ignored it. Thoby was insisting that she eat her breakfast, and Virginia, enjoying his attention, was refusing. Virginia, as a rule, does *not* eat her breakfast. But last week Dr Savage told us that eating is crucial if we are to avert another disaster. He was dismayed when Thoby told him that Virginia's room was at the top of the house. He suggested we either relocate her to the ground floor or nail her windows shut.

Scraping chairs. Slamming doors. The escape. Quick cat's-paw footsteps on the stairs, and Virginia barrelled into my sitting room without knocking and hurled herself into the low blue armchair.

'Ginia. I have asked you to knock in the mornings. *Just* in the mornings. Any other time, you may behave like the little savage you are and barge in,' I said without looking up.

'Nessa!' she said loudly. 'I am being *oppressed*! Thoby *forced* oatmeal down my gullet. *Libre Virginia!*'

The morning was off to a roaring start.

Later (after luncheon)

The interval before the second act. Adrian is down from Cambridge until Monday, and I will not let him out of the house until he unpacks his boxes from Hyde Park Gate. We moved six months ago, and they are *still* in the hallway. We walk around them like they are furniture. The servants shake their heads at us in disapproval. I can hear Thoby thumping around looking for his field glasses, and Virginia is out visiting Violet Dickinson in Manchester Square. Violet, older, calmer, and robustly good-natured, soothes her. And so we have peace.

A wobbly three-legged day. A current of expectation has rounded through the house since this morning. It races and puffs up the stairs, sifting through the bedrooms in a blur of undefined *something,* knocking us out of stride. Thursdays have become *important*, like a bump that defines a nose, or a fence that marks a field. Thoby's Thursday 'at homes' for his friends from Cambridge lend shape to the week. This will be Thoby's second at home—no idea why he chose Thursdays. He said Mondays were bulky and Wednesdays were flat. I do not mind. George and Gerald always try to frogmarch Virginia and me to a gruesome dinner or dance on Thursdays to meet the eligible young men of Belgravia and Kensington. It embarrasses our half-brothers to have such conspicuously unmarried sisters. George is less concerned about Virginia—at twenty-three she can get away with it—but at twenty-six, I am a desperate worry. Strangely, I am not worried. I hate wearing white gloves, and I always find the young men undercooked and sweaty. We were meant to go with George to a dance in Mayfair this evening, but I just sent round a note with my apologies.

I can't think what to do with the house tonight. Gaslights, which flatter everyone, or the harsh, unreliable new electric lights? Thoby, ever in favour of modernity, wants the electric ones, but they make Virginia and me look washed out and greenish as though we have been eating bad fish. My painting sits on the easel in the corner of the drawing room. Do I pack it away? Do I put away Thoby's books and Adrian's exam papers and Virginia's pens? Do I pretend that we four siblings do not live here? Stella would have ordered menus. Father would have received guests in his library. Mother would have sent out cards. We four will take our chances and see who turns up. Last week the last guest left at half past two in the morning. At midnight I told Sloper he could go to bed and Thoby's friends could see themselves out. Sloper looked appalled and ignored me.

Thoby's at homes have the soft, unpredictable feeling of a hat tossed high in the air. When we moved last autumn, not to a suitable address near the Round Pond in Kensington, nor to a pretty side street in Chelsea, but to the once elegant but now shabby Georgian squares of Bloomsbury, I did not realise what a shocking thing we were doing. Mother and Father's friends, feeling a sense of responsibility, tried to dissuade us from this bohemian hinterland, and of course George and Gerald objected, but we decided to ignore that. Because there is a sturdy beauty here. These Bloomsbury squares are set in their ways: no longer smart, no longer chic, they remain defiantly graceful. A good bone structure is hard to deny.

And what if people *are* shocked that we have no curtains and hold mixed at homes and invite guests who don't know when to leave? Only *we* live here, and we can do it how we like.

Just us four.

There is a lovely symmetry in four.

Mid-afternoon

I was in my sitting room working on my newest portrait of Virginia when Sloper came to tell me that the wine had been delivered as well as six crates of champagne and eight bottles of whisky. He was concerned, as we have never placed such a large order.

'And what time shall we expect Mr Thoby's friends?' he asked gravely.

What time indeed.

'Finished!' Adrian called up from the hall. He had unpacked the boxes. 'Nessa, I'm finished!'

Adrian still needs to be petted on the head and told well done as Mother always used to do, even though Mother has been gone ten years. Nothing is real for him until someone else approves.

'Wonderful,' I called down to him. Sloper winced and went downstairs. No one shouted in the house when Father was alive.

'Nessa,' Thoby said, strolling into my sitting room. 'Do you mind terribly? I think you and Ginia will be the only girls again. Lytton was going to bring his sister, but—'

'Marjorie?' I interrupted.

'Dorothy, I think. I always get the Strachey girls mixed up.'

'Is Dorothy the painter or the don?' I asked, pulling the canvas off the easel and tilting it to the light. It was still not right.

'The painter, but it doesn't matter because she isn't coming. We could ask Violet, but she is so patrician. She might make things stuffy.'

'Violet may be aristocratic, but she is not stuffy. You just think that because she is tall and unmarried. She is an eccentric. Stella used to say that Violet wore bloomers when she bicycled.'

Thoby, nonplussed at my mention of bloomers, came to stand beside me to see the painting. 'Are the shoulders a bit—'

'Wrong? Yes,' I said briskly.

'But the angle of her head is good,' he said. 'It is not that we *want* to invite girls, you understand. But you two live here, so—' He shrugged as if his comment were self-explanatory.

'Don't worry. It is much too late to ask Violet. Sophie is in a terrible mood and would never agree to make more sandwiches.'

Late (three in the morning)

They were invited for nine, and Thoby warned us not to expect most of them until after eleven, but a crowd of people arrived early. Lytton Strachey, his younger brother James, both down from Cambridge, Mr Clive Bell, Harry Norton, and Walter Lamb all trooped into the drawing room. They had been to the opera together and left at the first interval.

'*Andrea Chénier*. Giordano. Disaster,' Lytton said by way of explanation. He handed Sloper his hat and dropped into the basket chair by the window.

'You walked out?' Thoby asked as I poured Lytton his cup of cocoa.

Harry Norton and Walter Lamb had drifted to the far end of the room and were looking through the bookshelves.

'Yes,' James said, claiming the other basket chair. 'Lytton insisted we leave.'

'We *had* to leave. It was the most godawful cliché. Milkmaids. Shepherdesses. And there was a huge, puffy paper sheep on stage.' Lytton rolled his eyes. 'One must have limits.'

'The sheep was the best thing in it,' Harry said, settling onto the sofa. 'It was the singing that was dreadful.'

'Saxon saw it on Friday and told me that the fourth act is wonderful,' Mr Bell said, reaching for his drink. Whisky. I must remember for next week.

'Saxon has more patience than Strachey,' Thoby pointed out.

Nine exactly and Saxon Turner himself walked in. Saxon is never late. 'I, ahem, met your brother, ahem, outside,' Saxon said quietly to Thoby. Saxon prefers to speak to one person alone rather than address a room.

Thoby and I exchanged a brief look. George. The dance in Mayfair. I was sure he was annoyed that I had cancelled so late and had come to lecture me. Thoby quickly crossed to the door, hoping to intercept him, but he was not fast enough, and George stepped into the room. Hearty and obvious and unable to conceal his disapproval, George took in the scene. Six men and me in the drawing room at this time of night. We were suddenly playing by the old rules, the Kensington and Belgravia rules. I felt a slim wire of unease pull the room into a tense flat line.

'George,' Thoby said smoothly, 'come and meet some friends of mine.' He slowly took George around the room, making formal introductions. Lytton did not stand but offered up his hand like a Russian duchess. George's face flushed with insult.

'Thoby,' George said in a low, rapid voice, 'shouldn't the ladies have withdrawn?'

'Ladies?' Thoby said looking around. 'There is only Nessa. Virginia's not down yet.'

'You mean there were *no* other ladies invited to supper?' George said, his voice rising.

'No one was invited to supper,' Lytton added unhelpfully. 'We all just piled in afterwards. I am sure more people will pop along later, but I don't know if any ladies are coming?'

George's eyes bulged in outrage, and James shifted uncomfortably in his seat, but Lytton giggled and leaned forward to watch as if he were at a racetrack.

'It is hardly Thoby's fault, Mr Duckworth,' Mr Bell said, boldly stepping into the fray. 'We all dropped in unexpectedly, and Miss Stephen has been kind enough to make sure we are looked after. But you are quite right. It is late. We are imposing dreadfully and ought to be going.' I was amazed at how convincing he was.

'Sloper?' Thoby called downstairs. 'Would you get Mr Bell a cab?'

'I insist Mr Duckworth take the first cab,' Mr Bell said graciously.

'Yes, absolutely,' Thoby agreed. 'It *is* late, and George, you do have the farthest to go.' He led the way downstairs, and George could do nothing but follow him.

As soon as he left, the mood rose like champagne fizz, and Mr Bell, who had never had any intention of leaving, hurried back to the sofa and the party resumed.

•

Desmond MacCarthy, lean, shambling, and amiable, arrived and collapsed his long frame onto the sofa next to Mr Bell. Thoby questioned him about his newest article. Desmond has a tendency to put off everything, an unfortunate quality in a journalist, and Thoby has been trying to help him meet his deadlines. Last week, Desmond asked Thoby to lock him in his study until he finished his travel piece on Spain. It did not work.

'It was a poor choice of room,' Desmond explained, stretching out his long legs. 'There were so many interesting things to read in my study. It was an impossible place to work. Goth, we must find a more boring room.'

•

Eleven. Virginia and Adrian had promised to be down by ten, but of course they weren't.

I found them in my sitting room, arguing. They knew I would be back to fetch them. Adrian was being pedantic and trying to persuade Virginia to change into evening clothes.

'I do not see why I should wear a corset in my own drawing room,' Virginia said crossly. 'You can breathe. Why shouldn't I?'

'Because you are a *lady*, Ginia,' Adrian repeated.

'And therefore not entitled to breathe? Since I do not need air, I will swim around the drawing room like a fish. Then what will you do?'

Virginia logic.

I could hear the heavy front door open and close and the sound of voices and laughter drifted up as more people arrived. Anxious to get back downstairs, I quickly re-pinned Virginia's hair, smoothed her serge skirt, and clasped her jet cameo brooch to her blouse. It does not matter if she changes or not, Virginia is always beautiful.

Adrian stubbornly refused to go down without us and sat fidgeting in the blue armchair. Since he grew to six foot five, he feels awkward and oversized at parties. It cannot be easy to be the youngest and the tallest. Only an inch shorter, Thoby never looks or feels out of place. I pulled Adrian to his feet and tugged at his cuffs and straightened his tie. 'Lovely,' I said, hoping to encourage him.

•

By the time we rejoined the party, the drawing room was freckled with several more of Thoby's Cambridge friends, looking the way I always imagined Thoby's rooms at Trinity must have looked, with the intellectual young men draped all over the furniture. Their talk rang out with their affectionate university names for each other: Goth, Mole, Strache, Saxe.

Lytton Strachey had curled farther into his chair and was looking endearingly rumpled, with his round spectacles perched low on his nose and his frizzy red beard even bushier than usual. He was scolding sweet-tempered Morgan Forster about his novel.

'That was indecently quick, Mole,' Lytton said dramatically. 'You are meant to *suffer,* to *pine,* to *ache,* to *burn.* How is the work meant to be *art* if it arrives without *pain?*'

Lytton's own work, his unfinished fellowship thesis, is causing *him* considerable pain. This winter Morgan completed his first novel. It is to be published in the autumn. Everyone talks about writing a novel— Lytton, Desmond, and of course Virginia—but Morgan has actually done it.

Virginia had claimed the small velvet sofa and was sitting, silent and still, like a toad on a paving stone. I wished she would speak. I wanted Thoby's friends to see her dazzle the way she can when she chooses to rake the conversation into a leafy pile and set it alight. No one can burn up the air at a party like Virginia. I knew she was irritated that no one had mentioned her review of *The Golden Bowl* that was published in yesterday's *Manchester Guardian.* Father's friend Henry James wrote to her this morning to compliment her on the piece, and she had conspicuously propped the card up on the mantel. Adrian, recognising the problem, hurried over and congratulated her loudly, but that only made her more cross. Adrian has no sense of timing.

On the long sofa by the fireplace, Thoby was talking to Clive Bell about the Durand-Ruel exhibition at the Grafton Galleries. Only Mr Bell, wearing a beautifully cut tailcoat in the new style, matched Thoby's perfect ease in the room. Virginia thinks he is uncultured and blunt, and Lytton sometimes refers to him as 'Squire Bell' because of his penchant for hunting, and *everyone* teases him about his curly red hair, but I like his straightforwardness and the unhurried, fluent way he moves about a room. I stood nearby listening to him and Thoby talk of art. I had been to the Durand-Ruel exhibition twice, once with Margery Snowden and once on my own. Snow liked the pink-cheeked Renoirs, but I preferred the thick, muscular Degas. I knew Mr Bell was an art critic, and I was curious to hear what he made of the exhibition.

'Cézanne, Monet, Manet, Morisot, Pissarro, Renoir. Paul Durand-Ruel bought them all for practically nothing when they were first painted,' Mr Bell said. 'Incredible vision.'

'Does it take *vision* to understand *beauty*?' Thoby asked, tilting the conversation towards philosophy as always.

'Goth, it took vision to understand that they were the *vanguard*,' Mr Bell said with feeling.

As if anticipating my interest in the conversation, Mr Bell shifted up to make room for me on the long, low sofa. I sat as gracefully as I could and tried not to slouch.

'But does beauty always live in the vanguard?' Thoby asked. 'What if something is beautiful but never becomes popular? Would it still be beautiful?'

'Durand-Ruel *knew* that they were the next incarnation of painting,' Mr Bell replied. 'That takes a *visionary*!'

'Maybe he just liked them?' I said without thinking.

They both turned to look at me.

'Ha!' Mr Bell laughed. 'Simplicity is everything. Goth, your sister has trumped us all. That is the answer right there.'

I flushed with the praise. Not a potato tonight.

Friday 24 February 1905—46 Gordon Square (early—perfect light)

I waited for Maud to finish clearing up the detritus of last night and then brought my easel over to the window to work on my Virginia portrait.

A lovely room.

White walls. Right away I took to the white, white walls. Clean and punctuated with tall, fragile windows set in a light, straight row. This house has not such an anaemic leanness as 22 Hyde Park Gate. It is more generous with its proportions, a house that takes deep, pure breaths, lives on a diet of ripe melon and cold milk, and goes for brisk walks in the early afternoon. We front such a genial square. It is a square built for gardens and gossip and indiscreet summer evenings, with a curvy path slipping through its soft green centre. This square makes me feel part of the world and less as though the world were happening somewhere else.

Later (mid-afternoon)

George and Margaret just left. The lecture I avoided last night doubled in size this afternoon. Family quarrels are more tiresome than making amends, and so I will invite them to luncheon next week to make up. I will have to send a card. Our new sister-in-law is very particular about receiving an *invitation*—and of course we don't send out *invitations* any more. We should ask Gerald too. What would Mother and Father think if they knew that the siblings and half-siblings had split so cleanly into two camps? Duckworths and Stephens, unwound at the roots. It was not always like that. Stella was a half-sibling, and she was as much my sister as Virginia. But George and Gerald are not Stella.

And—I spoke to George about our funds, and he says that we should each have enough to travel next month. Ginia assumed I would go away with her and was annoyed when I announced that I was already planning to travel with Snow.

POSTCARD

THIS SPACE TO BE USED FOR CORRESPONDENCE

26 February 1905

Dear Woolf,

I have been dreadful. I received your letter before I left and had ample time to ship out my reply last week but didn't. Appalling laziness, and as there is no excuse, I shall offer none. Only my apology, which I send over the warm eastern oceans to you. Goth, Bell, and I went to the opera on Friday. Don Giovanni. We wish you could have come too. Please miss us? Letter to follow.

> *Yrs,*
> *Lytton*

To: *Mr Leonard Woolf*
    Cadet, Ceylon Civil
      Service
    Jaffna
    Ceylon

SERIES 8 NO. 6 SEASIDE DONKEYS AT BRIGHTON

1 March 1905—46 Gordon Square (late)

Tonight was our official housewarming. Our society debut. But I'm not sure I like society any more. And society certainly doesn't like trundling all the way to Bloomsbury. Everyone declared the house 'lovely' but bemoaned its location.

'So far from everything,' the Balfours said.

'But close to the British Museum,' said the Freshfields.

'Your mother would be heartbroken to see you here,' Aunt Anny said.

'It suits us,' Thoby said, closing the discussion.

Thursday 2 March 1905—46 Gordon Square (late)

Tonight's at home felt so *sincere* after the hollowed-china feeling of last night's housewarming party.

Last night the talk was about the *who* of everything, and it was dull. Dull. Dull. Dull. Who is marrying whom? Who is bankrupt; who is standing for office; who is having trouble with their cook; who is buying a motorcar? Dull.

Tonight the talk was purposeful, intentional. No one spoke unless there was something to say. When there was nothing to say, we made room for silence, like a thick blue wave rolling through the house. And then there were the arguments. Chewy, swift, *loud* arguments. I sat transfixed as the words sprinted through the room.

I watched Thoby argue with Mr Bell about art and Harry Norton and Desmond growl over a new translation of Racine. Lytton tried to provoke Morgan into a disagreement over publishing, but Morgan was too flexible to take up the bait. Then all of them pitched in and discussed the nature of *good*. Good in friendship, in art, in perception, in beauty, in words.

Snow was here too. She had meant to return home to Yorkshire for a few days, but I persuaded her to stay down in London another night so she could experience a Thursday at home. I was impressed by her composure. She surprised me by speaking about the difference between beauty and importance in painting. She had just read an article on the subject by Mr Roger Fry, the wonderful lecturer with the wild grey hair and the wire spectacles. Snow spoke, in her round, clear voice, with intelligence and conviction, and I sat back, feeling pleased that I had introduced a person of value to the room.

Virginia sat wrapped in weighted silence until well past midnight. Her reserve held fast until Lytton and Thoby began to talk about the death of Greek writers.

'Sophocles? Was Sophocles eaten by dogs?' Lytton asked.

'No,' Thoby said. 'That's not right. Aristophanes, maybe? And which one of them drowned?'

'Aeschylus,' Desmond guessed. 'I wish Headlam was here.' Walter Headlam is editing a new translation of Greek verse, but he has a head cold and could not come.

I could feel Virginia's gathering frustration. She has been studying Greek for years now, but I doubted she would correct them. I know she worries that her patchwork education at home does not hold up beside a university education like Thoby's.

'Sappho? I am sure Sappho drowned,' Desmond called out from the green chintz sofa.

'Sappho *leapt* to her death,' Virginia said, her voice cracked and low like a distant thunderclap. '*Euripides* was killed by dogs.'

Everyone leaned in to hear her.

'And Aeschylus?' Thoby asked, proud of her for knowing the answer.

'As prophesied, Aeschylus was killed by a tortoise that fell from an eagle's claws,' Virginia said without hesitation.

Later in the evening, Virginia found her pitch. Morgan asked her about her writing, and Virginia was brief, clear, and disarming. She spoke of rightness and beauty in the unfettered, clean phrasing she prefers. Her voice broke free of its rusted shell and slid like a deep river over rocks. I watched them watch her. She stands with them as an equal, even if she is afraid she doesn't. She looked particularly beautiful tonight. In the way a woman does when she does not know it.

Friday 3 March 1905—46 Gordon Square

A short note from Mr Henry James arrived in the second post. He has heard of Thoby's mixed evening at homes and wrote specifically to express his disappointment in my loose conduct. Virginia, it is assumed, sails under my colours.

MR SARGENT

5 March 1905—46 Gordon Square

'But why are you going to Portugal?' Lytton asked again. He had to speak up to be heard over the rain falling against the drawing room windows.

'Because I want to go to Spain,' Virginia answered, as if that made sense.

'Adrian wanted Portugal, Ginia wanted Spain, so they compromised and are visiting both,' Thoby said without raising his head from the newspaper.

Virginia and Adrian were leaving at the end of the month to travel on the Continent. They are an unlikely pairing, but Thoby has promised to go to the Lake District with Clive Bell and Saxon for a few days in early April, and I am going to France with Snow.

15 March 1905—46 Gordon Square, Bloomsbury

Snow, Thoby, and I went to see the great painter Mr John Singer Sargent in his studio in Sidney Mews. Snow and I studied under him at the Royal Academy, but my pen bolts at calling him anything less formal than his full name. His infamous portrait of *Madame* X hung in a prominent place. I have seen her several times and am struck each time by the artificial turn of her head. She is so *posed*. Striking, certainly, but the life in her seems to stem from her awkward, wrenching, haughty stance. I suppose that defiance is just the point he was trying to make?

I watched the practised, casual way the great man discussed his method but I failed to work up the nerve to ask him for criticism. I wanted to ask his opinion of my portrait of Nelly, still grandly called *A Portrait of Lady Robert Cecil*. The name feels stiff and Victorian. I asked Nelly if she really wanted to use the whole mouthful, but it seems she does. Or I suppose she does. In the last few years dear Nelly has become quite deaf and conversation is a struggle. Strange to think that she is only a little older than Stella would be. But Stella will always be twenty-eight.

Some days Nelly's portrait feels exactly, seamlessly right and others it slips and misses the mark. Does Mr Sargent fall in and out of love with his own paintings? I did not ask.

26 March 1905—46 Gordon Square

Ginia and Adrian left on the morning train. The day stretches out in front of me, empty and whole.

27 March 1905—46 Gordon Square

Thoby spent the morning marching about the house fretting about a hat that Adrian pinched and took on his trip. 'But your hat will benefit from a broader acquaintanceship,' I told him after breakfast. 'It will mix with urbane Spanish hats and come back lisping and tanned.'

'It will end up lost, stolen, smashed, or, worse, smelling of pork—everything smells of pork in Spain,' Thoby said with authority and went back to his book.

Now Thoby has gone birdwatching with Mr Bell. The house settles onto its haunches when Thoby goes; lays its head on its paws and waits for his return.

UNION POSTALE UNIVERSELLE
CEYLON (CYLAN)

4 April 1905

Grand Oriental Hotel, Colombo, Ceylon

Dear Lytton,

Travelled from Jaffna back to Colombo this week. They are recalling me and two other cadets to discuss ways to improve communications between the provinces. The summons took a fortnight to reach me.

I left Charlie-the-dog in the hands of my Sinhalese houseboy and am sure he will have gained a stone and picked up very bad habits by the time I return.

Has spring come to Cambridge?

Yrs,
Leonard

HRH KING EDWARD VII POSTAL STATIONERY

5 April 1905—46 Gordon Square (before breakfast)

Chaos. And dust everywhere. The mantel from Hyde Park Gate (one of the only things we wanted to keep from the house) is to be installed in the drawing room on the first floor, and the current mantel (thickset and literal) is to be dislodged and discarded. I had thought of moving it to Thoby's study downstairs but am afraid it might ruin the pretty, squared simplicity of that room.

Later

We dressed for dinner. It is becoming fussy and old-fashioned to change in the evening but I like it. I like the ritual grace of it, the sharp, circular breath of the fresh corset, the slim columns of lace and silk.

Thoby's friends call him the Goth as they think he looks like a gothic romantic hero, but in a starched evening shirt, crisp collar, white silk tie, and beautifully finished tailcoat, Thoby looks more like a monumental Elgin marble. Both our brothers are tall, but it is Thoby's golden proportions that give him that Acropolis look.

Even later (one a.m.)

Packing and cocoa. Packing in my nightgown. My toes grip the warm wood floor. I open the window. The square ripples with lilac. The chestnut trees lean protectively over the garden. The low grass is subtle and lush like a well-kept secret. Too much sensation. I close the window. The tautness of waiting. Curls of anticipation. Of travel? Of change? Of art?

No. None of these. The answer does not land like a bird in my hand the way I want it to.

Damn.

Waiting has become a habit with me.

A HOLIDAY IN FRANCE

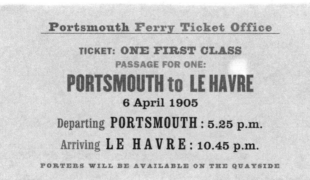

6 April 1905—Portsmouth (raining)

Where are they now? Seville? Adrian will be complaining of the heat, and Virginia will want to go bullfighting.

Eavesdropping. Two commercial travellers discussing riots in Madrid. *Worrying.*

POSTCARD

THIS SPACE TO BE USED FOR CORRESPONDENCE

9 April 1905

Dear Ginia and Adrian,

Waterworks have burst in Madrid and there has been rioting—turn back! All well here. Re-reading the Greeks in honour of spring and bicycling in the afternoons with Bell. Ginia, I borrowed your bicycle as my basket is broken.
> *With love,*
> *Thobs*

To: Miss Virginia Stephen
> *Poste Restante*
> *Seville*
> *Spain*

PS: Adrian, do you have my hat?

SERIES 12 NO. 6: BUST OF A ROMAN GIRL—THE BRITISH MUSEUM

---

10 April 1905—Hôtel de Ste Lucie, Honfleur (early—sky still pink)

I am sitting in the postage-stamp garden behind this crumbly hotel drinking cocoa from a handleless blue cracked bowl. Snow is painting on a bluff overlooking the harbour. I should be painting, or reading Balzac under a plane tree, but unromantically, I am doing our household accounts. They pass to the eldest woman in our family. Mother, Stella, and now me.

Was it right to let the house in Hyde Park Gate? Will those funds, plus the income from our inheritance from Father, be enough for our yearly allowance? And if it is enough now, will it be enough always? So far it has been all right, but Virginia's doctor's fees threaten to chip away at the capital, and George says we must be careful. Luckily, the rent in Bloomsbury is cheap. I meant to do the accounts before I left but ran out of time. It is absurd to be paying the bill for a butcher in Covent Garden when I am in Honfleur, but I am the eldest woman in my family, and this is what we do.

Virginia Stephen
46 Gordon Square
Bloomsbury

Hotel Washington Irving, Granada

11 April 1905

My Dearest Nessa,

Are you still in Honfleur? I forgot to write down your travel
dates.

Nothing went to plan. Boat broke and so took the train to
Lisbon. Is there anything so irritating as travelling without a book?
I left it in the last hotel, and there was not time to go back for it.
We saw only one church today and just two yesterday, but we had
a good proper walk this morning and saw: one woman who looked
as if she was late to meet her lover, two small boys selling turnips,
and seven nuns, so that makes up for everything.

I am second-guessing the article I sent in to Mr Maitland at the
Times. I should have sent the piece about Father and Tennyson or
the chunk about our childhood summers in Cornwall. Feeling the
thumping dread of a missed opportunity.

Are you well, dearest? Adrian has already caught a cold, and I
am quite concerned for poor Thoby, confined to bed in London
with diphtheria. His unhappy throat is swollen to three times its
normal size, and he can manage nothing but lemon custard and hot
chocolate. As you can imagine, he yearns for a carrot. Take good
care of yourself, my dearest Dolphin, and please do think of your
poor Billy Goat who is missing you terribly. I wish I had something
blooming and fresh to lay at your feet to show you how I love you.

Your
Billy Goat

PS: *Adrian has lost his luggage twice on this trip and his cases have only now caught up to us—naturally, but there is a piano in the hotel, so he is happy.*

PPS: *I look at the heading on the writing paper and it makes me miss the mechanical noises of London. Spanish traffic sounds so unbridled.*

Friday 14 April 1905—Hôtel d'Angleterre, Caen, France (the air smells of apple blossom)

There were Cornish fishing boats in the harbour at Honfleur yesterday. I see them and am dissolved into a thousand late days of summer fireflies and cool Cornish water sipping the rocky beach. It comes back wholly, sensually, in a way that no active recalling of a moment can do.

CARTE POSTALE

17 April 1905

Dearest Virginia,

Just a line to check that your meaty Billy Goat nose is still wet, your furry ears are tender monkey pink, and your sturdy mountain feet are as crusty and quick as ever in the chalky Portuguese heat. Are you feeling quite well, dearest? Sleeping well? Any headaches? Remember to cable Thoby or me at once if you have any of the old troubles. Promise me, dearest.

> *Your*
> *Nessa*

À: *Miss Virginia Stephen*
   Poste Restante
   Lisbon
   Portugal

SERIES 3 NO. 3—HONFLEUR LA CÔTE DE GRÂCE BY EUGÈNE BOUDIN

POST OFFICE TELEGRAPHS

Eyre & Spottiswoode, London.

This Form Must Accompany Any Enquiry Respecting This Telegram

OFFICE OF ORIGIN: Holborn, London

Office Stamp

International Cable

DEAREST NESSA. STOP. WILL MEET 6.15 TRAIN ON 23RD. STOP. I DO NOT HAVE DIPHTHERIA. STOP. VIRGINIA IMAGINING AGAIN. STOP. PLEASE BRING GRUYERE I LIKE. STOP. ALL LOVE. STOP. THOBY.

HN4GS7B—RECIPIENT MUST SIGN UPON DELIVERY

69 LANCASTER GATE

LONDON W.

> Trinity College, Cambridge—
>
> en route

Friday 21 April 1905

Dear Saxon,

I was delighted to see you last night, and I apologise for keeping you out so late. I can only imagine that an evening's deliciousness is soured when gainful employment looms in the morning. Did you make it in to the Treasury Office by nine?

Don't you think the Goth managed remarkably well last night without dear Vanessa's capable organisation? What a void those sisters leave when they fly away. Virginia's incisive, scathing chirps and Vanessa's level-hipped stability usually provide the contours for a Thursday evening. Do you suppose they know that the evening revolves around them?

Are you free to go to the opera on Tuesday? Do let me know.

> Yours,
> Lytton

Bureau De Bac De Le Havre

BILLET: UN **PREMIÈRE CLASSE**

PASSAGE POUR UN:

LE HAVRE vers **PORTSMOUTH**

23 Avril 1905

LE HAVRE DE DÉPART: 13.30 p.m.

PORTSMOUTH D'ARRIVÉE: 21.45 p.m.

LES BAGAGISTES SERONT DISPONIBLES
SUR LE BORD DU QUAI

Sunday 23 April 1905—46 Gordon Square

A train a boat a train a cab. There is nothing like the first bath after being abroad.

Later (after supper)

Mr Bell joined us for supper this evening. He and Thoby are still downstairs talking. He asked to see my paintings, quite directly and without preamble—as if he had planned to ask before he arrived. I was sure he was just being polite, but I surprised myself by unpacking the landscapes I did in Honfleur and Cassis. He looked at them, really looked at them, before he spoke. I like that.

Even later (can't sleep)

A slice of moon lights my room. Bright enough to read by. Bright enough to write. There is deep, true magic in nights like this. They are different from other, darker, more ordinary nights. I circle back to Mr Bell's comments. His suggestions were practical. He spoke to me about the unevenness of texture and the disorienting lack of depth in the landscape. He asked if I did it intentionally. Did I? No. I let instinct drive the scene. He waited, unhurried, for my answer. There is a completeness in his attention. It is not unnerving, but it is not familiar either. It is like a song one hears for the first time and wants to hear again.

Monday 24 April 1905—46 Gordon Square (Virginia and Adrian are back)

'So Snow was not too tiresome in the end?' Virginia asked pointedly. 'She wasn't too annoying or intimate? No awkward silences?'

'No,' I said carefully. Snow's gentle humour and level common sense have the uniform consistency of spring water. But it is a narrow precipice with Virginia. Too much affection given to someone else and she can topple over, too little and she gloats. 'It was quiet and not uncomfortable in the least.' I smoked a steadying breath of my cigarette. 'Of course, dearest, I would have much preferred to be with you.'

Later

Virginia received a letter from Mr Maitland, at the *Times Literary Supplement,* in the second post. He wants to call today and discuss her writing. Virginia is hoping he will invite her to be a permanent reviewer. I am crackling with harp-string nerves but trying not to show it.

Writing is Virginia's engine. She thrums with purpose when she writes. Her scattershot joy and frantic distraction refocus, and she funnels into her purest form. Her centre holds until the piece is over, and she comes apart again.

Later still

Mr Maitland just left. A mixed reception: while her latest book review for the *TLS* has been rejected—not academic enough—she has been invited to try again soon, and Mr Maitland has high hopes for her prospective novel.

Virginia's mood rocked gently at the tipping point. Relief. She won the day and fell towards the good of the moment.

THE NEW GALLERY

· ❦ ·

26 April 1905—46 Gordon Square, Bloomsbury

The exhibition opens today. I submitted my portrait of Nelly to the New Gallery over a month ago but never heard whether it was accepted. Mr Bell says that if it had been rejected, they would have sent it back.

'It probably won't be there. I think I would prefer it not be there,' I told Virginia over breakfast this morning.

'Nonsense. Of course it will be there, and of course we *want* it to be there,' Virginia said with brisk conviction, buttering her toast.

I was pleased to see that she was eating.

'Nelly loved the portrait. I loved the portrait, and you love the portrait. Ah!' She held up her hand to forestall my protest. 'You may not at this precise moment, but at some point between beginning it and now, you have loved it very dearly.'

I smiled at her. Yes, between beginning it and now, there have been moments when it pleased me. It is only now, when others are about to see it, that I doubt its worth.

I sipped my coffee. 'It might not be there.'

Later

Virginia set out after breakfast to get a catalogue for the New Gallery. This is Virginia at her best: loving, rational, engaged, sincere.

It *was* there. We stood in the gallery. Watching people watch the painting. It was exhilarating but mixed with an elusive bittersweet I could not place. *Nelly* looked lovelier hanging on that wall than she ever did resting on my easel, but she had grown unfamiliar in the weeks since I handed her over to the gallery. It is true that we do not understand the boundaries and dimensions of what we have created until it is consumed by another. I *loved* being an artist today.

Later (three a.m.—everyone gone)

The talk this evening was about me. *My* painting, *my* exhibition, *my* subjects, *my* work, *my* talent. Lytton, Thoby, Adrian, and Mr Bell went to the New Gallery this afternoon. Adrian and Lytton came down from Cambridge specially.

'On the first day?' I asked surprised.

'Of course on the first day,' Thoby laughed. 'When else would we go?'

'Well, you and Adrian, of course—' I said, moved that the others had joined them.

'Pfft,' Lytton said. 'Naturally I want to see it first. How else can I tell other people what to think?'

'Desmond and I are going tomorrow,' Saxon said. It was the first sentence he had ever directed at me.

'It was marvellous,' Mr Bell said quietly. He spoke as if we were the only people in the room.

Virginia did not say anything.

28 April 1905—46 Gordon Square (sunny and warm)

This morning my happiness was drenched by real life. I got entangled in a difficult conversation with Virginia. She was *determined* to discuss the morality of suicide—one of her favourite fallback subjects, but exasperating on a spring day when good things are happening. I was nervous as we were on the top deck of the Number 8 omnibus and her voice had taken on the specific, tinny shrillness that presages a mad scene—and this was not a good place for a mad scene.

We alighted near Green Park. I decided a long walk home might calm her. The traffic on Piccadilly clanged and kicked up dust, but behind the tall iron fence, the park lay in hushed splendour. Virginia noticed none of it. She was walking quickly, her long skirts flying and her hair slipping loose of its pins. Her small straw hat kept sailing off in the breeze. Twice I had to run after it into the road.

Up we went, along Piccadilly, past Devonshire House with its gilded animal gates, past the great stone cube of the Royal Academy of Arts, past the robin's egg blue of Fortnum and Mason. I knew Virginia wanted to stop in at Hatchards bookshop but it was better not to risk it. I had to get her home. When I steered her away from the glossy black doors, the tension in her body flared into rage, and I quickly asked the porter at Fortnum's to hail us a cab.

I know that chewing over a viscous, obstinate question is her way of recentring a day that is spinning out of her grasp. Trouble is, it takes *my* day along with it.

·

At home, she kept on talking; talking without stopping, talking for hours. She did not respond when spoken to and would not turn to look when we called her name. She just continued to talk. When she gets like this, her words rush and tumble like unskilled acrobats, landing up in a heap of broken nonsense.

A few years ago, Virginia talked for three days without stopping for food or sleep or a bath. We were still in Hyde Park Gate, and she sat up in her attic room speaking in low, frantic tones that rose and rose to shake the tall house by the shoulders. That time Virginia's words unravelled into elemental sounds; quick, gruff, guttural vowels that snapped and broke over anyone who tried to reach her. Her features foxed with anger and grew sly and sharp; her face twisted into something unfamiliar, and her hands bridged into white-boned nests. We waited until the third day before we sent for Dr Savage. A mistake. Virginia spent a month in the nursing home recovering.

Now I know better. After three hours of Virginia's unbroken talking, we sent for Nurse Fardell to come and administer a mild sedative—a draconian measure as far as Virginia was concerned. I stood outside the door and listened as Virginia evaded the nurse's starched ministrations. There was a huge glassy noise as the pretty bedside lamp crashed to the floor. Virginia howled, and the nurse spoke to her in a stern, efficient hospital voice.

Thoby came up the stairs with Mr Bell and, joining me in the hallway, asked what was happening. Virginia, not realising that she was in outside company, shrieked, 'The Goat's mad!' from inside her bedroom by way of a reply—her war cry. Virginia hates whispering and always reacts dramatically to sickroom voices. Mr Bell, not the least discomfited, drained the tension clean away by laughing a loud, easy laugh and politely enquiring if we had any other farmyard animals convalescing at Gordon Square.

Tuesday 2 May 1905—46 Gordon Square

The sedative worked, and Virginia slept for eighteen hours straight. Sleep rights her as surely as the lack of it derails her.

Virginia—irritated at her outburst—is now sulking, reading three books at once, each about Spain, and speaking only in Spanish.

Thursday 4 May 1905—46 Gordon Square

A busy at home tonight, but everything went wrong. Twice I showed my hand and revealed my staggering ignorance. Who knew Tacitus was Roman and not Greek? 'Listen to the name,' Virginia said, as if she were teaching a child to spell. I nodded but did not answer. Herodotus. Theodorus. Tacitus. I don't see it.

5 May 1905—46 Gordon Square

The house was quiet today. No one mentioned the date. It has been ten years. Thoby and I remember it all, but what of Virginia and Adrian? She was thirteen, and he only twelve. What do they remember? The long night before when no one slept? Beautiful, calm Stella, her hair pulled back in a blue kerchief, sitting by Mother's bed? Mother's dry, steep fever and her digging, racking cough? The doctor arriving just before dawn? Thoby was so angry that Father had not sent for him before. 'Your mother would not allow it' was all Father said.

Mother died just after eleven in the morning. Sophie had made roast chicken for luncheon, but we did not eat until after midnight.

Friday 12 May 1905—46 Gordon Square (late)

Virginia came in to talk as I was writing in bed tonight. I had to quickly pull the coverlet up over this notebook. Since the *Manchester Guardian* accepted her article on the inn in Andalusia earlier this month, she has been even more insistent about who is the *writer* and who is the *painter*. Letters are public and mine naturally get compared to Virginia's. My appalling spelling, my clunky phrasing, my mismatched metaphors rolling around like loose boulders, my handwriting that slopes uphill no matter how squarely I face the page—invariably, they do not equal Virginia's hammered prose.

And—Dinner with the Balfours tomorrow with George and Margaret. No doubt they have several eligible young men they would like us to meet. A white glove and seed pearl evening. It will be dreadful.

Thursday 18 May 1905—46 Gordon Square

Restless and unable to settle this afternoon. I know my demons are out in force because it is another Thursday, and after last Thursday's disaster, I am nervous. Last week my newly shored-up confidence broke away like wet sand. In four hours the serious, literate men will arrive, and while Virginia will amuse them with her circus acrobatics of witty, well-turned phrases, cleverly layered and underscored by her ruthlessly subtle mind, I will worry if the cocoa is served and if Lytton likes the fish.

I think in *mass*. In colour and shape and light and volume and texture. Not in words. Words delicately sewn around an abstract idea leave me feeling large and awkward and with nothing to say. *What is the meaning of good?* My mind asks, 'What is the colour of good? What size? What light? Where to put the bowl of poppies?'

Later

Not good. Wombat would not stop barking, and Lytton did not care for the fish. He would have preferred chicken.

1 June 1905—46 Gordon Square

Working on my portrait of Virginia and thinking about the effect of thickly layered paint. How to do it without losing the light? The translucence? I want it to be heavy but not dull, or perhaps thick but not heavy? Whistler does it and creates a finely blurred texture without the weight. I want the paint to mix right there on the canvas rather than safely on my palette. Homer's ocean in *Breezing Up* has the thickened quality, but the effect is a threatening underwater darkness rather than slides of light laid against one another. I wish for depth done with more paint rather than less.

I will ask Mr Bell about it.

5 June 1905—46 Gordon Square (a warm evening)

'But Nessa, do you think it's true?' asked Virginia tenaciously, sitting on the edge of the bathtub. The window was open, and I could hear the rumble of the Number 16 omnibus.

'I don't know, Virginia,' I said, wrapping my breath around a patch of calm. 'I only did a semi-rest cure, and I certainly did *not* fall in love with my doctor.'

The bathwater was beginning to cool.

'Elizabeth Robbins says it is inevitable,' Virginia persisted. 'A certainty.'

'Well, it wasn't inevitable for me,' I answered, gathering my hair in my wet hand and twisting it into a messy knot at the back. Virginia's eyes dropped unembarrassed to my exposed right breast as I raised my arm, and I quickly slid deeper into the soapy water.

'Nessa, do you think it's true?' she repeated in a mechanical, deliberate voice.

'It must be,' I conceded. 'If Mrs Robbins claims that in her—what is *The Dark Lantern*—a novel?'

Virginia nodded.

'Then it must be true.'

Satisfied, Virginia left me to finish my bath.

IN A CAMBRIDGE GARDEN IN JUNE

. ꙮ .

Sunday 18 June 1905—Grantchester Inn, Cambridge

'Virginia?' Lytton said, offering her a sugar bun. 'Mmm. No. I thought not.' Lytton wiped his fingers on one of the blue napkins and replaced the bun in the basket.

They are so alike in their determined fastidiousness, I thought, watching them sitting side by side on the riverbank. Brilliant, awkward, delicate, charming fusspots. They have both fastened onto this idea of calling those in our closest circle of acquaintance by their Christian names—not just when referring in conversation, which we already do anyway, but in *person*. It has always been easy to be familiar with my female friends such as Nelly and Snow, but I am finding it challenging in mixed company. Mr Strachey is Lytton—but that is no effort, as Lytton is such a thin, pressed name and suits him so well. Flamboyant, dainty, and usually lovesick, Lytton is a hypochondriac who is always ill or reading French literature and never shies away from outrageous topics. It would be impossible to be formal with him when he is so determined to be *informal*.

I do not want to seem fusty and Victorian and am trying to remember to use Christian names but I keep misstepping. Yesterday I offered *Mr Bell* tea, sandwiches, and finally an umbrella. Virginia wished I would sit down and not fuss. *Clive* feels so personal, and the nature of the name is so loose and abrupt—like sliding on silk down a grassy hill and landing with a gentle thump. He never corrects me, nor prompts any untoward intimacy, and he keeps calling Virginia and me 'the Miss Stephens'. But my Miss Stephen is gentler, softer, more lit by sunlight and fragranced with honeysuckle than Virginia's dusty, bookish-sounding Miss Stephen. Terrible and meaningless, but I am pleased to be the more endeared for once.

I closed my eyes to the afternoon sunshine. Getting Virginia to Cambridge had been like moving a pound of ants. She became convinced that the train would derail, the luggage would be stolen, Wombat would get lost, Thoby would fall ill, she would catch it—and on and on. She can do that as she knows I will take up the slack, arrange the tickets, see to the luggage, find the porter, water the dog, speak to the servants, and pack the sandwiches—and of course I do.

Turning away, I watched as a pair of fat, curvy swallows dipped and fell through the summer sky.

Later—Grantchester Inn (eleven p.m.)

The talk at supper centred on the Apostles—who is and who isn't. I knew the Apostles were an elite, strictly by invitation, all-male (naturally) debating society of the brightest young men in the university. But I didn't know they were called the Apostles because there can only be twelve members at Cambridge at one time, although old members seem to stay involved for life. Lytton told me that the art critic Mr Roger Fry still comes back for meetings when he is in England. Thoby says that Desmond, Morgan Forster, Lytton, Saxon, and Mr Leonard Woolf, who is now a cadet in the Ceylon Civil Service, are all Apostles. Apparently Lytton's friend, the hugely brilliant Mr Maynard Keynes, who is reading economics at King's, just joined them as well. Thoby does not seem the least bothered not to have been asked, but I think the subject makes Adrian uncomfortable.

19 June 1905—Grantchester Inn

At the inn to change into a warmer frock and then tea with Walter
Headlam and his protégé, the beautiful Mr Rupert Brooke, who is another of Thoby's sparkling university friends. Mr Brooke's flexible skin
is smooth like rosebud china, and his glossy hair sits in heavy gold
chunks. His cloudy blue-eyed expression is distant, and his bearing is
aloof. At luncheon, I worried I was boring him and stopped talking mid-
sentence. He did not pick up the thread of the conversation, and we sat
in strained silence until Thoby swept him off for badminton on the lawn.

And—Lytton's cousin, the painter, Mr Duncan Grant, another slim,
beautiful, elfin man, has joined our party. Lytton will bring him to supper.

Later (two a.m., crickets outside)

It all came together tonight—the way one hopes an evening will do.
Virginia, when she chooses, can unify a party the way a comet does. She
never missed. Her words fell light as cream, and her high-boned face
invited rather than challenged. She was just enough. She was beautiful.

I sat back and watched as all the bright young men in the room fell
in love with her.

And—It was good to have another artist in the room. Duncan's hands
are long and soft, with a small, neat callus on his thumb from holding a
brush—the painter's hallmark. I felt it when he shook my hand.

21 June 1905—46 Gordon Square, Bloomsbury (hot)

Home, and I have begun sketching for another portrait of Virginia (a
small oil). This one is a simple composition: just Virginia seated in the
shabby green wing chair, her face quarter-turned to the right and resting
in her open hand.

The pink dusk brushed the moment with nostalgia. I remembered
Virginia sitting in that chair when it lived by the fireplace on our nursery
floor at Hyde Park Gate. She would sit just that way and wait her turn as

Nanny or Stella brushed my thick, tangled hair first. Virginia always wanted to go second. She said she loved to watch me getting my hair brushed.

She posed for an hour this evening, until the June light failed. Her eyes closed in comfort, and her face settled into her hand in a way it never does when she is in conversation. Her fine hair, a paler brown than mine, was swept back from her elliptical face into a loose knot and lay in the shallow curve of her long neck. She did not speak nor try to break the moment but kept impossibly still. When Virginia knows I am watching her, she does not try to be anywhere else.

UNION POSTALE UNIVERSELLE

CEYLON (CYLAN)

23 June 1905

Jaffna, Ceylon

Lytton,

Civilisation has found its way to my doorstep. Today my Sinhalese houseboy brought in my tin-lined crate containing my Voltaire, Johnson, Spenser, Herbert, Elton, Galsworthy, Trollope, Dickens, and Tennyson. I had given up hope it would ever reach me.

Elton's verses loop round my thoughts. 'Luriana Lurilee', like a summer hoop on a warm gravel drive. The Goth always recites it in June. I miss the restrained green of an English summer. Will the strangeness of this country always shock me?

Package of semi-finished prose that I am semi-pleased with to follow.

Yours,
Woolf

FLOWERS AT THE DOOR

Monday 3 July 1905—46 Gordon Square (a hot, close day)

The card was simple. Just his name and mine. No 'compliments'. No 'thanks'. No reason.

'Hothouse,' said Virginia, sniffing the fresh blooms.

'Mmm.'

'But you prefer wildflowers,' Virginia said.

'Mmm.'

Later (four p.m.)

It is an afternoon for Blake. Coleridge is too long-winded, Byron too close to the fleshy surface, Keats too mopey, and Shelley too soft. I want the thundering, ripped edge of Blake. Pacing in the garden, in my studio, down the long hall as if to the beat of a drum.

I left without explanation and took myself for a walk to Green Park. The fat bumblebees stepped on the early summer flowers, and two boys in matching caps were flying a white, white kite.

He does. He doesn't. He can't. He won't. Why would he? How would I? My mind folded and refolded the questions. The boys tipped their heads back to see the white kite sail over the trees, and their caps fell off.

Clive as a suitor. I sat on a damp wooden bench. Virginia will say that Clive is prosaic. She will compare him to Thoby's clean, marble nobility and find him meaty and overcooked. Why should I care what she says? What anyone says? Why indeed, and yet I do. It is a weakness. Thoby likes him enormously, and that counts for much. That said, I am not sure Thoby would rank him as a gentleman; *gentlemen* do not come from families who have *earned* their fortune and *built* great mock Jacobean heaps in the country. My Duckworth half-brothers will look down their noses at his lack of connection, but then George is getting anxious that I marry *someone* so maybe he would not mind? Lytton, I know, disparages Clive's noisiness, his sportiness, his indelicate energy, his new money and vulgar house, but enjoys Clive's company despite his complaints. Everyone enjoys being with Clive. In conversation, he is like the dancer who lifts the ballerina with great, invisible skill. He makes the lifted partner feel beautiful.

And me. What do *I* think of Clive?

I like him. But it stops there. I do not think I could love him. I remember Stella when she decided to marry Jack. I watched her with the critical eyes of a younger sister but I could find no flaw in her certainty. She was alight. She was sure. She *recognised* him. He was hers. She had been waiting for him. I do not recognise Clive. He is not mine.

•

Even after all this time I wait for Mother's firm hand on the door handle, for Stella's light, quick step in the hall. I keep my questions planted in a tidy hedgerow, in readiness for them. But now I am the sureness, the footstep, and the others keep their questions for me.

•

Flowers on my desk. They need not present a dilemma. They need only bloom, wilt, and go away. Dinner party tonight with George and

Margaret at her parents', Lord and Lady Carnarvon's great house in Bruton Street. I am sure I will be seated next to—

Much later (eleven p.m.)

We're back. No idea who I thought I would be seated next to. In fact, I was seated next to a pompous, braying man whose name I can't remember. I have no patience for these formal evenings any more. Tonight the butler stood by the door like a sentry and belted out the name of each guest upon arrival. That is how it was done when we were young, but now it strikes me as ridiculous.

All the wit and laughter eddied around Virginia, at the other end of the table. She can be so charming when she chooses to be.

I should go and help Virginia sort her seed pearls from her hairpins. Mother left her the four beautiful blue enamelled hairpins she always wore, and I am terrified Virginia will lose one. She always leaves her things in a tangle on the floor.

4 July 1905—46 Gordon Square

I had no idea Clive's flowers had upset her so much. I thought if I brushed the topic aside, it would disappear like dust and Virginia would forget about it. I know she is terrified I will get married, just as I am afraid that Thoby will get married. As soon as one of us goes, the thing unravels and the whole of us comes apart. But I thought she would realise that *Clive* could never hurt us. I would never give the four of us up for Clive. How could I?

I misread her mood yesterday.

'Nessa!' Virginia banged the front door shut. 'No, no, Sloper, I want to give them to her myself. Nessa!'

'In here, dearest!' I wiped my hands on the old blue cloth and stood back to look at the painting. The nose. I hate doing faces—the inexactitude. Better not to define them at all.

'For you.' Virginia held out a bunch of fresh-smelling wildflowers. 'To replace those hothouse impostors,' she said, frowning at Mr Bell's flowers in the blue vase.

'They are lovely, dearest,' I said, taking the prickly bundle. Dirt still clung to the roots.

Maud put them in the green glass vase.

'Place of honour, Nessa,' Virginia said. And so Mr Bell's flowers were moved to the windowsill. Wildflowers preside over my desk.

A THURSDAY EVENING AT HOME

Thursday 6 July 1905—46 Gordon Square (midday)

The birdwatching party has returned. Thoby brought me one of his beautiful jay bird sketches, this one with a pale touch of morning blue on its wing. Now I have three bird drawings from him. A triptych.

I want to tell him about Clive's flowers, but the moment has passed. I put the card inside my copy of *Middlemarch,* and Maud threw the flowers away when they began to wilt. Hothouse flowers never last long. Clive is coming to Thoby's at home tonight. I am worried I will be childish and awkward and avoid him.

And—Virginia is *finally* wearing her new spectacles, turns out they were in the china inkpot on her desk.

Later—4.15 p.m. (guests invited for nine)

'Nessa!' Thoby called from the bathtub. 'Did you tell Sophie how many?'

'I don't *know* how many,' I said from my sitting room. After working on my Virginia portrait all day, I was cleaning my brushes. I rinsed the turpentine from the bristles as Thoby counted aloud.

'Lytton, Lytton's cousin Duncan, Lytton's friend, Mallard something, Bell, Desmond, Saxon, Hilton Young, Lady Ottoline, I think.

What is that, eight, plus us, so twelve?' Thoby's voice was muffled, and I was sure I had some of the names wrong.

'Mallard? Like a duck?' I asked, coming into the hallway to stand outside the bathroom door.

'Duck?' said Virginia, running lightly up the stairway. 'Did Thobs bring a duck home?'

'No! For dinner tonight!' Thoby shouted from the tub.

'You killed a duck! Thobs, you are only supposed to *watch* the birds!' Virginia shouted back.

I knew she knew exactly what he meant. When Virginia is in a good mood, she enjoys hysterics. It is when she is quiet that one should be careful. The stillness that presages the squall.

'If I had known you were going to kill wildlife,' Virginia continued loudly, 'I would have hidden your shoes.'

Thoby's bath ended in defeat. I could hear his sigh of resolve and the thick thud of his book hitting the white-tiled floor.

Later—five a.m.

They have gone, and I am too finely tuned to sleep. It all came off very well. Virginia was loose and laughing instead of taut and bright. She spoke earnestly to Desmond about the eleven new pens she tried this week. Virginia is passionate about good pens.

Lytton's cousin Duncan Grant, a quiet, observant person, was a focal point. Without trying, he grounds, pulling interest and conversation to him like a cape. Lytton is obviously half if not wholly in love with him, and everyone else just wants to see Duncan made happy. When you meet him, his well-being instantly becomes your concern. Unusual that he can accomplish so much by doing so little.

Despite my worrying, I was not awkward with Clive at all. We stepped out onto the shallow balcony and talked of last winter's Whistler exhibition, and painting lemons in Paris and flowers in Berkshire and picnicking on rocky beaches in Studland and reading

Victorian novels on trains, but were interrupted when Lytton called us back into the room.

I never found the right moment to thank him for the flowers.

And—'Mallard' turned out to be Maynard Keynes, Lytton's young economist friend from Cambridge—with whom I understand him to be occasionally involved? But then, I may be wrong. I often am.

69 LANCASTER GATE
LONDON W.

7 July 1905

Dear Woolf,

These Gordon Square evenings always start off with a delicious twinge of awkwardness, a hesitant lining up at the starter's marks. Throats are cleared, equipment checked, strings tightened, shoulders set, and we are off!

Each in our own way tries to pretend away such bourgeois discomfort. The Goth muscles through it in his large-scaled, country house charm sort of way, robustly enquiring after books and health. Saxon, blinking into the middle distance, adopts the air of a man who does not expect to speak or be spoken to. I know he must communicate with people all day long at the Treasury, but I can't picture it. Virginia rises above it like a bony wraith waiting impatiently for a good reason to come down. Desmond, unhurried and late, sits on the farthest sofa and stretches forward his loosely jointed limbs. I am sure he spends the evening hoping that no one will ask about whatever article he has failed to turn in this week. I sit in one of the basket chairs by the tall windows looking over the square and do my best to say shocking things. All assembled, we begin.

Darling Duncan—a new initiate—is urbanely unbothered by the tension. My dear, there is ferocious tension—a paramount need to say important *things and discuss* worthy *subjects: Good, Beauty, Truth—all very Keatsian. The stakes are high. One feels quite gladiatorial stepping into this arena of ideas. It is not an easy win. A subject is introduced but often flames out. Another is offered, volleyed, but fails to catch. But from these clipped efforts grows a rhythm, an unshelling, a feeling of group endeavour. Eventually the air takes, and the evening finds its shape.*

Bell, usually so bluff and unflappable, has been out of step recently. I met him last night on my way to Gordon Square. I do not often bump into him, as he approaches from King's Bench Walk and I come from Gray's Inn Road, but yesterday I found him lurking in the square behind a boxwood hedge. We stood in the shadows like assassins and he told me the source of his agitation. It is Vanessa, the Goth's sister. It is, I think, obsession rather than love but he insists it is the one wrapped in the other. He is determined to act despite almost certain failure. He sent flowers that were either ignored or misconstrued and then were elbowed out by some of Virginia's meadow weeds. He is now in search of a more telling declaration and is talking about armfuls of roses. He might have remained in Paris overlong.

I do see it. Vanessa is an ocean of majestic calm even if she does not know it. Virginia envies her sister's deeply anchored moorings. Nessa is powered by some internal metronome that keeps perfect time, while the rest of us flounder about in a state of breathless, pitching exaggeration, carried by momentum rather than purpose. I do not see her accepting Bell, but I was touched by his earnest, lemming-like determination.

Must go and nap as the afternoon is so hot.

Yours,
Lytton

Saturday 8 July 1905—46 Gordon Square

Clive stopped by to see Thoby again today. The third time since Thursday. Our conversations are broken, short, and familiar. Great swathes of a subject go unsaid but are understood just the same. We spoke of *Wings of the Dove*.

'So much more *there* than in *The Ambassadors*,' he said while he was waiting for Thoby to come down. 'I understand how Kate could risk him in order to keep him. She believes that if they really love each other, they can go through anything. The thing with Milly wouldn't matter. Shouldn't matter.'

'But how could it *not* matter?' I interrupted him. 'She loves him. How can it be irrelevant?'

'James comes back to that subject, doesn't he?' Clive said, leaping up to pace the drawing room. 'Look at *The Golden Bowl*.'

I was aware of Virginia listening. Books are her domain.

.

We speak only for a moment or two while he is here, but once he goes, I press Thoby for news of him. What am I hoping to discover?

And—I have been thinking. Since we have already shocked our more conservative family and friends with our racy, mixed Thursday literary at homes, perhaps we should take it further and have a Friday evening club for artists?

Later

Thobs says that Clive hated the Watts exhibition at the Academy. So did I. I feel of a pair. But I do not feel a certainty. I cannot see my life ahead with this man, or any man, really. But then, I do not imagine myself becoming a spinster. I thoughtlessly assume I will have a husband and children, but I do nothing to make that happen. I do not understand how one gets from here to there.

Neither of us has mentioned the flowers. Perhaps he has forgotten?

46 GORDON SQUARE

BLOOMSBURY

TELEPHONE: 1608 MUSEUM

Sunday 9 July 1905

Dearest Snow,

A dullish week. My painting feels flat and obvious, the brush leaden, the paint slushy and thick. The rich colours of the square turn muddy and pedantic on my canvas. I am waiting for something.

I am thinking about starting a Friday evening club for artists. Much like Thoby's Thursdays, but I am hoping we can show our work as well. What do you think? Who from the Academy and the Slade would you suggest? I am sure many of Thoby's Thursday evening guests would be happy to reappear on Friday. It could begin when we return from Cornwall.

Would it draw you to London?

Your
Vanessa

10 July 1905—46 Gordon Square

Luncheon at Rules with Thoby (who had to leave early), Violet Dickinson, and Virginia. I always forget how very tall Violet is. She is at least six feet and sturdily built but so rooted in herself. Her gestures are large, and her gait has a musical swing. Although she is well past forty, people turn to watch her when she walks through a room.

Violet was able to fix Virginia's twisted spectacles and then took her off to the powder room to reassemble her messy hair. Thoby and I were left at the table awash in a rare moment of comfortable sibling quiet. I love this restaurant. I love its bookish history and practised indifference. Thoby says that Dickens, Thackeray, and Henry Irving all came here. Knowing that makes a room more fun.

But lunch on the whole was not fun. It was *trying*. When with Violet, Virginia tends towards baby talk. Virginia has pet names for everyone, but then I suppose I do that too. I am her Dolphin, her Maria, her Nessa, and she is my Goat, my William, my Billy, my Apes. While my pet names can be taken or left, Virginia's are serious. It is her way of making herself singular, memorable, lovable.

It was a tricky atmosphere. Virginia sulked over Violet's impending trip around the world. Panic skipped through the conversation. Violet settles her so much better than I do. Sometimes even better than Thoby can. But then Violet has had so much practice. Virginia's vitriol towards me during her terrible breakdown last year was more than I could manage, but I still regret packing her off to Violet. I know Violet's big-bodied reassurance sets Virginia on her feet while my frantic flappings knock her flat, but to think of that time makes me twist in discomfort. Remembering how I palmed her off like a library book, or a fish, unhooked and thrown back into the lake. I was relieved to be unburdened of Virginia and able to get on with the business of moving into the new house—horrible of me. Virginia sensed my relief and took to shrieking unflattering things about me from her bedroom window. Now when I am with Violet, I suffer waves of embarrassment thinking of all she has heard of me.

Virginia feels no such discomfort. Her breakdown was medical and her ranting unavoidable and so not shameful. I watch the easy way Violet talks with her—without fear of misstep.

UNION POSTALE UNIVERSELLE

CEYLON (CYLAN)

11 July 1905

Jaffna, Ceylon

Lytton,

I was promoted to Assistant Government Agent of the Hambantota District. Charlie-the-dog is pleased. I am no longer a lowly cadet

*and can afford to buy him better cuts of meat. I thought I would be
happier. Instead I am still waiting for the puzzle pieces to fit—for a
sense of achievement and commencement. I lack the feeling of
rightness we enjoyed at Cambridge. Right place. Right purpose. I
am increasingly certain that my life here lacks (among many glorious, modern, and convenient other things) a rightness. I have realised that it is possible—without misery or alarm—to lead the
wrong life and allow the right one to live somewhere else. This letter may not make it past the censors. My apologies to all unexpected readers.*

Yours,
Leonard

HRH KING EDWARD VII POSTAL STATIONERY

13 July 1905—46 Gordon Square

'When do we leave, Nessa?' asked Virginia. We were sitting in the garden in the late afternoon summer sunshine.

'Tenth of August.' I pulled my newspaper closer.

'Nessa, are you sure we cannot go back to Talland House?' Virginia,
sensing my shorthanded answers, had begun to repeat herself.

'I have told you, I could not manage it, dearest. The house is let.'
True, I had tried, and the house was let, but I had not tried terribly hard.
I wanted to be somewhere new and untilled. We must be careful in
Cornwall. After thirteen happy childhood summers, all our ghosts will
be waiting for us there.

'But Nessa, will it be *near* Talland House?' Virginia asked.

'Quite near, dearest,' I reassured automatically, when in fact I had no
idea. 'St Ives is not a big enough place to be too far from it.'

'What's the house called? Trevor something?' Thoby asked, dragging
a wicker chair over the stones to sit down.

'But is it on the same side of the bay?' Virginia persisted.

'Trevose View, and yes, it is on the same side of the bay,' I said soothingly. I could feel Virginia pulled taut, on the brink of something, and I was not up to a mad scene today.

'Are you sure we could not stay *in* Talland House?' Virginia repeated, unfolding my newspaper and spreading it over her knees. The page I had been reading slipped to the ground.

'Ginia, if Nessa could have fixed it for us to stay there, she would have,' Thoby answered, with the unthinking authority of one who does not anticipate an argument. He set his lemonade down on the wrought-iron table and leaned back in his chair. He opened his book. 'When do we leave, Nessa?'

ONCE FOR LUCK

· ·

Saturday 15 July 1905—46 Gordon Square

A ferocious argument rippled below the surface last night but did not break the skin.

I suggested Snow come with us to Cornwall. A mistake. Snow has a steady grace that gets on Virginia's nerves. Women without a light fingerprint of malice are too foreign for Virginia. Snow, with her thick mahogany sheet of hair and her low, rich voice, is one of those women who grows more beautiful as you get to know her. Virginia hates that.

23 July 1905—46 Gordon Square

Lytton's sister Pernel—her real name is Joan, but she uses this one, bizarre—is unable to come. Virginia keeps swearing that she has diphtheria and threatens to send her soup. But then Virginia is always swearing that people have diphtheria. And Thoby's friend, Henry Lamb, Walter's eccentric artist brother, is also unable to make it.

POSTCARD

THIS SPACE TO BE USED FOR CORRESPONDENCE

30 July 1905

Dear Woolf,

Bell is resolved. He loves her straight through.
He would rather fall at her feet and live on her
doorstep than settle for less. Comfort is of no
value, he says. Uncomfortable, thorny passion is
where he will pitch his tent. Surprisingly, I wish
him luck. Unusual, when I think she is ten times the man he is. But his con-
viction has won me. How wonderful to feel such pure decision.

> *Yours,*
> *Lytton*

To: Mr Leonard Woolf
> *Assistant Gov't Agent*
> *Jaffna*
> *Ceylon*

SERIES 4. SUNFLOWERS IN PROVENCE

1 August 1905—46 Gordon Square (packing—cases everywhere)

I am surprised and not surprised all at once. I must have known it was coming.

The evening began beautifully.

After a wonderful dinner in his rooms—just he and I, very bohemian—he walked me home. The thick scent of roses sweetened my skin. He had bought hundreds of roses. Buckets of them. They overwhelmed his rooms at King's Bench Walk, perching on narrow shelves and slim windowsills. The effect was potent, visceral. I was touched. He had taken Virginia's knifing criticism and had gone out of his way to find roses that smelled of roses.

His rooms were not what I expected. Original Toulouse-Lautrec lithographs shared the mantel with invitations to shooting parties in Scotland. The bookshelves were crowded with a mix of Dickens, Shakespeare, Roman and Greek history, and books about fish. The conversation was unexpected too. I discovered he loves one of my loves:

Jane Austen. Unusual for so outdoorsy a man to be interested in the indoorsy lives of women.

He walked me home. In the square, he paused by the large lilac tree he knows is my favourite. Wordlessly brave, he knelt and asked.

A silent beat. And another. I took a shallow breath, held very still, and tried not to think. A tide of instinct roared through me.

I kissed the top of his head and told him no. I could not understand yes, could not envisage yes, so it had to be no.

'No? Just no?' Clive asked, fighting to keep his voice level.

'No for now is cruel, don't you think?' I asked. I was anxious to have the question settled.

'No for now is kind,' he said standing, without letting go of my hand.

'But when does *now* end?' He had no answer.

Later (half past three in the morning)

Clive guessed right. No for now is the truth. But is the truth fair? I do not want him to go, but I am not sure enough to go with him.

2 August 1905—46 Gordon Square

I have written to Snow. A long, crass, flighty letter that I regret. I was not genuine, and I hate that. Wrong of me to write at all. This sort of business is best kept between those it concerns.

Saturday 5 August 1905—46 Gordon Square

I have not told Thoby but feel that I must. He mentioned that Clive was not himself yesterday at lunch. I want to reach out to him but do not want to give the wrong impression. But then what is the wrong impression? Surely the right impression can only be the truth?

And—Terrible news. Thoby just told me—Theodore Llewelyn Davies drowned. Thoby says he was in love with a girl called Margaret.

9 August 1905—46 Gordon Square

Limbo: packed but not gone. Exhausted but not travelled. I still have not told Thoby but he keeps mentioning Clive's ongoing strangeness. Clive leaves for Scotland on Thursday. Thursday, and no one will be at home.

GODREVY LIGHTHOUSE

10 August 1905—Trevose View, Carbis Bay, Cornwall (seven p.m. —exhausted)

We are here. The house is *not* beautiful but it is many-windowed and set apart in a crook of Cornish seascape. I have taken the large blue bedroom overlooking the bay. I was feeling selfish and was going to cede it to Virginia but found she liked the writing desk in the yellow bedroom. Thoby is shouting in the hallway—

12 August 1905—Trevose View, Carbis Bay

We have forded the brook, swum the bay, scaled the wall, crawled the brush, and snooped the old house. Really we just took the footpath and looked over the escallonia hedge at Talland House, but Virginia insisted it was a great adventure, and her enthusiasm changed the day. The old house looked entirely the same. We did not see the occupants, but the accoutrements were familiar: striped bathing towels, bathing costumes, sandy buckets, and straw hats dropped on wooden chairs.

I told Thoby, and he was unsurprised. He worries for Clive.

17 August 1905—Trevose View, Carbis Bay

We have settled into the rhythm of the sea.

69 LANCASTER GATE
LONDON W.

Great Oakley Hall, Kettering

25 August 1905

Dear Bell,

Oh my dear. The angels and I weep for you. The Goth—only after much hounding and gnashing of teeth—finally told me of your thwarted suit. Brave man, to have ventured such a question to such a formidably lovely woman. Quel courage, mon brave. Hold tight to your conviction. If there is a symmetry—and I suspect there is—a righting of wrongings will follow. Be sure you are prepared to live up to her love, should you win her.

As I told you before, she is a cautious creature. Given to bone-shattering honesty. Believe all her words. The Goth told me she has said no but left bread crumbs for you to find her? To horse! Storm the castle and take the keep, for she does nothing by accident. Nor is she careless, like her sister. Virginia would set the house on fire just to watch everyone come running out in pyjamas. Vanessa might not know herself what she wants, but she will show you her muddle. I like that about her.

I have also found a clear ringing passion. It is Duncan, my beautiful cousin. He is also given to brutal honesty, but his sincerity rides a capricious horse. He lacks Vanessa's self-perception. He will break my heart into a thousand glassy shards. How maudlin I am today. Forgive me.

Yours,
Lytton

PS: Terrible about Theodore. He was such a man, and I fear he will be remembered only as a lost boy.

30 August 1905—Trevose View, Carbis Bay, Cornwall

I was wrong. The sea does not offer its rhythm, nor its colours, lightly. It is a snarling blue beast in one moment and a frothy jade pool the next. It is disinclined to sit for a portrait.

Later

Life *by* the sea, on the other hand, has taken on a predictable, lolling rhythm. In the mornings: I paint, Virginia writes, Thoby reads, and Adrian does whatever mysterious things Adrian does—and then we play piquet. We gather for a simple, elemental luncheon: bread, salami, cheese, fruit, tea. In the afternoons: more painting, more reading, more writing, some beaching, some bathing, some walking, more tea, and then more piquet.

7 September 1905—Trevose View, Carbis Bay, Cornwall

We are remembered in the village—many people recall us running on the beach as children and many more remember Mother—and this morning we were scooped up into a conversation with the new owners of Talland House. The grocer introduced us. The new tenants are an artist couple. Their children are just the ages we were when we last lived there. Symmetry. That house reaches for artists to weave into its magic.

Later

A difficult conversation after supper tonight. Thoby spoke of how Mother was the quieter and the more reserved of our parents, yet how *everyone* still remembers her best. Virginia felt compelled to stand up for Father's crashing, keen, razored intellect. Adrian looked stricken, as he does whenever we talk of Mother. He was her last baby, and her favourite.

POSTCARD

THIS SPACE TO BE USED FOR CORRESPONDENCE

8 September 1905

Dear Leonard,

Why did I do it? Why did I encourage Bell in his relentless pursuit of Vanessa. Pity? Can only be. He has been loafing about pining for months. He swears that he loves her to his deepest depths. But Bell's deepest depths just won't do. I have been watching her, it is impossible not to watch her, and I know that she is not someone to love lightly. She rings low and true in a single, pure note. And Bell? I know you care for him, as does the Goth, and that says much. He is a charming man. A winning man. But I am not convinced he has the weight to balance her. Luckily, I also think he lacks the gravity to pull her away from her family. Just as well. I wish you were here. You see these things so clearly.

Yours,
Lytton

To: Mr Leonard Woolf
Assistant Gov't Agent
Jaffna
Ceylon

YOUNG MEN ON BICYCLES IN BRIGHTON

8 September 1905—Trevose View, Carbis Bay, Cornwall

'But she only sent two chapters! What am I supposed to do with two chapters—and not even the first two!' Virginia said, striding into the room, waving loose pages in her hand. Nelly had sent her unfinished novel to Virginia for criticism. I collected it from the post office this morning.

'Mmm.' Not a satisfactory answer for Virginia. I was trying to flesh out a rambunctious bit of the sea by adding undertones of red and ochre. Whistler often used that technique to much better effect. My sea now looks like a shallow puddle flocking over river mud.

'Nessa!'

'And what do you think of the pages?' I asked, dipping my brush in turpentine.

'I have not read them, of course. How can I? It is incomplete.' She thumped down onto the striped canvas deckchair.

'Maybe you should try?'

Later

Now Virginia *likes* the chapters. Her brisk weathervane shifts leave me dizzy.

'They are very good,' Virginia pronounced, crumbling her teacake rather than eating it.

'Even though they are not the beginning?' I asked with a light hand of mischief.

She sat very still. 'You know they could be. Why not? Why must a novel begin at the beginning? Who declares such a rule? Who defends it?'

I looked at her, concerned. 'You sound medieval when you talk like that.'

'I feel medieval. Like an armoured knight on a roan warhorse riding into the blood-soaked fray.'

'The blood-soaked fray being Nelly's novel? Not much of a warrior—she's deaf,' I said.

'No, the wider, oppressive fray.' Virginia's voice was growing louder. 'The can and can't, do and don't fray of convention in literature that I hate.'

'And you are going to take it on?' I could not keep the scepticism from my voice.

'Yes,' she said, and walked off towards Godrevy Lighthouse.

I watched her pick up her lean, snapping gait. Virginia is always in motion. Her tempo is staccato and quick. Even when her body rests, her mind tumbles over and over like a lock. Her way is acquisitive. She is always interested in more—more affection, more attention, more contact, more safety, more warmth, more secrets. Her writing never catches its breath either. As soon as she has settled on a style, she grows bored with it. The freshness lost, she discards it and seeks something new. I worry she can never be still and happy at the same time. Her imagination feeds itself on motion.

Very late—my blue room, chilly night

I do not doubt Virginia's talent. I *know* she is gifted. But mine is a deliberate, remembered knowing: as if it is a hat I must try not to lose. And then sometimes she is changed. Sometimes she arches away from me and wears a light halo of genius about her. Then she is not *my* Virginia at all. At those times I feel horribly earthbound and built of base metals.

TENNIS WHITES

POSTCARD

14 September 1905

Stephens,

Arriving on 10.15 train.
Do not worry about meeting train.
Delighted to walk. Will thoroughly enjoy
getting lost and found again.
> *Yours,*
> *Saxon*

To: Stephen Family
Trevose View
Carbis Bay, St Ives
Cornwall

No. 4: MAN ON BICYCLE IN A STRAW BOATER

POSTCARD

17 September 1905

Saxon,

10.15 train on what day? You can't possibly walk
as you will get lost but never be found. Let me
know the day and a Stephen will be waiting for
you at the station. Please do not wander off and
make Stephen chase you through the underbrush.
> *Yours,*
> *Thoby*

To: Mr Saxon-Sydney
Turner
Treasury Department
1 Horse Guards
Parade
London

GODREVY LIGHTHOUSE, ST IVES

20 September 1905—Trevose View (hot and bright)

He was waiting at the small country rail station. Naturally, it fell to me to fetch him as Thoby and Adrian had forgotten his arrival and gone walking. Virginia was in the midst of a paragraph she could not put down.

Sunday 24 September 1905—Trevose View, Carbis Bay, Cornwall

Packing up for our return. I salt away the least noticeable items first. Virginia is unravelled by change and will start to fret. She has taken to walking out to Godrevy Lighthouse in the afternoons, and that is when I nip round the house lifting a beach towel here and an already-read book there.

FIRST TO GO:
>   Flower vases
>   Bedroom slippers
>   Dickens

LAST TO GO:
>   Striped bathing costumes
>   Straw hats
>   Austen

Later

Saxon has not changed the rhythm of the house at all but has moulded himself to fit it. He is a man who chases his own interests and does not consider what anyone will think.

26 September 1905—Trevose View, Carbis Bay (bright blue day)

'Ant. Ant. Ant.'

I looked over at Virginia. She was sitting on her lawn chair, loosely holding her pen but not writing. Her index finger was smudged with ink.

'Ant. Ant. Ant. Ant.'

'Dearest?' I asked gently. 'Ant *who?*'

'*Ant* ant,' Virginia said, as if stating the obvious.

Thoby came round the white stone path and dropped into a chaise longue.

'Ant. Ant. Ant,' Virginia directed at Thoby.

'Yes. Good word, "a-n-t",' he said, drawing out the small, sharp, pointy sounds. Saxon ambled over and flopped onto the blanket in the grass.

'Ant,' said Virginia to no one. Saxon turned to look at her.

'Ant? Tricky word in crosswords. Always more of an ending: "defend-*ant*, account*ant*".'

'Ant?' asked Adrian coming up the lawn, his hair still wet and smelling of the sea. 'Ginia, have we got ants?'

I looked at Virginia. She had grown bigger in the last few minutes. Rounded and settled, like a spider who is sure of her breakfast. She had caught everyone in her nonsense web. They were each wrapped and bundled and waiting for the spider feast. And she did it with a tiny word.

Virginia has been invited to teach writing at Morley College this term. She will charm her students into sailor's knots.

28 September 1905—Trevose View, Carbis Bay

Sat on a long summer lawn and watched Thoby and Adrian play tennis. The last few days of the holiday are always the sweetest. The unspent mornings are more precious, and the days more frugally divided. The rules break, and the habits bend out of shape. These were the days when Mother would allow us to have nursery tea with sandy feet and salty fingernails as we four wrung the last hours of tumbling sunshine from the summer.

Now the trunks lie half-open all over the house, and my canvases will never dry in time. Annoying, but I had to work on them today in the last of the loose blue-gold Cornish light. I will have to have them sent on next week. I will miss it here.

FRIDAY EVENINGS IN AUTUMN

5 October 1905—46 Gordon Square (summer dusk)

We are back.

Somewhere else, the tide rolls in. The tide rolls out. London's elegant lines are printed in street dirt. I only want to paint the sea.

7 October 1905—46 Gordon Square

The colours in my head, the colours in my heart, and the colours in my hours do not match up. My head wants to play with the textured gloss of clear white: the bruised shadows of pink, and the silver of the sunlight riding on the wave. My heart wants to plunge into the open-water freshness of the richest, purest, *bluest* blue, and my hours are muddied with the wrangling, tangled, starling browns of my family.

Thoby cannot get enough peace to work although *what* he is working on remains a mystery. He is meant to be reading for the bar but I am sure that on most days he is not. Adrian likewise professes his need to get 'work' done, but instead he is nearly always playing the piano. Virginia rolls her eyes, lifts her brows, and talks of offices and deadlines and bylines—as if to proclaim her work to be authentic in the face of their play work. I suppose it is true, as she so often reviews for the *TLS* now.

My work I keep to myself. Painting does not qualify as work in this family of literati. Work is not work where *words* are not involved. The unfixed mark of paint alters when it alteration finds. The distribution of colours is a curious sort of hobby to them. A lightweight experiment with insubstantial shade instead of the integrity-bound dimensional shape of letters on a page.

'Writing is real expression, Nessa,' Virginia said, refusing the rosemary potatoes Sophie had made especially for her.

'Virginia, those were made at *your* request,' I said steadily as Maud took the covered dish back down to the kitchen.

I knew Sophie had used the last of her squirreled-away rosemary on them this afternoon. Sophie is always worried about 'Miss Ginia' and her tendency not to eat. She shakes her head and makes noises about Lady Stephen disapproving of wasted food. It is true. Mother did hate to see food wasted. But even Mother could not get Virginia to eat. Only Thoby can do that.

'No good, Ginia? They looked good to me,' Adrian said gamely.

Nothing.

'Dearest, try. You know we all want you to eat,' I said, automatically cajoling her into nutrition.

'Violet says she is heading towards the savage land of Oklahoma, where water buffalo run through the town and people dress in feathers and paint,' Virginia said loudly to no one.

'Dearest, I think that was in the last century,' I said, trying to rope Virginia back into the realm of the everyday.

'Violet wrote and told me that she was taken captive and held at arrow point for two days.'

'And then got diphtheria, I suppose?' Adrian asked with a crackle of menace.

'Do just eat, Ginia,' Thoby said, laying down his book.

Maud, hearing Thoby's intervention, sensed her cue and returned with the potatoes.

POSTCARD

10 October 1905

Dearest Duncan,

My Cambridge life has bitten the poisoned apple. Failure: I am not to become a fellow. My dream will now sleep for a thousand years. I can only hope that I am rescued by seven deliciously small manual labourers and whisked off to a cottage in the glen. If so, please storm the forest astride a white stallion and move in with us.

> *Yours,*
> *Lytton*

To: Mr Duncan Grant
  22 Rue Delambre
  Boulevard Raspail
  Paris
  France

PS: Spending lots of time with Maynard, whom you will like. Please be jealous, chérie.

NUMBER 8. CAMBRIDGE COUNTRYSIDE

---

11 October 1905—46 Gordon Square

We have been home a week and I am still restless and unsettled. I have the loose-ended feeling of looking, *looking*. What am I looking for? Looking for substance, looking for a moment I do not understand. Is that just how life is? Do we ever have the sensation of *finding*, of arriving? I worry that life is always in the future and I am always here, in the preamble, straightening up the cushions so that life will go smoothly once it does begin. How does it *start*?

I have the outstretched feeling of wanting to seek Clive's advice, on the Friday Club, on my paintings, on my hats. Perhaps because I know he would have a definite opinion. He does not waffle as I do. He speaks and then acts. I like those short, explosive verbs.

No. Vanessa. Descend a storey. Round the stone steps of the curtain wall. Do I just seek an excuse to speak to him? I rummage for the truth and find handfuls of my own deceptiveness. Yes, no? Even I do not know the answer.

Later (past midnight)

He told me I am beautiful. Our family ostensibly values brilliance over beauty. Of course, underneath, Father expected beauty too. Tonight I closed the door and sat at my dressing table and looked in the glass, looked to see what Clive sees. I have never felt beautiful. I compare myself to the women in my family. I suppose all women do that. Mother was too hollowly drawn to be pretty, but she was arresting. Stella's good nature made her far more alluring than the sum of her features. Then there is Virginia. Everyone turns to look at Virginia. Narrow and ethereal, Virginia's beauty haunts.

And me? I look critically, as I would at an artist's model. My face is a pure oval. My eyes are heavily lidded, and my mouth turns down at the corners, giving my expression a gravity I did not earn. Overlarge for my face, my eyes are a widely set soft blue-grey, like washed slate. My skin is apple pink because I never remember my hat. My conker-brown hair escapes the loose knot at my neck and is never tidy. My hands are strong but long and white. I have paint under my nails. My figure is more womanly than Virginia's ascetic frame. I try to like it but often feel lumpy rather than purposefully curved. I look unfamiliar.

Friday 13 October 1905—46 Gordon Square (still warmish)

Tea with Aunt Anny and Virginia this afternoon was huge fun. My God, she is an eccentric old thing. Today she spoke to Virginia and me at length about the great merits of wearing woollen underwear and comfortable shoes.

Later, over dinner, I described the conversation to Thoby and Adrian. 'That'll be you someday, Nessa,' Adrian said as Sloper cleared away the soup bowls, 'dropping round to make sure I clean my ears and change my socks.'

Everyone laughed but me. I do not want to become that someday.

And—At homes start up next week. Must order more cake. I feel nervous and restless and out of practice. It has been three months.

Monday 16 October 1905—46 Gordon Square

Friday nights—for artists. Shape. Colour. Light. Depth. The fractured, messy journey of image.

I hope people come. I want so much. I want these nights to be brave. I want to elbow words out of the way and give art the floor. In Cornwall, I felt wrapped in such a sense of what was possible. Each canvas soaked up the paint hungrily. The brush thrummed with purpose. It was not the outcome that mattered but the doing. I want to bottle that feeling and serve it to my guests.

But will the evening work? I hope Friday catches some of Thursday's magic like a sniffle on an omnibus. Maybe Thoby is right and conviction is everything.

My rules are simple and clear. We must dispense with insincere politeness—that vapid veneer of untruth that smothers London drawing rooms. Our well-mannered social deceit must not die a private death but a court-ordered hanging in the public square. The anarchic animal that is left will be a dangerous and hot-blooded thing. Unruly and impossible to predict. But alive.

And—I have hung Great-aunt Julia's best photographs in the upstairs hall. A long, slim row. The talented women of my family give me credibility. Why do I fret so? I tell myself it is only a party.

Friday 20 October 1905—46 Gordon Square (unseasonably warm)

It worked. The result was good. Not incandescent, but solidly good. The Thursday friends blended with the Friday friends, and the result was complete. The evening happened. Arts and letters: circles drawn and understood. Lytton hurled himself headlong into the spirit of the thing and interrogated Mr Derwent Lees—a young Australian painter who looks enough like Duncan to cause Lytton distress—about the nature of *blue*.

Gripping the young man's hand, Lytton wailed, 'The melancholy, the drama, the pure forlorn character of blue undoes me. Ugh, Mother needs her hankie.' The astonished Mr Lees tried to retrieve his hand. Poor man. He was taking the brunt of Lytton's unhappiness over Duncan's increasing silence.

Clive rolled his eyes and mutely appealed to Desmond, the good-natured diplomat, for help in rescuing the unsuspecting painter.

'Yes, but another blue, a clear, French, new-day blue, can speak of promise and renewal,' Desmond called out, rising to join the discussion.

'How Napoleonic,' Lytton said, shooting him a sulky look of spoiled fun.

'Yes, *how* Napoleonic,' Desmond said, dropping into the other basket chair, taking the statement at value, and plunging into the question. 'Red, white, and blue—the Americans and the French both chose their revolutionary flags from the same energetic palette. There must be some concealed engine in that tricolour combination.' Desmond can talk to anyone about anything and make it sound both vital and charming.

Clive proved a masterful puppeteer. He is the truest bridge of arts and letters I know. He brought butter-yellow roses. I was so pleased to find him at the door and would not have preferred wildflowers at all.

And—Clive spent a long time looking at the photographs in the hall. He had had no idea that Julia Margaret Cameron was our aunt. He recognised her work immediately.

Later (late, curled in my dressing gown with a mug of milk)

In a roomful of friends, artists, and colleagues, I look for Clive. When we speak, I do not look over his shoulder and worry about the sandwiches or the coffee or the comfort of the other guests. I am no longer the ringmaster, urging the circus horses forward. I am where I need to be and that is enough—the rest can take care of itself.

Clive. I am on home ground when I am with him. Perhaps it is because Clive blends artistic sympathy and family friendship as no one else in the room does? No. Not even I believe that. Love, then? Is this what it feels like? Safety? Warmth? Comfort? Is that enough? Can I live without the thudding in the blood, the thrashing drama I always expected to feel? Maybe I have left it too long and am too old for that now? Perhaps. But I am not *ready* yet, I think. I am not done with this free, four-step, Stephen part of my life.

69 LANCASTER GATE

LONDON W.

3 November 1905

Dear Woolf,

Our weeks have grown more exciting. Intrepid Vanessa has devised a Friday evening at home to round out our Thursday thorniness. But she is uninterested in any particular brand of artistry. It is conviction and risk that compel her. She is not a disciple of any school but carefully selects sacred tenets for her three-dimensional faith from many temples. Likewise her salon does not endorse any one methodology, but rather it endorses effort. Effort and discipline are her twin gods.

Her evening changed the pitch of my week—gave it more verve and substance. The hungry young artists were so animated. One young painter actually beat his chest to make his point—thrillingly primal.

Virginia sat in the centre of the room, pinched and silent and affecting a bored expression. Her only comments (fired at close range into an unsuspecting crowd) centred on language. Her meaning was clear: image must lay flowers at the feet of text. She expected support from me and looked shrewish when, instead of taking her juicy bait, I threw myself headlong into a discussion of temperature: the loveless coldness of a world painted in blue. The loveless coldness of a world without the ripe, warming undertones of Duncan.

Bell was Vanessa's champion. Backing her utterly, he juggled the writers and artists, pairing unlikely people and ironing the night smooth. He made the party memorable. Guessing that Bell held Vanessa's strength, Virginia went for broke and attempted to bring the circus tent crashing down. It is her way. Do not mistake me. Beautiful Virginia is full of malice, but she is not malicious. It is just how she is built. She is governed by different forces than we. This is important to understand as I do so want you to like her. In fact, I think you ought to marry her. Was that too unexpected? Should I have let you come to that conclusion on your own? Dommage.

I do not think, in this case, Virginia meant actual harm; she just could not bear to be irrelevant. Virginia lives to be essential. That is the only way she is comfortable. But this was an evening for art, rather than books: not her forte. And so with honey sweetness she sought to upstage and invited Bell for a walk around the square to smell the last of the dying summer roses. Bell countered her by suggesting we go promenading en masse. And so like a herd of low-slung dachshunds, we trotted out into the autumn night to go flower sniffing. I look forward to next week, especially as Vanessa has promised to serve my favourite chicken.

And you, dear Leonard? How go the wilds of empire? Amazing to think of you battling through the brush, trading in the most basic elements of survival, while we sit in symmetrical squares and tinkle our teacups. You are much missed, my dear. Come home to us soon.

Always your
Lytton

PS: Duncan's affection is slipping—I am not imagining it. I expect the worst. I am bracing myself for tragedy and spending time with Maynard. He is a man of total self-conviction, much like the Goth, but his roots rest in a mathematical earth. He sees life, love, and human interaction as a series of knowable equations—how alarming.

PS encore: The Mole's novel came out last week. Where Angels Fear to Tread, from the Alexander Pope line that I don't much care for. The publisher put down his large inky foot and insisted on a title change, and the Mole is put out. I would be too. Sales good so far, and another printing is expected. I am vert with jealousy.

8 November 1905—46 Gordon Square

Virginia would not get out of the bath, so we were dining late, but it was not meant to be a dinner party. It was a simple family meal of pea soup, cold chicken, and green salad vegetables. Maud had just cleared the soup when the knocking began, and in they tumbled.

'No, the Goth must read it first,' James Strachey said, handing the paper to Thoby.

'But the girls are here,' Clive said, as if that statement made sense. I could tell he felt awkward about interrupting our meal. We are all keen to break with convention, but arriving during dinner grated upon his sense of decorum. We expected them at ten, and it was only quarter past eight.

Thoby scanned down the page of the *Daily News*. 'Ha! What a review! Where is he?'

'Still fussing with the cab, I think. You know how he dawdles,' James said.

Lytton and Morgan walked into the dining room.

'He was not dawdling,' Lytton said, smacking his pipe into his palm. Poor Lytton is rather storm-tossed at the moment. 'He was making an *entrance*.' Lytton bent to kiss my cheek. 'Hello, dear one.' Straightening, he said, 'Clive, you philistine, the great auteur cannot just march into a room sans trumpets. Goth, my dear, fix Mother a whisky?' He dropped gracefully into a dining chair.

Thoby stood to fix Lytton a drink.

Morgan looked even more slight and frazzled than usual. 'I was trying to sort out the tip for the cabbie,' he said. 'He is still waiting. Does anyone have sixpence?'

I nodded to Sloper, who went out to pay the driver.

'Mole, you have outdone us all!' Lytton said, pulling Morgan to him for a waltz. I stood and pushed in the other dining chairs so they would not get knocked over. Round and round the table they went in small uneven ellipses. Maud fetched more place settings and brought back the soup tureen.

'*Remarkable! Mastery of material! Keen insight!* Mole! This is brilliant!' Thoby said, reading fragments aloud. Virginia, brittle and still, was silent.

'I don't like the title,' Morgan said, as Lytton released him from their dizzying waltz.

'You wanted *Monteriano*?' I asked. It was the fictitious name he had chosen to conjure the very real towered city of San Gimignano. I think it does capture the cadence and height of that hillside town.

'The *Manchester Guardian* called the title "mawkish"—awful,' Morgan said, fretfully, folding and refolding his neat slim hands.

'Well, I think it is splendid,' Virginia said, unexpectedly. Thoby and I looked at each other, surprised. When Virginia says 'splendid', that is rarely what she means.

20 November 1905—46 Gordon Square (late afternoon, getting chilly)

Clive wants me to go to Paris with him. In fact, he invited the four of us plus Lytton and Saxon, but it is me he wants.

'It is electrifying! Such an exhibition could never happen in England. We must go!' Clive said, pacing between the drawing-room window and the fireplace, rolling and unrolling the news-sheet into a tight cylinder. I had never seen him so agitated. 'Now, Nessa! We must go *now*! It is a *moment*, Nessa! All Paris is talking! The Salon d'automne is turned upside down by this bunch. Vauxcelles, the French art critic, notoriously hard to please, is calling them the *Fauves*.'

'The . . . beasts?' I translated tentatively, never sure of my French. 'Is that a *compliment*?'

'The *wild* beasts,' Clive corrected. 'Of course it is a compliment.

They have taken the Salon by the scruff of the neck and are giving it a good shake—as wild beasts do. Henri Matisse, I met him a few years ago at a dinner party—marvellous man, bold painter, beautiful colours, can drink everyone under the table.'

I loved watching him lose his urbane calm and get boyishly excited by something.

'Nessa!' He pulled me out of my reverie. 'We have to get on to Cunard today!'

Clive calls me Nessa now. Thoby smiled when he heard it. Virginia did not.

Later

When Clive went down to Thoby's study, I read his tightly rolled-up article. M. Matisse is receiving terrible press for his shocking *Woman with a Hat*. No matter how groundbreakingly new and daringly bold he is, bad press must wound.

The exhibition finishes in four days, so there is no time. And where would we stay? An unmarried woman and unmarried man travelling alone together? Neither Thoby nor Adrian nor Lytton nor Saxon can go, and Virginia would only make matters worse. Travelling alone with a single man? Even I am not bold enough to break that rule.

25 November 1905—46 Gordon Square (late)

Clive just left with Thoby. The Steins—Gertrude and Leo, Clive called them—have bought Matisse's *Woman with a Hat*. I am glad, as M. Matisse must feel cheered up. Clive told me Mr and Miss Stein (brother and sister and not husband and wife) also bought M. Picasso's work, spending a huge sum of money. Clive said it was lucky, as last winter M. Picasso had no money to buy coal and so burnt his own drawings to keep warm.

Tonight Clive brought me an article by Mr Roger Fry, the art critic who has just been named curator of the Metropolitan Museum in New

York. It was a piece about the *Fauves,* and it was Clive's last-ditch effort to convince me to go to the exhibition in Paris with him.

I dined with Mr Fry once at Desmond MacCarthy's, and although his scholarly reputation intimidated me, I liked him enormously. He had to leave early as his wife, Helen, was unwell. I think she had had a serious breakdown some months before. All through dinner, she was unable to speak to anyone on either side of her and sat in an agitated silence. Her husband watched her anxiously from the other side of the table, and as soon as it was possible, he announced their departure. Just as he was leaving, I rose and, taking his hand in mine, asked him to take good care. I wanted to say that watching over a beloved who is prone to insanity is a treacherous, guilty, and lonely road, but I did not presume that far.

Reading his words, I was reminded of his quick bright manner and sincere expression. Mr Fry's article was visual, visceral. It nearly convinced me to discard convention and go with Clive to Paris. Nearly.

UNION POSTALE UNIVERSELLE

CEYLON (CYLAN)

25 November 1905

Jaffna, Ceylon

Lytton,

Do not be alarmed. Before you read further, know that I am well—well enough to have had eggs and ham for breakfast and be sitting on a sunny verandah writing this to you.

I have had typhoid. Terrifying, I know. The very name of the dreadful disease waters one's bowels. But in a one-room hospital, with a nurse who would not come closer than eight feet to me and a doctor who visited once a day, I am cured. The doctor diagnosed me and then said sternly 'If you eat nearly nothing and do not move at all, in twenty-one days your fever will return to normal, and you will be cured.' My fever was 103 degrees when he said it, and do you know what? On the twenty-first day? 98.6. I have renewed veneration for country doctors on bicycles.

> *All love,*
> *Leonard*

HRH KING EDWARD VII POSTAL STATIONERY

6 9 L A N C A S T E R G A T E
L O N D O N W.

6 December 1905

Dearest Leonard,

The Goth just told me that you had an encounter? Quoi? Avec qui? Do you think my stealthy use of French will disguise our subject du jour? Innocence lost. Experience gained. Blake would be so pleased. Milton, I fear, would not. Milton was such a prude. About time, I suppose. Dearest, at twenty-five was innocence wearing thin? And with a woman no less—that makes it official. Did you tell Goth and not me as you thought I would not understand such things? I demand a full account at once. Do write in specifics, dear. Such voluptuous gossip is no fun without specifics.

And how am I? I have recently become obsessed with Gluck. I fear I have lost my Eurydice to a great beefy Frenchman who probably smells of onions and cheese.

> *Yours,*
> *Lytton*

PS: Your postcard just arrived! Typhoid! My dear friend. Thank God for angels on bicycles. Get that doctor's name and ship him here at once. I have need of such a man.

Thursday 7 December 1905—46 Gordon Square (late, can hear birds in the square)

Morgan Forster (I cannot call him the Mole—it makes him sound like a beauty mark) was in high spirits tonight as another printing has been ordered for his lovely little novel. It is a slender narrative with an enormous scope. I am haunted by it. The great central tragedy skips across the water of the story with only the smallest stone. Virginia read it and pronounced it *Edwardian*—damning criticism.

We celebrated at Gordon Square.

'The Mole must drink champagne!' Lytton pronounced from his customary basket chair. He was looking more ramshackle charming than usual in his drooping red bow tie and brown velveteen coat.

'And how is your novel, Virginia?' I asked, knowing she would want the conversation brought round to her own writing.

'It has a healthy constitution,' she said mysteriously. 'Changed the title, though. I am thinking of calling it *The Voyage Out*.'

'I like it,' Morgan said, rising to go. He always leaves first. 'It feels suspended in air and ends with a good sliced consonant.' Without saying goodbye to anyone, he put out his cigarette and left.

'Has he always done that?' I asked once he had gone.

'What, left abruptly with no goodbye?' Thoby asked. 'Always.'

'Goodbyes make him anxious,' Desmond said, picking an apple from the fruit bowl. 'And competition undoes him completely,' he said, without looking at Virginia. 'Every time a rowdy discussion broke out in college, he would suddenly stand up and announce that he had to catch the train to Weybridge.'

'What's in Weybridge?' I asked, offering a pear to Virginia but knowing she would refuse.

'His mother and sisters, I think. Although they might have moved. It is just something he says.' Desmond accepts everyone wholly without criticism. Questions, yes. Criticism, no.

Virginia Stephen
46 Gordon Square
Bloomsbury

8 December 1905

My Violet,

I am concerned I may have lost track of your precise goings and more goings and am formally requesting a detailed itinerary. I like to know where you lay your beloved head down to sleep each evening, as well as where and with whom you dine. If I am to be deprived of your bolstering company, then I would like to know where to direct my jealousy.

Your only, only, only,
Virginia

PS: I think Clive is winding up to take another swing at Nessa. Vive la Nessa! Courage pour la résistance! Thankfully, no one has asked to marry me yet, but I feel the question of my future beginning to hover.

19 December 1905—46 Gordon Square (more snow)

'Nessa!' I could hear the door slam and Thoby's heavy footstep thumping through the house.

'In here!' I stepped back to look at my morning's work. I was pleased with the vase, although the tilt of the apple still felt wrong.

'Do you hear it?' Thoby banged open the door of my studio without knocking.

I stopped to listen. A Christmas robin, singing in the snowy garden.

UNION POSTALE UNIVERSELLE
CEYLON (CYLAN)

25 December 1905

Jaffna, Ceylon

Lytton,

How wonderful for the Mole. How easy he must rest. He has done something significant. Probably not all he will do, but very definitely something significant. I am envious. I am not sure I am doing anything here at all.

My writing has taken on the jungle tempo of the East and no longer belongs in draped drawing rooms. Happy Christmas, dear Lytton. Please tell Bell that I have faith that he will prevail. I feel it is too personal a thing to write him myself.

Yours,
Leonard

PS: Be careful. Duncan will always break a heart. He knows no other way. He softly roars with selfish truthfulness and tears apart all that is tender in his ruthless drive to be genuine. The only heart he understands is his own.

HRH KING EDWARD VII POSTAL STATIONERY

PART TWO

The Stephens
Go Abroad

..

1906–1907

'Thoby sends his love.
So does Nessa—but Wallabie love is
the nicest kind to get.'

(VIRGINIA STEPHEN TO VIOLET DICKINSON,
26 NOVEMBER 1906)

IS IT WORTH IT?

New Willard Hotel

1401 PENNSYLVANIA AVENUE

Washington, D.C.

3 January 1906

To my Beloved Wife,

An extraordinary afternoon. Went with J. P. Morgan to the White House for lunch with the President. J.P.M. was unimpressed by such august company but I kept worrying about using the right fork. Did you know, they turn their dinner forks up in this country? I am staying at the New Willard Hotel on Pennsylvania Ave. in Washington. Cable <u>at once</u> should you need me. I left you feeling wonderful a few weeks ago but I know how quickly these things can turn. Although I had a letter from Mother today and she commented on how well you looked. She even said you were painting! I am thrilled, my darling.

Please write soon, dearest. I only sleep well once I have had a letter from you.

Your own,
Roger

PS: J.P.M. wants me to arrange for him to buy Farinola's Botticelli.

5 January 1906—46 Gordon Square (snowing)

Cricket has taken over our house this week. It is the only sport Adrian and Thoby truly love. That means that meals are dedicated to talk of runs and wickets and bats and bowlers. It is what comes of living with brothers.

'One wicket!' Thoby repeated, refolding the newspaper in disgust. 'And South Africa wins it. Revolting. Sloper, is there any more of the grapefruit, or did Mr Adrian finish it?'

Sloper returned to the dining room with a sliced grapefruit on a tray. (Fresh grapefruits are Thoby's newest obsession, following closely on the heels of ripe figs and sugared walnuts.) 'Mr Bell is here—'

'Bell!' Thoby bellowed from the table. 'Get in here!'

My hand flew to my hair, hastily twisted into a messy knot. Regretting my faded skirt and fraying blouse (I was planning on staying in to paint this morning), I discreetly wiped the jam and ink from my fingers before shaking Clive's hand.

20 January 1906—46 Gordon Square (smells like snow)

Thoby's friends now collect here most evenings rather than just on Thursdays. One can walk into our drawing room and find any assortment of guests milling about after supper.

This evening Virginia had just returned from teaching her class and was still wearing her slouchy Delft blue hat when she launched headlong into the discussion of the new book about Byron's incestuous affair. 'Incredible that they did it! Marvellous. Great gumption,' Virginia said.

'And he knows for certain?' I turned to Desmond, who was sitting on the green chintz sofa. 'Irene Noel would know. What was Byron, her great-uncle?'

'We don't need to ask Irene. She doesn't like to talk about family history,' Thoby said.

'Lord Lovelace is Byron's grandson. He wouldn't have written it if it weren't true.' Desmond shrugged. 'Anyway, Lovelace's book is not about Byron's whole life, just the separation from Lady B. and his affair with Augusta.'

'Augusta was his whole sister or half-sister? Half, wasn't it? That makes it better, surely?' said Morgan from the doorway. He was late, as usual.

'Does half make it better? Does it need improving?' asked Virginia, relighting her cigarette. '*Manfred* makes it plain that they knew they were up to no good but went ahead. But it was love. If they'd had any courage, they would have gone out and faced everyone down.'

'How awful, to feel that way about a sister,' I said to no one in particular.

'Is it?' Virginia countered. 'He could have loathed his sister—that would be worse.'

No, I thought. That would not be worse.

Thursday 25 January 1906—46 Gordon Square (icy)

Virginia's 24th birthday today. She insisted on collecting her customary one hundred birthday kisses. *Trying*. Thobs got fed up after three and refused to donate any more to the cause. Affection is so much easier to give when it is not owed.

Saturday 3 February 1906—46 Gordon Square

Desmond is engaged! He is going to marry Miss Molly (or Mary?) Warre-Cornish, the daughter of the Vice Provost of Eton. Virginia says she is a crisp sort of a person. Will this change everything? Is this when it begins to happen? Will we singular Stephens become an anomaly? Will we become extinct? In the last years I have felt of a set, a breed— young, adventurous, artistic—unmarried. Outside our set, I am a spinster.

Desmond gave a talk this week at the Friday Club about his friend Mr Roger Fry's stance against Impressionism. Desmond agrees with him that it is not necessarily bad so much as it is *over*. If Mr Fry were not in America, I would ask Desmond to invite him.

Later—(eleven p.m.)

'Exciting,' Clive said, tapping his cigarette on the rim of the ashtray.
  'Exciting, yes, but so sudden,' I said, discomfited by the subject.
  'Takes daring for Desmond to lurch into it so suddenly.'
  'Does it?' I asked, trying not to read his comment as criticism.
  'Yes. To trust like that? Extraordinary courage,' Clive said quietly.
  Yes. That is true. It takes courage.

Later (writing in bed)

If there is courage, there must be risk. If there is risk, there must be doubt. If there is doubt, it is better to wait. But to wait at this age requires courage.

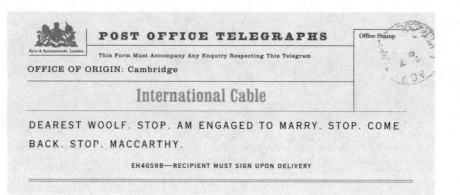

POST OFFICE TELEGRAPHS

Eyre & Spottiswoode. London.

This Form Must Accompany Any Enquiry Respecting This Telegram

Office Stamp

OFFICE OF ORIGIN: Cambridge

International Cable

DEAREST WOOLF. STOP. AM ENGAGED TO MARRY. STOP. COME BACK. STOP. MACCARTHY.

EH4GS9B—RECIPIENT MUST SIGN UPON DELIVERY

Friday 20 April 1906—21 Granby Road, Harrowgate

I included all of Snow's address (where I have been since yesterday) as I think it is a marvellous address. It sounds exactly like a bumpy country road—which is what it is. It is also cold, dark, damp, and cosy. We talk of paint, brushes, texture, light, and colour the way engineers talk of iron, belts, and bolts. The unrestrained fluency of a common language.

25 April 1906—46 Gordon Square

Back in London to a heap of post—nearly all bills that just sat on the hall table gathering dust while I was gone. One would think—no, actually, with Thoby, Adrian, and Virginia, one would not think.

Saturday 5 May 1906—46 Gordon Square (end of a long day)

Virginia asked Violet for a table. Such an innocuous sentence, but what a rumpus it has caused. It is apparently a particular favourite of Violet's and a valuable antique to boot. Virginia just thundered in to tea one afternoon and told Violet that she would quite like to have it. Mother would be so distressed. Thoby and Adrian are appalled—'One simply does not go about asking for other people's things, Ginia!'—and I am now resigned. I was unsettled at first, wary as I am for any signs of imbalance or incongruity in Virginia, but seeing that it was just one of her peculiar moments of directness at work, I relaxed. Violet was an utter dear and had the table delivered the next day. Virginia is planning to have two of the legs sawn off, which makes the gift quite irreversible.

And—Virginia, after listening to a stinging lecture from Thobs, has written twice today, pestering poor Violet for the price of the table.

And and—Desmond is bringing Miss Warre-Cornish this Thursday. He says she is not nervous—how extraordinary. She ought to be.

WINSOR AND NEWTON LTD: Art Suppliers

37–40 Rathbone Place, London W.

BY APPOINTMENT TO HER MAJESTY QUEEN ALEXANDRA

9 May 1906

TO BE DELIVERED TO: Miss Vanessa Stephen,
46 Gordon Sq.

Class III Fugitive Colours (Oil):
Retail 4d each

'Jaune Brilliant' (1 tube)

'Monochrome Tint, Cool No. 1' (1 tube)

'Sap Green' (1 tube)

'Mauve No. 2' (1 tube)

Total: 2s/2d

Thursday 10 May 1906—46 Gordon Square (late)

It was an awkward evening.

'No, I do not agree,' Miss Warre-Cornish said clearly. Her fearless diction was startling.

'Do *not* agree?' Thoby repeated.

'But surely, Miss Warre-Cornish, a writer, for example, must transform his medium? Just as anyone striving for excellence must transform his field? Miss Warre-Cornish, how can there be excellence without progress?' Maynard said, tugging on his moustache. Miss Mary, or Molly, or whatever Warre-Cornish had not yet invited anyone to discard her great double-barrelled bear of a surname, and it was distracting Maynard from his argument.

'Mr Keynes, a writer can succeed by conforming to the constraints of a medium without challenging the parameters. Success can be measured by how well a writer meets certain requirements rather than dismantles them.'

Lytton snickered. Saxon's head swung back and forth, following the exchange as if watching a tennis match he had no interest in joining. Desmond did not fly to his fiancée's rescue. But then she hardly seemed to require rescuing and did not look to him for reassurance anyway. Desmond did not seem at all concerned that his intended had upended a core tenet of our revolutionary faith.

'Miss Warre-Cornish,' Maynard said, regrouping, 'I just do not understand such passivity.'

She shrugged, ignoring the taunt.

'But surely an artist, any artist, must challenge all boundaries? They *must*, don't you agree?' Adrian spluttered.

'Why?' Miss Warre-Cornish said. 'Why would others care what boundaries are broken in *this* house?'

Lytton stifled a giggle. Saxon blinked in surprise. Virginia kept her face carefully blank. Maynard sat back, stumped. I honestly do not think it had ever occurred to him—to any of us—that what we did was unimportant.

POSTCARD

THIS SPACE TO BE USED FOR CORRESPONDENCE

11 May 1906

Dearest Woolf,

Do you know? Of course you do. MacCarthy must have cabled and insisted you return for his grisly nuptials. She is prickly. Not porcupine prickly but snapdragon prickly. That makes no sense. Dommage. She envies Vanessa. She hankers after her calm and her centrality. Nessa bore her brutal sidelong assault with the ease of a wave. I do not know how I shall ever like her, and I miss dear Desmond already. As I miss you.

> *Yours,*
> *Lytton*

To: Mr Leonard Woolf
> *Asst Gov't Agent*
> *Jaffna*
> *Ceylon*

PS: I am going to Paris with Maynard, but my heart goes rambling for Duncan. What a good sentence. You do keep my scribbles, don't you?

12 May 1906—46 Gordon Square

I spent the afternoon hat shopping with George's wife, Margaret. As sisters-in-law go, I think we did quite well. Two hats later (one with feathers and one without) we went to Fortnum's for tea, gossip, and cake.

'Does she mean to start arguments?' Turning to the waiter, Margaret ordered petits fours. 'Six, I should think, Nessa? Can you manage three?' She went on to order them before I answered.

'I am not sure. She clearly views us as a self-satisfied clique and means to tip the boat rather than beg entry. A courageous move, but it will certainly set Virginia against her.' The cakes arrived on a small gold-etched plate. 'Thoby and Adrian won't notice, and Lytton is already having huge fun with the disruption.' I chose the pink cake with the white flower.

'You are not an easy group, I will say that,' Margaret said. 'And you do give off a sense of being very pleased with yourselves. No, not easy in the least.'

I knew just what she meant. Seeing us as an outsider would—we must seem like closed, arrogant ranks.

Later (home and wet—it started raining)

Thinking about us. What we look like. Is there really a we? There is a Stephen we, but a larger we? Yes, I think there is. And we are a surprising company. For all our confidence, only Morgan has *done* anything of any note in the outside world. The rest of us are still living on the borrowed fuel of potential and so far have not left deep footprints. But together we carry a brackish air of importance. As if we are doing something worthy in the world. Maybe how we live our lives is the grand experiment? Mixing company, throwing out customs, using first names, waiting to marry, ignoring the rules, and choosing what to care about. Is that why we matter? Or perhaps Miss Warre-Cornish is right and we do not matter in the least.

Even later

Lytton. So finely sketched in groups, he can crumple and blur in singular company. I think I prefer the more fractured, muddled Lytton to the clear, quick, brilliant Lytton. He, Thoby, and Virginia went walking in the park, and I stayed home to paint in well-lit quiet. I have been working on a layered seascape and have only just discovered that there must be figures in order for the composition to have meaning. Annoying. I am considering figures but not faces, as faces always prove troublesome. I think they alienate rather than connect. But how to manage it? Perhaps to define expression and character through the set of the shoulders or the droop of the neck? Virginia's mood rests in the tilt of her head and the tempo of her hands. The key lies somewhere in how we recognise a figure from a distance. In any case, Lytton returned early from their walk.

'I saw him,' he said flatly. 'Duncan. We dined at Mon Plaisir in Monmouth Street and then went home separately—disaster. He swears it is over with us.'

Duncan, the beautiful, elusive cousin he loves. I can see how Duncan throws sparks with his clear, slim-boned loveliness but fail to understand how they could catch flame into love. Duncan is too remote for love.

'The equilibrium is off,' Lytton said, pulling at the fraying blue damask of the armchair. 'I fall, and he floats. It can only end with me hitting the ground with a very rough thump, and that is no fun if there is no one to pick you up, dust you off, and love you afterwards.'

I did not answer, as what do I know of this?

And—The table is definitely now Virginia's. She has had two of the legs sawn off and had it bolted to the wall of her sitting room. She is talking about having Mr Shaw, the carpenter, come back for further improvements to her wondrous table—something about inkpots and ledges. Thoby and Adrian came rushing in when they heard the sound of wood splitting, but they were too late.

And and—Violet refused to disclose the price of the table, so Virginia sent her vegetables instead. Adrian, who enjoys fresh vegetables, is mollified. Thoby remains outraged—but then he doesn't think much of vegetables and prefers cheese.

Wednesday 30 May 1906—46 Gordon Square (early, sky still pink)

There will be noise and friends and music and champagne and gifts and flowers and cake and dancing—later. Adrian will play, Thoby will sing, Virginia will kiss, Lytton will sparkle, Maynard will smoke, Saxon will watch, Clive will charm, Morgan will leave, and Desmond will laugh—but later. For now I am going to sit wrapped in my dressing gown, watch the sun light the trees in the square, and feel what it is to be twenty-seven years old.

I have a wanderlust. This year I want to travel—Greece? The drums of marriage are sounding. We four must clasp hands and flee.

LEMONADE SUMMER

15 June 1906—46 Gordon Square

'Enigmatic,' Clive said, reaching for his cigarette case. 'That is the right word.'

He offered me a cigarette. I shook my head.

'Enigmatic?' I rolled the word round my mouth and then washed it down with iced mint tea. It was not a tasty word. 'But I am not mysterious. I do not try to be. For that you must look to Virginia or Lytton.'

'Mysterious is different. Mystery implies deceit. You are enigmatic because you only say what is absolutely true. Often contradictory, partial, incomplete, nonsensical, and thorny, but true.'

His courtship has taken a turn for the bizarre.

.

Enigmatic. I do not know if I can be friends with that word. I am not sure what word I would prefer. Instead I would like the leeway to change my word randomly and without warning. Is that normal? Surely other women would be happy to live inside one full, sweet word? It is not that I do not like him, because I do. It is not that I do not like to be in his company, because I do. It is that once the choice is made, it cannot be unmade. The potential fulfilled. The who of my life will be defined. I know lots of women take lovers and reinvent the who, but I am not such a woman.

Vanessa. Latin for 'butterfly'—Father chose my name. Am I meant to change?

19 June 1906—46 Gordon Square (warm but not hot)

'Think they'll lift the ban after this?' Thoby asked, coming through the back door carrying three glasses of lemonade and stepping over the loose paving stone. We were seated in the sun-warmed garden enjoying the last of the summer afternoon and discussing last night's performance. Oscar Wilde's *Salome* opened to a small private audience. Saxon, Clive, Lytton, and Thoby all went to see it.

'The play is banned?' I asked, then instantly regretted it, as everyone seemed to know that but me.

'Yes, the beastly Lord Chamberlain banned it in the nineties. Dear Oscar never got to see it. He was already locked up by then and sending lovely limericks from Reading Gaol.' Lytton took a long drink of lemonade, getting bits of pulp wedged in his frizzy beard.

I watched Lytton carefully. He was discussing a play written by a man who loved other men and went to prison for it. I sometimes forget how very close to a keening wind Lytton sails.

Duncan has decided to spend most of the summer in London rather than return immediately to Paris. (Virginia suspects it is cheaper for him to stay with his parents in Hampstead than live *la* impoverished *vie bohème* in a Parisian garret.) Duncan will not see him alone, and so Lytton is running away to Cambridge. 'Clever move,' Virginia said, when I told her about Lytton's retreat. 'Disappearing is the only way to make Duncan notice that he was ever there.'

*Saturday 30 June 1906—46 Gordon Square (summer evening—
butterflies everywhere)*

He asked me to go walking in the park, and I suggested the drawing room. He asked me if I would like champagne, and I asked for lemonade. He asked if I still loved roses, and I said I preferred peonies. He asked if I would like him to shut the window, and I asked him to open the door.

He asked if I would marry him and I said no.

He did not respond to my no but stood by the mantelpiece quietly considering me. I felt self-conscious: of my hair, upswept but untidy, with long waved tendrils escaping over my shoulders; of my dress, a sprigged green muslin I am fond of, but the lace on the right sleeve is smeared with grey oil paint; of my cheeks—a rubbed fresh pink, as always when I am with him. But now when he looks at me, I feel beautiful. It is not a familiar sensation. This time he had no speech and did not kneel. Instead, a conversation.

'So today it is no,' he said, setting down his glass.

'Tomorrow it will also be no.'

'Yes, but it is still today,' he said, looking at me with his new peculiar, concentrated calm. 'Now shall we walk?' he asked, crossing to the door.

Our business over, we resumed the day. I was outfoxed. I do not understand the shift in footing: I feel translucent to his bold brushstroke. When did this happen? The signal must have come from me. I must have given ground somewhere in the invisible air between us. Twenty-seven. Should I be so cavalier with marriage proposals?

And—I have spent the spring planting seeds of Greece and perhaps even Asia in the family imagination, and it is time to pick the fruit. Thoby thinks travelling this autumn would be 'splendid', and when I asked about Greece, he said, 'Why not?' Wherever Thoby goes, we all want to follow.

Later (everyone asleep)

No? No. No? No. Really? Clive wants me to write a letter to explain my no. He is right. It is no longer a single straight-syllabled word solidly built and painted in the primary colours of conviction. Instead it is a tumbledown cottage of a word, furnished in curiosity and thatched in doubt.

1 July 1906—46 Gordon Square

I have written a letter to Mr Bell. I tried for decorum but am better suited to honesty. Every time I try for Elinor Dashwood, I wind up as Marianne. I decided to tell him only things that are true:

That I like him better than any man *not* in my own family.

That he ought to go away for a year to make me miss him as I am too selfish and lazy to understand my own feelings if he stays here.

That I can not marry him now.

Quick—send it, Nessa, before common sense returns.

•

Telling the whole bald, messy, unflattering truth suits me, whether it leaves me enigmatic or not. Easy to remember and unnecessary to defend—one coat of thick, pure paint.

69 LANCASTER GATE

LONDON W.

2 July 1906

Dear Woolf,

It is July, and after the hard, brilliant whites and rioting fuchsias of the south of France, England's gentle rained-on summer seems decidedly unimpressive. But then our rain must be a teardrop trifle next to the fearsome monsoons of the East. Can't fathom a monsoon. It seems biblical in its indecent lack of moderation. It isn't the volume of the rain but the punctuality. From this month to that month, I shall be wet. Oh my dear, no.

What is my news, you asked in your last letter? My news is grim. Duncan has returned to London and taken refuge with his family in Hampstead (yes, near to my family in Hampstead— torture), and so I am taking refuge with Maynard. It is not really a practical solution as it only further muddles a muddle.

Desmond is moving to the country with his épouse. It is the end, my petal, the end.

In happier news: the Gothic family are on the march. The newest plan is Greece in the autumn and then perhaps on to Constantinople. Vanessa has such a determination to live—I admire it. Unfortunately my determination is only to love— and that never ends well, does it? All bad things must end too, surely?

Yours,
Lytton

5 July 1906—46 Gordon Square (in the garden, hot—finally!)

Off to Eton, and what Virginia refers to as 'the Cornish wedding' on Tuesday. I am pleased for Desmond and terrified of his bride. She is permanent. She is not someone one must suffer as a dinner companion and then escape. She has our Desmond forever.

Saturday 7 July 1906—46 Gordon Square (in the garden square)

'He really loves you, you know.' Lytton was sitting on the worn park bench beside me.

'Yes, so he says,' I said. I did not know how much Lytton knew.

'No, Nessa. He really loves you. And this is not how Clive usually loves.'

I was startled. It had not occurred to me that Clive had loved elsewhere. I felt a forward jolt of jealousy. How complacent of me to assume I stood alone.

'Not how he *usually* loves?' I asked, kicking the sandy gravel of the path and scuffing my shoe.

'No. Clive usually loves in character, not as himself.'

'Character? I keep repeating you—forgive me.'

'Yes, he plays the urbane, genial host of a vaguely intellectual dinner party. Haven't you noticed?'

No, I hadn't noticed. The Clive I know is limned by sincerity. It is bone deep.

Monday 9 July 1906—46 Gordon Square (hot!)

Shopping again all morning. I asked Virginia to come with me, as I am buying travelling clothes for her as well, but she refused.

'I want *you* to dress me, Nessa. I will like the clothes so much more if you choose them.' Exasperating.

I ordered travelling suits, muslin day dresses, four blouses, navy serge skirts, plus belts and two evening dresses (black silk with a pearl neckline for Virginia and grey chiffon with roses at the shoulder for me). I also ordered white lawn dresses and bathing costumes (red-striped for me and navy sailor for Virginia).

BLO' NORTON

3 August 1906—Blo' Norton Hall, Norfolk

This house, which we have taken for the month, is low-slung with peaked roofs at either end. Like a child standing between her parents. Inside it has a stripped-down, bleached, Elizabethan feeling. The stair-cases creak and the raw beams shift and resettle. The taps in the bath splutter but, after coaxing, produce hot water. It is a welcoming, rumbling, tolerant place.

Later

Thoby and Adrian joined us this evening. It snipped the encroaching tension between Virginia and me. She asks about Clive at least three times a day, and it is only when I reassure her that I will not *ever* marry him that she lets the conversation go—exhausting. The boys leave for Italy in a few days.

4 August 1906—Blo' Norton Hall

We wear old cotton dresses and come down to luncheon marked by our pursuits: I am dipped in paint, Virginia is stamped in ink.

The house is quiet again. Too quiet. I miss the vigorous, heavy tread of my brothers. Thoby and Adrian have gone to ride horses down the Dalmatian coast. I wanted to go with them, but Virginia is not up to it. We had a row. Virginia is insisting on bringing Violet to Greece. A bother, as I was hoping it would be just us. I should have more patience with Virginia, but I am restless. By the afternoon, when the day is scratched and broken in, I am done with it and anxious to start a fresh one. I want to be in motion: on a ship, a horse, a train, a truck—it does not matter. I want to be moving away from here, where I worry about letters I will write and receive.

And—A note from Desmond. They are moving out of London. And so it begins.

7 August 1906—Blo' Norton Hall (sunny and mild)

Virginia walks for miles. She has a map and sets out like a surveyor to meet the countryside. Sometimes she bicycles (and gets grease on her hem), but most often she walks. She comes back breathless and muddy, telling tales of leaping fences and storming churches. I know I should not fret and just let her ramble as she chooses, but when she says she is writing and then does not write, I worry.

14 August 1906—Blo' Norton Hall (windy but sunny)

Virginia keeps talking about the two of us being on 'our wedding tour' and I try to encourage the description into 'holiday'. It is not the affection but the belligerence that frightens me. She is driven by the need to footprint, to own, to possess. A wedding tour is by nature a pairing, an exclusion.

Later

It came in the first post. Clive has responded to my messy, unflattering letter. He has developed an uncanny sureness, a certainty that I will change my mind and marry him. He is happy in his conviction, and perversely, I am happy that he is happy.

Virginia saw his handwriting on the envelope and twice over breakfast asked me to promise that I will *never* marry him. Rather than shoring up my decision to reject him, her persistence is having the opposite effect. I can't think why I am rejecting him now. I *like* his company. As far as I know it, I like his character. It is not rapture, nor even love, but a balanced liking. Is that something that should be thrown away with such vehemence?

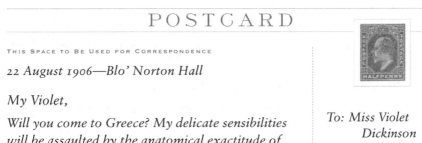

POSTCARD

THIS SPACE TO BE USED FOR CORRESPONDENCE

22 August 1906—Blo' Norton Hall

My Violet,

Will you come to Greece? My delicate sensibilities will be assaulted by the anatomical exactitude of antiquity—no fig leaves for this family. I am delighting in anticipation. The having is never so good as the almost having, don't you think?
      Your
      Virginia

To: Miss Violet
      Dickinson
      Burnham Wood
      Cottage
      Welwyn

PS: I have fallen in love with a story.

LANDSCAPE: THE VILLAGE OF EAST HARLING AT DAWN

25 August 1906—Blo' Norton Hall

Now she *is* writing. Every morning she stands and smokes and writes. She is using her travel desk from home. The wood is worn on the left top corner, where she pulls and paws when she cannot find the right word. Writing settles her. It gives her day a shape, a tempo. I hope she is working on the novel and so can keep her drumbeat rhythm for months and years instead of watching it eddy away as it does after a short article or review.

Later

'Rosamund Merridew. What do you think?' Virginia asked this afternoon.

We were walking to visit the village church, which is meant to be pretty, but I have not yet seen it.

'Rosamund Merridew? Floral. Is she a floral woman? What does she smell of?' I asked, not looking up. The road was muddy and pitted, and I worried for my new kid boots.

'She smells of earth, coffee, and raspberries. She is a *fascinated* woman, a hunting woman. She is bound up in the history of another woman who lived four hundred years before,' Virginia said cryptically.

'Careful, Virginia,' I said as I untangled her skirt from a roadside hedge. Virginia would have just torn it in her impatience to keep walking. 'Who is the four-hundred-year-old woman?'

'Joan Martyn. She kept a diary following one year in her life.' Virginia leapt over a grubby puddle. 'The year she decided to get married.'

There it was.

Even later (after supper)

We received a letter from Thoby and Adrian. They have had perfect weather and have ridden as far as Montenegro. Now they are headed south to the baked island of Corfu.

Virginia and I are back in London on Monday.

7 September 1906—46 Gordon Square (evening, too chilly to open the windows)

Violet *is* coming with us. She is travelling in Italy at the moment and will meet us in Athens. We have also decided to stop and see Irene's family, the Noels, in the Greek islands.

We leave tomorrow and meet the boys in Olympia on Thursday. Olympia: where the men meet the gods.

And—Virginia's story is about acceptance and alienation. What does it mean to belong to a place or country or family? What is it to be English? Why do certain places hold an emotional charge and others allow the current to pass right through?

TO ANTIQUITY

·⚜·

POSTCARD

THIS SPACE TO BE USED FOR CORRESPONDENCE

20 September 1906

Dearest Woolf,

The Gothic family have gone a-roving and I am twenty-five miles north-west of Lairg—Where? Exactly. It is Glencarron Lodge, Bell's abominable family's Scottish hunting box. Bell is pre-dictably tweedy and takes gruesome delight in shooting pretty winged things. His Parisian decadence was a façade; he fooled us all. He is a sportsman interloper snucked into our cosmopolitan midst. But his unsinkable good humour as ever redeems him. He has become sure of

To: Mr Leonard Woolf
Asst Gov't Agent
Jaffna
Ceylon

Vanessa. Some internal critical balance has tipped. I hope to meet Maynard in a few days and am longing for his anaemic, effete aversion to nature. Only the Goth can pull off indecent good health, outdoor pursuits, and indoor cultivation.

Duncan has inherited obscene amounts money from a dead aunt and is returning to Paris. My soul is in ruins.

Yours,
Lytton

LOCH MERKLAND, LAIRG, SCOTLAND

POSTCARD

THIS SPACE TO BE USED FOR CORRESPONDENCE

24 September 1906

My dear Keynes,

Help. I am abandoned in the rocky wilds of Scotland with Bell, who is either floating on his back in a rowboat, hatching beastly plots to entrap Vanessa, or out stomping through the bushes loaded for bear. None of it makes for good company. I am also trapped with his ghastly, robust family who grip their cutlery tightly in their meaty fists and discuss horses ad nauseam. Rescue me at once.

To: *Mr Maynard*
Keynes
6 Harvey Road
Cambridge

Yours,
Lytton

PS: Thoby and Adrian have reached Corfu and are frolicking in the sea. We should have gone with them. I am in need of a Greek frolic.

THE ISLAND CHURCH AT LOCH MERKLAND, LAIRG, SCOTLAND

1 October 1906—Palace Hotel, Athens

It all began well.

Ferry to France, and then bumping, rattling trains through Italy, to the bare, hot southern tip. I am pleased with the green-lined parasols. They do cut the glare of the endless white. And the earth paused, and then came the ocean. And what an ocean. This blue bilingual water knows itself. It is a weighted, fresh, crystal blue. I meant to read but was unable to look away from such a blue.

We changed boats at Patras, much the way one changes trains at Norwich. A small Greek man, with a thick Greek moustache, boarded the boat and organised us in perfect English. Travellers, trunks, parasols, and papers, he strapped our luggage to a small, wiry boy, sent him on ahead to the next boat, and instructed us to follow. This boat, the *Peloponnese*, was smaller, tinnier, and grubbier but sailed the same gemstone sea.

When the boat docked, we landed among the ancients. Our brothers, suntanned, white-toothed, and sweaty, whooped from the shore. Thoby has become even more expansive in this country. Dismissive of Baedeker and his kind, he relies solely on local advice. He believes in it like a religion. He speaks to everyone: milkmen, postmen, taverna owners, bankers, bakers, waiters, farmers, fishermen, toymakers, tailors, bus drivers, and the police. And being Thoby, he is instantly invited in for coffee, ouzo, olives, and cheese. He is returned to us flushed, happy, noisy, and full of ideas. 'We must visit *this* temple, on *this* mountain, on *this* day. We must eat *this* cheese from *this* goat on *this* farm. We must drink *this* wine from *this* region at *this* price.' And so we do. This family. We sail and swim in *this* sea under *this* sun, together. Even with an extra Violet, I feel the balanced symmetry of four.

In Athens we checked into the awful Athena Hotel and had to change immediately. There was a rat in Virginia's bathtub, and Adrian's window had no glass. We moved to the Palace Hotel—fusty but clean. Curvy gilded chairs, ornate beds, and tall open windows—I like it here.

I shared with Virginia and we looked out over the Acropolis. Thoby and Adrian looked over the square and were disappointed. But we did not stay long and quickly moved on to the ruins of Mycenae; Eleusis, the birthplace of Aeschylus; Epidauros and the beautiful crumbling amphitheatre; and sleepy Nauplia with its Italianate architecture.

And there, among the chalky ruins and the hot light, my appendix began to complain. And so we returned to Athens. Violet (who had a slight indisposition from the oily food) and I stopped here, and the others went on to visit the Noels in Euboea.

Violet is surprisingly easy to be with and much different on her own than with Virginia. She tries less and laughs more. I like her much better than I expected, but that might also be a product of being away. Familiar people become much more endearing when one is away.

Later

The doctor was here and thinks whatever is troubling my midsection is being agitated by a nervous condition. 'Do nervous conditions run in your family?' he asked in thickly rounded English. Don't they just. I must relax, he says. He charged next to nothing and prescribed four large glasses of champagne a day.

Virginia Stephen
46 Gordon Square
Bloomsbury

Achtmetaga, Euboea

9 October 1906

Dearest Dolphin,

We have fallen onto a seahorse-shaped island in the Aegean Sea, and I feel nestled in the bounty of Greek goddesses. I am sure we are surrounded by light-footed forest nymphs who will braid flowers through our hair and throw garlands round our necks should we fall asleep.

Today our host, Mr Frank Noel, took us picnicking on a grassy slope by a pine grove. He and Thoby discussed local birds for hours, and I lay reading Byron in the grass. When staying with the descendants of Byron, one cannot read Wordsworth, no matter how immortal one feels. How Byron loved this country. He died not far from here, in Missolonghi, but I do not think we will have time to visit there. I must rush back to you, my summer Dolphin, and have a stern discussion with your unruly tummy.

> *Your*
> *Billy Goat*

PS: Do you know, they have his writing desk. Oh, the saucy things that saucy man must have written at that desk.

14 October 1906—Palace Hotel, Athens (hot!)

They return tomorrow, and I am determined to be well enough to go on to Constantinople. You can set one foot in Asia and one in Europe, and I am *not* going to miss it. I have been reading about the Church of Santa Sophia and the Bosphorus, and my dreams are lit by spice.

15 October 1906—Palace Hotel, Athens

They are back. Virginia presented me with three letters she wrote to me but did not have time to send, and Thoby gave me a small square drawing of a lark. I love Thoby's birds. Adrian lost his hat and got terribly sunburnt.

Wednesday 17 October 1906—Palace Hotel, Athens

It was a sparkling morning, and we were breakfasting on the hotel terrace. I came down but was already regretting moving. Virginia was not eating her breakfast. I was drinking my prescribed champagne with orange juice and was not in the right mood to get tangled up with Virginia. I left it to Thoby.

'Virginia, of course they don't speak ancient Greek. Stop embarrassing everyone,' Thoby said, sipping his coffee and reaching for the English newspapers.

'Why *wouldn't* they speak their native tongue?' Virginia said obstinately.

'It is *not* their native tongue. It was, two thousand years ago, but not any more. Do you speak Anglo-Saxon?' Thoby said, disappearing behind his paper.

'If Sophocles or Aeschylus had written in Anglo-Saxon, then yes, I would be fluent,' Virginia pronounced, opening her guidebook.

Later (in the hotel drawing room—after ten p.m.)

'Nessa?' Thoby asked.

I waited.

'Do you miss him?'

There was no need to ask whom he meant.

I could not answer. *Yes,* but I do not want Virginia to know? *No,* I do not miss him enough to marry him? *Yes,* but please don't ask me about it?

Seeing my confusion, Thoby squeezed my hand in sympathy. 'Not yet. You do not have to think about it yet. Bell is patient. He is a huntsman. He understands the value of waiting. He loves you, Nessa. I think he would wait forever.'

Roger Fry
The City Club of New York
55–57 West 44th Street
New York

20 October 1906

My dear Mother,

The new gallery was finally finished on Wednesday, and the opening reception was held tonight. We had an awful time getting it ready. In the end, I was mixing the paint colours for the decorator myself as he would not get on with it. I have become an expert in haranguing contractors and electricians and printers. But tonight's gala was a success. The gallery looked beautiful. We borrowed a Cipollino table and placed it in the centre of the smaller room, and I scrounged up two lovely Rodin bronzes to sit majestically on top.

I feel increasingly entrenched in this country. I am no longer surprised by the wrong-sided traffic or the flat-vowelled bellowing, the wide avenues or the tightly gridded cities, but I never feel at peace. As soon as I have a letter from Helen, I count back to the day she sent it and breathe relief that she was all right on that day. But then my mind pitches forward and the brief respite is over. I count the days since, and the fretting begins again. I do not think I can keep this up much longer. I feel such a gathering pull towards home.

> *Your loving son,*
> *Roger*

THE EAST

Sunday 21 October 1906—Tokatliyan Hotel, Constantinople

What an exotic family we are. I was too ill to walk to the boat and so was carried in a litter. Carried in a *litter*. It is nearly impossible to be graceful in a litter. It bounces and yanks, and your head bobbles and your stomach drops. It would have been better to walk. The boat was gruesome. When one is afflicted with a stomach sickness, a boat is not the answer.

Later

Adrian has lost his luggage, naturally, and is wearing Thoby's clothes, which look ridiculous on him. No one but Thoby can carry off Thoby's clothes.

Virginia Stephen
46 Gordon Square
Bloomsbury

Tokatliyan Hotel, Constantinople

21 October 1906

Dearest Nelly,

I began this letter to you at six o'clock this morning when I stood
on the deck of the steamer and saw the Orient for the first time.
Wrapped in a fur-trimmed coat and feeling a bit Russian, I settled
down to write you a long letter. I got as far as the date and
stopped, as there it was: Constantinople, like a marzipan feast
glimmering on the wave. Santa Sophia floated in the centre like a
wedding cake; three golden spheres of impossibly ripe architecture.
How can something so definite be made of such rounded stuff?

Closer and closer, and it did not disappoint. Do you know, I
was not expecting the East. Never having left Europe, I feel like a
freshwater fish who hadn't realised there was an ocean. I did not
understand that such a place was possible. There is a story waiting
for me here. A story of magic and change.

Tomorrow morning we go to see the view of the city from Pera.
We will look down from a tower called Galata upon a river city of
misted gold.

By the way, I just read that Cortés, bloodthirsty, Aztec-
murdering Cortés, was the first man to bring tomatoes to Europe. I
thought you would want to know.

Missing you dearest,
Virginia

25 October 1906—Tokatliyan Hotel, Constantinople

The air feels different here. Gritty and tinted with a dusty light I do not yet understand. Today we visited the Church of Santa Sophia. What to do with such a building. A church and then a mosque and then a church. But she is still none of those things. She is entirely herself.

And now we will be four: three Stephens and a Violet. Thoby has to return to London early and will be taking the boat train tonight. I was hoping he would change his mind and stay, but he had promised to meet Lytton and Saxon in the Lake District, and it cannot be put off as the cottage is already paid up.

'Bother the cottage,' Virginia said.

I did not want him to go either but recognised the inevitability. Virginia ignores inevitability and refused to let the subject drop.

'But if you stay with us, you will get to ride home on the Orient Express. To come so close and then miss it? People will think you lack imagination,' Virginia said, her voice rising steeply. I saw Thoby tense. We knew that tone.

'Or, Ginia, they will commend me for my imagination. How rare a person it must take to get so close and then *not* go? That takes a rare man,' Thoby said, pulling her to him. 'I will miss you and be very sorry not to be here,' he said into the top of her head. She calmed. It was what she was waiting for.

Later (after supper)

We sat in the hotel drawing room. There was an odd assortment of travellers, Violet, and us. I poured coffee for Virginia but did not expect her to drink it.

Virginia was sullen but controlled. Thoby had said goodbye to her last. To be saved for last is very important to Virginia.

28 October 1906— Tokatliyan Hotel, Constantinople (hot and close!)

Ill again. Desperately ill. Adrian and Virginia are taking me home.

And—The train is booked. Adrian was able to rearrange our seats for tomorrow morning instead of next week.

Later

I managed some soup and a little bread tonight. My fever spikes up quite suddenly, and I lose my way in a thought. We are leaving for London early tomorrow. It will not be an easy trip, and Adrian and Virginia are both worrying about it, which is only making me more uncomfortable.

Clive. Now, when I feel so unsteady and far from the familiar crutches of home, I miss him terribly.

29 October 1906—The Orient Express (late, everyone asleep)

The rocking of the train is soothing as I write this. Everyone is settled into sleeping compartments, and the black, shadowy scenery flashes past the thick glass window. Such a long day.

This morning:

'It is a regular train,' Adrian said, stating the obvious.

Virginia shot him a withering look.

I looked up from my book. 'Should it be something else?' I too had been disappointed by the train. Black with peeling gold lettering, the outside was not promising. Inside there are relics of its fabled past. Elaborate Tiffany-style lights and curved divans upholstered in cracked red velvet. At night I am sure it can pass for luxurious, but in the inflexible daylight, it looks worn through.

'No, no, I just thought it would be *more* than a train,' Adrian said, clearly wishing he had never made the remark.

Virginia was enjoying his muddle—it distracted her from missing Thoby.

'I know what you mean,' I said, rescuing Adrian. 'It is the *Orient Express*. One expects it to be drawn by elephants.'

Virginia rolled her eyes.

THE RETURN

❧

GEORGE. STOP. NESSA ILL. STOP. NOT SERIOUS. STOP. RETURN-
ING EARLY. STOP. ARRIVE 1 NOV DOVER. STOP. YRS VIRGINIA.

DEAREST SNOW. STOP. RETURNING ILL. STOP. THOBY AWAY AND
VIRGINIA HOPELESS. STOP. PLEASE VISIT LONDON. STOP.
ARRIVE 1 NOV. STOP. ALL LOVE NESSA.

1 November 1906—46 Gordon Square (chilly and wet)

A small, mousy nurse was waiting for us upon our return to Dover. A nurse! George must have arranged it. She held a sign that read 'Miss V. Stephen'. 'Well, that could mean either of us,' Virginia said. I did not take the bait. I was too tired. The nurse proved more cumbersome than she looked, but at least she could help Adrian sort out his lost luggage.

I was irritated and just wanted to get home. A nurse was all so unnecessary, and I made the mistake of saying so. Virginia gave me a triumphant look. I am always telling her that her nurses *are* necessary. No use arguing. I felt like telling her that if I were raving mad and running all over the house shouting nonsense, as she does, then I would absolutely require a nurse—but I didn't.

And then we returned here and were shocked. Instead of finding the house empty and Thoby gone to the Lake District, we found him here and very unwell. Not serious, the doctor assured us, but uncomfortable. George, who picked us up from the station, insisted the doctor examine me as well. The doctor announced that I was recovering but not quickly enough and must go to bed at once. I did as he asked but looked in and kissed poor Thobs on his feverish head. Virginia is delighted to have us both invalided for a bit. She asked me not to 'recover too fast or I won't get enough chance to spoil you'. The idea does not improve my nerves.

And—Bother. The doctor also said I had to gain at least eight lbs and brought a weighing machine for me to use every third day.

2 November 1906—46 Gordon Square

Thoby has malaria, a bad case apparently. Dr Thompson just came in and told me (he is replacing Dr Savage, who is away for a few days). The dreadful disease has been nesting inside Thobs for weeks. He must have had fever in Greece but never said. But the doctor has instructed us not to worry. An atmosphere of *calm* will speed his recovery. This was said

to me but aimed at Virginia. She is genuinely shocked by Thoby's diag-
nosis but is doing her best, I can tell. I am also shocked. Thoby is the
deep ground, and we are the fickle, flexible tree that rests upon it. How
can the ground fall ill?

And—Now wishing I had not cabled Snow to visit as I am not the
one who needs looking after.

Saturday 3 November 1906—46 Gordon Square

Clive came again today. He has been stopping in every day, and is the
one who insisted poor Thobs go to bed and not to the Lake District. I
am grateful.

This afternoon:

'What if I just leave the offer on the table, like a fruit bowl?' he said,
sounding amused rather than nervous.

'A fruit bowl? Did you just compare your marriage proposal to a
fruit bowl?' I shifted on the sofa, tucking the thick cream blanket around
my legs. I am meant to be in bed, but Snow allowed me down to Thoby's
study. I am glad she is here, although her unruffled calm is annoying
Virginia.

'Yes. Why not? Fruit symbolises the offering of love and devotion,'
Clive said with a look of wry dignity.

'And knowledge. Fruit gets women into trouble,' I said carefully.

And—Weighed every other morning now. Gained one lb. As I get
weighed in my nightgown, I have moved the weighing machine into my
sitting room.

Later—back upstairs

Clive has been considering my suggestion that he go away for a year to
jolt me into understanding myself. Perhaps Paris. As I heard him talk
about it, I felt a shiver of jealousy. Good. I will nurture that. Perhaps it
may grow into something useful. But he will not leave now. He will not
leave Thoby while he is so ill.

Clive Bell
12, King's Bench Walk
The Temple

5 November 1906

Strache,

Get down here. Bring Saxon. Get Desmond. The Goth is ill, and while the doctor swears it is malaria and just miserable, rather than threatening, I am beginning to think the man is a charlatan and want to get a second opinion. Goth doesn't look like a man with malaria. His face is waxy and slack, and his great bear's body has rather sunk in on itself. Looks bad.

The girls are all right. Virginia is fixated on what he eats and sees each spoonful of coddled egg and clear broth as a sign of immediate recovery. Nessa herself is very ill and has not been allowed to see him. She is a quieter, fragile Nessa, and I only love her more. Adrian is pragmatic and dogmatic and hell-bent on not questioning the doctor. Frankly, I am surprised these Stephens are not panicked, given their history of losing people. In over my head, Strache. Hurry.

Yours,
Bell

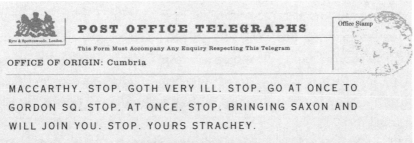

POST OFFICE TELEGRAPHS

Eyre & Spottiswoode, London.

This Form Must Accompany Any Enquiry Respecting This Telegram

OFFICE OF ORIGIN: Cumbria

Office Stamp

MACCARTHY. STOP. GOTH VERY ILL. STOP. GO AT ONCE TO GORDON SQ. STOP. AT ONCE. STOP. BRINGING SAXON AND WILL JOIN YOU. STOP. YOURS STRACHEY.

N4H7C—RECIPIENT MUST SIGN UPON DELIVERY

8 November 1906—46 Gordon Square (early—everyone asleep)

'Dearest?' I touched his foot so he would know I was there. I was not meant to see him, but I had to.

'Nessa,' he said, turning his face towards me. His eyes were open and glassy. He had not been sleeping after all.

'They are all here. Lytton, Saxon, Desmond, and Clive. They have all come to see you.'

I knew the arrival of his friends would mean much to him. His face lit with a faint smile. Like a pale pool of gaslight on a fogged street.

'Good men, Nessa. They are all good men,' he said, his voice dwindling as he used up his strength. His chest rose and fell rapidly with the effort. 'Bell. Bell is especially good.'

'Yes, dearest,' I said, taking his hot, papery hand. He closed his eyes, and we fell into the comfortable silence of siblings.

I thought many times I had heard Thoby and his friends discussing the nature of good. By whose standard should good be measured? By whose count should good be counted? Thoby's good is good enough for me.

Later—early evening (my sitting room)

'Virginia.' I struggled for patience. 'All I know is what you know and what the doctor told us. I did not receive any more information than you.'

I closed my eyes. Keeping them open is very difficult these days. My appendix appears to have improved, but my strength refuses to return. I am meant to be taking the rest cure but find bed more exhausting than not bed. And so I get up. I bathe but then get into my nightgown and blue silk wrapper again. I never manage to get my hair up and just leave it in a long braid snaking down my back. Virginia came in today and tied a black ribbon at the bottom to hold it together.

I am sure it was just the travelling that wore me out and nothing more sinister. Dr Thompson has prescribed an invigorating tonic for nerves, and rest, complete rest, which is of course a huge bother.

'Virginia,' called Clive from the hall. 'Virginia, she is meant to be asleep. Come away, please.'

This is how it is now. Clive roams all over the house like a member of the family. This morning I saw him upstairs without his jacket—such informality would have been outrageous a month ago. He speaks to Dr Thompson about the medical treatments and then discusses them with us. We have come to rely on him. Yesterday Snow went to *him* to ask if he thought she was still needed or if she ought to return home. It is probably best that she go, as she gets on Virginia's nerves. Clive told Snow he would send a telegram at the first sign of trouble, and in the meantime he promised to look after us and so drove her to the station. Should I mind such intimacies? I find I do not. I am relieved. Yesterday I found him and Virginia discussing enemas in the drawing room: glycerine versus turpentine—dear God. Had no idea what to make of it and so returned to bed.

·

In my furthest reaches, I recognise this malaise of mine. It is from nursing Virginia last year—when she went really mad, and I had to hand her over to Violet. I was unravelled to my core but did not have time to collapse then. It is an old debt that has to be paid sometime, and I may as well pay it now. Virginia said tonight that she is sure Thoby is improving. She says she heard the doctor say so. She also said Thoby ate nearly half a chicken, which must be a good sign. Thoby could hardly manage toast and weak tea yesterday, so I do not imagine he has already moved on to chicken. Virginia must be mistaken.

And—Violet has typhoid. Ghastly. Virginia is writing to her now.

9 November 1906—46 Gordon Square (two p.m.)

He's awake! We sat in Thoby's room talking of nothing: the new field glasses Thoby wants to buy, Adrian's stolen bicycle, Virginia's pens, and my nerves. Clive and Lytton had gone to luncheon and it was just us. Just us.

Saturday 10 November 1906—46 Gordon Square (after lunch)

'I want to tell him, Nessa.' Virginia has been increasingly strident since Snow left. She has run the enemy out of town and must dance to celebrate. The doctor has recommended that she spend no more than ten minutes twice a day visiting me.

'Tell who what?'

'Tell him—that thing, Clive—that he is not good enough.' Her venom spilt, she sank back into her chair. Frankly, I was surprised. I had thought her attitude towards him had improved. But I knew better than to try to shift her opinion. She had the look of a commanding general who has measured the enemy and found them wanting. She looked coiled and oiled and dangerously excited.

'Virginia, Clive has been very kind—'

'Kind? You call sniffing round you like some great sniffing dog *kind*?' Her voice arced shrilly. 'He means *harm*, Nessa. He means to wriggle and fit and ingratiate until he has made himself one of us; now, while we are too disrupted and different and ill to defend ourselves. He is not *good* enough, Nessa. And it will *not* do.' Increasing in speed, her voice was pitching like a ship.

'Clive is—' I stopped. Clive is what?

'Clive is a great round ball of unrooted, well-decorated *nothing*. He has no *character*. He lacks *bottom*. And one day I shall sit him down and tell him so. I shall say, "Absurd Mr Bell, you lack bottom and are not good enough for us. Please go."'

She was sitting forward in her chair, her long, lean body curved like a spoon. Having arrived at her subject, her face had pulled into taut lines of precision and discord.

I lay back on the pillows, too exhausted to argue. She waited.

'What do you say to that, Nessa? What will you do when I tell your thing to go away, we do not want him?'

'He does not want us, Virginia.' I looked at her levelly, raising my head from the pillows. 'He wants *me*.'

THOBY

14 November 1906—46 Gordon Square (early evening)

They are all downstairs. I can hear them from my little sitting room. Thoby's friends. Our friends. They visit him in turns, but too much and he gets worn out, so mostly they prowl about the drawing room and nap in Thoby's study. Occasionally they arrive in my room bearing a tray or a book or a daisy. Their company immeasurably helps what cannot be seen but drains Thoby's strength. This morning Lytton's spirited story about an argument he had with a woman who did not believe in women's suffrage left Thoby grey with effort but so much happier. Even I can see he is not improving. Patience, Dr Thompson says.

Later (after midnight)

Dr Savage is back! The second opinion. Clive summoned him.

Even later (two a.m.—can't sleep)

Softened voices in the hall. Doors open, chairs scuff the floorboards. I hear Clive's voice, 'I do not want to wake her. We will tell her in the morning.'

Thursday 15 November 1906—46 Gordon Square (early)

'Not malaria?' I repeated.

'It seems not,' Clive said. He looked exhausted. I am sure he leaves this house, but I have no idea when.

'Do they know what . . . ?'

'Typhoid. Quite serious. They will operate today, tomorrow at the very latest.'

'Operate?' I gripped the arm of the chair.

'Yes,' Clive said, looking at me steadily. 'There is a perforation. Savage says it must be closed or the poisons will leak.' He did not lessen the statement nor flinch from the graphic verbs. He just stood next to me while I absorbed the blow. Did he hope to halve the impact? Perhaps he did. Perhaps it worked.

'Will you—'

'Tell the others? Yes. I will. I have told Adrian and will tell Virginia after breakfast. Strachey was here last night and spoke to the doctor as well. He and Adrian have agreed to help should I run into trouble with Virginia.'

He tried to pry my fingers from the carved arm of the chair. I looked down and was surprised to see that my knuckles were bone white, wrapped around the wood.

Later (Thoby's study)

Downstairs for a few minutes. It was good to be dressed. Though I needn't have bothered. Downstairs is so different now. All of them go without their jackets, and everyone follows their own pursuits without necessarily talking. This one will read, those two will play cards, another one will sleep. I am not up to painting, but I have been enjoying the simple friendship of this room.

'Woolf had it,' Lytton said, laying down his book.

There was no need to ask what 'it' was. The word *typhoid* looms large in this house.

'No medication of any kind. The country doctor in Ceylon bumped over on his bicycle, put him to bed, starved him, and told him to hold absolutely still for three weeks, and he would come through. And do you know what? He did. And so will the Goth. Strength of ten. I asked Woolf to ship me that doctor and his bloody bicycle, and he never did, damn him.' Lytton was speaking to no one in particular. Desmond was writing at the desk, and Adrian was reading music at the piano but not playing. I looked at Clive, who was smoking at the open window. Footsteps on the stairs: the doctor.

Very late (wrapped in a blanket)

They will operate tomorrow. Dr Savage says he can do it here. It is better not to move him. I must go and tell Virginia. Time to face the cannon. The others did it last time. It is my turn.

16 November 1906—46 Gordon Square (late afternoon, chilly)

Tried to write letters today: the aunts and Snow and the Asquiths and the Balfours and the Freshfields and so many other family friends who have heard of Thoby's illness and sent cards. But I couldn't do it. I let the ink dribble onto the thick spongy paper. My fingers hovered over the page as if they had forgotten the alphabet.

Later

The operation was quick and apparently successful. He is asleep. He must sleep enough for us all, as no one else can.

And—We are not a religious family, but tonight my wish, liquid and pure, became a prayer. Please.

Saturday 17 November 1906—46 Gordon Square (early)

'Coddled eggs, Virginia?' I asked. 'Are you sure that is what he wants?'

'Yes, he told me. And sausages.' Virginia bridled at my scepticism.

'He *told* you?' I looked at Adrian warily. I knew Thoby had not yet woken.

'Ask him,' Virginia said imperiously. Instinctively, I looked around for Thoby to intercede. He is the heavy artillery when it comes to Virginia. But not today.

His temperature is holding steady.

Still later (midnight)

Hopeful. I opened his door to watch his chest rise and fall with sleep before creeping back to my room. Virginia heard me and came in and sat on the end of my bed. I did not talk. I did not want to.

20 November 1906—46 Gordon Square (midday)

Thoby, you died this morning. You died on a Tuesday. When I heard Virginia's scream, I was just coming out of the bath. I had washed my hair, and when I leaned over to kiss you, I dripped water onto your chest. Your eyes were already closed. I do not know who closed them. Or maybe you were asleep? Did you wake up in time to see your last morning?

I need to go and tell you that you died today. To talk over the flowers and the cemetery and the verse and the drops of water on your chest. You are the only one I want to talk to about it. It is an impossible circle with no door.

I look at this sentence and I think . . . but how can I think, write, want *anything*, Thoby, when you died this morning?

21 November 1906

Oh Woolf,

My dearest man, please sit. I was going to send a telegram and then realised that there is no rush. Even if you left this instant, you would never see our Goth again. His malaria was not malaria but typhoid. The operation that was a success ultimately failed. He left us yesterday. Such a quick moment, but what a very final thing.

Vanessa is the centre we hold to, although she does not know it. Virginia bucked and wriggled like a dying fish in order to evade this awful thing, but Vanessa stood up when grief knocked at the door. She turned to it squarely and put out her hand and took its hat and coat. There was no need for an introduction. They had met before.

Funeral on Sunday. Golders Green Crematorium. Bell has just sent me a note to say that he cannot go and would I take special care of Nessa? He knows he cannot get through such a grisly moment whole and does not want to come apart before her. It is not pride, I think, but care. It would do her no good. And so he is going birdwatching, to look for Thoby.

Look up, dearest Leonard. You may see him.

Such love,
Lytton

YES

22 *November 1906—46 Gordon Square (sunny)*

Yes. He asked again, and I have said yes. Yes. *Yes*.

Later (early afternoon)

I have come back to bed to selfishly think about myself. Out there, the house is engulfed in a thick, choking grief. The friends have gone, and Thoby's study is empty. We are left to get on with it. There is nothing to wait for.

I will marry Clive. I turn the decision over like a dish, checking for flaws. After each death, Mother, Father, Stella, came a wrenching sea change; a new fiery alchemy, a different physics. I know it will happen again. I cannot lose Thoby and stay the same.

But Clive knows me now. Knew me before. There is no other man I could marry who would know *this* Nessa. And now I will not have to go through the next terrible part alone.

Outside I heard a robin singing in the square.

BEZIQUE

※

Roger Fry
The City Club of New York
55-57 West 44th Street
New York

22 November 1906

To my beloved Wife,

It is decided, I will return to you for the Christmas holiday. There
was some scuffle about dates and salary, but it is settled now, and I
shall be with you on Christmas Day. I have warned Mr Morgan
and the trustees that I cannot keep this up indefinitely and must be
allowed to work out of England. To be near you. Will you be
pleased? I hope so. Your letters have been vague, my dear. I worry
for you constantly. Please tell me the first moment you feel the
awful sickness coming, and I will book passage at once. I cannot
bear being so far from you.

Your own,
Roger

PS: I am sailing on the RMS Baltic in case you should wonder but I
know you will expect me when you see me. How patient you are.

25 November 1906—46 Gordon Square

The funeral. Friends he loved and words he loved. Mother. Father. Stella. And now Thoby. I was calm, removed, all my denial caged by defeat. We lost him.

Lytton took charge of Virginia, and I sat with Adrian and the aunts. Virginia was contained, and I had stopped fretting over her until she asked if anyone could smell burning. Aunt Anny blenched when Virginia began to sniff the air.

And—Letters: from Mr Henry James, Mr George Meredith, the aunts, and others. Famous others. The writers, the painters, the social lions. Father's literary friends; Mother's artist friends. I resent their interjection. Not yet, I think. I cannot bear to read them yet.

26 November 1906—46 Gordon Square (writing in bed)

There are whole moments when I am happy. How utterly absurdly inappropriate. I have even been happy thinking of Thoby. I am going to marry his Mr Bell. I feel as though I can slip out of bed, walk softly down the hallway, and tell him. But he is not there. Maud changed the linen on his bed today. The linen is changed on Mondays whether Thoby has died or not.

He was happy. All his life. *All* his life. There is an all now: beginning and end. But then I suppose no one gets out alive.

Lately, in the last years especially, he has been so happy. Surely that is a good life? That is enough? Dear God, I hope so.

27 November 1906—46 Gordon Square

George and Gerald were pleased when I told them.

'Good man, Bell,' George said bluffly. I was surprised, as Clive's passion is modern French art—not something I would think would impress George. He distrusts the French.

'You approve?' I asked.

'Man sits a horse well and goes to a good tailor. Says a lot about character, if you ask me.'

I think he is just pleased that I accepted *someone*.

Virginia is hollowed by grief. First losing Thoby, and now losing me. 'But I am right here,' I keep telling her.

29 November 1906—46 Gordon Square

It took me three hours to persuade Virginia to have a bath this morning. Her hair was hanging in matted clumps. Now Adrian is trying to talk her into breakfast. The day does not work, does not flow into itself without Thoby. The day stumbles and stutters and has forgotten its gait. Clive does not try to step in and replace him, and I am grateful. It would ruin everything for us if he tried to play the part of Thoby.

Later

Virginia is reading Catullus. She is reading the poem he wrote on the death of his brother. She copied out a single line over and over into her writing notebook. It soothes something in her.

Atque in perpetuum, frater, ave atque vale. I looked it up. *And forever, brother, hail and farewell.*

Had he lived, Thoby would have liked that. *Had he lived.*

Friday 30 November 1906—46 Gordon Square

Virginia left her postcard for Violet, who is still down with typhoid but is improving, on the hall table to be posted today. Adrian was to take it when he went out.

'*No change in Thoby's temperature, but he did manage some milk this morning.*'

Oh, Virginia. No.

1 December 1906—46 Gordon Square (late)

We were all in my sitting room, where we collect in the evenings now. Thoby's friends stop by more often now rather than less. The house has become a hub, a shrine. It is like a busy railway station. Friends arriving, hurrying, waiting, leaving. Packages, hats, umbrellas left. Plans and schedules and people criss-cross our day. When Virginia and I returned from tea with George and Margaret, I found Desmond and Lytton playing chess in Thoby's study, and Adrian and Clive were reading the evening papers.

Sophie is unimpressed with our irregular visitors. No one adheres to invitations any more, so we no longer offer them. Instead, we just negotiate the day as it comes and whoever comes with it. They all feel closer to him here. As do we. We are all clinging together. We are all pretending we know what happens next.

'And so you will leave on Sunday?' Clive leaned down to tuck the blanket a little closer around me. I caught the edge of Virginia's impatience. She cannot bear his propriety, his ease with me, and considers it temerity. Her mouth pressed into an obstinate line.

Lytton stretched his long thin legs towards the fire. 'Yes, Adrian, you'll come to Cambridge, won't you? Keynes and James will both be there, and Harry Norton and Hilton Young too, possibly.'

I looked quickly at Virginia. We have all known Hilton Young and his brothers since childhood, when their father and ours would go mountaineering together, but he has behaved differently towards Virginia recently. Although he still insists on talking about politics, he has taken particular care to speak to her at length. But Virginia betrayed no reaction upon hearing his name.

'Saxon is hoping to come up, but I can already tell he won't make it,' Lytton said, resettling his spectacles. 'James and Headlam want to go and see this wretched Greek play, full of keening women and heavy-handed prophecy no doubt, but that beautiful young Rupert Brooke is rumoured to get into a state of dishabille, and that is certainly worth the train fare.'

'Yes, I will come, if, if . . . that is all right, Ginia?' Adrian asked.

Virginia and Adrian are house hunting in Bloomsbury, as it has been decided that Clive and I will take over the lease of 46 Gordon Square on our own. Virginia is full of 'us and them' talk and does not like Adrian to stray far from town as they have so much to *do*. Adrian always looks a bit shrunken and diminished when Virginia is in this mood.

I am relieved not to be moving anywhere. Awful to admit but true, and as I am still taking the rest cure, the doctor does not want me to exert myself. I am hiding behind that, but then I moved us all here from Kensington—surely Virginia can manage to move round the corner?

'Walter Headlam is translating something from the Greek, isn't he?' Virginia asked, ducking Adrian's question. She knows very well that Walter Headlam is working on a new edition of Aeschylus. Adrian squirmed in his chair, too uncomfortable to ask his sister for permission again.

'Has Maynard found a job yet, Strache?' Clive asked.

'No. He is impossible. No employment meets his requirements. But then his requirements are absurd; something glorious and useful and of national importance? Ridiculous. He came second in the country in the civil service examination, something I find hilarious and he finds irksome. I hope he doesn't follow Woolf into the wilds of empire. That would *not* do.' Lytton pushed his small round spectacles farther up his nose in a gesture of disgust.

'But Strache, you are going to write for MacCarthy, aren't you?' Clive asked, steering the conversation away from the grinding stones of cynicism.

'I suppose I shall have to. It looks as if his strange little paper might actually happen. Extraordinary of Desmond to be part of something that functions.'

And—Virginia has asked everyone to write something about Thoby. Lytton says that it is more than he can bear. All his bright talk is skimmed over a huge deep of sadness.

7 December 1906—46 Gordon Square (icy)

I saw another of Virginia's postcards to Violet today. It was lying on the silver tray in the hall waiting for Virginia's afternoon walk to the post box.

'Not much change, but Thoby is cheerful today and asked for mar-malade rather than butter. A good sign, I feel.'

Dear God, Virginia.

Later

Clive and I play bezique now, a game for two. It drives her mad. There is a part of me that just wants her to shore herself up and get on with it. But that is not her way. Instead she is writing daily postcards to Violet, tracking Thoby's fictitious recovery.

'Shouldn't we do something about it?' Even as I said it, I could feel myself nestling into the word. We. Clive and I were playing cards in Thoby's study. 'And the worst thing is, I left it there on the tray. I did not know what else to do.'

'Shall I talk to her?' Clive asked, winning the trick.

I like that. His preference is always for action rather than discussion. 'And say what? She will deny it.'

'But we have seen the postcards—surely she can't disregard that. Bezique, forty points,' Clive said. A queen and a jack. 'Are you warm enough, darling? Another blanket?'

It is amazing how quickly the endearments have begun to litter our talk. 'She can. She can disregard anything she likes. The natural bound-aries you feel do not apply to her. Double bezique. Four kings,' I reached for the score sheet. 'Five hundred points.'

Still later

Adrian and Virginia found a house. 29 Fitzroy Square. George Bernard Shaw's old house. It is in an elegant square, designed by Adam. A circle in a square. A compelling, concentric shape. The neighbourhood is just over Tottenham Court Road and a bit shabbier than here. Theirs is the only house not yet broken into flats. Lytton says that Duncan Grant, who is planning to study at the Slade next year, has taken a studio a few doors down. A tiny dilapidated room in no. 22.

8 December 1906—46 Gordon Square

'I wasn't expecting it, that's all,' Clive said, humping my suitcase onto the bed. 'She just spun the argument round and round, and I got a bit lost.' He looked so surprised, not expecting to be fuddled by Virginia.

'It is her maddening charm. She can take what you assume is important and make it unimportant. Do I need a woollen dressing gown, do you think?'

I was laying out clothes for Maud to pack. Clive and I are going away for a few days to meet his family. I am terrified to meet them all. Lytton makes them out to be great hearty farm people who have converted to the genteel country life with huge unappealing zeal. But all he says can't be true, surely?

'Yes, I could see it was charm, but there was no logic there, no order. I don't understand her,' Clive said, handing me my washing kit.

'Oh, order irritates her hugely. Be careful about suggesting it.'

And—Violet read about Thoby's death in the newspaper and was appalled at Virginia's deception and heartbroken for us. Virginia is contrite.

9 December 1906—46 Gordon Square

Virginia and Adrian signed a five-year lease at £120 a year, which leaves some money in their budget for repairs and improvements. And they will need some improvements. I met the architects today. Virginia was supposed to come but decided to stay and write, so Adrian and I went alone. I am feeling much stronger, but we still took a cab over there as Virginia and Clive both insisted. Clive said not to bother going at all and to let Virginia and Adrian sort out the renovations, but I know they won't. The new house has electricity but needs a bath installed, so it really cannot wait.

We walked through the house, and besides the plumbing, several rooms need painting and the banisters and the floor in the hall need to be refinished. Virginia will have the whole of the second floor. I have tried to speak to her about paints and furniture but with no luck. We could clearly hear the clatter and boom of the traffic and noise from the street. They should have double windows put in.

When we got home, Virginia did not ask about the house.

10 December 1906—46 Gordon Square (cold and Christmassy)

This afternoon, over luncheon with Clive at Rules:

'And she just . . .'

'Yes, she accepted the reasoning and promised to correct it—not that it needs so much correcting now that Violet knows, but she has promised to apologise. Once she explained it, it was all very understandable, really,' Clive said, motioning for the waiter. 'The lamb as well, darling?'

I waited for him to finish ordering and said, 'What is understandable? How can Virginia writing letters to Violet every day describing Thoby's recovery'—I stumbled over the word—'be *understandable*? She actually told Violet that she, Adrian, *and Thoby* were off to the New Forest this week.'

'She simply wanted it to be true. She wanted to pretend. And she did not want to frighten Violet. Remember, Violet is battling typhoid too, although Virginia says she is on the mend. This wine is excellent.'

I looked at his sleek, unbothered calm and felt snaking irritation.

'I also would like it to be true. I would like my brother to be recovering in his room right now,' I finally said. 'I just do not give myself the luxury of pretending that he is.'

'Virginia has such an *imagination*—it is easy to see how it could happen.'

'Imagination?' I asked through gritted teeth.

And—Rules. The last time I went there, I was with Thoby. Each first without him sweeps my breath from me. But I am terrified to run out of firsts. Once they are gone, they cannot come back. It feels like I am leaving fresh, crisp footprints in new snow and marking up the clean white sheet of our life before. Soon there will be nothing left of the old life.

Later

We have started on the books. Virginia is taking all of the books. All of the books from Mother and from Father. I went upstairs to her sitting room tonight, and there were towers of books stacked *everywhere*. We did not mention Thoby's books. It is understood that they will never leave Thoby's study.

Books require bookshelves, and Virginia's sitting room will not have nearly enough. I added bookshelves to the list for the architects.

UNION POSTALE UNIVERSELLE

CEYLON (CYLAN)

10 December 1906

Jaffna, Ceylon

Lytton,

I have a confession. I burnt your last letter. I did not want it to exist. Inexcusable and I apologise. One must square up rather than run.

All is the same here. Charlie-the-dog has forgotten wet English winters and lives only for chasing fat Indian mice. They are brave and quick and drive him wild. I wish I could say I was coming

home immediately. I wish I felt pulled in a direction absolutely.
Please congratulate Maynard for me. A fellowship at Trinity
sounds excellent.

This letter has little point, I realise. I send it only to greet you,
my friend. I think of our June days in Cambridge with the Goth
reciting 'Luriana Lurilee'.

Your
Leonard

HRH KING EDWARD VII POSTAL STATIONERY

11 December 1906

Away, away away. Virginia, chastened and apologetic, has written Violet
a truthful letter. But it no longer concerns us as we are going *away*.

Treasures have emerged from the packing rubble. The missing copy
of Elizabeth Barrett Browning's *Aurora Leigh* (inscribed to Father, although the ink is faded and blurred now) turned up amongst the Hardy
novels, and letters from Tennyson and Disraeli to our great-grandmother
Pattle slid out of Mother's threadbare copy of *Villette*.

The work on the Fitzroy Square house is set to start the week after
Christmas. I am leaving detailed lists with Adrian as Virginia is reluctant to visit the new house.

And—We chose a date. St Pancras Registry Office, 7th February,
1907, half past ten. I will wear blue. I have not yet decided on a hat. We
will invite no one.

POSTCARD

13 December 1906

Dearest Woolf,

He has done it. Beastly Bell has snatched Vanessa, and they are affianced. Gruesome, ain't it? Virginia is reeling a bit at the prospect of her florid new brother-in-law but is taking it much better than I would have thought. The dreadful day is set for February. In other news of our general decomposition, Virginia and Adrian are moving to Fitzroy Square, the Mole has gone travelling, and MacCarthy has moved to Suffolk. I only see him on Tuesdays and Thursdays when he comes into town. Luckily, Virginia is keeping up the Thursday nights. Is this to be the way of things? Letter to follow.

> *Yours, Lytton*

To: Mr Leonard Woolf
     Asst Gov't House
     Jaffna
     Ceylon

SERIES 7: ROWBOATS IN SUMMER

THE BELLS OF WILTSHIRE

Friday 14 December 1906—Cleeve House, Seend, Wiltshire (wet and cold)

Well, what did I expect? They are country gentry, live in a country house, and like country sports. So, the house: the house is *not* beautiful. I'm sorry, house. The house is also *not* original. Whatever was here isn't any more, as Clive's father pulled it down to build this mock Jacobean mess, and I think it must be a pity. Anything old and gracefully crumbling would beat this great Victorian scalloped heap any day.

And the family? The mother is most likely lovely, but I never see her alone as she is always with her brute of a husband or Clive's unbearable sister, Lorna. Lorna sounds exactly like a hunting horn and moves with a great barrelling efficiency that I find unnerving. Even though the house is comparatively new (although one would never know it, as there is a freezing oak-panelled great hall *and* a minstrels gallery), it is not modernly equipped. The water supply is unreliable, and we are encouraged *not* to bathe—extraordinary. The parlour maid is called Meeks and the chauffeur is called Ovens. It is all too good to be true and would seem contrived in a novel. I must tell Morgan.

Later

I've been put in a freezing gothic bedroom complete with walls studded with decapitated animals. There is a cosy smallish dressing room for me and the same for Clive. We will use his dressing room as our studio. I will paint and he will write.

15 December 1906—Cleeve House, Seend, Wiltshire

Good god. A gong sounds, and we are to present ourselves in the chilly breakfast room. Only it isn't for breakfast but a family sermon. The servants, in their starched black uniforms and frilly white aprons, keep to one side, and the family keep to the other. There is a reading, followed by a lecture, followed by the Lord's Prayer. I was startled when the servants, on cue, dropped to their knees at the correct moment with a unanimous bang. The icy floor is rough on the knees, I should think. And then they go out and bring back coffee, tea, porridge, and eggs. We are to do this every morning?

I still collect funny things all day long to tell Thoby. I know Virginia and Adrian and Clive and Lytton do it as well, but grieving has become a private business. The wound seeps, but we no longer speak of it. Instead, it rests like an iron anchor on a thick chain dropped under the water. To speak of it, everyone, all together, would drown us.

But the habits remain, and I cannot keep from saving bits of news for him. He would love to hear about the pompous Bell country household. It would have made him like Clive more rather than less. I can hear him saying that it takes gumption to rise above such determined mediocrity. Although even Thoby could not have forgiven Clive for this ugly house. I cannot share that with Clive, I don't yet know when it is all right to poke fun at his family. I wish I could ask Thoby about it. That slight wobble of unfamiliarity just makes me miss my brother more.

And—Walter Headlam has asked if he can dedicate his translation of *Agamemnon* to Virginia. He is at least ten years her senior and we have known him since childhood. What an unlikely suitor.

46 GORDON SQUARE

BLOOMSBURY

TELEPHONE: 1608 MUSEUM

Cleeve House, Seend

16 December 1906

Dearest Snow,

My God, what a family. Dorothy, the younger of his sisters, is pleasant enough but Lorna, the elder sister, is a struggle. Double everything Lytton said and multiply it by three. Not that it matters. Clive and I are so wrapped up in our new togetherness that even if they were a marvellous family, we would still ignore them.

I want to know everything about him. Everything fascinates me. I am astonished. And the moment I want to know something, I ask him. No hesitation. No stumble. Does that sound like me? Utter freedom. I have been holding my breath for twenty-seven years. Virginia would be desperately hurt to read that line, whereas you, my dear, I know, understand perfectly. What can I tell you about my days? They are not mine but <u>ours</u>, and they are peppered with our Victorian family encounters. Otherwise they are spent writing and painting and reading and walking together. Throughout all of it there is a taut thread of unbroken conversation. Even in the silence, we keep pace.

So happy. When I am finished writing this, I will go straight to our shared study and tell him that I wrote to you, without pause or preamble. Can you imagine me doing that?

Do not worry about travelling down for the wedding, as we are inviting no one. The aunts and George and Gerald are all put out; to say nothing of Virginia. Adrian took it all with good humour.

Yours,
Vanessa

19 December 1906—Cleeve House, Wiltshire (after luncheon)

'I cannot keep up. If she keeps writing like this, my only news will be that I have responded to her letters.' I flopped down in the armchair next to Clive.

'She misses you. All her life you have been there, and now you are not,' Clive said evenly, laying down his book. It was a collection of essays on Rodin.

'We have been separated before. Two years ago she went off travelling with Adrian, and there wasn't this monsoon of correspondence.'

'Yes, but now it is not just distance that separates you. You are not coming home to her. You are coming home to *me,*' he said, pulling me out of my chair and onto his lap.

I looked around to see if his family were looming. They tend to loom. Although why I should care, I don't know. We will be married in a few weeks.

'Yes, I am coming home to you. Home to you. Home to you. Doesn't that just sound right?'

Later (everyone in bed)

Can't sleep, and the giant animal heads on the walls are not helping. I am sure Clive's mother insisted I have this room to acquaint me further with the country sports I do not like. There are seven unhappy deer heads in the hallway. I counted.

Virginia. Virginia. Virginia. I worry about the effect all this change will have on her, but I cannot quite talk to Clive about it. I know Virginia would hate that, and it feels like betrayal. And so I cannot sleep. During the last go-round, when we lost Stella and then Father, she went mad. It hangs over my head like Damocles' sword. That Virginia will go mad.

And—I unpacked Thoby's small drawing of a nuthatch. I brought it from Gordon Square. I must have known I would need a touchstone.

21 December 1906—Cleeve House, Seend, Wiltshire

Clive just showed me a terrible letter from Virginia. He is not quite sure how to handle it and so came to me. I am pleased she is writing to Clive (as I have asked her to), but I am *mortified* by her subject. Virginia has written to ask him to please cite his good qualities so she may know if he is enough for me. And then she invited herself here for the Monday after Christmas. She wants Clive to placate her and me to scold, but I know that trick. Once again she would be invited into us—into the us-ness of us—to mediate, arbitrate, and make camp. No. It will not do. I will ignore it, not mention it in my next letter, and suggest Clive do the same.

22 December 1906—five a.m. (snow)

Clive came into my room early to wake me in time to hear the Christmas robins singing in the snow. He listens for them too.

POSTCARD

22 December 1906

Dearest Ginia,

These country days are calm but framed by a mealtime anxiety. If you struggle half so much when I insist you finish your lunch, dearest, then I have been dreadfully ignorant of your anguish. Here their appetites are so robust, and I feel like a wilting Victorian. How can anyone eat six cheeses, three meats, and afters at one luncheon? Darling Goatus, did you notus how very much I miss you?
      Yours, Nessa

To: Miss Virginia Stephen
46 Gordon Square
Bloomsbury

PS: Another letter has just arrived from you by the second post and so all my news is out of date. There is also one for Clive—sweet of you, dearest, thank you.

LA BELLE ÉPOQUE

· ❧ ·

6 February 1907—46 Gordon Square (frosty)

Just back from the opera—*Fidelio*. Virginia conjugated Latin verbs all the way home. It is, as she keeps reminding me, our *last* night. She says it mournfully like a lamb due to be separated from its mother in the morning. She says she has written me a letter. It was a weighted sort of sentence, the kind that gives me a rolling dread.

Later

Virginia knocked on my door but entered without waiting for an answer. 'You must read it, Nessa. *Before* . . .' Virginia held out the folded paper. There was no envelope.

'Before?' I was being difficult. I knew very well before what. Before I marry Clive tomorrow. Before I become a Bell and no longer a Stephen. Before Clive and I go away together and leave her behind.

The tickets—I looked around for them. We leave for the train from the registry office, and I do not want to forget the tickets. My mind had already drifted away from her letter to tomorrow.

*   *   *

Good God. For the rest of my life, I will pretend I have never read this letter. I will show no one, tell no one, and never think of it again. She calls herself 'my humble beasts'. She speaks in multiples. She wishes I had married them. And if I will not, perhaps I will take them as my *lovers*? Too much, Virginia. Too much. I will not let you spoil tomorrow as you have spoiled tonight.

7 February 1907—Paddington Station (beautiful winter sunshine)

Two sentences. Two signatures, and I am Mrs Vanessa Bell.

'Happy?'

'So happy.' I pulled one small white rosebud from my tightly wrapped posy and handed it to my husband.

The Bells, the Bells.

POSTCARD

THIS SPACE TO BE USED FOR CORRESPONDENCE

7 February 1907

Mon Ange,

The newly minted Bells are to honeymoon in Manorbier and then go off to Paris next month. I have given them your address. Please take good care of them as they are precious to me. Clive is so Clivy, but you will get used to that. Vanessa is a pure, whole person. You will like her. I will pack her off with bottled kisses and boxed hugs for you. Maynard will also be in Paris soon, and I will send him along to you like a love note. Do not mistake me. I understand my irrelevance. Nevertheless, I mean to entangle you in ropes of friends and family to keep you close should you ever decide to love me again.

Yours, Lytton

To: Mr Duncan Grant

Hôtel de l'Univers et du Portugal

10 Rue Croix des Petits Champs

Paris, France

SERIES 5. NUMBER 19: TRAFALGAR SQUARE

Virginia Stephen
46 Gordon Square
Bloomsbury

8 February 1907

My Violet,

How are you feeling today, my dearest? Are you eating custard and waxing round and plump with health? I hope so. I need you to conserve all your strength. You will need it to love me mightily this spring. For I am alone. She did it. She is Mrs Clive Bell. Not one syllable of that name bears any trace of Nessa. I am trying, dearest Violet. You must believe that I am. If you were here, I would curl at your feet and ask you to brush my coat until it shone. The Goat stands alone. It sounds like a farmyard nursery rhyme.

I have done my best to love him. No, that is not true. But I will do my best to love him. It is the only way. I think it will take some doing to divide them, don't you? I know just what you will say to that: be happy for your sister as she would be happy for you. Quite pedestrian advice, if you ask me. I expected more from you. You see, Nessa and I are more than just sisters. We are different—exceptional.

For now, I will see my new brother-in-law for all his best qualities and forgive his piggy faults. I will love him and write to him and charm him and bring him into our family. If he loves Nessa, then surely he will love me too? It will help. I am sure it will.

Your
Virginia

PS: This ought to be the last letter you receive from me on this writing paper. 46 Gordon Square is now the address of the Bells. The poor Stephens are shunted to the outpost of Fitzroy Square.
PPS: Mr Headlam has become pressing. I can't quite see it. Can you?

CLOSERIE DES LILAS

12 February 1907—Sea View, Manorbier, Wales

Who knew I would like sex as much as I do? It is neither awkward nor embarrassing nor dull—all things I was sure it would be. I have discovered that I am not a fragile woman. There is a humid, delicate closeness, a tangible, animal instinctive us-ness that wraps us together in these moments, and I know in that brief time, I am free to be everything that I have ever been or ever will be; all my Vanessas brought home to roost. It is as though all I feel for him is given a verb: a visible, shattering verb that thrums through us, making us different from other people— alone and of a kind. I have never known such safety. I feel rooted in another, all my selves and secrets held in trust. I had not realised until now that I have been lonely all my life.

Clive is frankly stunned by my response. I questioned him endlessly about his expectations. He expected duty and diffidence. He thought I would require huge coaxing. 'But you like it, and me, you are pleased it is *me*. I am . . . surprised,' he said yesterday as we were talking about it over supper. It is a subject that consumes and fascinates us long after we leave the villa.

'Did you think I would not like you?' I asked.

'After all the proposals, I thought you might not see me as other than a companion—a dear friend, but not a lover.' He blushed a furious pink as he said it. His blushes are absolute, and he does not pretend they are not happening.

I had not realised how deeply my rejections had hurt him. They burrowed through all the soft flesh of insecurity and curled into his heart.

•

I am sure the staff are laughing at us. We keep leaving for the day and returning in a matter of hours. We do not want to be with other people. Other people are hugely annoying. I feel as though we have made a great discovery—but then all new ex-virgins must think that? Clive has vast experience, I discovered. He was meticulously instructed by an energetic Mrs Raven Hill. I am not in the least jealous (Clive has assured me that she now sports several double chins and an enormous prow of a bosom) but am grateful to her. Her thoroughness is impressive.

31 March 1907—Hôtel du Quai Voltaire, Paris (Easter Sunday)

Clive is in his element here. I can see that he is a Parisian born in Wiltshire. We dine with friends and artists and art dealers. Clive was disappointed to find that Mr Augustus John and Mr Wyndham Lewis were not in Paris at the moment, but he has had telegrams from both, and they will all meet soon in London.

Clive speaks of paint and sculpture in lush, primitive words. His ideas are simple but revolutionary. He is interested in what happens when one sees art. Sometimes I worry that I am boring him with my questions and colours, but my security returns when he kisses me.

Later

Supper at a tiny brasserie on the *rive gauche* with Duncan Grant and Henry Lamb:

'But Clive, it is impossible to categorise what happens!' Henry said loudly. He had drunk the better part of a bottle of wine. 'It is different for everyone, every time! That is how art must be!'

Duncan and Henry both had the roasted lamb cutlets, and Clive and I ordered fillet of sole *pour deux. Tout est pour deux.*

Later

Now I see it. Lytton's compulsive love of Duncan. I didn't before tonight. His charm is subtle and wears a sharpened blade, but it is not his charm that compels. It is in the deep nature of his stillness that the steep cliffs lie; birds above, sea below, he holds the rocky space between. His is a nerveless, animal quiet that cannot be learned but lives in the bedrock of instinct. When he asks a question, I feel that rather than answer *quickly,* I must answer *truthfully.* The stakes are high with him, and the gulls shriek in faraway warning, cautioning against the misstep of artifice. There is a challenge in his delicate beauty, a light-boned absorption. Suddenly there is nothing you need do, nowhere you need be, and instead a small inner shelf falls away, and the moment emerges clean, pure, unabridged.

He changes the chemistry of a room, reverses the gravity. It is no longer the ground that draws one close but Duncan. Everyone feels it but pretends they don't.

Clive is a magnet turned the other way. His direction is outward. His reach is warm and long, and his generous humour encourages risk. I grow bigger, bolder; more inclined to speak a thought before it is polished hard and bright. The stakes are low, and the turns endless. Clive is home.

Lytton is planning to travel in France with Duncan this summer. Dangerous. Duncan takes him up and loves him only to let him go again. But that sense of precipice must be part of Lytton's love. Is it in him to wholly love someone who loves him wholly in return?

And—Walter Headlam has been writing to Virginia. Could she truly like him? She has not said. Could she see him as other than a friend of Father's? Clive says he is too bookish for her. Can someone be too bookish for Virginia?

UNION POSTALE UNIVERSELLE
CEYLON (CYLAN)

7 April 1907

Jaffna, Ceylon

Lytton,

Just finished an early copy of Morgan's second novel. MacCarthy
sent it me as you were too lazy. The Longest Journey feels a bit like
a nothing title, and the story feels fractured but sensitively
wrought. Again the shattering event is relayed is sparse detail—
beautifully done. Is the drowned Robert a tragic nod to Theodore
Llewelyn Davies? I hope so. Rickie is clearly Morgan in an ill-
fitting disguise. I find Morgan is someone I miss more rather than
less; surely the mark of a good human?

Desmond tells me Virginia Stephen wants me to write something about the Goth. I do not think I can. I do not know Vanessa,
as I have only met her a few times and just imagine her character to
be a slighter version of the Goth's. If that is true, she will suit Bell
superbly well.

Staying on at least another year. Hoping to transfer away from
Jaffna, but I would be unlikely to be promoted again so soon.

Yours,
Leonard

PS: I keep forgetting the Goth is gone. As long as I do not return to
London, he is there in all his broad-shouldered good humour, wait-
ing for me. It is a childish feeling that I do not discourage. Not yet.
I cannot let him go yet.

HRH KING EDWARD VII POSTAL STATIONERY

Sunday 7 April 1907—Hôtel du Quai Voltaire, Paris

Home is encroaching. Virginia and Adrian have come to Paris. Unusual to have guests on your wedding tour, but Virginia's letters were getting frantic and so I relented. They arrived yesterday, and Clive and I met them off the train. I could feel Virginia looking me over, checking for any outwards signs of change. She is terrified I will become some other unfamiliar Vanessa now that I am married.

Today the four of us breakfasted at Closerie des Lilas on the Boulevard de Montparnasse. Clive (and I) were hoping to meet M. Guillaume Apollinaire, who is a frequent patron, but he was not there this morning. It was warm enough for us to sit under the trees in the spotted shade. Clive persuaded Virginia to have a soft-boiled egg and was inordinately pleased with himself. Virginia's egg was brought out in a delicate enamelled egg cup with great ceremony. Adrian and I had coffee and buns.

Virginia told us over breakfast that she has chosen grass-green carpets and deep red *brocade anglaise* curtains for her sitting room. I am afraid it will look like Fortnum's at Christmas. But I do not have to live there.

Clive and I received so many wedding presents, and we have bought so much here in Paris, I am afraid Gordon Square will become hopelessly cluttered. Yesterday alone we bought a huge silver Venetian looking glass for our room and several small paintings for Clive's study. Each time I resist, Clive wins me over to the purchase by telling me that when we are old and grey, we will look back and remember that we bought it on our wedding tour.

I chose pale mauve curtains with butter-yellow linings for the drawing room—perfect.

POSTCARD

30 April 1907

My dear Strache,

Received a postcard from Virginia about next Thursday in Fitzroy Square. Virginia wrote that Clive would be coming and how wonderful to hear all their Paris news. Can only assume Nessa will be there too? Oddly worded note, I have to say. Does one take a wedding gift if there was no church wedding? Not sure. Please advise. Counting upon you and Desmond to be there. If not, I shall make excuses. Saw Maynard at the India Office, and he cannot make it.

Yrs, Saxon

To: *Mr Lytton Strachey*
 67 Belsize Park
  Gardens
 Hampstead
 N.W.

SERIES II. NUMBER 20: COVENT GARDEN FLOWER MARKET AT DAWN

THE
WESTERN UNION
TELEGRAPH COMPANY INCORPORATED

24,000 OFFICES IN AMERICA. CABLE SERVICE TO ALL THE WORLD

This company transmits and delivers messages only on conditions limiting its liability. The Company will not hold itself liable for errors or delays in transmission of unrepeated messages.

NUMBER SENT BY RECEIVED BY CHECK 379 MR R. FRY to LADY M. FRY: PAID

RECEIVED AT: 9 PALACE HOUSES, BAYSWATER RD, LONDON, N.W. ENGLAND

Message:

MOTHER. STOP. RECEIVED CABLE. STOP. BOOKED PASSAGE ON THE MAURETANIA AT ONCE. STOP. PLEASE TAKE HELEN HER LAVENDER SHAWL AND CHILDREN'S PHOTOS. STOP. WHEN SHE WAKES IN HOSPITAL SUCH THINGS HELP. STOP. WILL ARRIVE THURS. AND MEET YOU AT ASYLUM. STOP. ALL LOVE. STOP. ROGER.

ALWAYS OPEN. MONEY TRANSFERRED BY TELEGRAPH. CABLE OFFICE.

HOME

· ⚘ ·

BUREAU DE BAC DE DIEPPE

BILLET: **D E U X PREMIÈRE CLASSE**
Passage Pour DEUX:

DIEPPE VERS **DOUVRES** 1 Mai 1907
DIEPPE DE DÉPART: **13.30 p.m.**
DOUVRES D'ARRIVÉE: **21.45 p.m.**

LES BAGAGISTES SERONT DISPONIBLES
SUR LE BORD DU QUAI

10 June 1907—46 Gordon Square

We entertain at home together now.

Once Adrian and Virginia left, the air cleared and Gordon Square felt like home for Clive and me. As if it had always been that way. No. That is not right. The part when Thoby, Adrian, Virginia, and I lived here together is very clear and precious. But the murky bit, when Virginia, Adrian, and I tried to lopsidedly carry on here without him, has become opaque and distant.

It was not easy to get them out. Virginia is sour with envy and irritation. She hated leaving and was as unhelpful as possible. She unpacked her book boxes twice in a disruptive effort to find her copy of *Middlemarch*. I repacked the boxes, and Clive shifted them. I folded the linen, and Clive rounded up the wellies. I collected her silver brushes, and Clive stacked her hatboxes. I know if it had been just me, I would have been flattened by their resistance to moving. But Clive and I did it together, and we withstood the flood.

I collected Mother's jewellery from the bank at Virginia's request when she wanted to take it with her and then returned it to the bank at Virginia's request when she decided she did not. Clive hauled her favourite houseplants to Fitzroy Square in the rain. Sophie, Maud, and Sloper were over there every day for a week sorting out the lumpy furniture and damp kitchen. I went over most afternoons to harass the builders into finishing on time. The double windows reduce the noise enormously and were worth the extra week's wait. Adrian was no help at all and just clucked about nervously, obviously dreading Fitzroy Square.

Now it is just Clive and me and Thoby here. He drifts about the house like a protective ghost.

18 June 1907—46 Gordon Square (beautiful summer day)

I looked at the calendar today and counted backward. Three weeks. But three weeks can mean anything, surely?

27 June 1907—46 Gordon Square (nine p.m.)

A month. I told Clive. He was startled. He recovered quickly and said all the best things, but he gripped my hands so tightly that I wonder if he meant them. Is that how it always is? Is that how husbands react?

When Clive asked me to marry him, I did not see it right away. Perhaps this is the same? The pieces pause and hover before they snap into place?

I do not feel different yet. No, that is not true. My body feels entirely the same, but now I feel that we are no longer a couple but a *family*.

Later

We stayed up talking, and then Clive gently nudged me towards bed. He was ginger and faint with me, not at all showing his usual roughhewn ardour. It was all wrong, and I asked him to please stop it. Clive looked at me, surprised and pleased and so relieved. He swept me upstairs to our room and slipped free of his cautious shell. And we became us again.

30 June 1907—46 Gordon Square

The doctor confirmed what I already knew. He gave me a long list of instructions:

> Do wear a corset.
> Don't read too much.
> Do smoke cigarettes.
> Don't cut my hair.
> Do take omnibuses.
> Don't put my arms over my head.
> Do sleep with the window shut.
> Don't eat too much.

The last should be easy to follow given the long list of foods I am *not* to eat. I must avoid: hot chocolate, sour foods, rabbit, cherries, ice cream, and salt. Very boring, but I am determined to follow the doctor's advice meticulously. Clive is pleased that champagne is encouraged. I did not ask the doctor about sex. If it is prohibited, I don't want to know.

1 July 1907—46 Gordon Square

We received our friends in our bedroom today. Shocking, ain't it? We were having the loveliest, rainiest summer afternoon tucked into bed when we heard the barbarians rattle our gate. Sloper tried to tell them that Mrs Bell was not at home, but that never works any more, and

Virginia, Duncan, Maynard, and Lytton trooped in. I started to get up, but Clive stopped me. 'If they want to come and visit without an invitation, then they get what they deserve,' he said, pulling me back into bed.

They left after ten minutes, and we went back to talking about baby names.

Later (after midnight, can't sleep)

I lay awake thinking about this afternoon. Spooling my thoughts like thread. It was the determined, *possessive* way Clive set out to shock our friends today. As though he wanted everyone to know that I am his, that we share a bed. Clive is territorial when I least expect it. A few weeks ago, at a Thursday evening in Fitzroy Square, Clive overheard Henry Lamb drunkenly flirting with me. When I asked him about it, he laughed and was not bothered in the least. 'Henry is not the threat,' he said breezily. 'Why should I mind?'

If Henry is not the threat, then who is?

PART THREE

VANESSA BELL

..

1908–1909

'Have you ever noticed that there
are people who do things which are most
indelicate, and yet at the same time—
beautiful?'

(E. M. FORSTER)

JULIAN HEWARD BELL

POST OFFICE TELEGRAPHS

Eyre & Spottiswoode, London.

This Form Must Accompany Any Enquiry Respecting This Telegram

OFFICE OF ORIGIN: Holborn, London

Office Stamp

MOTHER AND FATHER. STOP. SON SAFELY ARRIVED. STOP.
WILL COME TO WILTSHIRE SOONEST. STOP. VANESSA WELL.
STOP. CLIVE.

WC1HS9B—RECIPIENT MUST SIGN UPON DELIVERY

Wednesday 5 February 1908—46 Gordon Square (late)

Now we are three. Exhausted. It was bone on bone getting him out. Why did no one tell me?

But now he is here, and I can't imagine a world without him. The name came instantly. When I met him, I knew. I would know him anywhere: *Julian*.

'Yes,' Clive said. 'Julian. Julian Bell.'

And—Born on a *Tuesday*. The things that shake my life happen on Tuesdays.

8 February 1908—46 Gordon Square

Visitors today:

'Not Thoby?' Snow asked, pulling the soft white blanket back to see our son's squashed red face.

'Thoby's first name *was* Julian,' Clive said, reaching for our tiny son's curled egg-cup hand.

Wednesday 4 March 1908—46 Gordon Square (icy—not that I go outside)

Julian has been with us a month today. I get distracted by the miniature, perfectly developed beauty of him. He has soft fleshy pads around his wrists, dimpled knees, and fat, stubby arms that reach out and dissolve me into small, pure particles. I did not expect it. I did not think I had rooms enough in me for this kind of love. I was wrong. Quite, quite wrong.

I found the violence of the whole thing deeply shocking. First the great tearing away of having him and then the huge roar of ferocious love that swept through my ragged senses. I awoke a lioness.

A lioness now, but my God was I a whale. That is not an exaggeration. I was, I think—a large, blue-veined whale. For the last four months, Virginia refused to comment upon my size, appetite, or the impending event. She would crumple her nose in distaste when I waddled across a room. I admit, I exaggerated to gain a reaction. Virginia has always been appalled by any human—or worse, female—function, the most offensive being pregnancy. To make my condition palatable and put it within an acceptable context, she kept referencing various resplendent Greek and Roman fertility goddesses when she spoke to me or of me. She still does it even though I gave birth a month ago. I find it wearing. She also referred to unborn Julian as a parasite that was draining me of my Nessa-ness. Very crass.

But since he arrived, Virginia has been friendly enough to Julian. She announced this morning that she has decided to love him. As if the jury have been deliberating and have returned with a verdict. 'I shall love your barbarian angel dearly. I shall lean over his cradle and bestow one hundred kisses like a great, good fairy.'

I suppose, with his huge appetite and atrocious table manners, he is a barbarian. It is the *idea* of Julian that really bothers her. The fact that there may be someone I love more than her.

Later

Clive just left. He is unsure and tender and anxious for life to return to normal. He surprised me and was wonderful throughout the nine months, professing to find me 'fertile, Rubenesque, and sexy'. Bless his dishonest soul. But now he is having some trouble adjusting to fatherhood. In the beginning he was reluctant even to hold the baby. 'I may drop him' was his only defence. He believes that babies fall squarely into the female sphere. But this week he has held the baby twice (both times when Julian was asleep), and that is better than nothing. Virginia goes on about my soft, placid nature, the nobility of motherhood, and how some women are just *born* to it—like a cow meant for breeding. All meant as a dig at me.

As of today, my customary month of convalescence at home is over, and I am to rejoin the wide social world. I know Clive expects it and is looking forward to having me with him in the evenings. And so, supper tonight at Fitzroy Square with Virginia, Lytton, and Adrian. I must keep from mentioning the baby. It only sets Virginia off.

And—Clive has slept down the hall all this week as he cannot sleep through Julian's crying in the next room. I miss his weight in the bed but cannot bear to move Julian farther away.

THE
WESTERN UNION
TELEGRAPH COMPANY INCORPORATED

24,000 OFFICES IN AMERICA. CABLE SERVICE TO ALL THE WORLD
This Company transmits and delivers messages only on conditions limiting its liability. The Company will not hold itself
liable for errors or delays in transmission of unrepeated messages.

NUMBER SENT BY CHECK RECEIVED BY CHECK 567 MR R. FRY to LADY M. FRY: PAID

RECEIVED AT: 9 PALACE HOUSES, BAYSWATER RD, LONDON, N.W. ENGLAND

Message:

DEAR MOTHER. STOP. HAVE RESIGNED MY CURATORSHIP. STOP.
TRUSTEES WILL NOT ALLOW ME TO WORK FROM LONDON. STOP.
UNDERSTAND HELEN GETTING WORSE. STOP. WILL BOOK PAS-
SAGE AND CABLE ARRIVAL DATE. STOP. TELL HER I LOVE HER.
STOP. ALL LOVE. STOP. ROGER.

ALWAYS OPEN. MONEY TRANSFERRED BY TELEGRAPH. CABLE OFFICE.

10 March 1908—46 Gordon Square (raining hard)

After a few false starts, we have formed a new group: The Play Reading
Society. It will be good to speak of grown-up things. We actually formed
it in December but were interrupted by Julian's birth. So far I have loved
The Relapse and disliked Milton. Much depends on the reader. Adrian
and Lytton are wonderful, but Virginia gets very nasal and takes too
many long pauses.

I suggested to Clive that we start with the raciest plays first, just to
get any inevitable, squirmy, anatomical awkwardness out of the way,
and he has repeated it to *everyone*. Lytton was delighted and promptly
began to use the word semen around me as often as he could. I trumped
him by swearing bugger when I spilt the sugar. I am liking the role of a
risqué married woman.

And—Clive held the baby for twenty minutes this afternoon, until
Julian began to cry, and he quickly handed him to the nurse.

Later

Lytton dropped by this evening. The conversation turned to sex, as it often has lately. In flat, medical, and gloriously unpretty words, we talked about copulation. My marriage to Clive and the incontrovertible proof of Julian have gained me admittance to the room. Lytton is full of graphic stories and rude details, and he is always having sex with some-one we know, so that makes it especially interesting. He reports back about this man's excessive furriness or that man's foul breath. We sit up late and say wild, inappropriate things. Clive finds it hilarious and joins in with relish (he always has questions about the mechanics of sex be-tween men), but Virginia grows uncomfortable and often asks Adrian (who is much more adept at such talk than I would have predicted) to take her home.

And—Clive only touches the baby when people are watching. When we are alone at home, he does not go into the little nursery next to our bedroom. It means that our paths rarely cross, as I never want to be where Julian is not. So be it. Clive will come in when he is ready. For now, he is mourning the loss of our two-ish life. I am impatient when I should not be, but I do not have time to manage Clive now. He is a grown man and ought to manage himself.

15 March 1908—46 Gordon Square (wet and cold)

'He sucks like the very devil, Nessa. How can you stand it? Don't you want him to get some backbone and go and find his own food?' Virginia had insisted on following me to the nursery. I do not know why, as seeing me feed Julian repels her.

'It won't be for much longer,' I said, calming her.

'Just as long as there is some Nessa left for me when the little mon-ster has finished,' Virginia said.

It is true. I cannot nurse for much longer. My milk is drying up. Prob-ably best. Virginia and Clive, initially tolerant of my outlandish desire to feed my own baby, are running out of patience. My life happens in three-hour instalments, and it drives them mad. I cannot go out to sup-per *and* the opera as it is longer than three hours. I *can* go to supper in Bloomsbury but *not* in Chelsea as it takes too long to get back. I refused an invitation for a Saturday to Monday at Desmond and Molly's the other day as I did not want to leave Julian. I can see how it is trying for them. There is talk of a Stephen and Bell family holiday in Cornwall this spring, so we will have plenty of time together then.

And—I feel the much-put-off visit to Clive's family in Wiltshire is imminent. So far I have pleaded cold weather. I am dreading it. It will be ghastly.

16 March 1908—46 Gordon Square

On Tuesdays, Virginia and Adrian are taking German lessons with a Miss Daniels. I thought they would call her 'Fräulein', but apparently she is from Surrey. I wish I could get more enthusiastic about that lan-guage, but the inborn gruffness of it does not sit well with me. Virginia occasionally practises her irregular verbs on Julian, and I wish she wouldn't, as it alarms him. But at least she and Adrian can talk about Goethe and Rilke. It is good for them to do something together.

Later

Just home from supper at Fitzroy Square. I did not think it was possible, but they seem to be keeping an even more informal house than ours. Virginia never dresses in the evening any more, and the house is thick with cigarette smoke. Wombat is not house-trained and 'performs' all over the carpet. Messy.

Supper was not served until nine, and then, inexplicably, it turned out to be herrings and melon. Walter Headlam read aloud to Virginia from his new translation of Aeschylus, Lytton has a cold and drank cough mixture under a blanket, and Henry Lamb arrived with green oil paint in his hair. Desmond appeared after midnight and was hungry, so Adrian brought him scrambled eggs in the drawing room.

Tuesday 17 March 1908—46 Gordon Square

Elsie the new nurse started today. She was a great success with Julian and very firm with me. Her meaty forearms are straight out of Dickens. Clive insisted we hire her. He says he wants me to have time to paint. 'It is time to get back to our normal life, Nessa,' he keeps telling me. 'But this *is* our normal life now,' I answer.

Saturday 21 March 1908—46 Gordon Square (four p.m. already)

Tonight we are giving our first party since Julian. I am behind and distracted. I have still not spoken to Sophie about the sandwiches nor to Maud about the drawing room. It has not been used in weeks, and needs a good going-over.

Even later (one a.m.)

I was terrified we would wake the baby. But he was two floors up, and Clive was right, he slept right through it. We played the gramophone and *danced*. The Grizzly Bear, the Turkey Trot, and the Bunny Hug. Even Lytton got up out of his chair and stomped and growled and grizzled and clucked. Saxon wanted to dance the old-fashioned Irene Skipping Rope but we said no.

And—London is dismal in March, and Clive thinks we need a change. There has been more discussion of taking a holiday in Cornwall. I suggested St Keverne or St Mawes or even Polperro, but Virginia wants St Ives. St Ives without Thoby.

UNION POSTALE UNIVERSELLE
CEYLON (CYLAN)

22 *March 1908*

Kandy, Ceylon

Dear Lytton,

Julian. For the Goth? Good. Not that he will be likely to have much of the Goth about him. I am sure this baby will soon be saturated with Clive's aggressively Francophile bonhomie and by next year will be able to choose wine, discuss art, and speak French better than either of us.

I am not surprised Adrian is a talented reader. He was always quietly theatrical. I also imagine Virginia can easily hold an audience. I remember her low, musical voice. Does Saxon actually read aloud? Difficult to picture.

Yours,
Leonard

HRH KING EDWARD VII POSTAL STATIONERY

Monday 30 March 1908—46 Gordon Square

Just back from 29 Fitzroy Square. Adrian and Virginia are not a natural domestic fit. The atmosphere is not breezy and comfortable but rather tight and unsaid, and the air around Virginia crackles with irritation. Poor Adrian. I wish they would find someone else to move in to cut the tension.

Elsie had a toothache so I left her here and took Julian to visit Virginia. It was awful. I held him and rocked him and bounced him, but he still fussed, and Virginia soon adopted a martyred expression.

I walked him in slow blunt squares around the room. Virginia said I was making her dizzy. Fortunately Clive called in for me and told Virginia amusing stories that gave her the opportunity to make witty and incisive observations.

I was left undisturbed to cope with Julian. When he is uncomfortable, I cannot keep my thoughts on the spinning conversational plates. They get tossed my way and I let them crash to the ground. Finally Clive put me in a cab. Best I went home alone. Julian's crying unsettles him anyway.

And—I have sent the cheque and signed the lease. We are going to take Trevose View in Cornwall again next month. Virginia and Adrian will go down early, and Clive and I will follow after a short stay with his parents in Wiltshire. I cannot bear that my baby will be introduced to wall-mounted stag heads before he is introduced to Manet and Schubert.

Later

Clive stayed on to supper at Fitzroy Square and came home after the baby was asleep. We curled onto the sofa and gossiped. I love that my husband is an avid, unabashed gossip. Only Lytton outdoes him. He retold the stories he told at Fitzroy Square and made me feel missed and wanted. Apparently Virginia has been asked to write several more articles for the *Times Literary Supplement*. And so she has decided to give up her Morley College teaching and concentrate on writing. Odd that she did not mention it when I saw her this afternoon.

A cosy conversation with Clive this evening. I think he will sleep in our room tonight—

31 March 1908—46 Gordon Square

Yes, he did, until four a.m., when Julian's crying woke him up and he went back to his own bed.

3 April 1908—46 Gordon Square

The news: Sir Henry Campbell Bannerman resigned as prime minister today because of ill health. H. H. Asquith is to bump up from chancellor to PM. I must send a note.

Lytton brought his eccentric but strangely beautiful friend Lady Ottoline Morrell, who lives around the corner in Bedford Square, for tea today. She has an affected, lilting voice, long, melancholy features, and wore an astonishing hat. I was startled when she said a quick grace over her sugar bun. Lytton is not religious, and I was surprised he would be so friendly with anyone who is. When she left, Lytton told me that she was the mother of twins, a boy and a girl, but the boy died of a haemorrhage a few days after his birth. Awful. I can understand her belief in God. Lytton said the little girl survived and is called Julian. I was pierced through. *Julian.*

11 April 1908—46 Gordon Square (raining)

Moving a family is exhausting. Clive will help when I ask him to but cannot seem to be able to look around and notice what needs to be done in order to relocate our son to his parents' home.

In the end, I decided to buy all new clothes for Julian as he is growing so rapidly. I do not want to risk shopping with Clive's family. I feel piecemeal and disorganised.

And—We were hoping Lytton and possibly Saxon could come to Cornwall, but it is not to be. We will all meet in London when we return.

Thursday 16 April 1908—Cleeve House, Seend, Wiltshire

The train journey was ghastly. A tasteless man held forth on the evils of interracial social mixing—loudly, for the benefit of the entire carriage, ad nauseam. Hideous. Luckily I had Lytton's latest draft of rude poetry to entertain me.

When we got here, it was hardly any better. Clive's bully-boy father gave Cory, Clive's brother, a tremendous dressing-down at luncheon today. It was appalling to see Cory, a grown man and such a nice one, get belittled like that. Clive's nervous, rabbit-faced mother could do nothing to stop the onslaught. Cory and Clive, accustomed to such scenes, just sat in silence and waited for it to end. I am terrified that this loud, volatile house will affect Julian, but he seems as placid as he was in London.

Luncheon with the Raven Hills and the Armours tomorrow. Curious to see what she looks like. The men should be interesting as well—Mr Raven Hill and Mr Armour are *Punch* artists.

And—Bottle feeding. Am using binding and am still terribly sore.

17 April 1908—Cleeve House, Seend, Wiltshire (nine p.m.—the grisly supper ritual over)

Mrs Raven Hill is as double-chinned, flat-bottomed, and vulgar as I could hope for my husband's former lover. But she is also direct, and I liked her immediately. She and Mrs Armour and I had a blunt and shocking conversation about sex: birth control, childbirth, husbands, and lovers. It seems once one is married with a baby, the jig is up, and we are allowed to speak frankly about sex with anyone. Clive's eyebrows lifted up into his red curls when he heard us. I must remember to tell Lytton all I learned. The intricacies of female sexual plumbing fascinate him.

Later

'She suggests I kiss your eyeball,' Clive said, apropos of nothing. We were having coffee in the small library. He was seated in the musty armchair opposite, reading a letter while I sketched.

'Who wants you to kiss my eyeball?' I asked, looking up.

'Virginia, of course. Who else would say such a thing? Not only your eyeball: your earlobe, elbow, temple, and collarbone. She is very specific.'

'She wants to be included,' I said. A year since the wedding, and I had hoped Virginia would have accepted that marriages are restricted to two people, but so far this essential truth has eluded her.

'I do like your elbow,' Clive said, laying aside his letter and crossing to lightly kiss my neck. 'And your collarbone is nice too. She chooses well.'

We left our coffee on the tray and went upstairs.

∙

We stayed up to see the sunrise, curled in the heavy warmth of our bed. We talked of Lytton's heartbreak and Maynard's lack of empathy, Duncan's clean selfishness, Desmond's ongoing renovations, and the expensive new windows needed for the nursery at Gordon Square. We talked of Julian's cold, and the early-blooming pear tree in our garden, and Clive's lost grey overcoat, left on a London train. And then we whispered about our work: my new canvas, his new essay, the new exhibitions we are planning to see in Paris next spring, the things we have done and will do together. We are such a together sort of together. A very whole whole. A family.

Virginia Stephen
29 Fitzroy Square · London W.

17 April 1908

My Violet,

Nessa has eloped to Wiltshire with her true love, Baby Julian. She permitted Clive to accompany them but only on the understanding that he sleep down the hall. I find it elating to see him ousted from the crook of Nessa's heart. She does not even realise that she has done it. I hope it lasts. Nessa invited me to join them on this visit to the terrifying Bells, but I nimbly leapt aside to avoid the hurtling threat. Clive's rambunctious family of overfed philistines offends every sense I have.

Lytton came for lunch today. I was very brave and boldly discussed the menu with Sophie (lent by Nessa, as our new and beastly cook is ill). She wanted lamb and I wanted fish and I prevailed. Do you remember Mr Strachey? The narrow-framed, rumpled, outrageous one with a frizzy red beard? He slides his spectacles farther down his steep-sloping nose when he intends to say something audacious. He and Nessa have been trading rude words for the past few months and are enjoying their déclassé be- haviour immensely. Lately he has been salaciously graphic about his lost amour Duncan Grant (fey, artistic, vague) and his current but erratic amour Mr Maynard Keynes (bright, sleek, selfish). Nessa's marriage has opened the door for this sort of liberal, anatomical chat. Do you know, before Julian was born, the Bells of 46 Gordon Square received guests in their bedroom? While they were lying down on the bed? Hurry, my Violet! Swoop down like the great, good eagle you are and snatch up your little wallaby from the maw of such brutish corporeal talk. Too bad eagles do not have marsupial pouches. Wallabies need snug pouches. I could curl up inside and read Swinburne.

And you, my decent Violet? I imagine you at Welwyn potter- ing amongst dear Ozzie's azaleas, offering them sturdy biscuits of oatey common sense dipped in sweet milky wisdom. I am sure your brother owes his garden's happiness to you, however splen- did a gardener he may be. Adrian and I are holed up here in Fitzroy Square, the shipwrecked siblings awaiting rescue and speedy removal to Cornwall. Shall you visit, my dearest? Shall you come and smooth my soft wallaby ears and kiss my velvet wallaby nose?

Your
Virginia

18 April 1908—Cleeve House, Seend

'Her mind is so subtle,' Clive said, handing me the lighter. 'I am not sure I realised before.'

He was reading a letter from Virginia, no doubt full of literary allusion and editorial questions. I am pleased they have this in common and hopeful that she might think better of him at last.

'Yes, it is subtle, but be careful. Do not mistake that subtlety for discernment. She can often miss what is right in front of her when she is aiming to impress and be clever.'

'Do you think—'

'Julian,' I interrupted. Instantly alert to the sound of his crying. I took the stairs two at a time.

After tea, I asked Clive what he was going to say before I rushed up to check on Julian, but he couldn't remember.

Clive is sleeping in his dressing room here. If he stays with me, his sleep is fractured by either Julian's crying or my listening for Julian's crying. We breakfast and work together through the mornings as normal, but the afternoons and evenings I am alone with my sweet baby. Bugger. Have I become one of those mothers?

And—Reading Virginia's manuscript of her *Life of Violet*. It is rigorous but full of affection for Violet's big-hearted, romping spirit. Virginia was kind enough to send two copies: one for Clive. Perhaps she is accepting him at last—a relief.

Later (three a.m., Julian just stopped crying)

Clive reminded me that Virginia leaves for Cornwall in the morning. I had forgotten. I forget everything this spring. Luckily, Clive remembered to book her seats on the train, as I forgot to make her travel arrangements. It was thoughtful of him. Clive does take good care of me and my family—just as he promised. I have married a good man.

I dread to think what Virginia packed for herself. I doubt she had the courage to ask her new maid to do it for her. She is even more terrified of the servants than I am.

Sunday 19 April 1908—Seend, Wiltshire (late, alone in bed)

A note from Snow. Am I painting? No. I am daydreaming. And another scathing note from Virginia regarding Clive. She cannot forgive him for hurling me to these ravening, unlettered Wiltshire beasts. So she has not come round as I had hoped.

67 BELSIZE PARK GARDENS

HAMPSTEAD, N.W.

TEL.: HAMPSTEAD 1090

21 April 1908

Dearest Nessa,

Two a.m. Keynes was here all evening—grindingly dull conversation but very good otherwise. And then a shock: midway through the strawberries and cream, he told me that he is off to Cambridge in the morning to visit my brother James and is travelling up with Duncan. Duncan? Duncan who is meant to be in Paris but is clearly here, Duncan? Duncan to whom I introduced the wretched Maynard? I feel doubly and possibly triply jealous. Jealousy is such a creeping low feeling. I ought to be thoroughly cosmopolitan and not mind, but mine is a parochial heart. Sharing is anathema when love is involved. I can only hope that Duncan will find Maynard to be a clodhopping piece of arithmetic and not an exciting, savage brute. I am so fruitlessly petty today.

Before she decamped, I was visiting your sister. She is a

distracting creature: vain, brilliant, elusive, and bright. But she is not you. Come back at once.

Yours,
Lytton

PS: My cold has got worse.

WHERE THE LAND ENDS

22 April 1908—Cleeve House, Seend, Wiltshire (three more days)

I have written to Virginia asking her to arrange to receive two boxes. The first: Julian's bath and cradle, the second: his linen, clothing, and pram. I know she will be unravelled by such practical tasks. It was Clive's suggestion. He thinks she is made of sterner stuff than she lets on and can manage just fine. I hope he is right.

He is enjoying her manuscript and says he sent her detailed editorial notes. Letters fly between them like summer bees. She is privately cruel about him, but as long as she is kind to his face, I am content. Peace at last.

And—Sir Henry Campbell Bannerman is dead! His wife, Lady Sarah Charlotte, must be devastated. They had no children and were, it is said, very much in love. Dead only nineteen days after he gave up politics. Nothing good ever comes of retiring from what you love.

Eyre & Spottiswoode, London.

This Form Must Accompany Any Enquiry Respecting This Telegram

OFFICE OF ORIGIN: Seend, Wiltshire

Office Stamp

DEAREST GINIA. STOP. ARRIVING ST IVES TOMORROW 7.10 P.M. STOP. PLEASE MEET TRAIN. STOP. ALL WELL HERE. STOP. YRS NESSA.

N7H7F—RECIPIENT MUST SIGN UPON DELIVERY

67 BELSIZE PARK GARDENS

HAMPSTEAD, N.W.

TEL.: HAMPSTEAD 1090

25 April 1908

Dearest Nessa,

My dear, he's done it. Maynard has stormed in, and with a ruthless mathematical cruelty, he has stolen my darling boy. It seems it began when they went to visit my brother James a few weeks ago. Do you remember? Maynard dropped by my rooms in Belsize Park tonight and made gratuitous reference to my darling Duncan's very pointy hipbone. A hipbone that I was not aware he was previously acquainted with and now obviously is. Mon dieu. Mother needs her smelling salts. I will save the anatomical precision for when I see you. Needless to say, I was destroyed. And yet, perversely, I wanted to hear everything. Why does one press for details that can only wound?

I long for Duncan. He is back in London. What exquisite torture to be so close to the exquisite torturer. I had hoped I was more recovered from him, but it seems I am not.

Yours,
Lytton

27 April 1908—Trevose View, Cornwall

Virginia and Clive are out walking, and the nurse has taken Julian up for his nap. This is my time. The intellectuals depart for a long seaside wander, and I paint in the airy quiet. Julian takes up enormous space for such a small creature, but I begrudge him none of it. He occupies my days and thoughts and ears and arms. I know Clive is feeling neglected, although he would never admit it, but I do not know what to do about it. Julian needs me so much just now, but it won't always be like this. Surely Clive understands that?

Virginia is also feeling put out by the baby. She complains that I am not paying her enough attention. I do not fix her hair, read her new writing, visit her lighthouse, walk her shore, run her bath, fret over her, watch over her, ask after her as I should. I allow the housekeeper to bring her tea and offer her the cake that she will never eat—an insult. Virginia likes to reject the cake that *I* offer.

Later (everyone is asleep)

It is not just Julian she resents but Clive. Tonight, when I thought she was asleep, I brought Clive a mug of cocoa. I set it on the desk where he was working and kissed his forehead. He wound his arms around my waist and pulled me into his lap, growling and biting my neck. It is a way he has. He chases and I run. I wriggled to get away and looked up to see Virginia on the stairs. Instantly, Clive released me. I was relieved. He can sometimes be belligerent and hold onto me when she is watching; even though he knows it upsets her. Why rattle Virginia when it takes so long to unrattle her?

Virginia came down the last few stairs and sat primly on the faded gingham wing chair but refused to be engaged in conversation. We tried. She picked up a book that I knew did not interest her and would only answer the most direct questions: Are you *well*, Virginia? *Hungry*, Virginia? *Writing*, Virginia? *Bathed*, Virginia? *Tired*, Virginia? Have you read *this* article? Seen *this* star? Heard *that* cow?

When at last she did answer, it was alternately in Greek and German. Trying. Clive changed tack and, switching to French and Latin, asked her questions I did not understand nor care to understand. Sometimes her determination to disrupt is monstrous. Exasperated, I went to run a bath. Is that—

•

It was not Julian but the housekeeper's son. I have developed oversensitive ears. I am sure I never heard so many babies crying before? In any case, I got out of the bath and was calmer. Clive had coaxed Virginia from her temper and nudged her towards speaking in English. Fragmented voices rose up the stairs.

  '*Galsworthy . . . better than Hardy.*'
  '*But neither as good as Eliot.*'

Fine. It was more than I was willing to do. Clive is just learning the secret language of Virginia. Even though I was sure he was still irritated by her childishness, I could hear the admiration in his voice and felt perversely proud of her learning and witty exactitude. My sister captivates and does not ransom her prisoners lightly. Virginia has a vibrancy about her that makes time spent with her seem inherently more valuable than time spent away from her; minutes burn brighter, words fall more steeply into meaning, and you feel you are not just alive but *living*. I have understood this Virginia equation all her life—but I also understand what Clive does not. There is no rational, logical, reachable Virginia lurking beneath, and eventually Virginia becomes exhausting.

Since my marriage, she is determined to be her most Virginia. No longer able to dissuade me from Clive, she seeks to ingratiate herself into our marriage. Does she think to charm Clive into relinquishing me? She does not know that a marriage does not work on charm but trust. I watch her trying to win a place in our marriage when there is no place to be had.

I do try. I pretend that I am not newly happily married with a new and happy baby. I do my best not to call attention to what she calls 'my real family'. I try not to discuss painting with Clive in case she feels excluded. I steer clear of their literary discussions so that she may shine brighter. I try not to go running when I hear Julian crying. Does she notice all this effort? Why should I do it when she does not take the same care of me? But then, I remember what Mother and Father always told Thoby and me. When one has a sister as extraordinary as Virginia, one must put up with a fair amount of inconvenience. True, but it does not make her any less exasperating.

And—I wanted to speak to Clive about Julian tonight. Since we left London, Clive has been growing increasingly unhappy with my distraction. I think he hoped that coming away would bring us closer together. I do miss him. And I miss us, but I am unwilling to give up huge swathes of time with Julian when he is so young. Some time, yes. Most of the time, no. I tried to explain it to him tonight but failed. How to explain something that feels so obvious? I must try harder.

Tuesday 28 April 1908—Trevose View, Carbis Bay

'I did read it!' Clive said as they came in the garden door from their walk.

'But did you read it when *I* suggested it?' asked Virginia. She looked relaxed; pink-cheeked and wind-tossed from the tangy sea air. 'Or did you say, ah, that Virginia Stephen, what would *she* know about what to read?' Virginia smiled her Virginia smile.

'That Virginia Stephen—' Clive laughed but, sensing he was beaten, did not finish his sentence.

'Read what?' I asked, without setting down my brush. I was working on a small portrait of Clive, and I was finding the perspective challenging. They both looked up, surprised to see me. Normally I would be putting Julian down for his nap at this time, but I was making an effort to be less consumed with the baby. I knew it would please them both.

'Greville's *Life of Sidney*,' Clive said, brushing my hair back to drop a kiss on my forehead. He leant over me an extra moment, smelling my hair. Clive loves the smell of my hair. 'Baby all right?' he asked, pleased I was downstairs.

Disrupted, I laid down my brush.

'Yes, I asked Elsie to put him down so I could be here when you got back.' He kissed my forehead again and nuzzled my neck.

'Sir *Philip* Sidney,' Virginia answered tartly, bringing the conversation back to literature. She always gets like this when Clive mentions the baby. With specific purpose, she brushed my hair back as well to deposit a damp kiss in the same spot. Virginia was not in the mood to be outdone. 'Poet. Elizabethan. Died early.'

I bristled and tried not to feel patronised, but grew quickly bored with her competitive bid for attention. Why should I prove that I knew who Philip Sidney was.

'Don't look like that, Nessa,' she said, dropping onto a cushion at my feet. 'There are several Sidneys. You can't be expected to remember them all.'

'True,' said Clive, pulling a book down from the bookshelf. 'His sister, Mary Sidney, was very bright; wrote longer, did more. Mmm, Apuleius?' He handed Virginia a thickly embossed volume. 'You might like it.' This is how it is with them now. A kind of literary shorthand has cropped up.

'Would I?' she asked, resting her head, Virginia-like, on my knees and not looking at him, happy to have navigated the room back to her sphere. She drew closer. Virginia is a burrowing animal in search of perpetual notice. At least their book talk enlivens them and keeps them from discussing me. I am not the only one she competes with. Virginia seems determined to prove that she knows me better and has for longer than Clive. It is absurd. She is my sister, and he is my husband. They know diffcrent Nessas. I prefer them to talk of words. They keep a constant literary conversation going now, like an unbroken shoreline. I went back to my paint. Not much time, Julian would be awake soon.

And—Virginia has begun a review of *The Life and Correspondence of John Thadeus Delane* for the *Cornhill*. Virginia is especially anxious that it be up to scratch, as Father used to be editor of the *Cornhill*. She and Clive talk of her articles endlessly. I find it dull but cannot admit that without sounding like a philistine, and so I just nod and wait for it to go away.

Later

Tonight the talk turned to Virginia's marriage—or the absence of Virginia's marriage. More and more, the discussion circles around Virginia's prospects. She does not shy away from the subject, but neither does she participate. She is a fixed, still centre and lets that conversation drift around her like well-cut silk. If it makes her uncomfortable, she does not show it. Good for her.

One a.m.

An argument with Clive tonight. With this new terrible upset over Duncan and Maynard, I want to invite Lytton down here to escape it. These things are always easier to face by the sea. Clive is resistant to the idea. He keeps saying that it is just *us,* and we ought not to ruin it by inviting anyone else. 'But it is not just us. Virginia is already here.' And I get nowhere. Maybe it is best? Without Thoby, I am not sure how well Clive and Lytton really get on any more.

67 BELSIZE PARK GARDENS

HAMPSTEAD, N.W.

TEL.: HAMPSTEAD 1090

The Green Dragon, Lavington

29 April 1908

Dearest Nessa,

My dear, there is nothing like a pastoral holiday to take one's mind off shockingly unpleasant news. I would have written my news to Virginia (who is not taken up with cumbersome marital obligations and ongoing baby nurturing and much prefers to be told news

first), but one cannot write the heart to Virginia—only the mind.
The heart veers towards you.

  Maynard has truly taken up with Duncan. They are always to-
gether now. And my soul broke over those unhappy rocks. I have
made an effort to remain friendly with them both—although why I
should I can't think. But I have fled, my darling, to Salisbury Plain
for a reading party with Morgan, Desmond, James, and several
friends of his from Cambridge, among them the delectable pink-
cheeked, yellow-haired fallen angel Rupert Brooke, a newly minted
Apostle. He is so beautiful, I think he must be doomed. The gods
do not give such gifts for long.

Yours,
Lytton

PS: Is it true that Walter Headlam is courting Virginia? He is a
great friend of Rupert's, but that alone cannot elevate him to
Virginia. Has he proposed? How unpleasant.

30 April 1908—Trevose View, Cornwall

I overheard a conversation between Clive and Virginia this afternoon.
On the verandah:

'Mr Headlam has always been a hypochondriac and is always sure
he will die before he finishes his next great *oeuvre,*' Virginia said, irritated.

'Yes, but once he survives to publish the *oeuvre,* he recovers, doesn't
he?' Clive said. I could not tell if he was teasing. Difficult to know with
him sometimes.

'He is also hopeless and cannot even manage his own holiday packing.'

'Virginia, have *you* ever done your own holiday packing?' Clive
asked, his question curling with laughter.

Ha. A point scored. I slipped away.

And—Another letter from Lytton. He suffers, and yet he sympathises.

Maynard apparently invited him out to see Isadora Duncan dance in an effort to help him forget the Duncan they both love. Seems a crass way to alleviate heartbreak, but any bridge between them is better than none.

1 May 1908—Trevose View, Cornwall (early and clear)

I asked her directly at breakfast. Clive has succeeded in coaxing her to sit at the breakfast table even if she only drinks black coffee.

Walter Headlam *has* proposed. She is thinking about it. How long has she been thinking about it?

Saturday 2 May 1908—Trevose View, Cornwall (Virginia left today
as she could not get a seat on the Sunday train)

Ten past nine. The train was due to leave at half past. We stood on the platform in the fresh Cornish-blue morning. The porter had already come for her trunk of books and travelling valise.

'Take it, Virginia, you may get hungry.' I pressed the small hamper of food into her hands. I had thought Clive would be impatient with my fretting over Virginia, but when I glanced at him, his face was softened by a sweet concern. 'Dearest, will you take her to her seat?' I jostled Julian on my hip, as he was starting to fuss. I was regretting bringing him.

'Of course,' Clive said, smoothly scooping up the hamper and taking her arm to lead her to the train.

At the edge of the platform, Virginia stopped and spun round. 'Delane! My book!' Virginia clutched at Clive's arm, appalled that she had left it. Clive did not hesitate but turned and raced to the motor. 'On my desk!' Virginia shrieked after him.

'There isn't time!' The train whistle sounded. 'Clive!' I yelled, upsetting Julian, but he did not hear me.

Later

I pressed the cold cloth onto Clive's bloodied knee. 'It serves you right, running off like that.'

He had just made it back to the station as the train was pulling away and handed the book up to Virginia's waiting white-gloved hand. And then, scrambling to get away from the moving train, he fell in the gravel.

'Yes, but I made it back in time,' he said, proud of himself. He winced as I ripped his torn trouser leg to get to the gash.

'She could easily have bought another copy in London. You were just showing off.'

Clive grimaced in pain as I dabbed the cut with iodine but did not deny it.

I smoothed white gauze over the wound and secured it with a clean linen strip. 'There. You don't need a stitch, but keep the bandage on it, as it will seep for a few days.'

Still later (the fire has gone out)

It was raining outside and snug and warm inside. Julian had had his bath and gone to sleep without fussing. I was finished and back down from the nursery earlier than usual.

'Quiet without her,' I said, looking up from my novel (*Mansfield Park*—again).

'Mmm?' Clive said, his head bent over a letter he was writing.

'Quiet without her,' I repeated.

'She will be there by now,' he said absently. His thoughts elsewhere. 'We will see her soon.'

4 May 1908—Trevose View, Cornwall

'Virginia is a *Sapphist*?' Clive said again.

'No,' I repeated for the fourth time. 'Virginia is *nothing* at the moment. I can see how she could *become* a Sapphist.'

We were sitting on the big wicker chairs in the late afternoon sun, discussing Clive's current favourite topic—Virginia. I had made the mistake of musing aloud on the nature of Virginia's love for Violet, and now Clive was unwilling to let it drop.

'But is she in love with Violet?'

'Virginia, so far, has not loved, kissed, or been held by anyone that I know of,' I said wearily. 'She likes affection from Violet. But then she likes affection from me too.'

Clive sighed, as if placated. 'Well, of course she is not in love with *you*,' he said, relaxing into his sun chair.

I did not answer. In my deep bones, I have always known that Virginia is in love with me.

UNION POSTALE UNIVERSELLE

CEYLON (CYLAN)

8 *May 1908*

Kandy, Ceylon

Lytton,

I am not going to sweep in and propose to Virginia Stephen to save her from Walter Headlam, whom she has known all her life. She is a ravishing girl from what I recall, and there are many much more suitable and closer-to-hand candidates who would surely be up to the task. I can't think she hankers after a Jewish civil servant whom she hardly knows and who is currently in the middle of the Indian Ocean. At least once a month you have suggested that I marry her. Do I sense a concealed agenda? Do you wish to be encouraged in that direction? Has your heart finally healed itself of Duncan? I can only hope that this is so.

I have been taking violent exercise; either squash racquets or tennis every day. I play with the Superintendent of Police, who was an Oxford Blue, and I have learned to play in inhospitable temperatures. I also occasionally play hockey with the Punjabi regiment. I am happy to report that Kandy is far more pleasant than Jaffna.

Yours,
Leonard

HRH KING EDWARD VII POSTAL STATIONERY

QUESTIONS AND ANSWERS

Sunday 10 May 1908—46 Gordon Square (warm and pink)

'And how is your valiant, wounded, book-fetching husband?' Lytton asked, settling into his customary basket chair.

'Busy,' I answered. It was good to be back. Our cases were hardly un-packed, and already the house thrummed with visitors. 'He is preparing an essay on Manet at the moment. How did you know about his fall?'

'Injuries incurred in the service of Virginia are not likely to remain secret for long,' Lytton said flippantly. 'She wrote to me, terribly excited that your devoted husband fell on his sword to please her. Although, more likely, it was to please you.' Lytton reached for a slice of Dundee cake. I had telephoned ahead and asked Maud to order it from Fortnum's for him.

'He fell in the *gravel*, less dignified than a sword,' I said.

'The gravel was next to a moving train,' Clive said, joining us in the drawing room. It was the first time I had seen him all day. He bent and kissed me, and I handed him a thick wedge of cake.

'And the *beau dauphin*? Is he well? Belching, teething, seeing to all those important baby tasks?' Lytton asked, daintily wiping his mouth.

'Asleep, at long last,' I said. Julian has been fractious lately. No won-der, with all the travelling he has been doing in his small life.

We talked on, of the opera (Virginia went four nights in a row last week) and the theatre and Saxon's current obsession with the Ballets Russes and then, when Clive went out, of Lytton's terrible Duncan-shaped heartbreak. I am glad I came home.

Later (nine p.m.)

Clive just told me that Maynard means to move into 21 Fitzroy Square. One door down from Duncan. It will be awful for Lytton.

15 May 1908—46 Gordon Square (late afternoon, sunny but chilly)

Virginia popped by to deliver an extraordinary rumour this afternoon. She looked like a child with an extra-special secret. Apparently, Father's friend Mr Henry James has been heard to say that he cannot believe one of Leslie Stephen's daughters strayed so far as to marry Clive Bell. Stray so far from whom? The half-witted, damp pink men George kept intro-ducing me to? Irritating. No idea where Virginia got such a rumour. She might have made it up.

Later

I was surrounded by my favourite buggers tonight. Lytton, James, James' friend Harry Norton, and Morgan all stopped by this evening. We played the gramophone, danced, gossiped, told rude jokes, drank, and ate chocolate biscuits until three in the morning. Clive stayed up in his study, saying he had to work. Unlike him.

Virginia Stephen
29 Fitzroy Square · London W.

20 May 1908

My Violet,

*Where are you now? New York? I hope so, as that is where I
am sending this letter. I am also sending a kiss that I ought to
dress in chic, narrow-shouldered, expensive clothes and equip
with a good cigarette holder to use uptown—is that a place?
Uptown?*

*My dearest one, I dislike being proposed to. Unless of course it
is you doing the proposing. Such a lot of affection and attention, I
ought to like it, but I don't. Walter Headlam will no doubt be coming next Thursday, and I am running out of things to say to him. I
am trying not to be wicked—you do know that, don't you? Trying
don't count for much when it comes time to pay up, I suppose.
I have refused Mr Headlam, but refused really is the wrong word.
Drifted. That is what I have done. He asked me early in the year,
and I prevaricated, sidestepped, and ignored it and let the subject
drift away. Eventually, he stopped asking. Wicked, I know. When
one is asked such a question, one ought to answer. But if one has
no idea what to answer? Then what?*

*I think it was my first proper proposal. There have been others,
but they lacked substance. Will it make me feel better to recount
the others? Shall you like to hear them? There was Lytton, who
asked me to marry him one evening at a Trinity Ball. That way we
could avoid having to dance with anyone else and make awkward
conversation. He also suggested I marry his long-absent friend
Leonard, but as that was a proxy request, I doubt it counts. Walter
Lamb also mentioned it once behind a potted palm at a dinner
party—I can't think whose. He said I would make an interesting
wife. Hilton Young has been nosing about, and everyone thinks he
will make a run at me, but I am not sure yet. I proposed almost*

daily to Nessa before she married Clive, but she always turned me down, however sweeping and sincere I was. And for symmetry, last week Clive tried to kiss me and told me he loves me—does that count?

Yrs,
Virginia

POSTCARD

25 May 1908

My Dear Strachey

Great things afoot. Just booked tickets to Paris to see the Ballets Russes at the Opera Garnier. Did you read the interview with Diaghilev in the Times last week? The man is a genius. Got a note from Adrian. I understand evenings at Fitzroy Square resume next week?

Yours, Saxon

To: *Mr Lytton Strachey*
67 Belsize Park
Gardens
Hampstead
N.W.

PS: Adrian told me about Maynard and Duncan. Bad luck. Sincere sympathy. Funny expression—sounds as though something died. But then I suppose, something has. Thoughtless of me—have I made it worse? I hope not. Please forgive.

---

30 May 1908—46 Gordon Square (my birthday—raining and cosy)

Lytton stopped in today. It was a quiet afternoon. Clive went out after breakfast and will not be back until early evening. Before he left, he sweetly put birthday roses on my breakfast tray. I am to have a treat tonight: Clive and I are leaving the baby with Elsie and going out for a supper at Rules and then to see Maurice Baring's *The Grey Stocking*. Lytton saw it and liked it but then told me that his taste is not to be trusted as he is too preoccupied to work up real disgust about anything at the moment.

Lytton is heartbroken. Touchingly, he has chosen to remain friends with both of the treacherous lovers—Maynard because they have been friends too long not to be friends, and Duncan because he loves him. Lytton understands the fundamental problem: 'How could one *not* fall in love with Duncan?' he asked me sincerely.

Our visit ended in laughter. Lytton tells me that ever since he found out about the affair between Maynard and Duncan, he is haunted by the smell of semen. 'It is everywhere, darling. Mother just can't escape it. Watch out at the opera house—it was definitely sprinkled in the dress circle. Someone was having a *very* good time in box six.' He says it is torturing him enough to put him off men. Perhaps he should marry Virginia?

31 May 1908—46 Gordon Square (six p.m.)

My fingernails are cutting into my palm.

I ought to put them back where I found them. I ought to go and check on Julian. I ought to open my hand and look at them again. But I cannot seem to put them down.

I was collecting Clive's jackets for Maud to press. For a man who cares so deeply about his appearance, he does not see to his clothes terribly well. But then, until recently he has always had a valet. We planned to hire one, but then came Julian and we needed a nurse instead. Clive has always resented that. And so I round up Clive's jackets and send them down to the laundry with Maud to be washed and pressed.

I checked the pockets. I always look, as Maud forgets. They were inside the breast pocket. Mother's blue enamelled hairpins: the ones Virginia always wears. Four of them lay in a row like toy soldiers in my palm.

And now I cannot seem to put them down.

Later

She may have left them in Cornwall. He may have found them when we were packing up. She may not know he has them. He may have thought they were mine. He may have. She may have.

It may be nothing. But nothing is nothing when it comes to Virginia.

Roger Fry
22 Willow Road
Hampstead, N.W.
London

1 June 1908

Dearest Mother,

I must thank you again for the wonderful bulbs you gave us this spring. The lily of the valley have been magnificent. And now may I ask you for yet another favour? Would you mind taking the children next week? Mr J. P. Morgan has a commission for me, and Helen is not up to having them at home without me there. She is recovering well but slowly and still has moments where she does not recognise me and, worse, does not recognise the children. And then there are the voices always. We had another of the dreadful violent episodes last night, but thank God, it passed quickly. I managed to restrain her, but she still struck her head against the wall with a terrible force.

I am so sorry to burden you with extra responsibilities. I only planned on going as far as Perugia this trip (to see about the Velázquez), but Mr Morgan has now asked me to bid for a Vermeer and a Hals held by a private collector in Rotterdam. I should be gone about three weeks.

It is good to be working for the Metropolitan Museum again,

even if it is only as an adviser. I have been finding myself at
loose ends since I returned. Caring for Helen takes considerable
energy, but beyond that, I feel stagnant. This Saturday, barring
mishaps, Helen and I are taking the children to Guildford for a
picnic. Do you remember the spot on the grassy hill where we
flew kites with Father? Just there. She loves it there. I am won-
dering if I ought to take all my latent restlessness and hurl it
into a grand project and build a house in the country? What do
you think?

> *All love,*
> *Roger*

PS: I have just heard from Burroughs, and the Trustees are de-
lighted with the Leonardo da Vinci drawing I secured for them last
month. We can learn so much from the sketches.

2 June 1908—46 Gordon Square (late)

A normal day. Clive has been working on his new article, and I worked on my still life in the morning and played with Julian all afternoon. Clive kissed my forehead at breakfast and talked about the new exhibition at the Grafton Galleries he wants us to see. I managed tea with sugar but nothing else. My stomach feels full of sand.

Maud brought Clive's ironed jackets upstairs, and I replaced the hairpins in the pocket where I found them. Ruffles of unease slip under my skin. Virginia wouldn't, I tell myself firmly. I am being overly suspicious. It is not like me, and I must stop it. Because Virginia wouldn't.

Sunday 7 June 1908—46 Gordon Square (warm enough to
have the windows open)

Virginia, Adrian, Lytton, and Desmond all came for supper this evening. Everyone talked about summer travel plans. Now that the weather has turned, we are all anxious to get away. Desmond and Molly are off to

Scotland, and Lytton will travel on the continent with either James or Pippa.

Clive and I will make our obligatory filial pilgrimage to Seend, and Virginia has decided to go to Wells alone to write. I don't like her travelling by herself, but Clive suggested Wells, as that way we won't be far, and we can all meet up for the day in Bath. And then at the end of the summer we will all go to Italy together. I want Venice, but Virginia and Adrian will want Florence. Clive will want to go to Rome.

Irrationally, I was hoping to travel alone with Clive. Absurd, when I was the one who suggested Virginia and Adrian come along.

Virginia was wearing her blue hairpins tonight.

Monday 15 June 1908—46 Gordon Square

'Bench? Shade?' Lytton pointed to the peeling black bench under the great plane trees. He has become monosyllabic lately.

'Aren't you meant to be writing today? Desmond says your review is due on Friday.'

Lytton is writing regular columns (book and theatre reviews mostly) for the *Spectator,* and Desmond is editing the *New Quarterly*. It is shocking to have both of them viably employed.

'It's nearly done. Just needs polishing,' Lytton said, settling himself onto the low bench.

'And by that, you mean you have not started?' I sat next to him, hooking my legs around the curved seat and wishing I had worn a darker colour, as I would surely get rusted paint flecks on my cream skirt.

Out of unstoppable habit, I glanced over my shoulder at the house. It was semi-obscured by the bushy lilac blooms climbing over the wrought-iron fence that wraps the garden square. I do not know what I was looking for, as the nursery windows are high. I had wanted to bring Julian, but he was asleep, and I did not like to wake him. Lytton was quiet. He does not look well, and I am concerned about him. I will talk

to Clive about it. Talk to Clive. Will that always be my instinctive reaction? No. Once it was to talk to Thoby.

Lytton sat with his eyes closed, face upturned to the summer trees. I
was also quiet. Silenced by a question I do not know how to ask. Perhaps there is no need to ask it? I know I have been distracted by Julian
this spring. I know I have neglected Clive and Virginia. She is my sister,
and he is my husband. The affinity is natural. I *asked* her to reach out to
him. If Clive could not spend time with me, then of course he would
look to Virginia. Do all new mothers worry about this? But all new
mothers do not have sisters like Virginia.

And—Damn. Adrian can't come to Italy.

Later (everyone asleep)

Clive just went back to his own bed. I feel rumpled and warm and happy.
I did not even mind when he left. He is used to it, he says. And I still get
up in the night to check on Julian.

We talked. I fell back into my habit of truth—unmitigated, brutal,
blunt, and whole. It is the only thing that heals.

What happened:

Four in the morning, and I would not back down.

'She is better read than I am.' I was lining up reasons for why Clive
might prefer my sister to me. I was not sure why I had taken this tack,
but it was too late to turn back.

'But you understand *art*.' He moved closer to me on the bed.

'She is better at conversation than I am.'

'But you understand *people*.' He smoothed my hair from my face.

'She is more beautiful than I am.'

'No one could be more beautiful than you.'

'But she is—'

'You are *my* Vanessa. We are a family.'

'Yes.'

It was what I wanted to hear.

Later (early morning)

Yes, but it does not square up. Yes, but he never said that he did *not* love her. Yes, but I know what families are capable of. I hate this feeling of sifting for truth.

Wednesday 17 June 1908—46 Gordon Square

No breakfast again today but calmer. Sex repairs. At least for the moment. Together in our room, now my room, I suppose, it was impossible to imagine, but in the raw daylight the picture slides out of focus, and I question everything.

Clive and Virginia. Virginia and Clive. It flows more naturally than Clive and Vanessa. I sketched Julian in the morning sun again today and neglected my still life. Life at the moment is not still. It is moving very fast.

Late morning

I painted Julian in oils. Should start on my portrait of Irene Noel, but I only want to paint my baby boy. The neat, tucked curve of his small head. I talk to him as I paint. Everyone tells me that he cannot possibly understand, but I know that he can.

Later

I have finished my letters, played with Julian, planned the menus with Sophie, cleaned my brushes, and given my new box of handkerchiefs to Maud to be edged. A domestic day so far. I left instructions with Sloper and Maud that I was not at home (and if Virginia asked, because she always asks, I am at the hairdresser—nothing will keep Virginia at bay like the hairdresser). The bell rang twice, but I did not go downstairs.

Doubts play in the thick trees but do not come out from hiding into the scraped bright day. I unstitch our conversation thread by thread. He did not say it was *inconceivable*. He did not say it was *impossible*. He did not say he could *never* feel such an emotion. I sent my questions flying over the net with long, sure strokes, and he returned my forehand every time. That ought to make me feel better. So why doesn't it?

Shocked. He was not shocked. That is the missing emotion. One *ought* to be shocked when asked about an affair with your wife's sister. He was careful, urbane, logical. His reasoning was cooked all the way through, with no raw uncomfortable truth left red on the bone.

After supper (Clive is reading in the armchair opposite)

I have been a perfect shrew today. I picked a quarrel over luncheon and then refused a walk before tea. Clive is pretending that I am behaving normally, which only makes me behave worse.

What did I want to happen? Why can't I accept his denial? I have told him that no matter what has happened, we can get through it if he is honest with me. Do I mean that? No, probably not, but I said it anyway. I feel as though I will say *anything* to snap him into honesty, and then we can see where we are.

I do believe truth heals, but sometimes only after it desperately wounds. It is a risky cure. Is that why I fight about the lemonade and the broken bicycle and the unposted letter and the bill for the grocer and the bad luck hat left on the bed? Because it is better than saying the things that cannot be unsaid?

Marriage is a binding, blending thing that runs on a low-burning fuel of habit and faith. Love, on the other hand, is unanchored and lissom in its fragility. I pull a thread and then carefully weave it back into place, keen to keep the shape of the whole. The way I did when I learned of his affair with Mrs Raven Hill before our marriage.

It is not in my nature to destroy. It is not in my nature to be suspicious. So I will do nothing. I will accept his reasoning and her innocence and fold the episode into myself—where it can harm no one.

It took so long to find this steady life. I lost each of my lives that came before. Each time the shattering blow on the slender new bone:

Mother, Father, Stella, and each time the terrible business of piecing together what was left over. Rebuilding the broken piecrust and hoping the dough will stretch.

But when we lost Thoby, I reinvented from scratch. I found something else. Something wide and new and safe. And it is all my own and so even more precious, and I cannot bear to smash it to look inside.

Later (two a.m.—the baby woke me)

I tiptoed into Clive's room after I got the baby back down.

'Julian all right?' he asked, sitting up sleepily in bed.

'Fine. He is asleep now.' I sat on the edge of the single maplewood bed. It used to be in the attic in Hyde Park Gate. Virginia and I hid from George and Gerald under this bed, I thought randomly. It creaked as I sat down.

'Elsie can get him back to sleep. You do not need to get up yourself,' Clive said, rubbing my shoulder, his hand large and awkward. 'You look tired, darling. You ought to sleep more.'

'Yes,' I said, and lay down beside him in the narrow bed.

Clive shifted uncomfortably. 'Nessa?' he asked. 'Are you going to stay?'

'No,' I said, kissing him. 'I just came to say goodnight.' And I crept back to my own room.

MR HEADLAM

Thursday 18 June 1908—46 Gordon Square (ten p.m.)

We were discussing our circle's migration to the country. Morgan, Desmond and Molly, Lytton, Lytton's sisters Pippa and Marjorie, Harry Norton, Virginia, and Hilton Young (at Virginia's request) came for supper tonight, and we were all enjoying whisky and coffee in the drawing room after a simple meal of roast chicken and new potatoes. Adrian was at the theatre, so the numbers were uneven, but I don't worry about such things now.

'The country has a majestic quality,' Desmond said as I handed him his drink. 'I prefer rural quiet to the busyness of London these days.'

'You have just purchased a house in the country,' Lytton said, re-lighting his pipe, 'and that renders you an unreliable judge. The country *is* lovely as long as one packs: good books, lively theatre, agreeable food, plenty of hot water, old friends, glittering conversation, and at least one like-minded Adonis to fall in love with—two to be safe.'

'And so you ought to visit more often, as we have all that,' Molly said with a straight face. She has lightened considerably since she and Desmond married, and I have difficulty remembering why I found her so awkward.

'Virginia, explain the poetry of a city to these country swine, would you? The music of a passing omnibus, the aria of the flower market?' Lytton teased from his basket chair.

'Ah, but Virginia *has* been enjoying a more pastoral life lately,' Clive said, rising to hand Virginia her coffee. I noticed, too late, he had given her the chipped cup I had meant to throw away. 'Where have you been this month, Virginia?' Clive asked, returning to his seat on the blue sofa beside me.

'So far, Hampton Court, not really rural but not urban either; Welwyn, Kew, Dulwich, and Hampstead,' Virginia recited neatly. 'And I have still made it back each night to get to the opera.'

'Then you have had the best of both worlds,' I said, and was rewarded with a sunny Virginia smile.

'Speaking of the glories of nature, Morgan, where is that flower shop you like in Hampstead?' Hilton asked. 'Are they better than Edward Goodyear in the King's Road?'

And the conversation moved off to other things.

Later

Siena is definitely on the itinerary, and naturally Clive is keen on Paris. He wants to see Matisse's new painting *Harmony in Red,* as well as the *Blue Nude* everyone is talking about. I adored the nudes in his *Le Bonheur de vivre.* Stunning shapes.

I am voting for Venice and Florence as well but doubt I will have my way. Virginia is being contrary and says she does not care for the light in Venice.

Three a.m. (in the armchair by my window, can't sleep,
stormy outside)

I watched more than spoke tonight, but I am comfortable that way. Clive, sitting beside me, also let the evening eddy around him without directing the currents as he usually does.

Interesting developments: Hilton spent a long time talking to Virginia, and I saw Lytton watching them keenly. I sometimes wonder if Lytton would consider marrying Virginia? He is not romantically interested in women, but sometimes it seems as though he could fall in love with Virginia out of sheer curiosity. He has always been fascinated by her. Clive was also tracking the interaction closely but did not leave my side. How she rivets, my sister. Virginia's conversation has taken on a hard, diamond brilliance. When did that happen? She plays to keep now: carving up the chessboard, fluent and calm. And each time the pieces move to defend their queen.

Friday 19 June 1908—46 Gordon Square

Tonight:

'Do you mind it?' Lytton asked, shutting the tall windows against the rain.

'Mind?' I asked, trying to find my glass from the many scattered all over the room. We had meant to have an evening alone, but Lytton called in after supper with James and Desmond, and then Virginia and Adrian popped by, and suddenly I was hostess again.

Now, Lytton and I were in the drawing room. Desmond had left early to catch his train, and Adrian had left with James. Clive was walking Virginia home. I told him it would rain, but she insisted that it was just too silly to get a cab around the corner to Fitzroy Square. I did not mention that she often *insists* on a cab to Fitzroy Square. Her capriciousness is best left unquestioned if one wants to avoid a scene. Lytton stayed behind, his eyes semi-shut and his red springy beard resting neatly on his chest.

'Yes, *mind*.' He calmly waited for my response and did not clutter the air with words we did not need.

The question swung like a trapeze through my thoughts, threatening to kick open my carefully boxed-away fears. Did I want this conversation? Even with Lytton? Even with myself? No.

My voice took on a challenging pitch. 'Of course I don't mind. Why should I? I would much prefer Virginia not walk home alone.'

'No reason, my dear. Absolutely no reason at all.'

Later

I asked him, and he said no. It is enough. I refolded the question and tucked it back under the shelf of my swollen fleshy heart. No good will come of half-believing. I have decided to trust this man—to hitch my happiness to our life together. When did I decide to do that? My happiness was always drawn by painting before. Before, I was in love with being an artist. Before, I was not in love with Clive.

Lytton is naturally wary of betrayal at the moment. It is the landscape he lives in.

20 June 1908—46 Gordon Square

Left Julian with Elsie and slipped out on my own for a peach ice at Buzzards. I sat in the shade and ate it slowly, feeling like a runaway.

21 June 1908—46 Gordon Square

Walter Headlam is *dead*. He was only a few years older than us. Clive rushed in to tell me. Apparently he went to the King's College ball and a fellows' party last week plus a cricket match at Lord's, and then yesterday he fell down dead. I teased him for his hypochondria. He must have known something that we did not. Clive left immediately for Fitzroy Square to tell Virginia. I ought to have gone, but she will either be hysterical or cold—neither of which is sincere.

Later

'She was upset—her sensibilities are so *fine*—but not in love with him, thank God. Did you know she had refused him?' Clive was standing at the mantel in the drawing room. Agitated, he was finding it difficult to light his pipe.

'I guessed, but did not know,' I said. On the fifth try, he lit it.

POSTCARD

THIS SPACE TO BE USED FOR CORRESPONDENCE

25 June 1908

My Dear Woolf,

Have you heard? Headlam. Up and died on a Saturday afternoon. He had been to a ball at King's, the cricket, and then kaput. He was always fretting that it would happen. Ghastly. I fret that it will happen to me too. Perhaps I should stop? I was right, he had proposed to beautiful Virginia, who from her lack of yes, I assume said no. I saw her yesterday, and she seems sanguine. But then, she is starting trouble in a different quarter just now. It really would be best for everyone if you married her. Letter to follow.

Yrs, Lytton

To: *Mr Leonard Woolf*
  Gov't House
  Kandy
  Ceylon

HATCHARDS BOOKSHOP

5 July 1908—46 Gordon Square

There was a small informal memorial for Walter Headlam today. I listened to Adrian and Virginia telling stories about our childhood summers at St Ives. We had known him all our lives.

ITALIA

Monday 17 August 1908—46 Gordon Square (hot!)

Virginia is off to Manorbier tomorrow. As usual, George and Margaret are appalled that she is travelling alone, but she is determined and says she needs the solitude to write. She is to stay at Sea View, where Clive and I stayed on our wedding tour. Last year—a hundred years ago. *Everything* before Julian feels like a hundred years ago. Virginia is cutting it finely. She will barely make it back from Wales in time for us to all leave for Italy in a few weeks. 'Did Clive suggest it?' I asked her when I stopped in this afternoon.

'Of course. He said I would enjoy Tenby, the little village by the sea,' Virginia answered without looking up from the letter she was writing. 'I told him it would make me miss you less to be in a place where I knew you had been happy. Won't it make you happy to know I will be thinking of you?'

Virginia logic.

20 August 1908—46 Gordon Square (late)

Another three letters from Virginia today. They were disastrous. She talks of cliff walking and slipping and imagines the sensation of her arms being torn back by the fall but reassures me that she has no wish to misstep. Does she mean to terrify me? Of course she does. I beg her to take care, and she basks in my protectiveness, but it only spurs her on to recklessness.

Saturday 22 August 1908—46 Gordon Square (ten p.m.—in the library, chilly without a fire)

Clive lowered the letter he was reading. 'She wants to know if you have finished your sonnet.' Clive uncrossed his ankles and stretched his legs in a great cat stretch.

'Sonnet? Am I writing a sonnet?' I put down my sketchbook.

'Apparently you are writing a sonnet about Julian's eyelashes?' Clive said, consulting his letter.

'Virginia?' I asked, already knowing the answer.

'Who else? She is now calling you "sweet honey bee" and would like me to kiss your, I can't make it out . . . *knee,* maybe? At once.'

'Only because it rhymes with *bee.*' I went back to sorting through my sketches of Julian.

'Perhaps, but ever the faithful brother-in-law, I am happy to oblige.' He popped out of his chair and kissed my knee. 'She also says that she is enjoying the *primitive* and *unbridled* setting of our wedding tour. Was it primitive? I don't recall?'

'Yes, it was.' I ran my hand through his reddish curls. 'The sea was wild, and the air never stood still. But *you* were the one who was un-bridled, if I remember,' I said.

We left our coffee on the tray and went upstairs.

67 BELSIZE PARK GARDENS
HAMPSTEAD, N.W.
TEL.: HAMPSTEAD 1090

25 August 1908

My Dear Woolf,

Mon frère, James has fallen for the rather garishly beautiful Rupert Brooke. We are in Scotland recuperating our demolished hearts. Our sisters Pippa and Pernel are joining us in a few days. Virginia writes that she has completed one hundred pages of her grand oeuvre and the Mole has nearly rattled off another novel. I shall ask him to send you an early copy. I am feeling slothful in my lack of productivity. Your physical exertions sound alarming. Do take care. Very pleased you are in a more comfortable situation but have no interest in your becoming so comfortable that you never return.

Yrs,

Lytton

PS: Do consider marrying Virginia. Apart from being lovely to look at, she is the most extraordinary company, and we do not want to lose her to an outsider. If Bell can make off with Vanessa, anything is possible.

Virginia Stephen
29 Fitzroy Square • London W.

Sea View, Manorbier
Pembrokeshire, Wales

27 August 1908

Dearest Nessa,

Is Clive keeping my letters from you? Is he stashing them under cushions and inside shoes? Has he locked you in a store cupboard and refused you pen and ink? Have you been jailed for duelling? Taken prisoner? Shipped to Australia? Chased up a tree, shot at dawn, or lost at sea? It is the only explanation for your continued silence. I have not had a letter in four days. I feel like Napoleon badgering Josephine.

I am writing well, dearest. One hundred pages of my novel and counting. It is something. I arrive back on the 31st and I understand we leave for Italy on the 1st? Would you send Maud round to un-pack and repack your disorganised Goat? I am meant to go to the opera with Saxon on either the Monday or the Tuesday (depending on when he can get a ticket). Would you and Clive like to go? If so, send a note round to him at once. I can make either day provided the train is on time.

Friends of Violet have just returned from Florence and report that there is a dangerous fever running riot in the city—but maybe that is just in the heat of summer and by next week we will find Italy bathed in the cool, clean air of autumn? What do you think? What does Clive say?

Yrs,
Ginia

And—Bliss! A letter from you in the second post. I did not wait but gobbled it up right there in the hotel foyer. I shall spend the afternoon composing a proper response, but for now, know that I am eating breakfast and not planning to fall off a cliff. Kiss your left shoulder for me. Rhymes with 'boulder'.

28 *August* 1908—46 *Gordon Square (hot!)*

Another letter from Virginia. Her letters amuse but ultimately infuriate. She is trying to provoke affection from me, and it is tiresome.

And—Clive was talking tonight about rumours of fever in Italy. Ru-mours planted by Virginia. Nevertheless, I am growing anxious about taking Julian. But how could I leave him behind?

Sunday 30 August 1908—46 Gordon Square

Just returned from Fitzroy Square, where I spent the morning sorting out Virginia's things for Italy. Siena, Perugia, Pavia, Assisi, and then Paris for a week. Clive is hoping to meet the famous Steins, M. Henri Matisse, and M. André Derain, who have been causing such a fuss. He also hopes to see M. Picasso again, but apparently he may be in Spain at this time of year.

Clive has decreed that Julian is to stay behind at Seend with his frightful family, and I have reluctantly agreed. Elsie is going to go with my sweet boy. For once, I am glad of her meaty efficiency and viscous spirit. She has promised to let the bathwater run until it is warm.

Later

It was glorious light for painting—substantial, fluid, thick, bright light—when Clive came into my studio waving a letter. 'Now she wants me to kiss your nose,' Clive said, settling into the low blue armchair. 'Are we to run through your entire anatomy? Not that that would bother me.'

'My entire anatomy at least twice, I should think,' I said, choosing a broader brush. I was still working on the still life—all pale greys and whites, and then a slash of poppy red. I am pleased with the effect, although it looks like blood on the snow.

Clive looked at the still life approvingly. 'Red is the only break in the palette?'

'Yes—too drastic?' I stood back from the easel to get a wider perspective.

'No, I like it. Reminds me of Derain.'

And—Clive just told me that Maynard has left the India Office and is trying for a fellowship at Cambridge. I half hope he does not get it, as it could salt the fragile soil between him and Lytton. If Maynard got not only the man Lytton wanted but the position as well? Awful.

Still later (after supper)

'Clarissa?' Clive asked. 'She thinks our next child will be called Clarissa.' *Another* letter had come from Virginia. I was having trouble keeping up.

'She knows I have always loved that name,' I said, handing the letter to Clive.

'And she dreamt the baby will be born with a complete set of teeth and be able to say "no objection" upon arrival?' he asked, looking up. Sometimes Virginia's letters alarm him.

'Yes, the vocabulary is fine, but the teeth might be a bit rough going,' I said, accustomed to Virginia's random nonsense. I looked over at Clive. His eyes were closed, his mouth slack. He was sleepy after a large supper. 'It is our last night alone,' I said, but he did not move.

And—Just before we went to bed, Clive asked me about Virginia and Hilton Young. Had he proposed to Virginia? Would he propose to Virginia? Would Virginia accept him? *Would* Virginia prefer Lytton? Who *would* Virginia like to marry?

And and—I woke up in the night with the thought: *Clarissa*. Is she trying to find out if I might be pregnant?

WINSOR AND NEWTON LTD: Art Suppliers
37–40 Rathbone Place, London W.

BY APPOINTMENT TO HER MAJESTY QUEEN ALEXANDRA

1 September 1908
To Be Delivered to Mrs Clive Bell, 46 Gordon Sq.

Transparent Oil Colours:
    Retail 4d each

'British Ink' (2 tubes)

'Chinese White' (6 tubes)

'Lamp Black' (2 tubes)

'Crimson Lake' (1 tube)

'Rose Doré' (1 tube)

'Polished Silver' (2 tubes)

New Travel Palette and Sketchbook

(Note: Do rush this order as Mrs Bell is to travel abroad)

CORRESPONDING

.⁓.

67 BELSIZE PARK GARDENS

HAMPSTEAD, N.W.

TEL.: HAMPSTEAD 1090

3 September 1908

Dear Woolf,

And they're off. The complicated Bell ménage has left for Italy, leaving England feeling deserted and passé. What is it about those sisters that compels? One craves their company, no matter how naughty Virginia can be. Clive has certainly married up. But my God is he making a pig's ear of it. Not content with marrying darling Vanessa, he is now hell-bent on landing Virginia too.

From what I gather, the Bells and the Stephens went to Cornwall, and because Vanessa was too taken up with the baby, Clive grew bored, and Virginia grew spiteful. It all came apart like a Greek tragedy, my pet. Act I—prophecy. Act II—betrayal. Virginia has always wanted to be part of that marriage, and here she was being invited in. Clive has never understood how desperately Virginia loves her sister.

The only part of this that gives me any pleasure is my absolute confidence in Virginia's awkwardness. Knowing her, I am sure that the liaison has teetered near the brink of sex but has remained largely a love affair of the mind rather than the body. Headlam said she really was the most god-awful tease last winter, lurking behind palm fronds and then refusing even a kiss. Not being able to have her is driving Clive bats with frustration. He has become unbearable again. It is his shamelessness that I find galling. He swore that all he needed in this world to be happy was one Stephen sister. Now he needs two? Several times I thought Vanessa was going to mention it, but she kept silent and went for stoicism instead—brave girl.

Clive is not stoic. I have received two letters from him demanding to know if I am planning to propose to Virginia. And if not, who is? And then the day before yesterday, I was lunching at Simpson's with Keynes, and in burst the sweaty, lovesick clod.

'Has Hilton Young proposed to Virginia?' he asked without preamble.

Keynes was delighted at this moist interruption.

'I've no idea,' I answered, irritated that my soup was getting cold—the sorrel soup with watercress they do so well.

'Well, as I am her brother-in-law, shouldn't he ask my permission first?'

Naturally, I promised him that I would forewarn Hilton that should he wish to propose to Virginia, he ought to ask her brother-in-law/lover before he does so. Ridiculous.

On the home front, things are even more hopeless. Harry Norton has fallen in love with my brother James, who is in love with Rupert Brooke, who seems to be in love with a woman called Noel, of all things. It is like an unhappy daisy chain. Missing you, dear Leonard. Come back.

Yrs,
Lytton

PS: You must not think this reflects poorly on Virginia. She is not an easy creature, but she is well worth the trouble. This current

flirtation is ill advised, but you must understand that it stems from inexperience and jealousy rather than malice. She cannot bear to lose her sister to this man. She really does have the most spectacular mind, Leonard. In a conversation, there is no one quite like her. It really would be best for everyone if you married her.
PPS: Morgan's new novel is out next month. I will send it on to you.

HÔTEL DU QUAI VOLTAIRE
19 Quai Voltaire
7éme Arrondissement
Paris

24 September 1908

My Violet,

I have run out of my own thick, creamy English writing paper, and so this letter to you, my dearest, arrives on wings of former French trees. Do you think these shaved, flattened French trees feel it when they are sent abroad? Do they miss Gallic comforts and familiar food?

Alors. Paris, encore. I will spare you the pavement café art talk as I am sure you are growing weary of my descriptions of paint-smudged young men wearing Breton stripes and straw boaters sipping absinthe in the sunshine. Or perhaps you are not? If you are not, board a train at once and join me here.

Nerves are frayed, and our Nessa is fractious and unreasonable. Madness runs in the blood, and I am quite concerned for her. Clearly it is being returned to adult company that has done this. Nessa, accustomed to the soft baby gurglings of her infant, is unused to the rigours of proper conversation. And <u>what</u> conversation. Clive has been reading my writing and has had several viable *suggestions for my novel. I am reinventing him in my mind as a cultured being. How generous you must find me.*

Home in a week!

Your
Virginia

HÔTEL DU QUAI VOLTAIRE
19 Quai Voltaire
7éme Arrondissement
P a r i s

30 September 1908

My dear Lytton,

I know you know, so there is little sense in pretending.

To answer your long-ago question, yes, I mind. My sister and my husband do little to hide their affair, and I am at last angry—very angry. Do they suppose I am a dim-witted woman? Do they suppose that as Virginia presumes upon every other aspect of my life, I would not mind sharing my marriage as well? Do they suppose that my trust in my marriage will survive this? We have all talked so much about the provincial confinement of conventional marriage and our desire for modern, broad-minded freedom. But we never spoke of what trust is broken when freedom is taken rather than given. I am released from my traditional marriage, whether or not I chose to be. Here I am.

Virginia has decided that my foul mood is a result of my nerves and keeps insinuating that I am having a breakdown. I am ignoring it. London in a few days, and Julian and work. For now I think in colour, in paint and pen and ink and shape. It is safer, and there are fewer lies. I know they find me distant. I know they find me changed. I know they do not think I know. And I know what they still do not: that betrayal is betrayal, whether the betrayed knows it or not.

Preoccupied with art and artists, Clive and I have much to talk about, but the small intimacies of loving each other are lost—that time of trusting and expanding as a couple is over. I presume that affection between us will survive in some form. It is more convenient that way. And Virginia? I do not know what to say about Virginia except that she cannot be other than she is. She never could. But then, she has never had to.

Dearest Lytton, you did warn me. And Virginia warned me. Only Thoby had utter faith. Perhaps because he drew out the best parts of Clive? I do not, it seems. Virginia was right. My husband is not good enough.

Burn this letter.

Yours,
Vanessa

12 October 1908—46 Gordon Square (late afternoon)

So far I have said nothing. Lytton looks at me anxiously when he thinks no one is looking, but we have not had a moment alone together to discuss my appalling letter.

I am the one who is appalled. To have expressed so much. To have lost my nerve and crashed through the thicket of all the carefully built calm. And yet Clive and Virginia seem to notice nothing. Nothing. Clive still comes to my room at least once a week, and Virginia still prattles on, inviting me to praise her, to hear her, to heed her, to love her. And I do nothing to crack the smooth eggshell surface of our life together. Why?

But then, a dying star can light the sky for centuries after her fall.

Clive has suggested another holiday to Cornwall. The Bells and the Stephens. Virginia clapped her lovely white hands and flashed her lovely grey eyes at the prospect. I am sure Clive truly believes this holiday was his idea, but I know better.

And—Elsie says that babies often say 'Mama' before they are a year old. Julian looks at me, and I know he knows who I am, but he has yet to speak. Should I worry? Perhaps I ought to ask Ottoline?

21 October 1908—46 Gordon Square (late)

Henry Lamb came for supper. Virginia, Saxon, and Adrian were at the opera, and Lytton was with Maynard, so it was just the three of us. Henry is less affected than he used to be and dresses like an eccentric. He is also less dogmatic and shrill when he speaks to Clive. He used to intimidate me with his unbridled conviction and utter absolutism. He is more civilised now.

Clive, Henry, and I stayed up and spoke about art until the early morning. Henry is now very much in the sway of Augustus John, has changed his approach to underpainting entirely, and has given up painting with black altogether. The result is a diffused, blended, less strict look. I like it enormously. Clive says that Virginia has commissioned Henry to do a portrait of me when he gets back from Edinburgh next month.

Clive insisted I show Henry my portrait of Lytton's sister Marjorie. Clive thinks it is one of my best, but I am still ambivalent about the angle of the pose.

'Oh, I like this,' Henry said, pointing to the way the figure's arm leaned over the table. 'I like the quarter-turned shoulders and the way you do not try to make her beautiful.'

'Isn't my wife marvellous,' Clive said, squeezing my hand with that familiar, possessive look of love and pride.

Henry was effusive in his praise and gave me some helpful advice about the troubling vase of yellow chrysanthemums. After supper we pushed back the furniture and switched on the gramophone so Henry could teach us the foxtrot. I caught on quickly, and Henry and I whirled around the rug, but Clive kept confusing the steps. He was always quick on the fourth beat when he should have been slow. Eventually, Henry took my place and danced with Clive until he got it. Lytton and Maynard stopped in at about midnight and, seeing Henry and Clive, began to dance as well.

Later (three a.m.)

I switched on the light, but he did not move. Clive is sleeping beside me in our old bed—in our old room—tonight it *feels* like our room, but I know now that that feeling will go in the morning. Tonight was like sharply recalling a distant memory—the affection, the sex. Is this where our modern view of marriage has dropped us? He flirts with my sister during the day and then sleeps beside me at night? Am I to take only what I am offered? I feel passive, as if my life is being decided by others and I will be a bother to everyone if I fuss. It will not do.

22 October 1908—46 Gordon Square (dawn)

Clive has gone back to his room. I asked him to. I could not let him stay. Sex, yes. Sleep, no. This is *my* room now.

25 October 1908—46 Gordon Square (late, raining)

Virginia and Adrian, Lytton and Marjorie, Ottoline and Philip, Gwennie Darwin and Rupert Brooke (down from Cambridge), Maynard, Duncan, Lady Katherine (Katie) Thynne and her husband, Lord Cromer, and Saxon for supper this evening. Virginia went quiet several times (each time that Clive called me 'darling' in fact), but Clive and Hilton took turns enticing her out. I watched Clive expertly knit the evening together. I watched him slip in and out of conversations, fuelling debate, laughter, and gossip. He makes people feel comfortable and heard. I felt flat and scattered. I kept losing the arc of the evening. Instead, I watched. I watched Clive watching Virginia.

27 October 1908—46 Gordon Square (late)

'Isn't this the first novel you started, Morgan?' Clive said, taking a sandwich from the tray. Virginia looked away. She can't bear watching people eat.

'Yes, I started this one in 1902. But it did not feel right, so I dropped it,' Morgan said in a low voice, wiping his hands softly on his napkin.

It is good having him back in London, however briefly. He is so often away, Greece last year, and now he is going to India. He sails on Monday.

'I began it after Mother and I travelled in Italy in 1901,' Morgan continued quietly.

'Why didn't you finish it?' Lytton asked from his basket chair, where he was having trouble lighting his pipe. He never cleans his pipes properly and then complains that they won't light. Morgan goes about his writing with such an unfussy, self-effacing grace that he is one of the few people for whom Lytton feels no real jealousy, only admiration.

'*A Room with a View* is a beautiful title,' I said, handing Lytton my lighter. I've been smoking far less since Julian was born but still carry Great-aunt Julia's chased silver lighter in my pocket.

'Thank you,' Morgan said. 'I like it too. I was pleased the publishers let me keep it.'

'Why didn't you finish it six years ago?' Virginia asked. She is bitingly jealous of Morgan and usually avoids discussing his novels, but curiosity had got the best of her.

'I couldn't,' Morgan said, uncomfortable at being the centre of attention. 'It would not come right. The end felt too neatly patched together and too, I don't know . . . resolved?' he said, his voice lifting into a question. 'The problem of how to go about things, how to live as one should, as one wants to, when one *can't* really. It was such a muddle.'

I looked at Morgan, astonished. It was a lengthy and deeply personal speech for him.

'Ah,' said Lytton. 'You mean how to live as a bugger when the world tells you not to?' Everyone roared with laughter.

'Yes, I suppose,' Morgan said, flushing. 'I suppose that is it.'

29 October 1908—46 Gordon Square (late afternoon—beautiful light)

We are going to Cornwall. We are booked in to stay at Penmenner House, a small hotel in an area known as the Lizard—seems fitting for my family at the moment. No, Vanessa. Too forked. Too spiteful. Too obvious, really. My jealousy is seeping through.

And—Lytton is coming with us. We will not be alone in our unhappy triangle.

Saturday 31 October 1908—46 Gordon Square (All Souls' Eve)

Just home from a supper party at Ottoline and Philip Morrell's magnificent Bedford Square house. It was a pleasant evening. Morgan was there, and we spoke some more about his new novel. I had thought that he had written himself as George Emerson, but it seems he is Lucy Honeychurch.

'Mr Emerson—old Mr Emerson—is that not you?' I asked.

'Ah, Mr Emerson. He is how I *ought* to be,' Morgan said. 'But being Mr Emerson takes huge courage.'

'Is he based on someone?' I asked.

'I met a man once, in Italy. A Mr Edward Carpenter.' Morgan stopped mid-thought, as he sometimes does. I waited for him to resume. 'He believed in love—all kinds of love. He was'—Morgan paused—'very wonderful.'

Later

I woke up in the night and, out of habit, checked on Julian. Seeing that he was sleeping, I came down to the darkened drawing room and sat on the long sofa overlooking the square. I thought about the conversation with Morgan, about the asymmetrical shapes of love, about the inevitable destructive quality of secrets. Morgan's ideal is to bring the muddle into the open. He does not try to solve the muddle, he just hopes not to hide it. What a small important thing he is doing.

12 November 1908—Penmenner House, the Lizard, Cornwall (early)

I relish writing our current address. It is a tiny serpent joy. Everything is different from the last time we holidayed here. But the activities remain stubbornly unchanged: breakfasting, painting, walking, writing, piquet, reading, and talking—always the talking. I really could do without so much talking. I have nothing to say. Instead I seethe. Have they noticed that I no longer talk? No. Because now we are translated into another language—a language of ragged-edged undercurrents and bitten-off consonants rather than the open-armed, snareless friendship of good.

Lytton watches them, fascinated by their boldness, by their shame-lessness really. Clive's pursuit and Virginia's encouragement. Their pre-texts are long-winded and their excuses reed thin. Each afternoon Virginia goes walking, and it is only Clive who joins her. Lytton is as-tonished. But he can't help being fascinated by Virginia.

Later

We stayed up late as Lytton and Virginia talked about his intended novel. From what I can tell, the plot involves a prime minister, a don's wife, a saucy footman, and some prostitutes. He won't actually write scenes of buggery, but he means to brush very close. He and Virginia sat by the fire hashing out ways for this unlikely medley of characters to believably interact. Virginia grew agitated (as she often does around good writers) and abruptly ended the conversation by asking Lytton to please confine his genius to non-fiction. Clive watched from the sofa looking stormy.

Friday 13 November 1908—Penmenner House, the Lizard, Cornwall
(early morning)

I went in to visit Lytton over his breakfast tray. His routine is un-shakeable. Soft-boiled egg, toast, coffee, and his letters all taken on a tray in bed.

'I have been thinking about triangles,' Lytton said, dunking his toast in his egg. 'We all love in triangles. Duncan, Maynard, and me. James, Henry, and Rupert. And now Clive, Virginia, and you. And Ottoline always has a triangle going on with some man or woman.'

'Ottoline is a Sapphist?' Did I know that?

'Only sometimes. She is having an affair with Augustus John at the moment. I don't think Philip minds, especially as he is always entangled in a romance of his own. You know she has a beautiful, long, low country home where she stashes them? Peppard Cottage. I have often stayed there.'

'And do you participate in these liaisons with Ottoline?' I asked, half-teasing.

'At one point I worried she might be expecting it, and I thought I would have to pack my bags and go as it would be too ghastly, but no. She knows I am a bugger.'

'Ha!' How I love Lytton's pragmatic indecency. I kissed his forehead and left him to his breakfast.

Later (four p.m.)

'Does he know he is making himself ridiculous?' Lytton asked, dropping into the wicker armchair opposite and picking up the thread of our ongoing discussion of Clive. 'He is becoming a buffoon. He was already mostly a buffoon, but now he is really finishing the job.'

'Does anyone know when they are becoming ridiculous? Is there such a thing as ridiculous, or is it just a social construction?' I asked. That was the sort of circular philosophical nonsense question that

Thoby used to ask during our earnest Thursday evenings. Now we mostly gossip and talk about sex.

'No,' Lytton answered. 'No, he does not know. Nor does he think that you suspect. You are playing the part of the unwitting wife perfectly.'

'And Virginia?'

'She *wants* you to know. It is your attention she's after, not his. She does not care about Clive. It is you she loves.' Lytton gestured out the window. Virginia and Clive were coming up the walk. Virginia's hat was off, and her cheeks were whipped raw with pink. They paused on the path, their heads bent close. Clive watched intently as Virginia pinned her hat back into place. Virginia waited as Clive tugged self-consciously at his jacket.

Lytton, also watching, leaned forward to me. 'You know *nothing* has happened between them, don't you?'

'No,' I said. 'It is not nothing.'

My sister and my husband opened the front door and let the cold air in.

VIRGINIA

20 November 1908—46 Gordon Square (London!)

Home and a raft of notes and cards were piled upon the hall table waiting for me. Invitations:

> Ottoline: yes
>
> Aunt Anny: yes
>
> Gerald: no

As well, there was a stack of post for Virginia. She still receives about half of her correspondence here. An envelope from Mr Cecil Headlam, Walter's brother. I will walk it over to her now.

And—My God, Thoby, it has been two years today. I feel decades older, and you are still a golden twenty-six.

Later (one a.m.)

Exhausted. It happened. I suppose it had to happen.

Tonight:

'Virginia, aren't you going to open it?' I asked, watching her toss Cecil Headlam's letter onto the kindling pile.

'No. I already know what it says, and I know I don't want to.'

Virginia slumped deeper into her wingback chair. It used to be Father's, and I can remember him adopting that same sulky position.

'Well, then, I will answer Cecil. What does he want?'

'He wants me to help write Walter's memoir. He wants to know if I have any particular memories I want included. And I don't.' Virginia pointedly took up her book. I looked at the spine. Eliot. *The Mill on the Floss*. She's reading it again.

'Dearest Billy Goat.' I could feel myself wheedling and stopped. If she wished to insult Cecil, I was not going to prevent her. Virginia is determined to behave badly in every quadrant of her life at the moment, and nothing I say seems to stop her. I picked the letter up out of the pile and began looking around for my hatpin, lost in the sofa cushions.

'Nessa, that is *my* letter. What do you want with it?' Virginia challenged.

'I am going to write to him, since you seem to be too ill-mannered to do so.'

I was shocked when Virginia leapt from her chair and snatched the envelope out of my hand.

'It is *mine*. Do not touch what is *mine*.' Virginia's face had taken on a feral malevolence. I should have called out for Adrian. I should have sent for Dr Savage.

'What is *yours,* Virginia?' I asked softly. I too could be dangerous. 'Do you want to discuss what is yours and what is mine? Do you really?'

But Virginia was trapped in a cyclone of anger and resentment by then and too far gone to hear my warning.

She was muttering to herself, '*Mine,* Nessa. You do not get to have everything and everyone. Some things are mine. Walter was mine. He did not love *you.* You think that everyone must love you? *You?* The perfect mother. The perfect wife. Walter didn't. Walter loved *me.*' She was pacing. For once I was unafraid of her madness. Unmoved by her fragile mind.

'Yes, Walter loved you. He even asked to marry you.' I watched her stride back and forth in front of the fireplace.

'Yes, yes, he did. He thought I was beautiful and brilliant. He told me I had a classically noble disposition, Vanessa. A *noble* disposition, unlike you, who have become some sort of breeding animal, dribbling milk and grunting at her piglet. How could you, Nessa, when you were so splendid.'

I stepped back, stung.

'Beautiful and brilliant,' she continued. 'He told everyone he thought so. Beautiful and brilliant.' She was repeating herself. A bad sign that I should have heeded, but I refused to bend to her instability. 'He said that there was no one who could touch me, no one who could best me. And so he asked me to *marry* him.'

'Yes.' I paused. 'Just as Clive asked me.' His name fell like a stone through the thickened air.

'Clive.' Virginia had stopped pacing. 'Clive and you.'

'Yes. And now it is Clive and *you*.' I held very still.

'That is not *my* fault, Nessa,' Virginia said, pulling at her hair and shifting from foot to foot. 'Not my fault. I cannot help how he feels.'

'No. I do not believe that.' I looked at her levelly, insisting she remain calm. 'You have pursued this, Virginia. And I could have forgiven you, had you fallen in love with him. Had you felt sincere passion or even real affection, I could have made sense of my sister doing this atrocious thing. But you are not in love. You are jealous. You can not bear to be left out. And so you have broken what you could not have.'

'And what if it is broken?' Her chin lifted in rebellion. 'He is not *enough* for you, Nessa. He is not up to being a man in our family. I am your *sister*. Our relationship is unbreakable. What does it matter what happens between you and that thing, Clive?'

'*Nothing* is unbreakable,' I said quietly.

Virginia stood still. All her wildness tamed.

Still later (three a.m.)

I go over it in my mind. How I should have said this, and this. How I should have raised all her terrible destruction to the surface like a ship-wrecked boat dredged up from the sea floor. But that would have given the fracture a shape, a dimension—a definite perimeter to the ruin. This way has a subtle cruelty. This way will torment. She will spend years trying to map the rift she caused and sound the damage. She will push on the bruise and grow frantic trying to repair the creeping remoteness. It is the unkindest thing I have ever done. And I will not relent. I will not do otherwise. Damn her. And damn him.

18 December 1908—46 Gordon Square

This morning, when I went to take Julian from Elsie, he looked at me and, with his voice full of purpose, said, 'Mama.'

PROPOSALS

⚜

Roger Fry
Chantry Dene
18 Fort Road
Guildford, Surrey

6 January 1909

Dearest Mother,

*I spent all yesterday with the architects, Mr Clemence and Mr
Moon, talking about the house I intend to build here in Guildford.
They suggested several wonderful innovations to make the home
more comfortable (radiators hidden under the floorboards!), and
the plans should be ready by next week. I will bring them when I
next come to London.*

*I feel sure that leaving London was the right thing to do. Here
Helen will be able to rest and recover in peace. She is still in hospital, but Dr Chambers is hoping she can be released by the end of
the month. Joan has taken the children to Bristol so that I can
work. For the last two weeks, the doctor has advised me not to
visit Helen, as her outbursts have turned violent again. I should
hate to see her restrained, even for her own safety. There are days
when I feel in the grip of crashing sadness. We began with such an
ignorant happiness. We had no idea such things could happen. And*

now. How could we have come to this place? I am choking in the
swollen dark.

And then I shake myself and return to my industry. It is the
only answer. I am working with my former assistant, Burroughs, in
New York to negotiate a marvellous Renoir for the museum, La
Famille Charpentier. It is an unusual composition and has so far
been undervalued. I hope this neglect persists long enough for me
to buy it. There is also a Whistler (a portrait of M. Théodore
Duret—wonderful—owned by King Leopold) that would be per-
fect for the Met. Burroughs (who has replaced me as curator)
agrees and is travelling over next month to see them both.

I hope you and Father are still planning to come for Sunday
lunch? Let me know the time, and I will meet the train.

All love,
Roger

Thursday 21 January 1909—46 Gordon Square (frosty)

'And she is fifteen!' Lytton lit his pipe and then handed me his lighter,
and sat back in his customary chair.

'And James is . . . ?' I relit my cigarette. We were having Thursday
night here tonight, as Julian has a cold and I did not want to leave him.
Since we returned from Paris, we have been meeting at Virginia and
Adrian's. It was still early. Clive was dressing, and Lytton and I were in
the drawing room discussing his brother's latest romantic misadventure.

'James is still besotted by Brooke, and Brooke is besotted by this
fifteen-year-old Miss Noel Olivier. Rupert is absurd, writing sometimes
three or four letters a day to this unsuspecting schoolgirl. But then if one
is in love, letters are a moment of relief until the frenzy subsides.'

I looked at him fondly. This autumn he has done his best to make
peace with Duncan and Maynard. It is a courageous thing.

'I suppose I see it in a carnal, objective way, as he is astonishing to look at, but I just do not see the *point* of Brooke. He is so self-satisfied and, I don't know, lazy—yes, lazy.' Lytton reached for another slice of cake.

'Lazy? You only say that because he is not interested in being friends with you,' I said.

'Do you know, we spent a month living on the same staircase at Cambridge, and nothing—he had no interest in speaking to me. I call that lazy.'

'But James?'

'James is in the death throes of the thing, and one can only hope it passes soon. Although it might carry James away with it.' He looked up at me. 'Not all of us have the willpower to survive these things, Nessa.'

UNION POSTALE UNIVERSELLE

CEYLON (CYLAN)

21 January 1909

Kandy, Ceylon

Lytton,

I am sorry to have neglected you for so long. We are having a disaster here. Rinderpest disease has broken out in several herds in the neighbouring province of Uva, and it will be cata-strophic if it spreads to our cattle herds. It is highly contagious and can wipe out thousands at a time. Cattle are people's most precious possession here, and to lose them is heartbreaking as well as ruinous.

I realise, writing this, how far I have strayed from who I was when I left England and wonder how, if ever, I could make my way back? I find myself wondering if your mythic Virginia is the answer, the magical civilising force that could make me happy. Is

that madness? Is that desperation? It is illogical, but often these
days, my thoughts find their way to her door. Perhaps it will pass.
I think of you often and hope all is well with you.

Yrs,
Woolf

HRH KING EDWARD VII POSTAL STATIONERY

25 January 1909—46 Gordon Square (frosty)

Virginia's birthday supper tonight. She asked for family only. Family includes Adrian, Clive, Lytton, Saxon, Desmond, Molly, Duncan, Morgan, Hilton, and Maynard. (Violet is at Welwyn or we would have invited her, and Virginia decided against Ottoline and Philip and their menagerie of lovers.) She says she wants to be with the people she loves best. Virginia is circling. She is seeking my forgiveness. I am civil. I am kind. She cannot fault my behaviour. Nor can she find me.

At one point, as it inevitably does, our talk alighted on the question of whom Virginia might marry. Hilton volunteered (I still think he might genuinely propose one day), and Lytton looked anxious and suggested Leonard Woolf again. Clive missed it, as he was seeing Morgan into a cab. By the time he got back, we were discussing Maynard's new position as a fellow at King's.

1 February 1909—46 Gordon Square (early morning)

'Is everything all right with you and Virginia?' Clive asked, coming into the dining room for breakfast.

'Of course.' I folded my napkin and put it next to my place setting. I did not want my eggs after all.

'Really? Virginia seems to think that you are angry with her.' Clive stood at the sideboard ladling out sausages from the warming dish.

'Virginia is mistaken.' I kissed his cheek and went upstairs to check on Julian.

4 February 1909—46 Gordon Square

I am painting well, given all that has happened. I am pleased with my quiet still life and have decided to call it *Iceland Poppies*. Each time I come back to it, I am surprised at how well I like it: the wintry palette, the antique medicine jar and pale matching bowl, the green glass poison bottle, and the contrasting poppy. Yes, they are right together. Of course, I could fall out of love with it in an afternoon. Rightness can be a transitive thing.

Clive wanted to know if the painting is about Virginia's suicide attempts. How very obvious of him. He did not see the triplicate nature of the canvas. The three stripes on the wall. The three vessels: two white, one green. The three flowers lying in the foreground: the two white, turned to the wall, and the one shorter-stemmed poppy facing outward and painted in a fresh bolt of red. I alternate. Sometimes I am the white flower and sometimes I am the red.

Wednesday 17 February 1909—46 Gordon Square (six p.m.)

Lytton *proposed* to Virginia this afternoon. And Virginia *accepted*. Disaster.

Lytton has just left. What a mess. He arrived wild-eyed and desperate to undo this fumbled proposal. It seems he went to Fitzroy Square this afternoon to escape his depressing bedsit in the crowded family house in Belsize Park. He was late with his article (for the *Spectator*), could not get any quiet to work, was disheartened at the prospect of Maynard having won a fellowship at King's, and was still suffering from his ongoing Christmas cold. He went seeking good company, luncheon, and a decent fire, and he ended up impulsively proposing marriage to Virginia in the drawing room.

'Did you kneel?' I asked.

'No,' he said, looking shocked.

'Did you speak to Adrian about it?'

'No.' Lytton slumped further into his chair; his body curved like a question mark. 'If I had had the forethought to ask Adrian, I would have also had the forethought not to do it. Tea and toast and French novels by a warm fire—it was just such a pleasant way to spend an afternoon, and then I thought, *all* afternoons could be spent that way if we were married, and then before I knew it I said . . .'

'Did you kiss her?'

'Ugh!' Lytton dropped his head into his hands, horrified by the thought. Apparently he was stunned and appalled that Virginia had accepted. He never expected her to accept. In all honesty, neither did I.

'As soon as I said it, I realised I am a bugger through and through. I could never marry a *woman*,' he wailed. 'And certainly not a woman such as Virginia.'

'Yes, I can see that.'

·

I cannot imagine that Virginia really wants to go through with it. I hurried him out and sent a note round for Virginia to call.

Later (eight p.m.)

I asked her to come when I knew that Clive would be out. He has yet to learn of the proposal, and it will be awful for Lytton when he does find out. And he will find out. Virginia and Lytton are not good at secrets. She sat in the armchair but soon crept to the sofa and laid her head on my lap. She shook and burrowed until I put my hand on her head. It rested there, calming her.

'Why did you agree?' I asked, smoothing her hair from her face.

Each time I stopped, she nestled her head until I brushed my fingers through her hair again.

'I shouldn't have,' she said, clutching at my painting smock.

I waited, knowing there was more.

'How will I ever do this, Nessa? Am I to live with Adrian for the rest of my life? Don't I get to have *someone* of my own? *Somewhere* of my own?'

I was taken aback. I had expected her to plead our recent rift. But this rang of truth. With the exception of my own husband, Virginia had never expressed a wish to have a man of her own or a place of her own. She was always violently against the family breaking up at all. 'Ginia,' I said carefully, 'plenty of men would love to marry you. Walter, had he lived. Hilton most likely. You must find the one *you* would like to marry. You must find a life for yourself. And then, of course, you will set up house on your own together.'

'I have never met a man I wanted to marry. I am not sure there is one,' Virginia said darkly.

'So, not Lytton?' I asked, gently steering her round to the current problem.

'Of course not Lytton. I would prefer his sister Marjorie over Lytton,' she said bluntly.

I looked down at her, surprised. Virginia's Sapphism has long been conjectured, but I was surprised to hear her state it so frankly. 'I said yes because I was happy to be *asked*.' She hunched her legs up under her long skirts and tucked her hands under her chin. A posture from childhood. 'I was so happy with just *us*—just our family,' she said softly. 'I wanted us to be all together.'

I know she was thinking of Thoby.

Ten p.m.

I bundled Virginia into a cab. She is meeting Lytton in a quarter of an hour at Fitzroy Square.

I was moved by Virginia's great distress tonight. Surprising that sincere affection can survive where there is no trust.

18 February 1909—46 Gordon Square

They managed what Lytton called an honourable retreat.

They dissolved the preposterous engagement, and when he got home Lytton wrote Virginia a very sweet note insisting that what mattered most was that they liked each other as friends. Lytton says that he has been urging Leonard Woolf to marry her. He says he will explain his inadvertent proposal, and Leonard will understand. Leonard Woolf must be an extraordinary man to understand such a thing.

I know she accepted Lytton to make amends for Clive. In her reasoning, if she marries someone else, she can erase all the harm she has caused. Since that day at Fitzroy Square, I have refused to discuss the affair. She treads carefully around me, waiting for signs of forgiveness. It is difficult to forgive when she is not finished transgressing. The flirtation is not over with Clive, hardly abated. I understand Virginia's logic. If she finishes with Clive now, she will lose us both. She will not end the affair until I agree to forgive her. She cannot be left with no one.

And—It seems that Clive believed me when I told him that all was well between Virginia and me. How unobservant of him.

Monday 1 March 1909—46 Gordon Square

They have just left for Cambridge. I decided not to go. Julian has caught another cold, and the weather has not yet turned, and I wanted a moment alone to paint. Virginia, Rupert Brooke, and Henry Norton have gone for the day to visit James Strachey in his rooms at Cambridge. James is in need of cheering up; he is still not over Rupert Brooke, who is still not in love with him. Lytton says a mountaineering Adonis called Mr George Mallory *is* in love with James, but James is too besotted by Rupert to notice. I suspect Lytton is a bit in love with Mr George Mallory himself. Mr Mallory has something of Duncan's slim, rumpled beauty, and he climbs mountains to boot. Lytton will find that hard to resist.

Clive wanted to go but is meeting a curator friend from Paris and had to stay in town. I am hoping they will all stay away until after supper and Clive and I can have an evening alone. I must tell him of Lytton's proposal. It will be a disaster for Lytton if Clive hears it from someone else.

And—Adrian told me that Duncan has ended his affair with Maynard. Lytton will be happy. Adrian seemed pleased about it as well.

Later (four a.m.)

Clive is still not home.

3 March 1909—46 Gordon Square

Everyone was here tonight except Clive. I am suspicious.

5 March 1909—46 Gordon Square

It is Mrs Raven Hill. They resumed their affair over our Christmas visit to Seend. Lytton told me this afternoon. He has been trying to tell me for months. I am exhausted by the deceit.

At least it is not Virginia.

Later (two a.m.)

Clive is still out. He told me that he was going to be with Maynard and Duncan, but they stopped in after supper and knew nothing about it. They looked uncomfortable when I asked bluntly if Clive was with Mrs Raven Hill.

6 March 1909—46 Gordon Square (late afternoon—lightly raining)

Clive came home this morning, unrepentant. Apparently, I have misunderstood our marriage. He never thought we would be constricted by provincial fidelity. He never thought I would be so narrow-minded, so Victorian, so unimaginative, as to confuse a marriage and a love affair.

He never thought I would interrupt his personal freedom in this way. He never expected to love just me for all of our lives. I had that wrong. But he knows I am not the kind of woman to love many men. I am built to love just one, passionately. Does he expect me to direct that singular love to someone else?

10 April 1909—46 Gordon Square (blooming)

A disastrous morning. Why did I do it? Ridiculous question—of course I was going to do it.

This morning Clive left early to meet Lytton at the Savile Club in Piccadilly. Maud and Sophie were both out food shopping, it is Sloper's half day off, and Elsie had taken Julian into the square to play on a blanket in the grass. I was alone in the house, and I am *never* alone in the house.

I did not hesitate. When I heard the front door shut behind Elsie, I ran quickly up the stairs to Clive's study. Taking care to notice the order of things and replace each letter exactly where it lay, I read them. I read them all. The new love letters from Mrs Raven Hill are stacked together with the older love letters from before we were married. Her passion is uncomplicated and straightforward—of the body rather than the mind. Her letters speak of arrangements and train times and seedy hotels in Paddington. He has bought her two new hats, a silk nightgown, and a small watercolour. Fine.

In the smallest drawer in the desk, tucked all the way at the back, are a stack of much-thumbed letters, tied in a pale blue ribbon. Virginia. They were as bad as I feared. No. They were worse. And they were all about me. I retied the ribbon exactly as I found it. A double bow with the ends looped around.

24 April 1909—46 Gordon Square (late afternoon—still light)

It has been a fortnight. I have not told him I have read the letters. What would be the point? I have asked all my questions about Mrs Raven Hill.

He has answered in half-truths, and I can guess the rest. Clive finds her a comforting and familiar convenience. She is Virginia's counterpoint. I feel superior because I know more than his lover does. It is a petty victory. I am sure Clive turns to her because Virginia refuses. *My* refusal or not is irrelevant. I am no longer a competitor in the match. I am conquered territory and have no currency. Annexed and occupied and without much value.

And rarely, delicately, Clive asks about Virginia. It takes great nerve and huge arrogance to ask me, but he does it anyway. He cannot help himself. Will she marry? Who will marry her? Who wants to marry her? His shoulders draw into tense defensive lines as he collapses his voice into an even pitch.

10 May 1909—46 Gordon Square

The New English Art Club accepted my *Iceland Poppies*! It will be on exhibition this summer alongside Augustus John and John Singer Sargent. So something wonderful has tumbled out of this appalling year.

And—How lovely, Duncan will be exhibiting as well. I know his portrait of James is to be included, but I am not sure of the other piece. His work has gained such authority and beauty lately. I think he will become quite famous. He is often among us at Fitzroy Square and comes here with Virginia and Adrian. The better I know him, the better I like him.

Tuesday 18 May 1909—46 Gordon Square

Virginia just returned from Cambridge. Hilton Young finally proposed. And she refused. So she is willing to wait for the right love after all. Clive is smug and relieved and has been whistling all day. He hopes she refused for love of him. He does not understand her at all.

I felt scooped out, hollow, and detached when she told me. I heard myself offer pale platitudes and empty words of confidence. I am becoming someone I do not recognise.

CLARISSA

9 October 1909—46 Gordon Square

Just back from Seend and the horrors of the Bells. His family do not improve with time. How is it that they are able to spend their days gossiping, shooting, and wondering if it will rain and then go to sleep, wake up, and do it again? It eludes me.

Now home and we are having a party. I say 'we', but Clive had to stay in the country. So who is coming? Ottoline and Philip, Walter and Henry Lamb, Lytton's sisters Pernel, Pippa, and Marjorie (Lytton is in Cambridge), Duncan and Maynard, Adrian, Morgan, Gwennie Darwin, Saxon, and Virginia, Bertrand Russell (but not his wife, Alys, whom he does not love any more), Irene Noel, and Tudor Castle, who is mild but very funny and definitely my favourite of Adrian's Cambridge set. Desmond and Molly missed their train this afternoon and so could not come. I know the evening will be fraught as Ottoline and Henry Lamb are having a stormy affair and poor Irene is desperate to catch Tudor's attention. It will be a grim coupled-off evening.

I wish Clive were going to be here to smooth out the social crinkles, but he has to stay in Seend to take care of some family business for his father. I know he is really going to be spending his time with his battleship-bosomed, double-chinned Mrs Raven Hill, but I was too proud to say so. She is an overblown, flashy, extroverted woman, but I remember her being amusing in a crass sort of way. Perhaps I was the exception all along and his tastes truly run to that sort of showy woman?

I suppose the real trouble for him is Virginia. I am certain that Clive has been unable to seduce her. Virginia's resolve is steeled by distaste rather than virtue. But it hardly matters. Intention is the thing that harms us.

Since the summer I have been trying to accept Clive's view of modern marriage. The notion forces me to run anticlockwise and upends all that makes sense in my mind, but at least we have honesty between us again. That alone sits well with me. He is Julian's father and my husband, and so there we are.

Later

It was an awkward party. I tried to coax the evening into a proper shape, but it refused. Ottoline and Henry sat far apart but kept staring at each other while Philip and Walter made stilted conversation. Pernel, Pippa, and Marjorie spoke to Bertie Russell and Morgan about women's suffrage *all* evening. They were uninterested in speaking to anyone else about anything else. Wonderful if one is at a political rally but difficult at a party. I know Maynard was disappointed, as he had just finished Morgan's extraordinary futuristic story, 'If the Machine Breaks', and wanted to speak to him about it but never got the chance. It is different from anything else Morgan has written. It is his answer to H. G. Wells, and it is terrifying.

Irene was laughing too loudly, trying to interest Tudor Castle, and Ottoline looked over disapprovingly. Ottoline draws her lovers in with a melancholy sensuality rather than a brash sparkle, but Irene does not have the nuance for that. Virginia tried to ignite a whispered conversation with me, but I refused. Beyond that, both she and Saxon remained stubbornly silent. Adrian and Duncan sat in a corner talking together, and Maynard and Hilton wandered out to the balcony. I was worried it would be awkward between Hilton and Virginia, but it was not. Virginia was in a difficult mood to start with so perhaps the tension with Hilton simply got folded into the mixture. I am sure she was put out that Clive was not here.

Saxon was the last man standing, and I finally went up to bed and left him in the drawing room. He can be difficult to dislodge, and it is best to leave him. The evening never *happened*. Not a success. I too wish Clive had been here.

67 BELSIZE PARK GARDENS

HAMPSTEAD, N.W.

TEL.: HAMPSTEAD 1090

19 October 1909

Dearest Leonard,

I have returned to Cambridge for the autumn and find myself wondering why we ever left. I have taken over a fallen angel's rooms for the term. George Mallory. He is not mine, but oh how I wish he were. I am staying at the Grantchester Arms, as beautiful Mallory does not vacate the room until next Friday.

I sat today in the autumn sunshine and thought of how happy we were in this small city. Life in London is uneventful at present. Or rather, it is lacking in pleasant events. Adrian is leaving for America. Clive has taken up with a terribly vulgar woman, and although Duncan has discarded Maynard, he does not want me. I speak of you often to Virginia. She has refused Hilton Young. I tell her she is waiting for you.

Yours,
Lytton

Tuesday 9 November 1909—46 Gordon Square

'You're back!' I said, pleased. He had stayed on to meet an artist and an art dealer in Bath, and I had not expected him until the end of the week. Clive crossed the room to kiss me and then sat on the small sofa and pulled out a handkerchief. It was one of the monogrammed ones I ordered for him last Christmas. I must remember to order some new ones this year.

'Yes, the painting was not nearly as good as I thought it would be, and the painter was unimaginative and thick. I missed you. Let's move to Paris.'

'Because the painting was poor?' I laughed, putting away the last of my brushes. Clive always wants to move to Paris.

'I am serious, Nessa. You and me and Julian. We could live in St Germain, we could breakfast at Closerie des Lilas, you could paint, I could write, and we could be part of the most fascinating circle of artists in the world. Let's move to Paris.'

He *was* serious. Clive suggests moving to Paris at least twice a month, and every time we go there, he looks at apartments. But we always come back to the security, convenience, and familiarity of London. I felt fragile green shoots of hope push to the sunlight. I know this was his attempt to save us. To repair us. But it is too big a risk. In Paris, Clive would just be unfaithful with some chic Frenchwoman, and I would be away from here and even more alone. No. I sidestepped the question.

'The painting was bad?' I asked, leaning down to kiss him.

'Awful,' he said, pulling me onto his lap the way he used to.

We went into our room and closed the door.

Wednesday 8 December 1909—46 Gordon Square

Julian has learned to climb up the furniture in the drawing room. I spent the morning moving all the ornaments off the lower branches of the Christmas tree as he kept breaking them.

Later (three p.m.)

Damn. On Tuesday, Adrian arrives back from his American holiday on the *Mauretania*, and Virginia has already invited Violet for supper that evening. I wanted to have them both over to celebrate Adrian's return.

Duncan had a postcard from Adrian last week. He has taken up fly-fishing, whatever that may be.

12 December 1909—46 Gordon Square

Home from an evening in Fitzroy Square. An interesting talk with Duncan. I told him how I hoped to show my work, and he cautioned me, 'Once you offer a painting to the world, it stops being yours.' His reputation has been gaining lately—he did not sound pleased about it.

25 December 1909—46 Gordon Square (Christmas Day)

'Virginia has gone to Cornwall,' Clive said, waking me up with my Christmas breakfast on a tray.

'What?' I had slept late and could not make sense of what he was saying. 'She was here last night and never mentioned it.'

'Yes, it seems she was walking in Regent's Park this morning and decided that being in London was silly when Cornwall exists, and so she went home, told Adrian, and hopped on a train.' Clive sat on the bed beside me. 'Adrian just sent a note round so we would not expect her for supper.'

'Did she take her spectacles? Book a hotel?'

'I can't imagine she did any of those things. She just left,' Clive said, concerned. 'Adrian says she did not pack a bag. She won't have combination underwear, her washing kit, her books, her spectacles, warm clothes, or anything.' Clive ran his hand through his hair in agitation. 'Nessa, does she even have her chequebook?'

'I have no idea,' I said, feeling flooded with guilt.

'I can't think why she would do this,' Clive said.

'I can.' I turned to face him. 'I should have told you before her, and I am sorry for that.'

'Told me what, darling? You can tell Virginia anything. I don't mind.'

'Clive, last night I told Virginia I was pregnant.'

Later (three p.m.)

Clive went out. I know where he has gone.

Tonight the house is not making that rattling hollow silence it usually does. Instead my mind thumbs through names. Angelica? *Angelica, archangelica.* Like roots and sky.

Even later (eleven p.m.)

Clive was with his whore. A brutal, seedy word, but it is how I have decided to refer to her. From what I can tell, it is an essentially unromantic relationship defined by sex, so lover is all wrong. If anything, Virginia is his lover, she is still the one he loves. And I am still the wife. If Virginia were not my sister, we would be a pedestrian cliché. Instead, we are a bohemian nightmare. Nevertheless I wait for his footsteps on the stairs, and the day does not feel over until he is home and the door is bolted behind him. The small day-to-day details of a family continue even when the heart of a marriage has broken.

I watch him. He does everything that a husband should. He speaks to me about the wine and the tailor and the traffic in the square and the new painters he meets and the draught from the nursery windows, but his affection is a habit now, a routine and not an engine. Our life has taken on the heavy immobility of a load-bearing wall. We are no longer an adventure.

I had fallen asleep on the sofa in the drawing room and did not hear him open the door.

'I'm sorry,' Clive said, kneeling on the floor beside the sofa.

'Why? What have you done?' I asked, sleepily.

'I think you know.'

'You were with Mrs Raven Hill.'

'Yes,' Clive said, meeting my eyes.

'I forgive you.'

'Why?' Clive said, surprised by my prompt response. 'I thought you did not subscribe to my modern ideas on marriage.'

I laughed. Infidelity was hardly *modern*. 'Do I have a choice? I am married to you.' I took a slow breath, deciding to speak the unspoken. 'Anyway, your affair with *Virginia* is what ended our marriage, not Mrs Raven Hill.' I paused, waiting for him to deny it but knowing he would not.

'Ended?' he ventured cautiously.

'Evolved. Is that a better word?'

'Evolved.' He considered the word a moment. The word was vague enough to placate him. 'Yes. Evolved. You are a rare and fine thing, Vanessa,' he said, looking at me as he sometimes still does. He affectionately tugged at the end of my messy night braid. He did not try to convince me that our marriage was unharmed. Nor did he pretend to be other than he was. My last hope fell from the sky.

'And you are really pregnant?' he asked.

'Yes.'

'Good,' Clive said. 'That can only lead to good.'

26 December 1909—46 Gordon Square

A letter from Virginia arrived in the first post. She has washed up at the Lelant Hotel in St Ives and is the only guest. She made no mention of the baby and insists that Cornwall is at its best in winter. She does have her chequebook, but forgot her spectacles. I shall have to ask Adrian to send them.

Later—after supper

'What about Clarissa?' Clive said.

    An olive branch name. He has never liked it, but he knows I do.

    'Yes. Clarissa.'

PART FOUR

Vanessa in Paint and Ink

..

1910–1911

*'If you came, as I think I have
mentioned, you could marry Virginia,
which would settle every difficulty
in the best possible way. Do try it.'*

(LYTTON STRACHEY TO LEONARD WOOLF,

27 MAY 1909)

A MEETING ON A TRAIN

·ᴧ⳼·

Sunday 9 January 1910—46 Gordon Square (two a.m.)

'It was splendid! He has the most magnificent mind,' Clive said, leaping up to refill Adrian's glass.

We were in the chilly drawing room at Gordon Square, discussing our encounter with the art critic Roger Fry. We met him this morning on the 9.15 train from Cambridge. I recognised him standing near us on the platform. He remembered me and greeted me warmly and knew of Clive from his recent article for the *Athenaeum*. He and Clive struck up an animated discussion about modern French art. I stayed largely quiet and marvelled at the way Mr Fry listened. It was an active, thoughtful listening rather than the passive pause while one waits his turn to speak that you see so often in great men.

'You know, he is really serious about this exhibition of modern French art,' Clive said, coming to sit by me. 'French art has moved beyond Impressionism. It is not relevant anymore. It is no longer *modern*.'

'Who is he looking to show?' Desmond asked. I had forgotten how sincerely he cares about paintings.

'Manet, Cézanne, Gauguin, and Van Gogh primarily, although he may include newer paintings by Matisse and Picasso,' Clive said. 'I hope he does—they are genius. You liked the Matisse we saw in Paris, Nessa, didn't you?'

I looked at Clive. He knew I had adored it. The bright palette, the thick paint, and the unexpected perspectives were astonishing. He was trying to include me. He had noticed my reserve and was trying to draw me out. 'Yes, I thought they were revolutionary and beautiful,' I said simply.

'Didn't you meet him at our house, Nessa?' Desmond asked.

'Mr Fry? Yes,' I said. 'At your dinner party, years ago. Before he left for New York. He was with his wife.'

'Sad business,' Desmond said, reaching out to squeeze Molly's hand.

'Is she at home now?' I asked.

'Helen Fry? I think since her relapse a few years ago, they have tried their best to keep her home, but she has had to return to the mental hospital for long stays several times,' Molly said. 'The last time we saw him, she was to come home to spend Christmas with the children, so she may be at their home in Hampstead now.'

'Darling, don't you remember, the Frys have moved,' Desmond said. 'Roger designed and built that huge Arts and Crafts house in Guildford— tall ceilings, heat under the floorboards, modern kitchen. I found it weirdly spare, but it grows on you. It is called Durbins. I am not sure if Mrs Fry has yet lived there or not.'

'Terrible thing to live with such uncertainty,' Clive said, looking at me.

'We should invite him to speak at a Friday Club meeting,' Molly said.

'I already have,' I answered quietly.

Clive looked surprised.

Just then Virginia and Lytton arrived. They came from the opera and had been caught in the rain.

And—It seems that Lytton's sister Dorothy and her husband, the artist Simon Bussy, have been corresponding with Mr Fry for years. Lytton did not seem impressed with our new acquaintance, but Lytton has been out of sorts lately.

Saturday 5 February 1910—Peppard Cottage, Oxfordshire

The trouble with a Saturday-to-Monday house party in the country in February is that it will probably rain. Since we arrived this morning, there has been a steady grey Oxfordshire drizzle—depressing. But the indoor amusements are not to be sneezed at. Ottoline chose her guests well. Lytton and his sister Marjorie are here, Irene Noel and Tudor Castle, who are not officially engaged yet, as well as Desmond and Molly. (Like us, they left their baby, Rachel, at home with her nanny.) Duncan, Maynard, and Adrian arrive tomorrow. Ottoline and Henry Lamb circle each other discreetly—I have noticed that Ottoline is much more circumspect when she entertains at home. We have spoken several times, and I find myself warming to her. Roger Fry has also come along, and he and Ottoline have been chattering about art and friends in common and country houses they both know and like. It gives a particular kind of pleasure to introduce people who then become friends.

And—Virginia has borrowed the name Rachel for her heroine. Now she has to come up with a surname. She says she wants something lean, slicing, and elegant, like a paperknife.

UNION POSTALE UNIVERSELLE

CEYLON (CYLAN)

5 February 1910

Kandy, Ceylon

Lytton,

I have such news, my friend! I have just secured a long leave to re-turn to England. Charlie-the-dog and I will be arriving in April or May of next year and will be home for several months. My mind flops like a fish with excitement. I would come sooner, but last year

*I embarked on an ambitious education project and have now made
primary school mandatory in the town. We are opening a government school to accommodate all the children, and it should be in
hand by this time next year. It is one of the few things I have done
here that feels like true good. I will sail for England as soon as it is
up and running.*

    *Do you think your beautiful Miss Stephen will agree to meet
me again? Will she remember me? Do you think she will still be unmarried and unengaged? So many questions about a woman I have
hardly met—forgive me. Please do not tell her this, but she is beginning to haunt my thoughts daily. Thank you, Lytton, for that, no
matter where it leads. It will be wonderful to see you, dear man.*

                 Yrs,
                 Woolf

HRH KING EDWARD VII POSTAL STATIONERY

*Sunday 6 February 1910—Peppard Cottage, Oxfordshire (still
raining)*

'Nessa?' Ottoline lightly rapped on the door to my room. 'Are you
awake?'

    'Yes,' I called. I was taking advantage of one of the few luxuries ac-
corded married ladies in formal households and was enjoying a breakfast tray in bed. Unmarried ladies like Irene have their breakfast in the
dining room. 'Come in!' I said, realising that she was waiting for my
invitation.

    'Clive went walking early with Roger and Desmond,' she said. 'He
asked me to tell you that he would be back before luncheon.' Ottoline
began to drift around the room, like a great paper bird. Her dark red
hair floated around her angular, strong-featured face in airy curls. She is
not pretty, I decided, but it is impossible to look away from her. She
looked, in truth, worn out. Her hooded eyes were circled with delicate
lavender saucers, and her shoulders sagged with exhaustion. Her clothes

stood out in defiance of her weariness. She wore a cinched poppy-red morning dress and a striking amber choker at her throat.

'Ottoline,' I began, not knowing quite what I wanted to say. 'Are you having a good time?'

My question caught her off guard. She abruptly sat down on the bed, jostling the breakfast tray. I was startled. Sitting together on the bed changed the tenor of the conversation. The room became charged, intimate. 'Not really,' she said. 'I tend to worry so when I give a house party.'

'Worry?' I asked, although I well understand the rankling, trivial worries of a hostess.

'About silly things. The food, the weather, the guests, the conversation . . .' She trailed off.

'And then, of course, there is the intrigue,' I said.

'Yes,' she laughed, plucking at the counterpane. 'There is always the intrigue.'

And then it all spilled out. Her difficulties with Henry: his unpredictable temper and her easily wounded heart, their tentative reunions, his flirtation with other women and her devotion to him, his dissolving marriage and her unexpectedly successful arrangement with Philip, his art and her artistry, his talent and her fine sense of beauty, and then there is their jealousy. This is not her first affair.

'Nine?' I repeated, making sure I had heard correctly. 'Nine affairs?'

'While I have been with Philip?' she asked. 'Yes, Henry is the ninth.'

There was a profound dignity in the way she said it. This is not a sordid nor a loose woman, but a woman searching for a particular brand of love. Love mixed with art and ideas. Love sketched in paint and ink. Love to share unreservedly with another human. She was not ashamed of her quest, only disappointed in her failure. And why should she be ashamed? I thought, reproaching myself for my instinctive disapproval. She was not betraying Philip. They had come to an agreement. I was startled. I had not expected such a brutally large number. We all talked of setting aside the constricting confines of traditional marriage and society in favour of genuine connection. We all talked about the paramount importance of personal relationships—but so far my steps have been small and my life tightly seamed with convention. Ottoline has quietly lived her life outside such structures.

'And you?' she asked, prompting my confession.

'None,' I said quietly. 'Until recently, I have found so much happiness in my marriage. And now Clive has been . . . distracted,' I said, hedging past the truth.

Ottoline looked at me with disappointment. I had met her honesty with evasion.

'Clive has become lovers with a Mrs Raven Hill,' I said with clear candour. 'And he has fallen in love with my sister.' I felt flushed with truth—purged clean of the shadowy secrets. But there was also a loss of control, of discretion; a diminishment. But why should I have control? Why should I be discreet? These are not *my* misdemeanours. I was stating what was true. I do not owe the world a happy marriage, a perfect family. That is not my job.

'And Virginia?' Ottoline asked with a pragmatic clarity.

'Virginia loves that he is mine. I do not think she loves him for himself.'

'Does it really matter,' Ottoline asked, 'why she loves him? Why she wants him? She is your sister. He is your husband. It is wrong. Does it matter *why*?'

'No,' I answered her. 'I don't think it does.'

HOAXING AT SEA

10 February 1910—46 Gordon Square (late)

'You *what*?' I asked, trying to understand what he was saying.

'It was terrific, Nessa,' Adrian said, rocking on his heels. He was too excited to sit down. 'Just wait—Duncan and Ginia will tell you. They will be here in a moment. They walk so *slowly*.'

Adrian is six feet and five inches. To him, everyone walks slowly.

'Nessa!' Virginia called from the hall.

'She's in here!' Adrian shouted back.

'Nessa, you should have come!' Virginia said breathlessly, hurling herself onto the sofa. She looked manic, agitated. 'It was amazing. No, only the first bit was amazing. After a while I think I started believing it, and the whole thing began to feel quite ordinary.'

'Until Guy's moustache started melting off,' Duncan said.

'Guy who?' I asked, getting irritated.

'Guy Ridley. You remember him, Nessa,' Adrian said. 'He helped us the last time we did this in Cambridge, when we pretended to be in the court of the Sultan of Zanzibar.'

It was an absurd stunt, and I remember Thoby being cross with him for doing it. While at university, Adrian and his friends had dressed up and pretended to make a state visit to Cambridge, posing as the Sultan of Zanzibar and his entourage. Sometimes Adrian goes along with things he really shouldn't. Now, it seemed, they had done it again. 'Did you—'

'Don't worry, Nessa. We didn't do the sultan again,' Adrian said breezily.

'Who were you this time?' I asked, trying to summon my good humour.

'The Emperor of Abyssinia,' Adrian said proudly. 'Tudor sent a cable from the Foreign Office, announcing a visit from the Emperor of Abyssinia to the HMS *Dreadnought*. We were to inspect the ship.'

Dear God. The *Dreadnought* is not only the biggest and most famous ship in His Majesty's Navy, but it is also captained by our cousin, William Fisher.

'It was fine, Nessa,' Adrian said, sensing my disapproval. 'Anthony Buxton played the emperor beautifully—very regal. Duncan and Ginia were court officials, along with Guy Ridley and Horace Cole—it was all Cole's idea really. And I was the translator. I was the only one without makeup, but I did most of the speaking,' Adrian said, leaning back in his chair.

'And what were you speaking?' I asked. 'You don't speak—'

'Swahili, we think,' Adrian said. 'Mostly Anthony and Guy just said "*bunga, bunga*" at regular intervals.'

'And what did you answer to "*bunga, bunga*"?' I asked, horrified.

'I "*bunga, bunga-d*" back, of course,' Adrian answered. 'Nessa, is there any Dundee cake?'

'He recited Virgil,' Virginia said. 'Mixed up with a bit of Greek. And he looked perfectly dreadful in an ill-fitting suit.'

'Like a commercial traveller,' Duncan agreed. 'But he spoke wonderfully, and what is more, Anthony Buxton, playing the emperor, caught on to the Virgil and spoke back.'

'No cake at the moment, but we have buns.' I rang for Maud. 'You were speaking Latin?' I asked, trying to keep Adrian on the subject.

'With some Greek and some German and some nonsense thrown in,' Duncan said. 'I think he used a bit of Lear's "The Owl and the Pussycat" translated into Latin at one point.'

'The owl and the pussycat went to sea . . . *Bunga bunga*!' Adrian shouted.

'Oh my God,' I said, appalled.

'No, it really was fine, Nessa,' Adrian reassured me. 'I think we were quite convincing.'

He looked happier than I've seen him since Thoby. Adrian has always adored practical jokes. As long as it is someone else's plan. I don't think he would like to carry the weight of the thing on his own.

'And they were wonderful hosts,' Virginia added, her face alight with the excitement of the day. I worried. She swings so quickly from melancholy to manic this winter. 'They laid out a red carpet for us, and everyone was in full dress. They even offered to fire the guns, but Adrian said no, thank you. Which I thought was exactly right.'

Adrian sat taller. He rarely hears praise from Virginia. 'They would have to clean all the guns out afterwards and that would be unsporting of us to cause them more work,' Adrian said. 'And we did not have any lunch either, although the salmon looked wonderful. We refused on religious grounds.'

'Then it started to rain, and we worried the makeup would run, so we left,' Duncan said.

Later (midnight)

Clive came home late. I thought he had been with his whore, but he was with Roger. Roger wants Clive's help in organising this exhibition of modern French artists in the autumn. Clive was hugely annoyed about the *Dreadnought* Hoax, as we are now calling it, and was very glad I did not take part. 'Virginia ought to know better,' he said icily.

28 February 1910

Dear Woolf,

Delightful man! I have grown so accustomed to singing for you like a siren beached up on a friendless rock. Whatever will I do with my time, now that I no longer need to lure you home?

What news of us, you ask? Lots. Remarkably, Adrian, Duncan, Virginia, Anthony Buxton (do you remember him?—he was a few years below us), and a few others whose names I cannot remember dressed up as the Emperor of Abyssinia and his entourage and toured HMS Dreadnought. It has all ended badly, as the papers have got hold of it now and are having a field day at the Royal Navy's expense. They are calling it the Dreadnought Hoax. Adrian is very pleased with himself, which I find off-putting, and Duncan feels badly about the whole thing, now that the Royal Navy has been made to look foolish. He keeps telling me how kind they were to the emperor, how they rolled out a red carpet for the emperor, how they showed such deference to the emperor, and I have to keep reminding him that there was no emperor. It all feels like Hans Christian Andersen.

In the end, Adrian and Duncan went to see Mr Reginald McKenna, the First Lord of the Admiralty. Duncan had convinced Adrian that the officers who had been so sweet to them on the ship were now headed for a military tribunal and were going to be severely punished. Duncan and Adrian went to apologise and plead for them. McKenna was quite wonderful and told them he did not hold the officers responsible at all and thought the Navy had behaved beautifully. Duncan and Adrian agreed with him and complimented him on the Navy's hospitality. McKenna also said he would see them locked up if they did it again.

In other news, dear Leonard, I have come down with an attack of violent jealousy. It is noxious stuff, my friend. Steer clear. A man has come into our midst, an artist and art critic. He is ancient and was an Apostle while we were still in short trousers. See how unkind I am? He is a Mr Roger Fry. Do you know him? I ought to check before I begin my rant. He is, as far as Ottoline and Vanessa are concerned, captivating. My sister Dorothy and her husband, Simon Bussy, are wild about him too. He is animated and learned and respected and accomplished, and I am irritated by his perfection. Even Virginia likes him, and she never likes anyone. Do not worry on that score, he is forever married to a truly unhappy woman who is always detained in some mental institution or other.

Ottoline has had him down to Peppard Cottage twice this month, and now he has begun attending the Friday Club meetings. He is frustratingly charming, and I feel slothful, unproductive, consumptive, and uninteresting around him. I would like him to return from whence he came and leave my darling women alone. I prefer them to be dazzled by my wit and my charm, not some interloper's party tricks. Vanessa, usually so intimidated by critics, glows with opinions around him. But then she has changed altogether lately. Clive, after he showed himself to be a pig by fornicating with his Wiltshire hausfrau, has grown less substantial and Vanessa more so. Her voice carries conviction, and the room looks to her for assurance. With humour and the lightest touch, she holds the floor without trying. It impresses Clive and annoys Virginia, whose plan to unravel her sister's marriage has misfired badly. Vanessa is more splendid for her forbearance.

You would settle Virginia wonderfully. And she would inspire
you with her sharp, quirky mind. How clever I am to see what a
happy couple you would make.

Yours,
Lytton

PS: It seems Vanessa is enceinte encore. I only wish it were the re-
sult of a frothy love affair and not a product of marital duty. She
deserves more fun than she gets.

1 March 1910—46 Gordon Square (early—sky pale pink)

I do not think I am a modern woman. At least, I am not modern enough
for this.

Last night Clive and Virginia stayed up until two in the morning in
our drawing room. Maud had lit the fire, but they sat on the far sofa.
Ostensibly, they were looking over Virginia's novel. In fact, Clive was
just looking at Virginia. The air around them snapped and took like a
brushfire. Virginia sat very straight but was careful not to meet my eyes.
She knew that if she did, I would look away. She is never happier than
when she knows I am watching.

I ought to have gone to bed. I should have known that Virginia would
not go home as long as I stayed up. Being alone with them, I felt pulpy
and skinned. I had thought I was coming to accept this awful new incarnation of my marriage, but I am not. It was all made fresh because I was
marooned in our unhappy trio. Lytton was meant to come last night,
but at the last minute he went to the ballet with Saxon and Desmond.
Lytton's steady, unspoken disapproval of the shameless pair helps. He
makes me feel bolstered and reasonable.

At three, unable to wait them out, I came up to bed. Five minutes
later, I could hear Clive outside hailing Virginia a cab. Why can't I learn
to walk away from them and show nothing? Galling that tomorrow
Clive will come down for breakfast and be perfectly charming as if
tonight were all in my imagination.

9 March 1910—46 Gordon Square (pouring)

Virginia found out. Adrian mentioned it to her without thinking. As soon as he realised, he came rushing over here in the rain.

'I thought she knew,' Adrian said, removing his soaked shoes. 'Lytton said *everyone* knew.'

'Lytton told you?' I asked, surprised. Lytton's opinion of Clive has steeply diminished, but I did not think he would discuss it with Adrian. We all still treat Adrian like our little brother who must be shielded from any unpleasantness that rears up. 'Never mind,' I said, sitting next to him on the velvet sofa. 'She was bound to find out. Clive and Mrs Raven Hill are not being discreet.'

I handed him a pair of Thoby's socks.

'Nessa,' Adrian said, digging his bare feet into the thick carpet, 'she is *furious*.'

Later

Furious. Because her almost lover, my husband, has taken up with his former lover. And why should she be furious? It is not as if he has stopped pursuing her.

But if I am worried about Mrs Raven Hill, Virginia will have lost some of her purchase in our marriage. Now she will work to reel Clive back to her. She is selfish but predictable.

At least she did not have a mad scene, I keep telling myself. Anything is better than that.

15 March 1910—46 Gordon Square (late morning)

Virginia joined us for breakfast, although she refused to eat anything. We were all off to Duncan's studio to see his *Dancers* before he shows it to Roger next week. It was meant to be just Clive and I, but yesterday Virginia asked to come too.

'And Mrs Raven Hill?' Virginia said with clear and sturdy diction.

'Will she be joining us to see the painting?'

Clive looked up from his paper, startled. I said nothing, unsurprised at Virginia's tactic and curious to hear his response.

He quickly recouped his composure. 'No, I don't think she is coming to town today,' he answered.

I looked at Virginia to gauge her reaction, but she was not looking at Clive but at me.

Later

Duncan's paintings. Besides his beautiful but unexceptional Matisse-inspired *Dancers,* we saw his *Bathers* and his *Crime and Punishment.* *Bathers* gives the viewer a sense of wild, irrepressible joy. *Crime and Punishment* shows a woman whose heart is broken. She sits with her face in her hands and has not bothered to take off her hat.

Clive saw it, and even though Virginia was watching, he wrapped his arm around my waist. Painting unites us.

Thursday 17 March 1910—46 Gordon Square (sunny and warm)

What a fiasco. We never found the house. Admittedly, it was raining and I was grumpy. Clive and I had had a ferocious row on the train. It was not a good day.

What happened:

'That can't be it.' We stepped under a broad chestnut tree, and Clive shook out the umbrella. 'It is too big and bald and new. The man is an expert in Italian painters. He would not build *that.*'

'It must be it,' I said, irritated that Clive refused to go and knock on the door and ask if this was Durbins, Roger Fry's house. We had been wandering the country roads outside Guildford for over an hour. I was annoyed that when Roger suggested he collect us from the station, Clive had refused.

'Why didn't you just agree when he offered to meet us off the train?' I asked again.

'I did not want to trouble him,' Clive said. 'I did not want to seem as if I needed . . .'

'Directions?' I interrupted.

'Assistance,' Clive said coldly.

This was no place for an argument, but it was inevitable at this point. 'Clive, that is absurd,' I said. 'His house has no number. It is newly built, and no one in town has heard of it. We have no map, and it is raining. *Of course* we need assistance.'

Clive ignored me. 'Let's go back to the station, and we can write Roger a note and explain. I am too wet to sit down to luncheon anyway.'

I looked at him. He was the one holding the umbrella, and he was drier than I was.

And—We heard the news when we got into Victoria. The king has collapsed in Biarritz! At a dinner party last month, Margot Asquith said that he smokes at least twenty cigarettes and fifteen cigars a day and that he has been coughing all winter. How awful.

Roger Fry
Durbins
Guildford

18 March 1910

My dear Mr and Mrs Bell,

Please forgive me! I ought to have foreseen your difficulty. Durbins is an easy house to find, once you know what to look for. I am absolutely sure you passed the house several times, looked at it, and dismissed it as impossibly ugly. 'How can that be the house?' you said. Do not worry. Neither my house nor I are the least offended. We shall win you in the end.

I would be delighted if you both could come for lunch this Sunday. I promise to meet you at the station, convey you easily to

my house, give you a marvellous lunch and a superb walk. Please
allow me to make up for yesterday!

Sincerely yours,
Roger Fry

Sunday 20 March 1910—Train from Guildford to Victoria

What is it about a train journey that makes one feel skimmed with city grit? Clive has drunk four cups of coffee and talked about Roger without stopping.

'What a brilliant multifaceted mind he has. It is not just the breadth of his knowledge—which would be impressive enough—but it is how he pieces things together. I am flattered he asked me to help him with the exhibition. It is going to change *everything*, you know.'

Roger has invited Clive to accompany him to France to help him gather paintings for his autumn exhibition at the beautiful Grafton Galleries. They are calling it 'Manet and the Post-Impressionists'. I am not sure exactly what Post-Impressionism is but did not want to say so at luncheon.

I agree that Roger has a wonderful, active, interested mind and a unique way of making conversations feel whole and important, but my experience of the day was different from Clive's. After lunch we went walking. I was reluctant to go, as my ankles were starting to swell. But Roger not realising I was pregnant strode ahead, and Clive did not stop to think that I might prefer resting to walking. The men marched ahead, and Mrs Fry—Helen—and I lagged behind. She had been silent throughout the meal, her hands folded in her lap, and her food growing cold. Until the coffee, when she jerked in her chair, her head spinning swiftly towards the door.

'They are not here, dearest,' Roger said, anticipating her question. 'They are with my sister.'

Helen looked confused, and Roger repeated the sentence. 'They are not here, dearest, they are with *Joan*. She has taken them to *Bristol*.' To us he said, 'She thinks she hears our children outside.'

Helen did not turn back to the table.

'We wanted to give you some time to settle back in. Remember? You have been away, and now you are home.' This was clearly a sequence of sentences he repeated several times a day. How patient he is, I thought, watching him wait for her face to register understanding.

The conversation moved on, and Helen faded into her own thoughts once again. When we spoke of Julian, I looked over at her nervously. I did not want to discuss my happy, healthy son, from whom I could not bear to be separated for long, in her hearing. It felt cruel.

After lunch, we walked down the grassy hill behind the extraordinary house. Midway down the slope, she suggested we go up to her sitting room instead. Exhausted already, I accepted. Along the upstairs gallery, she pointed out several small oils she had painted.

'It was a lovely thing,' she said, stopping in front of a small portrait of Roger. 'To be able to do that.'

'Yes,' I said. I looked closer at the painting. It was an expressive, intimate, beautifully wrought portrait of her husband. His head was bent over a book, and the painting captured Roger's absorption and joy. 'It is stunning,' I said truthfully.

'Thank you,' Mrs Fry said. 'I loved being an artist.'

It was a sad comment, spoken as though she no longer had the skill or artistry to paint. But said without self-pity.

She led me into a small, pretty room. 'How soon?' she asked.

'Soon?' I repeated.

'You are expecting a baby, aren't you?' she said, sitting on a curved velvet sofa. 'Men never notice these things. Roger has no idea or he would never have insisted on a walk.' She pulled a low embroidered footstool over. 'Please put your feet up. When I was pregnant with Julian, I could not go more than an hour without resting my feet. They would start to look like huge root vegetables if I didn't.'

'Your son is Julian?' I asked. Roger had never mentioned his son's name.

'Yes, my son is also Julian. And my daughter is Pamela.'

I put my arms around her. She had been there at the table, this sad, kind, talented woman. She had heard everything, but had been unable to speak to us.

Later—46 Gordon Square

We got home to find Adrian in the drawing room. He came to tell us that he had called Dr Savage. He says the voices have been at Virginia today, and she has been clawing at the skin on her neck. Clive and I went over right away.

Very late (four a.m.)

Dr Savage administered a sedative. She did not resist. She must sense that she is nearing a cliff. The doctor says she will be all right if she can stay calm and sleep.

3 April 1910—46 Gordon Square

She has found her way back to herself. In the last week she has slept and eaten more than usual. Not an easy thing for Virginia, and I am proud of her.

Tuesday 5 April 1910—46 Gordon Square (feels like spring)

'They would be wonderful together. I'm right, Nessa, you'll see,' Lytton said, tipping his face to the sun.

I was pleased he was outside. Lytton has been feeling unwell since Christmas. We were sitting on a bench in Gordon Square, and Lytton was explaining why Mr Woolf would be a perfect husband for Virginia. I am not sure. But then I don't really remember him. His name conjures the memory of an angular, serious, hawkish boy with floppy brown hair whom Thoby loved dearly. But *someone* has to marry Virginia. She is twenty-eight and can't go on living with Adrian much longer. I am sure it is at the root of her unrest this spring.

'And how does Mr Woolf feel about this?' I asked him.

'Oh, he is quite sure she is the only woman for him,' Lytton said.

'How is he sure?' I asked. 'He's only met her a few times, and that was years ago.'

'Yes, but he trusts me. And I am sure. You will be too. I know it.'

I do not trust his complacent logic, but there was no time to discuss it further. Ottoline has invited Lytton to Bedford Square for every Tuesday evening in April. Lytton has arrived.

And—Began a large painting of the seaside today. I think it is Studland Beach. Here is what I know: it is by the water; the figures will be a mixture of children and adults; the shoreline is stark; faces will be vague.

Later

We have argued. Clive came in to talk to me while I had my bath, and I wish now that he hadn't. He asked me about my day, Julian, my painting, and the new nanny we are planning to hire, but he became short-tempered when I told him that I spent the day with Lytton. He is increasingly hostile towards Lytton lately. I am sure it stems from Lytton and Virginia's bungled engagement.

KING EDWARD VII

12 April 1910—46 Gordon Square

I had returned from an afternoon of shopping—Whiteleys for more baby clothes, Hatchards for novels, and Fortnum's for cake and to order a baby cup, as well as a quick stop into the Royal Academy to see the new Titian exhibition—when Duncan turned up for tea. He had been in his studio and had flakes of green paint on his nails, but beyond that he looked as unruffled as ever. I look wild after a day in the studio; paint in my hair and on my nose, and stains on my dress even though I wear a smock.

We opened the new tin of cake, and Maud brought the tea. Duncan likes his tea very sweet. Our talk was surprising. He is about to go up and visit his parents in Scotland. From what I understand, they have a very happy if unconventional relationship. Each engages in prolonged but discreet love affairs but never deserts the marriage. It is equitable and functional. Duncan's voice held no judgement when he told me. I was flattered by the confidence. He rarely discusses his family. Nor does he ever discuss his own messy, heartbreaking romances. Duncan believes that love is a private business. The conversation left me wondering if I am the only woman in England who has not strayed from her marriage.

And—Now Desmond is also going to Paris in the summer to pull together the paintings for Roger's exhibition. It is turning into a holiday, and I wish I could go.

Friday 22 April 1910—46 Gordon Square (muggy)

'Nessa!' Virginia called from the downstairs study as I came through the door at Fitzroy Square. 'Nessa! Mr Fry has to go to Poland today!'

'What?' I looked at Virginia, surprised. She was not usually so exuberant.

'On Tuesday,' Roger said calmly.

'Poland?' I took a seat by the window. 'Why Poland?'

'I am buying a picture for the industrialist Mr Henry Clay Frick in New York. He has an extensive collection, and he wants this painting badly.' Mr Fry helped himself to another sandwich and sat forward in his chair. His mobile face animated with delight. 'Rembrandt's *The Polish Rider*—unique, beautiful. You would love the layered brushwork, Nessa,' he said, leaning farther forward. 'Stunning texture.'

Roger's plate was balanced precariously on his knees. Was it rude to reach out and steady it?

'Wasn't there a question of authorship?' I asked, wishing I could remember the circumstances.

'Yes!' Roger clapped his hands. 'Yes, wonderful! How clever of you to know the work! There *was* a question, but it has been resolved. It is thought now to be from Rembrandt's latest period, around 1654. A marvellous picture.'

'The scale is unusual, is it not?' I asked, flushed with happiness that I had said something clever.

'Yes, the scale is—'

'Yes, but tell her whom you are buying *from*,' Virginia interrupted, steering the conversation away from the technical aspects of painting.

'Ah yes. It is Count Adam Amor Tarnowski von Tarnów and his wife. They have a wonderful family collection.' To my relief, Roger set the plate on the low table.

'A Polish count married to a Polish princess,' Virginia said. She does not like to admit to it, but she is captivated by the aristocracy. Even Ottoline and her eccentric aristocratic relations fascinate her.

'I was telling your sister, the count's wife is the Princess Marie Światopełk-Czetwertyńska,' Roger said with difficulty. 'I shall have to practise her name over the next few days. Luckily, the count prefers to be called Adam.'

'How dull,' Virginia said. 'Names are so important.'

29 April 1910—46 Gordon Square (seven p.m.)

Back from Fitzroy Square. The conversation inevitably turned to names (baby boy names—I have thought of none). Virginia, keen to move the conversation away from babies, asked us to help her with character names for her novel. Today she has fixed upon the name 'Rachel Vinrace' for her heroine.

'It is not a sweet name,' I said.

'I do not think it is meant to be,' Roger said, looking at Virginia.

7 May 1910—46 Gordon Square (early)

The king is dead! Clive just came in to tell me.

The Prince of Wales told the king that his horse, The Witch of the Air, had won at Kempton Park. And the king responded, 'I am very glad.' His last words. He died late last night.

Friday 20 May 1910—46 Gordon Square (day of the Royal Funeral)

In the end, we went. *Everyone* went. We stood near Hyde Park Corner and watched the funeral procession. All his children were there, and every crowned head in Europe. They look alike—but then they all had the same grandmother, so I suppose they *would* look alike. The older generation are moustachioed and dignified (Kaiser Wilhelm and Tsar Nicholas of Russia both have magnificent moustaches), and the younger set, like the Archduke Franz Ferdinand and the Duke of Aosta, are dapper and bright. The children (all shouldering hefty names like Prince Heinrich something something of Prussia) marched along without complaining.

The whole day made me feel sentimental about the old king. We dined at Ottoline's later, and everyone was telling royal anecdotes. There were all the predictable old threads of gossip—Lillie Langtry and Alice Keppel—but there were other, less salacious stories I had never heard. Ottoline (who is distantly related to the royal family—I suppose you can see it with that extraordinary chin of hers) says that Bertie was a genuinely affectionate father, holding his children when they were first born and taking time to play with them as they grew up. Apparently he was devastated when his youngest son, John, died after only one day. He insisted on placing him in the tiny casket himself and by all accounts was openly weeping at the funeral. That made me like him very much.

67 BELSIZE PARK GARDENS

HAMPSTEAD, N.W.

TEL.: HAMPSTEAD 1090

23 May 1910

Dear Woolf,

Cambridge is wrapped in black. The colleges all sport huge mourning wreaths over the doors. The Edwardian era was brief but poignant. That sentence made me feel one hundred years old. I do not like change at all, but it feels as though it is afoot. My apologies, terrible form to complain while the nation mourns, but what to do? My health has faded away like spring fog. Virginia is headed straight for Bedlam, Vanessa is pregnant, Clive is an amoral pig, Duncan is being evasive, Maynard is a revoltingly successful new don, Saxon has gone silent, Desmond is procreating, my sister

Dorothy is annoyed with me, Henry Lamb is entangled with Ottoline, and I find all of England dissatisfying today. Complaining is the only answer. Could you possibly come home sooner?

With love,
Lytton

PS: *Virginia will surely be fully recovered by the time you return.*

30 May 1910—46 Gordon Square (hot and fuggy—all the windows thrown open)

'*Post*-Impressionist?' I asked Roger, who was sitting in Lytton's basket chair by the tall window.

'Yes!' he said, looking at me over his sketchbook. We were alone in the drawing room. Clive had gone out on one of his unexplained errands and would collect Virginia, who was joining us for supper, on his way back. Virginia has been dining with us most evenings. It makes more sense while her mood is so precarious and her madness looms. Lytton was expected soon and would also stay for supper, as would Desmond, who would be late as always. Julian was napping, and Roger was taking advantage of this small pocket of stillness to do some studies for a portrait of me. When I suggested he wait until after Clarissa's birth, he flatly refused and said, 'But you are so perfectly *you* right now. Why wait?' I could not argue with such tangled, kind logic.

'But what does it mean, *Post*-Impressionist?' I asked. 'Obviously it is the school of thinking that comes after the Impressionists, but what does that mean? What do they believe?' I sat forward, ruining Roger's composition. I have grown unafraid of looking silly in front of this man. I do not mind the stamp of ignorance, as I know he could never feel contempt. It is not within his spectrum of emotions. It is a relief to show myself to be brazenly uneducated with Roger. He never makes me feel stupid. Instead, he is consistently delighted in my questions and answers them all with somersaulting excitement rather than condescension. Strangely, I have grown self-conscious in front of Clive and am afraid of looking foolish when he is watching. It is not that Clive would criticise me, but I know he compares me to Virginia. Her clear mind against my illogical sentiment. Just as Father used to do. Sad, when Clive used to make me feel so free.

'Yes, that is just what it is,' Roger said, his eyes crinkling as he spoke. 'It is the work of the Fauves but so much more than that. These artists— Manet, Cézanne, Gauguin, Derain, Matisse, Van Gogh, Seurat, Picasso —they do not care for *replication*. If distorting a subject's features will reveal the artist's sensibility, so be it. They do not need to prove that they can accurately reflect what a subject *looks* like. Not for a still life, nor a landscape, nor a portrait. Instead they show us what a subject *feels* like to them. It is so personal. So courageous. It is remarkable.'

'Manet does not care for replication?' I asked. I had seen his wonderful *Olympia* and *Gare Saint-Lazare* again the last time Clive and I were in Paris.

'Manet is the starting point,' Roger said. 'The departure from Impressionism to all that has come later. I chose Manet because he was one of the very first to reject Impressionism. It was his own school of thinking, and he turned away from it. And so we are calling the exhibition "Manet and the Post-Impressionist."'

'It was the only name we could think of,' Desmond said lightly as he walked into the room. He was early—surprising. 'Roger wanted to call it Expressionism, but that sounded . . . what did I say it sounded, Roger?'

'You said it sounded unimportant,' Roger said.

'*You* could think of?' I was confused. I turned to Desmond. 'Are you in on this as well? I thought you were just going along to Paris to round up paintings.'

'Roger asked me to be the secretary for the exhibition. He seems to think I have a head for business. He is mistaken, of course.'

'I am not mistaken,' Roger said cheerfully. 'You managed to get the Grafton Galleries a twenty per cent commission on sales when previously they have only ever managed eleven. Remarkable. Nessa!' he said, refocusing on his sketch, 'stay just there. Lean back a bit. Yes! That's wonderful!'

But I could not stay there. It was uncomfortable, and I had to twist to speak to Desmond. Roger put down his sketchbook and selected a cake from the tray of pastries.

'Twenty per cent? Desmond, how did you manage twenty per cent?' I asked.

'Roger sent me into the meetings with the dealers, and I was totally unprepared. When they asked how much the gallery wanted in commission, I hadn't the faintest idea what was right. I asked for twenty, and they agreed. But the whole thing will fail, and I doubt any of the paintings will sell, so it hardly matters. But for the moment, I feel unexpectedly shrewd.'

I looked over at Roger, but he seemed perfectly comfortable hearing his exhibition described as a failure. He was enjoying his cake and getting crumbs all over his jacket. Roger always manages to look dishevelled. Clive says he can make the best clothes look awful, but I don't agree. I like his broken-in, rumpled look.

'You *really* don't think it will be a success?' I ventured.

'Oh no,' Roger answered, his good humour unaffected. 'The English public will *hate* it. The English artists will hate it, and I am sure it will be a commercial disaster. But it is the beginning of something. Something *important*. And that is what matters.'

And—I decided this morning that my seaside bathers will wear hats. The sand has become very clean. Flat. Uniform. The water is in the upper-right corner.

31 May 1910—46 Gordon Square

We've had *another* argument about Lytton. Clive came home and found Lytton, Virginia, and me in the garden drinking lemonade. I was pleased that Virginia was sounding more like herself. She has been so shaky and off-pitch in the last few months. Clive stood in the doorway but refused to come outside. When everyone left, I confronted him, but all he did was shout at me about 'that damned effeminate bugger'. His petty jealousy over Virginia's friendship with Lytton is absurd.

TWICKENHAM

· ⚜ ·

1 June 1910—46 Gordon Square (sunny)

Virginia broke a plate this morning. We were planning to go to the gallery space for the Friday Club exhibition (it is next week, and *none* of the paintings are ready to be hung), and she stopped in to Gordon Square to collect me. Sophie and Maud, worrying that Miss Ginia was looking too thin, insisted she eat some breakfast.

Apparently she was standing at the sideboard, looking out the window, when the plate dropped from her hand. It smashed at her feet, but she did not seem to notice. Maud called for me to come down and then swept up the hunks of china, but Virginia did not move. I found Virginia talking to herself in the dining room.

'Virginia?'

Nothing.

'Virginia?' I said again, putting my hand lightly on her arm.

'Is someone in the garden, Nessa?' she asked, without lifting her eyes from the window.

'No one is out there,' I said, gently tugging her arm, trying to draw her towards Thoby's study. We still call it that. I knew Virginia would feel safe surrounded by Thoby's things.

'No!' Virginia said sharply.

I went to get Clive.

Six p.m.

Clive came, and together we got Virginia upstairs to her old room. I tucked her into one of my nightgowns and settled her into bed. We debated sending for the doctor. By now Virginia was sitting up chatting with Adrian, who had come straight over when he received my note. She seemed better. In the dining room I had felt her resting on a knife's edge. Now she seemed easier in herself.

Virginia has been veering towards a breakdown all this spring. The danger lives in the small details: the way she waits a fraction too late before she responds to a question; the way she repeats herself without knowing it; the way her voice slides uphill when she speaks; the way she eats less and walks more; the way her face is mapped in blueish circles and sharp bones; the way she locks her hands together in her lap while on the omnibus; the way she is not writing.

It is not all the time, not every day, but it is enough to worry. The worry begins to grind and churn, and I watch her, vigilant, waiting for the moment when the boat capsizes in the dark.

Ten p.m.

Duncan, Saxon, and Adrian just left. We all sat up with Virginia. Maud brought cocoa and sandwiches and we had a sickroom picnic. Adrian and Duncan left first, and finally Clive took Saxon downstairs to let Virginia rest. I straightened the bedclothes around her and put the books she had requested from Thoby's study on the nightstand.

'Well,' she said, sitting back on the pillows, 'what do you think of the grand passion?'

'What?' I asked, startled. There are so many grand passions passing through the house this spring. 'Which one?'

'Duncan and Adrian! Haven't you noticed Adrian keeps talking about buggers?' Virginia said, rolling out the vowels in the word.

'Duncan and Adrian? Are they . . . oh god.' I had not noticed. 'Does

Lytton know?' Lytton is half infatuated with George Mallory and half with Henry Lamb, but still mostly in love with Duncan.

'I do not think *anyone* knows yet. I only know because I caught Duncan creeping down the stairs at five in the morning yesterday,' Virginia said, pulling the covers up around her. 'Hasn't Adrian spoken to you about inverts yet? He has been on about buggers all month.'

'No,' I said, feeling unobservant. 'I do not think he has mentioned it more than normal. Does Clive know?' I asked.

'Oh yes,' Virginia said. 'Of course I told him right away.'

3 June 1910—46 Gordon Square

Now Adrian has mentioned inverts. Guessing that I knew, he brought it up after supper last night.

'It really is wonderful, Nessa,' Adrian said to Clive and me, sounding too loud for the room. 'So much less complicated than an affair with a woman.'

I looked at him. Had he ever *had* an affair with a woman?

'Yes, I am sure it is.' I handed him his cocoa. 'And Duncan lives in the same square. That must be convenient.'

Clive rolled his eyes at me. I could hear how banal I sounded. Clive had so far remained noncommittal on the subject.

'So you don't object, Nessa?' Adrian said, sounding like himself.

'Of course not, dearest. I just want you to be happy.'

'I *am* happy,' Adrian said, relieved. He turned to Clive. 'Clive, I am sure you know, Virginia minds dreadfully.'

And—I went to see Dr Savage this afternoon to talk about Virginia. Voices, anger, visions, sleeplessness. These are the things we must look for. I do not know why I asked him. I know that list.

Later (one a.m.)

'What did he mean?' I asked Clive when we got home tonight.

We had been at a supper party at Ottoline's in Bedford Square.

Adrian and Duncan had sat close together and did not speak to anyone but each other all night. Adrian's hand rested on Duncan's knee. Lytton, sitting on the other side of the room, had noticed and left early. I watched him out the window, his lean figure stalking through the pale, gravelled square. I considered going after him, but that would only draw attention to his disappointment.

'What did who mean?' Clive asked, pouring himself a drink.

'Adrian. Last night. When he said that Virginia minded.'

'Oh, you know Virginia,' Clive said without irony. 'She does not like to be left out.'

'So is she going to seduce Duncan too?' I asked.

'I shouldn't think she would get very far,' Clive said, neatly evading the jab. 'You know Duncan does not care for women.'

I came upstairs. It is left to *Duncan* to curb Virginia. Virginia is not expected to control herself.

Wednesday 8 June 1910—The Moat House, Blean, near Canterbury

We have brought Virginia away. As well as not sleeping, she has been having her headaches again, a sure sign of trouble coming. Dr Savage suggested getting out of London to see if the country air might restore her mental balance. Clive took this cottage, and we arrived here last night. We are paid up through next Wednesday, but if Virginia does not improve, we may stay on. Clive and Virginia have gone for a walk. At eight months, I do not feel like a walk. Clive tells me I am my most beautiful when pregnant, but when I look, his eyes always rest on Virginia.

Later

A long discussion with Clive tonight. After Virginia finally got to sleep, we sat up by the fire, and I told him the rest of what Dr Savage had said. I could not tell him before, as we have not had a moment out of Virginia's company.

'And he thinks it may be her *teeth*?' Clive asked.

'He says there is some imbalance that comes from infected teeth,' I said. 'As Virginia has been running a slight fever this spring and has not been sleeping well, Dr Savage thinks it might get better if he removes some of her teeth.' I paused, unsure how to phrase my concerns. 'The theory is new, very new,' I said.

'Which teeth?' Clive said, evidently considering the aesthetics of the thing.

'What does it matter which teeth?' I said, irritated. 'Anyway, these are just things to try if the rest cure does not work.'

12 June 1910—The Moat House, Blean, near Canterbury

Not improving. She had one of her headaches this morning and hasn't eaten anything all day. I could hear her talking to herself, and twice she bolted downstairs to me.

'Virginia?'

'We have to go back to London, Nessa!' Virginia said, her words crumpling together like a carriage wreck. 'There is someone in my room. We must go at once!'

'There is no one in your room, dearest, but I will ask Clive to go and check as soon as he returns,' I said in my most soothing voice. Frankly, I prefer her down here with me. Her windows have no locks.

She insisted on returning to her room.

'Go away, Nessa!' she yelled when I followed her.

I took off my shoes, softly crept up to the landing of the stairs, and settled onto the floor. Three paces from her door. I hoped it was close enough to make it in time.

Later

She is shrieking in her room. Clive is fetching the doctor from the village.

Still later (six p.m.—Virginia with the doctor)

Clive pounced on the poor man as he came down the stairs. 'Well?' Clive said roughly.

'Not good, I am afraid,' the country doctor said, pulling on his coat.

'Not good how?' Clive persisted.

The doctor turned to me. 'Mrs Bell, your sister is in the midst of an hysterical episode. While I am sure this particular crisis will pass in a day or so, she seems to be on the verge of a significant nervous collapse.'

'And what will that look like? A nervous collapse?' Clive interrupted rudely.

I knew he was sick with worry, but he was not helping matters. I was surprised. He is usually so calm in the sickroom. But then the last time we dealt with illness, we lost Thoby. That must be it. He is terrified of losing Virginia.

'Delusions, headaches, voices, inability to eat or sleep, hostility, numbness, detachment, irrational behaviour, anger, and possibly an attempt at suicide,' the doctor finished quietly.

Yes, I thought, mentally checking the list against Virginia's past. Yes, that is right.

Monday 13 June 1910—The Moat House, Blean, near Canterbury

'No, Clive, she cannot come to us.' I took a deep breath. 'It is *impossible*,' I repeated.

'She is your sister, Nessa, and she is unwell.' Clive ran his hand through his fluffy red hair. It was riding high, puffed up by the wind.

'Yes, and so she must be looked after by her *doctors* and not by her extremely pregnant sister!'

'You will not have to take care of her alone!' Clive shouted. '*I will be there to help!*'

I looked out the window to see if Virginia was returning from her walk. It would do her no good to hear this row. I had been opposed to allowing her to walk alone, but Clive had insisted. I was anxious for her to return.

'Clive, I know you mean well,' I said generously, 'but you must see that she needs a proper facility. We are not equipped to care for her, and we will be even less equipped once the baby comes.'

'But she went to Violet the last time this happened,' Clive said, his voice rising. 'And *she* could handle her!'

'But I could *not* manage her! That is why she went to Violet! And even then it was only after she was released from the nursing home.'

Clive sat down abruptly. 'It just seems cruel, Nessa.'

'I know it does, but it isn't.'

'I want to help her to . . .' Clive's sentence trailed off, and his face resumed its cagey expression.

'You want to save her. I know you do. You love her, you want to be near her, and you want to rescue her. I do understand some things, Clive.'

Clive rose and wrapped me in his arms. 'What an extraordinary woman you are,' he said into my hair.

I must go to London next week to see my doctor. Clive has suggested that he and Virginia remain here.

Sunday 19 June 1910—46 Gordon Square (two p.m.)

In the end it was the only thing to do. Clive swears that he is up to the task of handling Virginia. I doubt that very much, but they were both adamant that I keep my appointment. My true reason for going was to be here to meet Elsie when she brings Julian from Seend this afternoon. I have hated to leave my beautiful boy with Clive's family, but between Virginia's illness and my pregnancy, I had no choice.

Clive and Virginia are alone in the Moat House. The thought intrudes, unwelcome, unbidden. They will sleep there alone tonight. All the way home, I tried to muster fury, anxiety, jealousy, indignation—but I could not. I do not think that their relationship has turned sexual. I am sure Clive is still hoping it will. Thoby once told me that Clive has a hunter's patience. Her illness will only draw him in further. Clive is drawn to fragile things.

But I know Virginia will not allow him near her now. She will invite him to love her but not to touch her. She becomes further removed from her body when she is ill. She cannot manage breakfast right now, much less a lover. Is that naïve? Is that complacent? Am I now accustomed to my husband's faithlessness? Perhaps. But not with Virginia. I will *never* accept his affair with Virginia.

And—Julian is home and delighted to find me here alone without Daddy or Aunt Ginia. We spent the afternoon playing with his toy trains.

46 GORDON SQUARE

BLOOMSBURY

TELEPHONE: 1608 MUSEUM

21 June 1910

My dear Snow,

I am sorry to have neglected you. It is dreadful of me to cancel at the last minute, but I will not be able to give you lunch on Monday. Everything has unspooled here. Virginia is not at all well. It is the old illness, and it looks set to stay awhile. I am meeting her doctor this week and will know more then, but I can already guess the outcome.

I could say that I will make it all up to you and come up to you, but I know I would be lying. I am getting to the uncomfortable stage in this lengthy process. Would you be an angel and come down for the birth? Clive, I have learned, is not a natural with newborns. He is much more comfortable when the child is able to bring something to the conversation. He is marvellous with Julian

now, but I know he will be inept when Clarissa comes. Have I told
you her name? Clarissa. Clarissa Julia Bell. Isn't that wonderful?
She should arrive on 25 July or thereabouts. Do say you will come?

> *Yours apologetically,*
> *Vanessa*

Thursday 23 June 1910—46 Gordon Square

I have just seen Dr Savage, and he prescribed the rest cure for Virginia—
not a strict rest cure but a milder, modified version. He says the stopgap
measure of taking her out of London will not cure the root of the problem and only put off the inevitable collapse. I did tell him that she has
many good days, but he thinks the headaches have come too frequently
this spring to be ignored. They herald madness.

There is a good private nursing home in Twickenham, run by a cultured and sympathetic woman called Miss Jean Thomas. Good. Virginia
does badly with officious matrons. Now, how to tell Virginia and Clive?

And—I flatly told Dr Savage to leave Virginia's teeth alone.

Later (four p.m.)

In the end, I wrote to Virginia. I did not wait to ambush her when she
stepped off the train. It was simpler and more honest. I dread to think
how she is taking it. Clive will have to manage her somehow. I sweep the
thought cleanly from my head.

I am going to the Friday Club exhibition tonight with Adrian and
Duncan. The last few times I have spent the evening with them as a
couple, something has felt out of joint. Their love affair makes me uncomfortable. It is not the ostentatiously furtive affection, nor the nature
of the thing that I mind—how could I? I am besieged by buggers. It is
the falseness. Adrian seems to be playing a part. His affection for
Duncan does not feel spontaneous and natural. It feels staged and
rehearsed, as if he is cast in the role of the young man in love and is

proud of remembering all his lines. I hope that I am wrong. I wish such true happiness for Adrian.

And—Duncan is exhibiting his wonderful *Lemon Gatherers* tonight, and so Lytton has fled to Grantchester with Rupert Brooke. The two have become friends at last—not lovers, but friends.

One a.m.

Saxon, Adrian, and Duncan just left. We came back here for drinks and sandwiches after the show. I wish I had not drunk so much coffee. It always gives me indigestion when I am this pregnant. I bought *Lemon Gatherers*. I feel bold. I had a moment of calm, clean decision. Clive will not be pleased. Is that why I bought it? The painting will be delivered when the exhibition comes down. Truthfully, I am shocked that I bought it. But it felt right. This painting is meant to live here. I also liked the work by Mark Gertler, the eighteen-year-old prodigy. Ottoline believes he will become an important painter. I shiver with envy when I hear painters spoken about in these terms. It is not the fame or the money but the position—the respect, the clearly marked seriousness. Duncan is also on his way to importance. He is regularly written up in the art journals, and his paintings always sell. I think it was clever of me to buy his work now.

Sunday 26 June 1910—46 Gordon Square

They are home. They came straight here from the train, and the three of us discussed the nursing home and Dr Savage's advice. Virginia submitted to the idea with little resistance. Clive looked scattered and shocked.

I painted while Clive took Virginia home. Still working on my seaside canvas. The little girl is now wearing a straw hat with a wide ribbon. I shall buy one like it for Clarissa.

Seven p.m.

Clive is back from dropping Virginia at Fitzroy Square and is truly upset. I don't understand. I have told him about the Goat's madness before. Did he not believe me? He says there was a terrible scene in Canterbury. Virginia did not take my letter well. Until yesterday, Clive had seen only the remote, endearing aspects of Virginia's madness. Now he has seen the dark, uncontrolled edges of her. It all began well. She wrote me a clear, sober letter, but soon after Clive says she went mad, and beat her head against the glass window. Then she lay for hours in a darkened room with a thrumming headache. Clive wanted to take the train down yesterday, but he did not dare move her. He is so happy to be home.

·

It is agreed. Clive and Adrian will take Virginia to Twickenham tomorrow, where she will undergo the rest cure for at least a month. By then Clarissa will be here.

And—Clive was *not* pleased about *Lemon Gatherers*. He would have preferred I spend the money on a French artist—more cachet. Clive always considers how a thing will or won't impress other people.

1 July 1910—46 Gordon Square

Spent the afternoon with Ottoline at Bedford Square. She is going abroad later this month. Philip is standing for election, and they want to get away before the upheaval of canvassing begins. I am hoping Clarissa will come before she goes. So few of my friends have children; it makes it difficult. I sat with Lytton for hours yesterday, gossiping and discussing Rupert's affair with that schoolgirl. I can usually tell Lytton anything, but he becomes acutely uncomfortable when I mention anything anatomical, female, and unrelated to sex. Pregnancy terrifies him.

Ottoline is practical, if not at all maternal. It must be protective, since she lost one of her twins. The boy was called Hugh. Her daughter, Julian, is a sweet, solemn child. Perhaps she and Clarissa can be friends?

．

Ottoline asked after Roger several times. She was more persistent and pointed in her questions than I would have expected. Have I seen him? Is his wife's condition improving? Do I think it will ever improve? Is his sister Joan still looking after the children? Was Clive going to accompany Roger to France to collect the paintings for the November exhibition? My information is hopelessly out of date. I did not even know the exhibition dates had been set.

And—Letter after angry letter from Virginia. The bed is uncomfortable. The hallways too loud. The food is inedible. And Miss Thomas is trying to convert her to Christianity. *And* it is all my fault.

31 July 1910—46 Gordon Square

No Clarissa yet. I feel sure she is fully cooked in there and ought to emerge any day now.

News from Virginia. Apparently she has set about seducing a Sapphic Swedish woman in the sanatorium—how alliterative—and apparently, half the ward is in love with her. Luckily, the amorous Swede was discharged before hearts were broken. Even with women, Virginia enjoys the mental seduction rather than the physical. Even the matron, Miss Thomas, a practical and sensible if overly religious woman, has also fallen headlong for Virginia. Virginia can be maddeningly charming when she chooses to be.

Later (hot and uncomfortable!)

Clive, Julian, and I went walking in Russell Square this evening. It is as far as I can manage. Clive and I sat on a bench, and Julian chased fireflies.

'Thoby loved fireflies,' I said into the soft dusk. Julian reminds me more of Thoby every day.

And—Miss Thomas plans to accompany Virginia on a walking tour of Cornwall once Virginia is declared sane again. Perhaps by the middle of August.

GRATIAN

20 August 1910—46 Gordon Square (hot)

Not a girl. And *not* in July. *He* arrived yesterday, 19 August—*three* weeks late. I was so sure. We had an understanding, a communication. It was one-sided, it seems. Julian has a brother and will be thrilled. I was startled, certainly, but recovered from my disappointment as soon as he lay on my chest. He is here, and he is whole. That is all I asked for. I have decided to call him Gratian. Too exhausted to write more. I do not remember being this undone by Julian.

Later

Snow left last Monday, after hanging about for two weeks, and I now wish she hadn't. At the time, I felt like an inadequate hostess for not producing the baby I had promised. Unable to pull the rabbit from the top hat, I asked her to go home. Now I have asked Clive to cable and ask her to return. 'Not Virginia?' Clive asked, hopeful.

'Not Virginia,' I said, standing my ground.

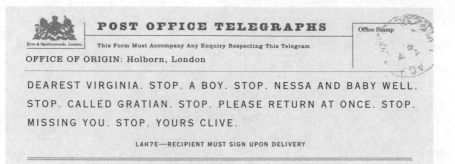

Eyre & Spottiswoode, London.

POST OFFICE TELEGRAPHS

Office Stamp

This Form Must Accompany Any Enquiry Respecting This Telegram

OFFICE OF ORIGIN: Holborn, London

DEAREST VIRGINIA. STOP. A BOY. STOP. NESSA AND BABY WELL. STOP. CALLED GRATIAN. STOP. PLEASE RETURN AT ONCE. STOP. MISSING YOU. STOP. YOURS CLIVE.

L4H7E—RECIPIENT MUST SIGN UPON DELIVERY

21 August 1910—46 Gordon Square

Everyone hates the name. Not indifference but dislike. I am wavering.

Later (six p.m.)

Clive is sweet but nervous and just as inept as I remember him being. He is reluctant to hold the baby. I told him to buck up. At least this time I know he will grow into his fatherhood. He left to write to Virginia, who has finished her rest cure and has begun a walking tour with Miss Thomas. Virginia wrote letter after letter complaining of this woman and then went on holiday with her. Strange.

And—I know babies often lose weight just after they are born, but Gratian is losing too much. He is spindly, frail. Worried.

24 August 1910—46 Gordon Square (ten a.m.)

'Hadrian?' Saxon offered. He had been sitting in the corner with Gibbon's Latin dictionary for the last three hours.

'No,' I said, annoyed by the subject. I am not up out of bed, but visitors are flocking in and out of my bedroom.

'Pausanius?'

'No, Saxon.' Adrian and Duncan had left for lunch, and Clive was off, most likely penning *another* letter to Virginia.

'Viggo?'

The baby's name is not sitting well with anyone, including the baby. I must come up with something else. Julian was such a Julian when he was born. His name settled on him like a wave on the shore. Gratian is bumpy and loose and not settling on my new baby at all.

Later

'Clive, you cannot just disappear!' I hissed at him. The house had not emptied. Saxon, Adrian, Duncan, Maynard, Desmond, Aunt Anny, Molly, and Snow were all downstairs. Lytton is still in Sweden for his health cure, and Morgan left to dine with his publisher but will be back tonight. Gerald and George and George's wife, Margaret, are due any minute and will be appalled by the collection of buggers in the drawing room. I needed Clive to stay and keep all the social feathers from ruffling, but he kept vanishing up to his study or out to meet art dealers, or out to meet Mrs Raven Hill for all I knew.

'I didn't *disappear*. I have been cooped up in the house for days,' Clive said irritably. 'You have dozens of people to help you. What do you need me for?'

'Clive, we have guests—lots of guests, and I want you to be the host. I cannot get out of bed and cannot control the rumpus downstairs. Could you please do that for me?'

'These people are driving me mad, Nessa,' Clive complained, dropping heavily into a fraying armchair. 'I am leaving for Paris in a few weeks. I am meant to be helping Roger organise the exhibition. Desmond does not have the least idea about how to put this all together. I have things to *do*!'

Later (two p.m.)

I decided to take a different tack. When Clive came in after luncheon, I tried to speak to him again.

'Clive, I know you have things to do. You need to get out. I understand.' I took a deep cool breath. 'But before you go, could you look in on the guests downstairs? And since you want to get away, could you make arrangements to go and get Julian from Wiltshire?' That is what I had been waiting to ask him.

'Nessa!' Clive leapt out of his chair and began to pace around the bedroom.

'Clive, you said you would go and get Julian from your parents as soon as the baby came. And now he is here.'

'Yes, he is. And I *will* get Julian. It is just not the right time *now*.' Clive was pacing between the window and the door.

'Why *isn't* it the time?' I asked, exasperated. 'Your Mrs Raven Hill? Is she away?'

'Yes,' Clive said, surprising me with honesty, 'she is, but that is not the point.'

'What *is* the point?' I shifted uncomfortably in the bed. I am constantly uncomfortable. I remember the month's rest after Julian being peaceful and happy. I do not remember this feeling of being pulled apart like wax and being unable to come back together again.

'The point is that there are things that need to be done in London!' Clive said, his voice rising.

'Clive—'

'No, Nessa. As you said, we have a houseful of guests, a new baby, a new nurse, you're in bed, and it just does not make sense to leave to fetch one more person into the house.'

'That one more person is your son,' I said icily.

'Of course he is,' Clive said, sensing his misstep. 'But Elsie will come back with him. I have no idea if Sloper and Maud have organised the new nurse's rooms—have they, Nessa? Did you see to that? What is she called? Margaret?' He sat on the edge of the bed, tipping the mattress down in a way that irritated me.

'Mabel. Of course I organised it. I put her in the room next to Elsie. Julian will be in the night nursery. Gratian is here with me. Snow is in Virginia's old room, and all the other guests go home and sleep in their own beds.'

'And Virginia?' Clive said, avoiding my gaze.

'Virginia is in Cornwall, as far as I know. *Is* she in Cornwall, Clive?'

'How should I know where she is?' Clive said quickly. Too quickly.

And—Should I try the other broad branch of the Roman Augustan tree? What about Claudian?

Much later (one a.m.—the baby just fell asleep)

'You asked her to come back. Didn't you?' I said, choosing to be direct. I was too exhausted for anything else.

'She is your sister. Of course I cabled her. I cabled your aunt and my parents and brother too—would you like to see the receipts?'

'Yes, but you asked her to come back, didn't you? You knew I did not want her here, and you asked her to come back.'

Clive did not answer. That is why he won't go and get Julian. That is why he is restless. He is waiting for Virginia.

And—The baby is not sucking as he should. He cannot grab hold of the thing. His instincts are off. Or my instincts are off? I am less adept this time around. He is smaller than Julian was. Less substantial. Terrified. Cannot sleep. The doctor is coming tomorrow.

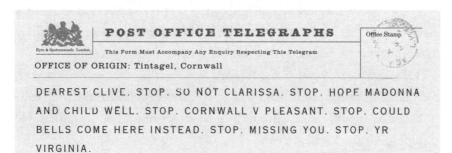

POST OFFICE TELEGRAPHS

Eyre & Spottiswoode, London.

This Form Must Accompany Any Enquiry Respecting This Telegram

Office Stamp

OFFICE OF ORIGIN: Tintagel, Cornwall

DEAREST CLIVE. STOP. SO NOT CLARISSA. STOP. HOPE MADONNA AND CHILD WELL. STOP. CORNWALL V PLEASANT. STOP. COULD BELLS COME HERE INSTEAD. STOP. MISSING YOU. STOP. YR VIRGINIA.

T9H8L—RECIPIENT MUST SIGN UPON DELIVERY

Roger Fry
Durbins
Guildford

25 August 1910

My dear Vanessa,

Congratulations! I just received Clive's note about the baby. How very wonderful. I hope you are well and taking very great care of yourself. Forgive me—how indelicate to mention such things. But it is such a very traumatic process. I hope you are being truly spoiled in care and affection. I would very much like to visit once the house settles and the little one has found his feet a bit. Please let me know when would be convenient. I really am very, very pleased for you and your family.

Yours sincerely,
Roger

26 August 1910—46 Gordon Square

Clive will *not* go to Wiltshire to collect Julian. We had a row. I am sure everyone—servants, guests, neighbours, family—all heard it, and I don't care. Clive is behaving appallingly. He wants us to go on holiday to Cornwall next month and to stop and collect Julian on the way.

I flatly refused. I am going to spend the rest of the requisite month convalescing in bed, and then I will go to collect Julian from Clive's horrible family myself since Clive refuses to go for me. Clive is stalling. He is hoping Virginia will appear.

Two p.m.

The doctor just left. This is the third time he has been here this week. He did not say anything new. Try to remain calm. Try to nurse. If it fails, try again. That is *terrible* advice. How can I possibly remain calm when my baby is starving? His weight has dropped again. Why is no one but me panicking?

And—A letter arrived from Clive's mother. She suggests I leave the baby with a wet nurse and take a short holiday. Clive must have put her up to writing that letter. I tore it up.

28 August 1910—46 Gordon Square

The baby was up all night again. He is not gaining weight. His indignant wails have given way to small yelps of misery. It is heartbreaking.

Later (three a.m.)

Everyone is still in the drawing room. How did I keep these hours before? I just checked on the baby, and Mabel is now upstairs trying to get him to sleep. Clive gets annoyed when I go up there. He does not understand why we are paying a nurse if I won't let her get on with it. He has a point, but I am too anxious about the baby to be away from him for long.

Tonight was amusing in glimpses but overall it was infuriating. Harry Norton ambushed me when I came downstairs and asked if I was 'bearing up all right'. I assumed he was referring to the trouble with the baby and was touched that he asked, but no. He said that he had had several letters from Virginia, and she implied that I was missing her quite terribly. Not five minutes later, Henry Lamb asked me the same thing. Galling.

29 August 1910—46 Gordon Square

'Stephen?' Adrian asked.

'His name already has Stephen in it,' I answered, handing him his coffee. We were still looking for the right baby name. So far I have been too distracted to focus on it. Clive is frustrated because he does not know what to tell his parents. I do not care what he tells his parents, but as they are giving us a gift of a thousand pounds, I know I should probably come up with something.

'Claudian?' suggested Saxon. Saxon was still going through the

Latin dictionaries. I like Claudian, but it feels too formal for a baby. It conjures Roman elephants.

'Quentin?' Duncan said. He had been eating cake, and his mouth was rather full.

'Quentin?' I repeated. '*Quentin.*' I rolled the word over my tongue.

Snow came in, holding the baby. She is leaving tomorrow, and I am desperate for her to stay.

'Mabel will be down in a minute, but I think he just wants you.' She handed me the squalling baby.

'Quentin Claudian Stephen Bell? Yes.'

46 GORDON SQUARE

BLOOMSBURY

TELEPHONE: 1608 MUSEUM

30 August 1910

Dearest Virginia,

Quentin Claudian Stephen Bell. Quentin for short. It suits his anti-quated spirit. Clarissa was a Trojan horse. Perhaps she will come another day. In the meantime, I am very glad to have my newest darling boy to take her place.

How is the ocean? Kiss it for me. I am afraid, with two small boys, we shall never make it to the seaside again. I understand that you have been encouraging us to holiday in Cornwall. I can hear you now, vehemently denying it. Be honest, Billy Goat. Did you suggest it to Clive? Did you imply that our summer would be far more pleasant spent by the sea? Yes. I thought so.

Write and walk, dearest, and enjoy the salty air.

Yours,
Nessa

PS: *Virginia, do stop alarming our friends. It is awkward when they*
hear from you that I am wasting away with missing you and then
see me in perfectly good humour and health.

31 August 1910—46 Gordon Square

A rare and beautiful evening.

Roger came tonight. Roger plus the usual mob that descends on our
house at nine p.m. Thursday nights have bled out into the rest of the
week, and now our circle seem to always be here. Desmond and Molly
were unable to make it, but Adrian, Duncan, Harry Norton, Henry
Lamb, Maynard, Lytton (just returned from Sweden), James, Ottoline
and Philip (also just returned from abroad), and Gwen Darwin were all
here. I had a long bath—ill-advised after childbirth, but I was desperate
to be scrubbed clean—and dressed for dinner. I am recovering my figure
quickly, but the weight is coming off in odd places, leaving me a different
shape than I was before. Not that I am worrying about looking appeal-
ing. I cannot focus on clothes or my hair or anything but the baby. Clive
had finally to ask me to change my dressing gown so that I would not be
receiving visitors in the same one three days running.

As I am still not supposed to get out of bed, the evening came to
meet me. I twisted my hair into a messy knot and left off the corset but
was dressed enough for decency. We sat and gossiped most of the night:
Morgan's new book, Ottoline's trip (exhausting), Lytton's health (improved), Duncan's painting (selling well), and naturally, Virginia's
Cornish adventures and the baby's new name. Around midnight, the
rain cleared and everyone went out into the garden square. I have asked
people not to smoke upstairs until the baby is a bit older. He ends up
smelling of smoke rather than of baby, and I do not think he cares for it
much. Clive went down to ask Sloper to fetch up more wine, and Roger
stayed to keep me company.

'You are well?' he asked anxiously.

'Yes, much better.' I was not sure how to answer him.

'Thin,' he said, looking at me carefully. I like that. I like that he looks at me and sees what is there rather than what should be there.

'*Worried*,' I answered truthfully. 'Quentin is not gaining weight as he should.'

'Oh my dear,' Roger said, understanding the problem instantly. 'How awful for you. Of course you are worried. How can you think of anything else?'

Moved by his raw sincerity, I began to cry. He was not embarrassed, nor did he try to quiet me. He sat beside me in sympathy. It helped more than any words ever could.

And—Letters from Virginia. It seems her walking tour is *not* a success. Miss Jean Thomas is apparently cloying, and the beloved Cornish coast is obscured by rain. At least the local doctor has declared her sane again. Dr Savage will have to confirm it when she returns to town.

And and—Clive is in a foul mood. He is always bad-tempered after an evening with Lytton. I don't think Clive will ever forgive him for proposing to Virginia.

THE POST-IMPRESSIONIST EXHIBITION

. ⚘ .

Sunday 6 November 1910—46 Gordon Square (eight a.m.)

'And you were up all night?' I offered Desmond a cup of coffee. He looked exhausted.

'I missed all the trains back, and so we kept working in the gallery. We were still choosing pictures at four a.m. There are two nudes that Roger wants to hang that I am not sure are a good idea.'

We were in the dining room. Sloper informed me when I woke up this morning that Mr MacCarthy and Mr Fry had arrived early in the morning. He had shown them to Virginia's and Adrian's old rooms but did not like to wake me, as I had been up most of the night with Quentin, who is slowly improving.

'They *are* a good idea,' Roger said as he came into the room. Even early in the day he has a lived-in look about him. 'Ah,' he said, sitting down opposite Desmond, 'Cooper's Oxford Marmalade. My very favourite. How did you ever know?' He spread the marmalade on a thick slice of toast. How like Roger to think that his hostess has gone to some trouble to locate his favourite jam. He always assumes the very best in people.

'Why not suitable?' I asked.

'Why don't you come with us this afternoon and see?' Roger said.

And—Virginia is back in London. Should I ask her to join me today?

No. There is something wonderful about being with Roger that I want to protect. Virginia will spoil it.

Later (seven p.m.)

I went. I did not understand what a tremendous thing Roger was doing when he invited me to the gallery this morning. Today was crucial, but still he took time to walk me through the entire exhibition.

When I got there, it was mayhem. And Roger was in the centre of it all. He was like an orchestra conductor, keeping a fraction ahead of the music. He was switching paintings ('I need the *other* Cézanne, not the mountain, the portrait of his wife, yes, up, down, a little to the left, *there*!'), talking to reporters ('No, I do not feel it is akin to pornography in the least'), installing lighting ('The chandelier should be brighter, we have to see the vibrancy!'); he was magnificent. I had not realised quite what a bold and important undertaking this was. Clive is right—it will change *everything*.

'Amazing, isn't he?' Desmond said, coming to stand by me in the midst of the chaos. 'The gallery curators do not know what to do with him, he is such a tornado of energy.' Desmond pointed to one of the directors of the gallery who was standing at the edge of the whirlwind trying to catch Roger's attention.

'How long has he been like this?' I asked.

'Like what? Roger is always like this.'

And—Clive was put out that I went to the gallery. Specifically, he was put out that I went without him. 'But Roger did not invite *you*,' I said. 'He invited *me*.'

And—Still working on my beachgoers painting. It plays a sombre song that comforts me.

8 November 1910—46 Gordon Square

The exhibition opens to the public today. Desmond and Roger decided not to hang the two Gauguin nudes. They stashed them in

Desmond's basement office instead. The right choice, I think. There is enough to excite the public as it is. Desmond is concerned that Roger reordered the paintings so many times, and the catalogue is all wrong. He is terrified that one of Van Gogh's curvy landscapes will be listed as *Station Master at Arles*, or worse, that one of Gauguin's lush tropical paintings of bare-chested Tahitian girls will be mislabelled as 'Cézanne's wife'. Roger trusts Desmond and is sure it will all turn out all right.

And—Julian and I watched the birds in the square this morning. He is so like Thoby. I have hung Thoby's lark and nuthatch drawings in his room.

Thursday 10 November 1910—46 Gordon Square (late)

'The reviews are awful,' Maynard said to no one in particular.

'But that is perfect!' Lytton said from his basket chair. 'The British public will rush to see something scandalous. My dears, they must see it. Otherwise how can they criticise?'

'But they are taking it as a *moral* affront,' I said. 'I knew they would not like it, but they are outraged.'

'Wonderful!' Clive said. 'That way they will be *sure* to see it.'

Roger Fry
DurbIns
Guildford

11 November 1910

Dearest Mother,

Please explain to Father that I am not exhibiting pornography. I am sure he will read the reviews of my show and worry that I am. Yes, the public are disconcerted, but that is how art must happen. It cannot

be a comfortable, smooth transition from one aesthetic to another.
It must bump and jostle and disrupt and shake the ground until the
ground gives way. My reputation as an Old Masters lecturer is sunk
for good after this. So be it. The old does not politely move over to
make way for the new; it must be roughly shouldered aside. If you
and Father would like to come one evening after all the crowds are
gone, I would very much like you to see the exhibition.

Thank you for writing to Helen. The doctor has been very kind
and helpful to me as well as to her. He encourages me not to blame
myself, and I sense that he is trying to prepare me for the worst. I
told him that I have been trying to prepare myself for this news for
years but cannot do it. The callus will not grow. I do not want it to.
What sort of person would I have to become to be 'prepared' for
such news? Instead, I must continue to hope. In each letter, in each
visit, there are moments, small and fragile as eggs, of precious nor-
mality. For that fraction of time the ice door opens and she is calm,
not violent, not rageful, but herself. I hang my heart on these mo-
ments.

Love,
Roger

14 November 1910—46 Gordon Square

They were right. The gallery is packed like a fish crate every day. Morgan
went yesterday and pronounced it 'confusing'. Morgan is traditional in
his tastes and gets startled when I say 'bugger' at a dinner party, so I am
not surprised he got muddled about the paintings. Maynard is seeing it
tomorrow. Duncan loved it and is enjoying the vocal indignation of the
public. Virginia has not been to see it yet (crowds make her nervous at
present), and Clive and I go daily.

And—I am experimenting with dark fragmented outlines around
my loosely drawn figures. It allows me to move freely inside a stricter
space. Like wild horses in a broken-down paddock.

Sunday 20 November 1910—46 Gordon Square (nine-thirty p.m.)

What Roger has done is remarkable. His reputation as an art critic will never recover from the mighty fury he has raised in London, but he does not care. He lives entirely in the present tense. It is astonishing, particularly given what he has been enduring this month. Desmond was here for supper. He has been staying here whenever he misses the last train back to Surrey. Desmond is chronically late and leads a mistimed life, so *often* misses his trains.

He said it quietly. He said it just to me. While Lytton, Maynard, Duncan, Adrian, Virginia, and Clive were enjoying a rowdy gossip about Ottoline and Henry Lamb, whose affair seems to be drawing to a messy close, Desmond leaned over and, in a low voice, told me that Roger's wife has finally been declared incurably insane and was placed in a permanent institution this morning.

'He has known it was coming for some time,' Desmond said softly. 'But I think that makes it harder when the day actually comes, don't you?'

I looked over at Virginia. All my worst fears for my sister follow this sea lane. It is lightless and choppy and the tide is strong. 'Yes,' I said. 'Hope is an unbreakable habit.'

Later (two a.m.)

I came up to bed and went to check on Quentin. They are all still downstairs. I keep thinking of Roger alone in the big house in Guildford. Desmond says the children are with Roger's sister in Bristol. I know Roger built that astonishing house on a hill for his wife, even though he never said so. 'Open spaces are better for Helen,' he said on the day we joined him for luncheon. 'She prefers to be out of London.' She lived there so briefly. It is a terrible thing to grieve for someone who is not dead, not in love with someone else, but just no longer there.

And—I watched Clive and Virginia tonight. Clive has behaved in a way that has released me from all the love I felt for him. But he has left me whole, intact. However can Roger go on after breaking his own heart?

21 November 1910—46 Gordon Square (late—everyone asleep)

I suppose it was inevitable. Clive and Lytton have never liked each other much. No, that is not true. I think Clive would very much have liked to be Lytton's friend, especially after Thoby died, but over the years it has become painfully clear that Lytton does not think much of my husband. Tonight they had a noisy row, and Clive threw Lytton out of the house.

The air between them was drum tight. Clive accused Lytton of spending too much time with his family—by that he meant Virginia and me. Lytton accused Clive of behaving like a pig of a husband. I was grateful that he left the specific details of Clive's bad behaviour unsaid. But then, there was no need to say them. Everyone knows.

22 November 1910—46 Gordon Square

We had breakfast as usual. Neither of us mentioned the row with Lytton. This is how our life is this autumn. We get on fine if things remain flat, routine, and dishonest. But I could not leave it at that.

'You know I mean to still invite Lytton here, don't you?' I said as he sliced his grapefruit.

'When?' he snapped.

'Whenever.'

'To annoy me?'

'No. I do not think it *should* annoy you.'

'But it does, and you won't change to suit me,' Clive said, sounding hurt.

'No, I won't. I love Lytton dearly and want him here. I am sorry.' The truth is best.

Later

I met Lytton at Ottoline's this afternoon. She left us alone to talk. She really does have the most marvellous tact.

'Are you going to try to make it up with him?' I asked him bluntly.
'No use,' Lytton said. 'He is angry about things that I cannot help.'

Thursday 24 November 1910—46 Gordon Square

The art gallery at Helsinki just bought a Cézanne from the show, the
Mont Sainte-Victoire, for *eight hundred* pounds! I am regretting Clive's
decision not to buy the Van Gogh we liked. He thought four hundred
pounds was too much. I am pleased wc bought the Picasso last month
for only four pounds. It is a small cubist still life with beautiful colours.
Ottoline has bought two paintings from the exhibition, though I am not
sure which ones. She has visited the gallery nearly as often as Clive and
me. It is strange that she never asks me to accompany her. Our friendship has mellowed to a kind civility. I am disappointed. To my surprise,
I enjoy her company very much.

Later

Clive came home with lots of gossip. Ottoline and Henry are through,
although they always say that and never really are, and Bertie Russell is
in love with Ottoline. He and his wife, Alys, live entirely apart now. I did
not tell Clive but I suspect Ottoline has begun to care very much for
Roger. Roger notices nothing. This month, how could he?

Roger Fry
Durbins
Guildford

1 December 1910

My dear heart,

Yes, I have received your letters. I am sorry not to have replied. I was acting under the doctor's advice. He thinks you will settle in better if you have less news from Durbins. But I know it pains you not to hear from your family. I ought to have written. It was wrong. Forgive me? I am stumbling, my dear, and you must believe that I am doing my best.

The children are still with Joan, and both asked me to send their very best love. Joan is teaching them to ride, and they are learning quickly. I have been very much occupied with the new exhibition in London. It has brought a riot of anger and derision down on my head, but the bad press has only increased our sales. It is all painters you have long loved and I am sure you would approve. There is a Matisse you would adore and two Gauguin nudes I chose not to hang in the end. You would have included them, but then you are braver than I am. You always have been.

How I miss you, my dearest one. How you are threaded through my thoughts. I wish I could take you away to a world of colour and light. Perhaps things will change and you will grow well enough. I hope only for that.

Sleep well, my dear,
Roger

20 December 1910—46 Gordon Square

Leaving for Wiltshire to see Clive's family for Christmas and am resentful. Virginia and Adrian are staying at the Pelham Arms in Lewes for a week's holiday, and I am being hauled off to face the dragons.

Quentin is doing a bit better but still does not weigh as much as he should. I do not like taking him out in midwinter.

THE RED TRAIN

⚘

15 January 1911—Little Talland House, Firle, Sussex

Virginia has rented her own house. She found it while she and Adrian were spending Christmas in Firle and took it on the spot. I came down to see it right away. 'My own first proper home,' she said, happily trotting from room to room. Having a place of her own has already done such good. It settles her, calms her, just knowing it exists somewhere on this earth. Predictably, she has renamed it Little Talland House after the house Father rented for so many years in Cornwall. We have been scavenging for furniture for the last three days, and Virginia is fed up. She has found a wonderful stand-up desk, very like her desk in Fitzroy Square, and so considers the house furnished. Her books are stacked in towering piles on the floor of her new study.

I worry that Adrian will be a bit adrift on his own at Fitzroy Square, but Virginia told me that he spends nearly all his time with Duncan anyway. Good.

25 January 1911—46 Gordon Square

Virginia's birthday. She is visiting Lytton's sister Marjorie for the night. Clive, who said that he was in Wiltshire last week to see about some family business, was most likely either in Sussex at Virginia's new

country house or with his Mrs Raven Hill. I made the mistake of working on my painting of the bathers today. I am sure I ruined it. So I sent a
note round to Lytton, who came over, and we ate cake.

30 January 1911—46 Gordon Square (early)

'He gave letters of introduction to meet who?' I asked, pulling Clive's
socks out of the drawer.

'To meet *whom*,' Clive said pompously. He is always correcting my
speech.

'To meet *whom*, then,' I said, looking for the other brown sock.

'Miss Stein and a Mr Matt Prichard. I am sure I have met him before
but cannot remember when. How many pairs of shoes, Nessa? Three?'

'Two, just in case one pair gets wet,' I said, handing him a soft cloth
bag for his shoes. Clive always takes too much. We were packing for his
brief trip to Paris. Roger has given him letters of introduction for this
Mr Prichard and his good friend, the American, Miss Gertrude Stein.
Roger says hers is the only letter one ever needs in Paris. Once you meet
Miss Stein, the rest of the city follows. Clive has been wanting to mix
with that set for years. How like Roger to effortlessly open such a door.
I would love to go with Clive, but Quentin is just coming through the
worst, and I do not dare leave him.

Later (seven p.m.)

Clive caught the six o'clock train to Dover. He will spend the night there
and take the first ferry in the morning. Julian, Quentin, and I had nursery tea at the scrubbed kitchen table. Julian dunked his toast in his milk,
and Quentin dropped boiled egg on the floor. I ate nothing but jam
tarts. Clive insists that we eat a proper meal in the dining room and that
the children eat earlier with Nanny. I prefer it my way. Four whole days
before I have to meet Virginia in Firle.

1 February 1911—46 Gordon Square

Roger stopped by in the late morning. He had read Clive's unsigned article in the *Athenaeum* yesterday but forgot that Clive is still abroad.

'I went to see the sculpture exhibition he mentioned in the article, the one at the Chenil Gallery? And now I am convinced your husband is quite, quite wrong,' Roger said, moving Julian's toy motorcar out of the way so he could sit on the sofa.

'Wrong?' I asked, sitting in the armchair opposite.

'Oh yes, very wrong. He claims that the artist is only "half educated" artistically and therefore dismisses the work. I disagree entirely. I thought his work showed profound imagination.'

'Why does—'

'Nessa!' Julian came running in and jumped onto my lap. 'Nessa, look!' He held out his finger.

'What am I looking at, little one?' I asked, holding his finger up to the light.

'They call you Nessa?' Roger asked.

'Julian does, so I am sure Quentin will too when he can speak. I don't know how it happened. Darling,' I said to Julian, 'I do not see anything wrong with this finger.'

'Elsie stood on it,' Julian said, studying Roger. 'Who is that?'

'*That* is Mr Fry. Stand up and shake hands, darling,' I encouraged, aware that Clive would be appalled at his son's terrible manners.

Julian climbed down from my lap and stood in front of Roger. Roger got to his feet and leaned down to shake his small chubby hand.

'How do you do?' Roger said sincerely.

'Well. Thank you,' Julian said formally. 'Do you like trains?'

'Very much. Particularly red trains. They have such style.'

'I have a red train,' Julian said. 'Would you like to see it?'

'I would like that very much, thank you.' Roger understood the importance of the invitation, and they swept out of the room.

Later

'His nanny came to take him for his nap,' Roger said, coming to find me in my studio.

'Yes.' I shifted Quentin on my lap. He had fallen asleep after lunch.

'I must be off,' Roger said. 'I have an appointment with an art dealer on Bond Street. He is interested in seeing one of the paintings from the exhibition before it gets shipped back to Amsterdam.'

'Which one?' I asked, ringing for Mabel. She came and took the baby upstairs.

'One of the Van Goghs. His sister, Madame Gosschalk-Bonger, is selling off his paintings. One hundred and twenty pounds for some of his beautiful sunflowers. They could go for four times that much. Outrageous.'

'*Gosschalk-Bonger?* That is really her name?'

Roger giggled. 'I have been struggling to say it with a straight face. How was I?'

'Terrible—your mouth twitched.'

He looked startled, surprised that I had been studying him so closely. 'Would you like to see it again? The *Sunflowers*? You could come to meet the dealer just now.'

I was pleased by the invitation. Clive has never asked me into that sealed world of dealers and auction houses.

How I love the saturated colours of Van Gogh's painting. I have been struggling with colour lately. Nothing is as vibrant as I would like, and I am experimenting with stark white to offset the flatness.

'Yes,' I said, boldly. 'I would love to go.'

And so I went.

3 February 1911—train to Sussex

There is something relaxing about train journeys on one's own. Something hidden and safe. I am on my way to Virginia's new house, where it will *not* be relaxing.

5 February 1911—Little Talland House, Firle, Sussex

Two days of pure Virginia. We have her bedroom, library, and small drawing room organised so far. She has conceded to bookcases rather than just stacks of books heaped all over the floor. She is smoking more and eating less, but she is writing.

Monday 6 February 1911—Little Talland House, Firle, Sussex

'Virginia, I *can't* stay,' I explained again.

'Why not? I always stay with you,' she answered illogically.

'Yes, and that is lovely, dearest, but I have a family. I must get back.' Perversely, Virginia was sitting on my coat.

'I am your family too,' Virginia persisted.

'Yes, I know, dearest, but you know what I mean,' I said, exasperated.

'Yes, I know what you mean. Children. A husband. A *real* family.'

A real family. I know she is getting nervous. We all shed the conventions of our class, but spinsterhood is a clingy grey spectre that hugs the body and chokes the soul. I know Virginia is afraid. For years we have all speculated about who might win Virginia in the end. Walter Lamb is clearly keen, but she has no interest in him. Hilton Young seems to have moved on. Saxon never speaks to her—or to anyone else for that matter—and Lytton escaped with his life. Who does that leave?

And—I finished Morgan's beautiful new novel on the train. It is about sisters: one wild and uncompromising but breathtaking in her courage. And one practical, reasonable, and unhappily bound by her good sense. Elinor Dashwood and Marianne. Margaret and Helen Schlegel. Even the name is haunting: *Howards End*.

10 February 1911—46 Gordon Square (late)

It was a strange evening.

Ottoline gave a dinner party for the poet Mr William Yeats tonight. It was a difficult mix of people with several of Philip's colleagues—all MPs—sitting in one corner and Ottoline's aristocratic connections making camp in another. Clive is in Paris until tomorrow, and Virginia is still in Sussex, so I sat on a sofa with Lytton and Duncan. Ottoline spent the evening talking to Roger. I saw her lightly rest her large, bony head on his shoulder.

Duncan was watching too. 'Are they . . . ?' Duncan asked, leaning towards Lytton.

'No, his wife is in a mental hospital,' I said, answering for Lytton.

'*Permanently* in a mental hospital,' Lytton corrected.

I sat up a little straighter, invisibly bristling. 'He wouldn't,' I said firmly.

•

Later Lytton walked me home.

'He *would,* you know,' he said gently.

'Has he?' I tried to conjure the image of Roger in bed with Ottoline and instantly regretted it.

Lytton shrugged. 'Maybe not with her, but he *would.*'

A textured warmth roiled up my spine. He would.

Saturday 11 February 1911—46 Gordon Square

Clive is home and surprised me by announcing that Roger is coming for supper tonight. It was arranged before Clive went to Paris. I felt sliced by an irrational jealousy. A visceral sense of possession thudded through me. When Quentin was so ill, Roger saw what Clive did not, and it changed things, the way a dinner that becomes a stay-up-until-sunrise kind of night changes things between two people. Clive tumbled away, and Roger stepped into clear focus. His friendship, his respect, his opinion, his *affection* have become essential to me. They nurture the seeds that grow the plant. Regardless of what Lytton thinks, I know that Roger and I could never slip beyond the high walls of friendship—he still loves his wife. It lives in the way he says her name. Helen. Beautiful, lost Helen.

And—And then I shake myself out like a dog which has been swimming in the sea and remember: I too am still married. But I no longer *feel* married in the way I did. I feel alone.

Three p.m. (beginning to rain)

I was looking for stamps in Clive's desk and found a letter he wrote to Lytton. Dear God. It is riddled with acrimony and written in rage. He must not send it. So much will break if he sends it.

Later

Roger is staying the night. As is Desmond. Unusually, Desmond actually thought he might make his train and went dashing out into the rain, but he was back again in half an hour, drenched. I gave him a pair of Thoby's flannel pyjamas. Lytton looked at them sadly when I fetched them, but I handed them over without grief. Thoby would give them gladly were he here. He would not want to become a museum—carefully dusted and lovingly preserved. He would want to be remembered and included. The reflexive thought gave me a brisk snap of happiness.

Lytton ignored Clive all evening, but as it was mutual, it lent balance to the occasion. Normally he would delight in unnerving Clive, but Lytton was not joyful tonight. He seemed put out that Roger was here. Roger makes him feel displaced, and nothing I say rights it. Ironically, Lytton makes Clive feel exactly that brand of left out and irritable. Or perhaps I make Clive feel left out and irritable? And then I think, what are we all vying for?

Virginia singled Roger out and began her inevitable campaign to charm him. I pulled her aside and reminded her that his wife is in an institution. It is not right. Roger sought me out several times, but I slid away. I am transparent. I don't want Virginia to see how much I enjoy his company. She would stop at nothing to make him love her.

And—Exciting. A trip to Constantinople is in the works. I did not think I would want to go back but I do. Roger has been wanting to go and is looking for travelling companions. I said yes, as did Clive and Harry Norton, who popped by after supper.

67 BELSIZE PARK GARDENS

HAMPSTEAD, N.W.

TEL.: HAMPSTEAD 1090

15 March 1911

Dear Leonard,

Things are so dull here. Couldn't you leave sooner? It is awkward in London at the moment. Duncan and Adrian are together, but I am hoping that such an unlikely romance cannot last. I do not even think Adrian really is a bugger at heart. He simply finds women terrifying—which of course, they are—and has gone with the devil he knows. In any case, I do not see how it can go on much longer with Duncan. Adrian is too tall. The physics of the thing boggle the mind.

I have had a blazing row with that great pink pig Clive and can only slink to Gordon Square when I am sure he is either out forni-cating or drunk. The other night I tried to spend a civil evening in his company and found it exhausting. What a bore. He claims that he does not like me to spend time with his wife, but it is when I am in Virginia's company that he goes berserk. The row the other day was sparked when he realised I had been down to see Virginia in her new and quite hideous country cottage in Sussex. Steam from the ears, my dear. Comme un teapot.

I have just received your letter. No, of course Virginia is not

planning to marry Saxon. How could anyone marry Saxon? That
is an absurd notion. I could not tell from your tone; are you wor-
ried that someone else will marry her before you meet her again, or
are you panicking and trying to palm her off?

It is nerves, Leonard. You are coming back, and after hearing
about her for so long, meeting her again is a daunting prospect. I
understand fully. But you must persevere. Buck up. You are the best
man I know. You are her equal as very few men could ever be. We
have already lost one of those delicious sisters to an unsuitable
oaf—we mustn't lose two. That would be careless. Virginia is
exactly right for you. I cannot explain how I know this, but I do.
You will see, and then you will be astonished by my perception. I
am looking forward to that.

Now. Are you packed? Have you booked your passage? Have
you booked your dog's passage? I do not want any last-minute
hiccups or apologetic telegrams. You must board the ship, dear
man. No lollygagging in exotica. Enough is enough. Time to come
home.

Yours,
Lytton

28 March 1911—46 Gordon Square (raining)

'And you are definitely going to Constantinople? Again? Extraordinary,'
Lytton said, crossing his thin ankles. He had folded himself into his
chair like a stork, the way he does when he disapproves.

Clive was out, but this morning I told him pointedly that Lytton was
going to stop in this afternoon. He did not say much but just picked up
his umbrella and left. Everyone is plotting how to navigate the two of
them back onto the shoals of friendship. Virginia wants to hold a
masked ball—dress Clive up as a guardsman and Lytton as a ballet
dancer and persuade them to waltz. She is sure it will solve everything.

'It has all happened so *fast*,' I said to Lytton, laughing. 'Roger does not waffle the way we do. He makes a plan and then buys tickets. Clive and I usually mull over a trip for weeks before doing anything about it.'

'And who is going on this Asiatic adventure?' Lytton asked, relighting his pipe, his face pleated in distaste.

'So far it is Clive, Roger, Harry Norton, and me. I am sure I will get stuck talking to Harry the whole time while Roger and Clive debate the finer points of art criticism,' I said. 'I am just happy to be going abroad. Clive and Roger have been nipping over to Paris all winter, and I have been stuck in England for a hundred years.'

'And Virginia?' Lytton asked.

'Virginia is happily nesting in her new country house. She wouldn't want to go. She has had such a rocky year. It will be better if she just keeps on doing what she is doing.' I marvelled at how cleanly I delivered the lie.

Later

Clive had the nerve to ask, and I flatly refused. I will not go if he invites her.

Friday 31 March 1911—46 Gordon Square

We have been to Cook's, arranged the post, bought the tickets, and packed the bags. Roger and Harry Norton leave tomorrow for Calais and then on to Ghent. We are to meet them at the Gare de l'Est and together take the Orient Express to Constantinople. They refurbished the entire train a few years ago, apparently, and returned it to its belle époque glory.

At the last minute I went out and ordered a new silver evening dress, four crisp white shirts, and two serge skirts. They make me feel starched, clean, prepared, and snapped together in the way that only new clothes can do.

We leave for Wiltshire to drop Julian and Quentin with Clive's parents tonight. I am dreading it.

Later—Cleeve House, Seend, Wiltshire

It was not as bad as I feared. Elsie and Mabel will be with the boys, and the weather is warming up enough for Julian to go outside in the afternoons. I have learned to ignore Clive's ruddy robust family. I hope my boys will learn to do the same.

PAINTERS

. ⚜ .

4 April 1911—Calais

Seasick. Terribly seasick. Clive is fussing and wants to turn back. I am ignoring him. Paris in a few hours. Clive has promised me supper in Montmartre before we meet the others at the Gare de l'Est. I hope I can keep it down.

5 April 1911—the Orient Express (somewhere outside Strasbourg)

We made it—just. The ferry ride went on and on and was awful. And naturally Clive began to panic—lately he goes to pieces when I am ill. It has not been an easy journey thus far: first he thought we would miss the train to Dover, then he thought we would miss the ferry to Calais, and then he was sure I was going to die of nausea on the boat. He is recovering; lying down in our tiny berth like a consumptive prostitute in an Italian opera.

And in the lavish dining car, Roger and I *paint*—the blurry scenery outside and the faces of the other passengers inside. We use simple words and uncomplicated grammar but have exemplary conversations. Harry has been buried inside his newspaper since Paris, but Roger is exuberant and jolly. I cannot think why he ever frightened me so. He is unlike anyone I have ever known. He is *game*. Game for painting anything: the light, the sea, the people, the goats, and for discussing anything: babies, families, books, art. No suggestion is ever too silly or too impossible. He will consider anything. I am unused to such a lack of cynicism.

Friday 7 April 1911—Hotel Bristol, Constantinople

The day went to Roger. And it was a perfect day. We boarded a rickety boat with two rowers and headed up the Bosphorus into the East. Breakfast in Europe, luncheon in Asia. We landed up on a rocky beach and all tumbled out of the boat onto the slippery dock. Clive's expression was sour as he picked his way over the damp planks.

Roger and I found a dry spot away from the others and set up our makeshift easels. We work quickly and efficiently together.

'Nessa?'

'Mm?' I was trying to capture the small boy fishing from the dock. His skinny legs dangled over the water, and his head was thrown back, his face tipped towards the bleached, hot sky.

'Today makes me . . . happy,' Roger said hesitantly, guiltily.

I put down my brush. 'Good.'

I know he has not had many happy days this year. Perhaps he no longer feels entitled to them?

Later (seven p.m.)

'Nessa?'

'Mm?'

'What shall I do when we go back to London?' Roger asked thoughtfully. We were seated on a stone bench, watching the sun set in a riot of fuchsia.

'Anything you like. You can hardly go back to lecturing on Old Masters now,' I laughed. Roger is taking his expulsion from the conservative lecture circuit with customary good grace. After the fury he caused over the exhibition, no one wants to hear him speak about anything other than modern art. Unfortunately, the people who want to hear about modern art cannot afford to hire Roger to speak.

'True,' he said. 'But then I would not want to go back. I prefer to go *forward*.'

'Forward how?' I asked. I know Roger is still asked by private collectors to help them find and purchase particular pieces. He is also writing a good deal. 'Would you write another book?'

'I think I ought to put on another Post-Impressionist exhibition, don't you? I could talk to the Grafton Galleries. I know they are anxious to have me back.' He spoke, his face in profile, turned to the gashed pink sky. 'Would you show your paintings with me?'

'In your second *Post-Impressionist* exhibition?' I asked carefully, reverently, trying to make sure I understood him clearly.

'Of course. Your work is *important*, Nessa.'

Important. Not beautiful or lovely or charming—important. I did not turn to look at him. The birds in my rafters took flight. 'Yes, I would like that.'

'Good,' he said, taking my hand impulsively and bringing it to his lips. 'Good.'

46 GORDON SQUARE

BLOOMSBURY

TELEPHONE: 1608 MUSEUM

Hotel Bristol, Constantinople

11 April 1911

Dearest Snow,

Today Roger and I painted eleven portraits between us. Roger wedges stacks of canvases under his arms, and rather than carrying his paintbox, he stuffs it into the pocket of his Ulster coat along with handkerchiefs, a sketchbook, a novel, and any other assorted bits of wreckage from his day. His coat ends up looking distorted and lumpy, but Roger refuses to be weighed down. He walks quickly, his bright eyes wide with interest and his long hair flying behind him.

Wherever we go, we promptly set up easels and bully the public into sitting for dashed-off oil sketches. I feel like a penny portrait-ist at a country fair. Harry and Clive grow bored and wander off in search of culture or luncheon or both. I did not know that Roger would prefer to paint rather than talk about painting. Clive confines himself to talking about painting. Why take part in the artistry when you can sit back and judge? How catty I am—forgive me?

Our days are colourful and busy. Roger has become our host, even though he does not know this country. He can communicate with anyone. It reminds me of Thoby. He arranges day trips and mule pack picnics and boat rides and Roman baths and gains entry into secret Byzantine churches that have burst into mosques. We keep company with ancient Greeks and Ottomans and Crusaders and kings. At first Clive wrangled for control of the party, and then, sensing a more competent traveller was among us, he conceded the field. He was outgunned. Although Clive has admitted defeat, he has not accepted it. He thumps around begrudging Roger his ingenuity. I am a terrible wife and find it endlessly amusing.

But none of that matters in a place such as this. The sun sets differently here. It does not discreetly slip behind the trees in a gen-teel wash of lavender, as it does in England. It goes down swinging in a ball of roaring firelight. It would be presumptuous to paint it. It is too beautiful. I can only witness and hope to remember.

It is an unspoken agreement between us. At a quarter to seven, Roger and I put down whatever we are doing and go outside. We meet on the hotel terrace and wind down the gravel drive to the rocky bluff overlooking the sea. We do not speak much. I do not take his arm. The sun sets. We hold very still. And then we return.

*We leave for Brusa, the ancient capital of the Ottoman Empire,
tomorrow to see Mount Olympus and the mosaics. How I miss you.*

*Yours,
Vanessa*

PS: *Roger calls my chunky black outlines 'slithery handwriting'. He
likes the way they stop and start, which is my favourite bit about
them too. I have found a style that suits me.*

12 April 1911—Hôtel d'Anatolie, Brusa

We took a Greek steamer and then a German train. The train crawled
uphill through tangled olive groves and bare hillsides to Brusa while we
lunched on bread, cheese, and sweet oranges. With sadness and sympathy, Roger and I talked about madness.

'She turned violent. That is when the doctor finally persuaded me that
Helen, my Helen, was gone,' he said quietly, his back to the train window.
'Have you ever had to make such a terrible decision?'

'We have brushed very close. So far Virginia has always come back.'

He nodded as the train pulled into the station. Even if we never
speak of it again, it is comforting to be with someone who understands
so well.

UNION POSTALE UNIVERSELLE

CEYLON (CYLAN)

12 April 1911

Kandy, Ceylon

Lytton,

*I sail next month and should be with you by mid-June. I will take
the first train to London and find you straightaway. We shall dine
and we shall talk and it will be marvellous.*

I am no longer afraid to meet her, Lytton. Instead, I feel an apprehension born of unfounded ironbound certainty. It is borrowed conviction, and it stems from you. I know very well it may dissolve into dust when your Virginia steps out of myth into flesh, but like a light left burning in a window, it has been enough to lead me home. Thank you for remembering to love me so well and so consistently. You have a rare gift for friendship.

> *Yours,*
> *Leonard*

PS: *I find I am packing the things I love best, in case I never return.*

HRH KING EDWARD VII POSTAL STATIONERY

15 April 1911—Hôtel d'Anatolie, Brusa

A strange and important day. It may be because we are in the hometown of the Olympian gods, but things feel weighted here. Predestined, foretold.

Today I lost the ring Clive gave me when we became engaged.

We spent the day as usual: Roger and I painting on a hillside, and Clive and Harry kicking about looking for ruins. We sketched a Turkish man and his wife in a palette of dark oils against the bright backdrop of a sun-whitened wall. I painted the wife, and she and I were delighted with the dramatic result. The sweet couple asked us into their home for tea and invited us to rinse our hands in well water. I removed my rings, including the pretty French antique engagement ring, and put them in my lap. I forgot they were there, and when I stood, the engagement ring fell into the long, deep well. The couple were terribly distressed, and the man fetched a pane of glass to try to see into the dark water, but it was hopeless. The wife burst into noisy tears.

I tried to calm the distraught couple and told them that it was all right and they must be sure to remember me when it surfaces one day, but when the wife understood that it was my engagement ring, she could not be consoled. When I turned to find him, Clive had slipped away.

16 April 1911—Hôtel d'Anatolie, Brusa

We have become a subdued group since the business about the ring. Clive did not mention it again, and neither did I.

Later—seven p.m. (in my room)

Came to bed early with a sick headache and fever. Worried I ate something I oughtn't, but then the whole day has felt off.

18 April 1911—Hôtel d'Anatolie, Brusa

Ill. Dreadfully ill. Roger is here with me.

19 April 1911—Hôtel d'Anatolie, Brusa

Wretched. The doctor is coming.

TÉLÉGRAMME

OFFICE OF POSTAL DELIVERY

BRUSA, ANATOLIA
INTERNATIONAL CABLE

DEAREST VIRGINIA. STOP. VANESSA ILL. STOP. PLEASE COME TO BRUSA. STOP. NOT THREATENING BUT WOULD RATHER YOU WERE WITH US. STOP. ARRANGE THROUGH COOK'S. STOP. CABLE ARRIVAL DATE AND TIME. STOP. WILL MEET THE TRAIN. STOP. ALL LOVE CLIVE.

GBSW1H99075—RECIPIENT MUST SIGN UPON DELIVERY

20 April 1911—Hôtel d'Anatolie, Brusa (sunset)

It is still our hour to talk, but now we stay in while everyone goes out to see the sun set. Roger pulls his chair close to the bed. He twitches the sheet and straightens the blankets. I rewrap my dressing gown and smooth it tight. The tea grows cool in the cups. We do not want it. We do not bother. This is our hour alone.

Friday 21 April 1911—Hôtel d'Anatolie, Brusa

'London to Paris, Paris to Naples. Naples to Athens. And then the boat from Patras to Constantinople and the train on to Brusa,' Clive said, reading the cable. 'She will be here by Monday.'

'Yes,' I said, resigned. I felt I had the energy to speak to Clive only in few words. *Yes* was less complicated than *no*.

And then Roger gently shooed Clive from the room.

He can do that. It is audacious, but he does not mean it to be. It is just a truthful recognition that Clive is not handling my sickness well. When Thoby was ill, Clive swooped in like a bureaucratic angel, organising doctors and specialists and servants and patients. As my husband rather than my lover, he has lost that kind, firm touch. He has forgotten the specifics of me, of us. Instead, hamfisted and melodramatic, he overplays it, and Roger will not permit theatrics when I am so ill.

Roger has come into his own. He sits with me during the day and sleeps in a chair by the bed at night. Calm and generous, he has shepherded me through my discomfort. It was a fever, most likely brought on by the water or something I ate. Not a terrible fever but frightening for a family such as ours. We know what can come of a fever.

Roger rises to the moment. He meets the world so beautifully. Our talk runs unbroken, like a vein of water under the ground, punctuated by sleep and deep, comfortable silence. Level and dignified, he tells me of his wife. He tells me of the callus that refuses to grow over his love for her. He tells me of his brief, mistaken affair with Ottoline. I felt a thin white current of jealousy, but it subsided when I realised that the intimacy it took for him to tell me about their affair trumped the fleeting intimacy he had shared with her.

And he tells me how he loves me. The first time, he said it cleanly and with pride. He loves me. I see that now. He says he has known from the beginning. From the day on the train. 'It was in everything you did *not* say,' Roger said. 'It was in the way you listened. It was the way you occupied a room. The way you held the floor without knowing it. You overwhelmed me.' His is not a light, airborne love. It is anchored deeply, resting comfortably on the sea floor. 'It has only happened once before,' he said, gently sitting on the side of my bed.

Helen. There will always be Helen.

Later

We love but are not lovers. Moments appear, light-footed and indistinct, where we could manoeuvre into sex, but not yet. It is not time for that. I wait for his regret, his guilt, but it does not come. He is a man who always sees the good in things. And in his mind, love is always good.

REGRETFULLY YOURS

·⚜·

22 April 1911—Brusa

I asked Clive to cable and intercept Virginia. The English doctor says it is definitely not typhoid, but just a fever. He prescribed rest and toasted bread only. The local doctor also says it is a fever and prescribed rest and citrus fruit. It is agreed, I will recover. She does not need to come.

'But you *need* her to come. You need *family*, Nessa,' Clive said plaintively. I need to be nursed by someone other than Roger, he means. Clive looks at me differently. It's not the hungry, thwarted look from before we were married. But differently. It is a regretful, lost look. I have seen this look on Julian's face, when he puts down a toy and Quentin picks it up. That underestimation. Now that Roger loves me, Clive sees my value again. I am meaningful because I am loved by a man he respects. Carefully, gingerly, he plies me with affection. It is impersonal. It is too late.

ON A SWING

24 April 1911—Brusa

'Nessa!' Virginia called from the hallway.

She and Clive burst into my room. Roger rose to greet them. I watched Virginia do the sums in her head. She noticed everything: Roger's chair pulled close to the narrow bed, his reading glasses on the nightstand, his rumpled clothes and unslept-in cot in the corner, my flushed cheeks and blue silk nightgown. But she does not know Roger well enough to muster disdain. Instead, she began to flirt. It is her instinct. It is not the keen-bladed intellectual taunting she employs with Clive. Instead she softened with Roger and grew coy.

Clive watched, woolly and confused, from the doorway as Virginia fussed and deferred to Roger. Roger was not flattered, because he did not recognise what was happening. Things that do not matter to him are invisible.

Later

The tables have turned quickly. Virginia snaps at Clive. She seeks only Roger's attention. We all had supper on trays in my sickroom. Clive watched Virginia and me the way one watches a ship bearing loved ones pull away from the harbour. He seems to understand that it is over with them. I hope he understands that it is over with us.

Still later

They have all gone to look at the moon. Virginia was buoyant and elastic tonight when talking to anyone but Clive. This afternoon she told us about an evening she spent with Lytton last week. Leonard Woolf has taken ship from India and is on his way. Lytton has been dropping by Fitzroy Square to give Virginia daily bulletins. By today, he is packed. By today, he is in Colombo. Virginia finds Lytton's certainty endearing if a little strange.

'I feel like an Eastern bride who has been matchmaked. Is that a word?' she asked Roger, knowing of course that it isn't.

'Lytton is perceptive,' Roger said amiably. 'You may want to consider it.'

Tuesday 25 April 1911—Brusa

'Yes, see the mosaics,' I said. 'I will be fine.'

'Yes,' said Virginia, looking at Roger. 'I would hate to miss them.'

I did not point out that the last time we were here she refused to see them.

'Nessa?' Roger asked, leaving the final decision to me. Virginia watched, envious. Clive sat quietly, his face difficult to read.

'Go,' I said.

Later (six p.m.)

Virginia asked Roger to take her to see the sunset, and Clive came to see me.

'Fever staying down?' he asked officiously, shaking the thermometer.

'I just did it, honestly. There is no need to do it again,' I said.

Clive sat in Roger's chair. 'Virginia seems well,' he said flatly.

'Yes.'

'Nessa,' Clive said, gathering himself like a diver from a spring-board. 'Nessa, I would like us to try to have a real marriage again.'

'Clive—'

'Please, let me finish.' He stood and began to pace. He thinks better when he is in motion. 'I was careless and selfish, and I should have been happy with only you. I am sure I *could* be happy with only you.'

'Not Mrs Raven Hill?'

'Not Mrs Raven Hill.'

'And not Virginia?'

'There never was a Virginia, it turns out. It was you she loved. It is *always* you they love. I ought to have seen that,' Clive said, sitting heavily on the bed. 'Roger sees it.' When cornered, he chooses honesty. It is one of his best qualities.

'We have our beautiful boys,' I said. 'We have a happy life together. We have a modern marriage—just what you wanted.'

'Your answer is no, then?' Clive said, turning to it squarely.

'My answer is no.'

We sat together a long time, settling into the new silence of well-meaning friends.

27 April 1911—Brusa (early)

'Nessa?' Virginia said quietly, in case I was asleep.

'I am up,' I said, although I really wasn't. 'Where's Roger?'

My first question. The corners of Virginia's mouth swung together primly, like curtains at a play.

'Organising our visit to the river, I think. Do you need anything?' She stood and began fluffing pillows.

'Yes,' I said sharply. 'I need you to leave him alone.'

'Who?' She sat quickly in the chair. Rapt. 'Clive?' She was buying time.

'Roger,' I said, letting the name drift slowly to the ground between us.

'Dearest, I never . . .' Virginia laid her head on the bed, wanting to be petted.

'No, Virginia. Sit up.' I would not resume the foggy, affectionate animal habits until she understood. 'You have been flapping about all week trying to pander to him, to flirt with him, even though he is oblivious.'

'Nessa!'

'No, Virginia. You *ruin*. You ruin whatever you see coming between you and me. Roger is *not* my lover. He is my friend, but that hardly matters. We have a fragile, particular friendship, and you will destroy it if you can. As you destroyed my marriage. You cannot help yourself. You do not want something of your own. You want what is mine.'

'But I thought that it was all all right now,' Virginia said desperately.

'No, Virginia,' I said. 'You are my *sister*. It will never be all right.'

It will never be all right. I had not understood until that moment. An even tide rolls in with the certainty of fracture. The boat ripped to the keel. The anxiety over. The balance tipped. It can *never* be all right.

Monday 1 May 1911—Hotel Bristol, Constantinople

Train in an hour. We came back to Constantinople for two nights and are to take the Orient Express back to Paris this evening. Harry, Roger, Virginia, and Clive have gone to the bazaar to look for exotic fruit to bring back for the boys. I am parked in a deckchair on this sun-washed terrace overlooking the blue sea until they return. I do not mind. After the constant rumble and hum of travelling companions, it is luxurious to be alone. I am not waiting. I am not waiting for anyone any more. It was me I was waiting for.

Today I have the sensation of being on a swing, sailing high over the ground. Below, Roger is waiting to catch me in his warm, capable heart. Clive lounges against a tree and, if he thought he could, would snatch me from falling too far through the open air. Perhaps there are others waiting. Others watching.

But then, perhaps I do not need to be caught.

PART FIVE

THE BELLS AND
THE WOOLVES

..

1912

'Memory,' he often said,
'is an excellent compositor.'

(DESMOND MacCARTHY)

RESOLUTION

⁂

Opening day. The Second Post-Impressionist Exhibition.

Roger let me into the gallery. With long neat fingers, he traced the bones of my face, and, bending, kissed the soft patch below my ear, the spot he loves. And then he slipped away. He knew I wanted a moment alone. His deft understanding is my North Star.

Two rooms. My footsteps crack the velvet silence. *Nursery Tea* is bearing up well in a room full of Matisses, Picassos, Braques, and Cézannes. I worried she would look provincial and domestic in this company, but just as Roger insisted, I was wrong. She is holding her own. I close my eyes and say goodbye. I wish her well. In three hours she will no longer belong to me. Her brushstrokes will grow unfamiliar, and our history will be wiped clean. She will start fresh. That is what happens when a painting puts on her boots to meet the world. Duncan tried to explain that loss to me long ago.

Duncan's jagged poster hangs in the window, announcing the exhibition. I have the early sketches he made for the design. Roger brought them over last week, folded and crumpled in his pocket. I smoothed them out under some heavy books. Clive wants to frame them.

Three hours. And then the crowds will come. They will be more prepared now. Last time they were taken wholly unawares by Cézanne's stark mountains and Gauguin's plush Tahitians. They were too startled to be urbane. They will try not to make the same mistake twice, but Roger thinks that Picasso's cubist *Girl with a Mandolin* alone will stump up plenty of fresh outrage. I do not want to see that. The red faces and meaty fists. Roger can describe it to me later when we are alone.

In three hours, Virginia will be the first through the door. Leonard has been Roger's secretary for the exhibition, and since last spring Leonard and Virginia do everything together. The Bells and the Woolves. There is a lovely symmetry in four. Before Virginia and Leonard married two months ago in a poky room at St Pancras registry office, I could not quite see it. They seemed mismatched, like odd socks. Bound together by decision rather than affection. Leonard is so inflexibly good, so direct, so sincere, and so grave. Virginia's wit frothed around him like a party dress.

The wedding day bulged with thunder and split wide with lightning. The sheeting rain washed the greasy pavement clean. Clive, soaked with misery at losing both Stephen sisters, hardly looked up from the salmon carpet as I sat with Julian and Quentin and watched the bride and bridegroom. Dear Leonard wore a sun-faded suit, as he could not afford to buy another, and Virginia spoke her vows in a voice too low to be heard over the storm. She stood willow-stripling straight, and hawkish Leonard curved towards her like a moon. All her life Virginia has been in terrible motion, as if she runs on the belief that there is always a better place to be. She charms and sparkles and binds us to her on her way, but she does not slow her pace. But standing beside Leonard, she gathered in one level grassy place, and I watched him tense with the lean, sharp hope that she would stay.

Now I see it. He moors her. He is Virginia's to the bone. And someone needs to be Virginia's. Perhaps it will change us. Perhaps she will grow safe, and I will grow trusting. Or perhaps we will go on as we are: Leonard will wait for Virginia, and Virginia will wait for me.

I breathe in the freshly dusted room, the bold paintings, and the clear lights. The bell rings, the gallery door opens. Roger is back. I will stay to watch the first wave of people break over the gallery floor, and then I will leave.

'Ready?' he asks gently, careful not to disrupt the cathedral air around us.

'Ready.' I love being an artist today.

5 December 1912

Dearest Ginia,

Now Quentin has caught Julian's cold, and so I do not think we will be able to come down after all. Shepherding one drippy, runny child to Sussex is a challenge, but two is impossible.

Yes. You are the woman in the painting. I can see you are different. I can see you are changed. Your happiness makes you supple and warm.

But you are on the far bank, Virginia. I am replanted in different earth now. Look for me. I will be watching you from here. You are my sister, and in that we are twinned always. But to begin again? No, Virginia. There can be no beginning again. The problem was never in the beginnings, but in the ends. It is the ends that are always the same.

Vanessa

AUTHOR'S NOTE

ADRIAN STEPHEN

In 1914, Adrian married Karin Costelloe, a fellow of Newnham College, Cambridge. When military conscription was introduced to England in 1916, the couple became conscientious objectors and spent World War I working on a dairy farm in Essex. After the war, Adrian pursued a medical degree and went on to become one of England's first psychoanalysts. During World War II, Adrian renounced his pacifist views and volunteered as an army doctor at the age of sixty. He died in 1948.

OTTOLINE MORRELL

At the outbreak of World War I, Ottoline and Philip Morrell declared themselves to be conscientious objectors and invited fellow pacifists Duncan Grant, Clive Bell, and Lytton Strachey to live with them at Garsington, their country house in Oxfordshire, for the duration of the war. The Morrells maintained their harmonious open marriage until Ottoline's death in 1938. Her lovers included Dora Carrington and Bertrand Russell. She continued to support artists and writers to the end of her life, among them Mark Gertler, Aldous Huxley, T. S. Eliot, and Siegfried Sassoon.

DESMOND MacCARTHY AND SAXON SYDNEY-TURNER

During World War I, Desmond MacCarthy worked in naval intelligence. After the war he returned to journalism, writing a weekly column under the name 'The Affable Hawk'. In 1920 he became the literary editor of the *New Statesman* and eventually went on to become the literary critic for *The Sunday Times*. He never finished his novel. Saxon Sydney-Turner never married and never left the Treasury Office.

MAYNARD KEYNES AND E. M. FORSTER

Maynard Keynes went on to marry Lydia Lopokova, a ballerina from the Ballets Russes. He became arguably the most important economist of the twentieth century. E.M. Forster published five novels and then stopped writing fiction at the age of forty-five. He lived for another forty-six years, publishing non-fiction. His sixth novel, *Maurice*, was written in 1913 but was not released until 1971, a year after his death. It tells a story of homosexual love in the early twentieth century.

ROGER FRY

Vanessa Bell and Roger Fry became lovers in 1911. She did exhibit her work at his Second Post-Impressionist Exhibition in 1912. Their affair continued until the end of 1913, when Vanessa transferred her romantic affection to Duncan Grant. Roger Fry was heartbroken, and letters written years after the affair speak clearly of his profound attachment, yet he and Vanessa remained dear friends. He was close to her children and often a guest at Charleston, her home in Sussex.

Helen Fry was never released from the mental hospital. After her death in 1937, it was discovered that her insanity was caused by an irreversible thickening of the skull. Roger wrote to her every week for the rest of his life.

When Roger Fry died, after a fall in 1934, his ashes were buried at King's College Chapel, Cambridge, in a casket designed by Vanessa Bell.

CLIVE BELL

Clive and Vanessa Bell never divorced. In 1919, when Vanessa gave birth to her third child, Angelica, by Duncan Grant, Clive claimed the child as his own. Clive had a string of relationships for the remainder of his life, most notably with the writer Mary Hutchinson.

In 1914 Clive Bell published *Art*, developing the theory of significant form and earning a reputation as an influential art critic and theorist.

The Bells' elder son, Julian, named for Thoby, became a writer and poet and served as an ambulance driver in the Spanish Civil War. He was killed in 1937 at the age of twenty-nine. Quentin Bell became an artist and author. He wrote several books about the Bloomsbury Group, the most well known of which is a biography of his Aunt Virginia.

LYTTON STRACHEY

During World War I, Lytton Strachey applied to be a conscientious objector but was exempted from military service on health grounds. He spent most of the war at Garsington, Lady Ottoline Morrell's country home.

In 1918 Strachey published *Eminent Victorians*. It was an immediate success, and his career as a biographer was established.

In 1917 the young painter Dora Carrington fell deeply in love with Strachey. She and her husband, Ralph Partridge, lived in a romantic partnership with Lytton at Ham Spray House in Wiltshire. Lytton died of undiagnosed stomach cancer in 1932. Dora Carrington committed suicide two months later.

VIRGINIA AND LEONARD WOOLF

Lytton Strachey did begin suggesting that Leonard Woolf marry Virginia Stephen as early as the spring of 1909. Leonard Woolf and Virginia Stephen became engaged in the summer of 1912 and married that August. Like Vanessa, Virginia refused two proposals before she said yes.

Virginia Woolf published her first novel, *The Voyage Out*, in March 1915. The same year, she and Leonard moved to Hogarth House in Richmond and later founded the Hogarth Press, which published all of Virginia Woolf's subsequent novels, each with a cover designed by Vanessa Bell.

When Virginia committed suicide in 1941, she left two letters, one for Vanessa and one for Leonard. She wrote to Leonard, 'I don't think two people could have been happier than we have been.'

VANESSA BELL

Vanessa Bell and Duncan Grant lived in a partnership defined by painting and friendship until her death in April 1961. They moved between various houses in Bloomsbury and Charleston, her farmhouse in Sussex. Virginia and Leonard Woolf settled at Monk's House in nearby Rodmell.

Vanessa Bell never forgave her sister for the liaison with Clive. Years later her daughter, Angelica, remembers the wariness with which her mother treated her Aunt Virginia. And from Virginia, Angelica always sensed 'a desperate plea for forgiveness'.

Vanessa Bell's paintings now hang in museums all over the world.

·

It is not easy to fictionalise the Bloomsbury Group, as their lives are so well documented. They were prolific correspondents and diarists, and there is a wealth of existing primary material. For me the difficulty came in finding enough room for invention in the negative spaces they left behind. The characters in the novel are very much fictional creations. The broad external chronologies and events are as accurate as possible, with the exception of a few small adjustments and alterations I made to better tell the story.

Vanessa and Clive's second child was initially named Gratian and then for a period of time was renamed Claudian before he was ultimately called Quentin some time after his first birthday. I call him Quentin for the sake of clarity. Many of Vanessa Bell's early paintings were destroyed in a fire at her studio. Apart from *Nursery Tea*, *Studland Beach*, *Iceland Poppies*, the sketches of Julian, and the portraits of Virginia, the paintings I describe are fictional but are based on descriptions in her many letters, and are subjects and themes she would return to in her work throughout her life. The internal landscapes of the characters are completely imagined and Vanessa Bell never kept a diary.

Many of the unlikelier details in the novel are rooted in fact. Virginia did appal her family by requesting a valuable table from Violet. Virginia also did write to Violet for weeks after Thoby died, outlining the various stages of his fictional recovery. Violet did in fact learn of Thoby's death from the newspaper. Virginia, Duncan, and Adrian did dress up as the entourage of the Emperor of Abyssinia and tour the *Dreadnought*. Vanessa did lose her engagement ring down a well just before she began an affair with Roger Fry.

The choreography of the complicated romantic lives of the characters as much as possible follows the historical template. And remarkably, within the group, they all remained close friends. Duncan did have love affairs with Lytton, Maynard, Adrian, and finally Vanessa. Maynard and Lytton also had an early affair. Roger and Ottoline had a brief liaison just before he left for Constantinople. Clive did rekindle his affair with Mrs Raven Hill and simultaneously pursue his sister-in-law in the same year. And Vanessa wrote amicably to Clive in 1909 and cheerfully referred to Mrs Raven Hill as 'your whore'. Virginia and Clive did write suggestive, flirtatious letters alluding to their affair for several years after the family trip to Cornwall in 1908. Judging from their letters, it is likely that, although Clive clearly would have preferred it otherwise, the affair remained platonic.

I took one important detour from recorded history with the argument between Vanessa and Virginia over the affair with Clive. We do not know whether it was ever mentioned between them, and Vanessa never referred to the liaison in her letters. However, in 1925, Virginia Woolf wrote, 'My affair with Clive and Nessa turned more of a knife in me than anything else has ever done.'

ACKNOWLEDGEMENTS

I would like to particularly thank:

Kaleem Aftab, Olivier Bell, Sarah Blake, Dr Sarah Carpenter, Claude Christian, Judy Clain, Darren Clarke, Sophie Deveson, Eve Ensler, Sarah Hall, Emma Healey, Lisa Highton, Nancy Horan, Howie Kahn, Anthony Mason, Jainee McCarroll, Paula McLain, Naomi Nicholson, Sharon Kay Penman, Matt Pycha, Katy Raffin, Tamar Rydzinski, Dr Roger Savage, Helen Simonson, Noah Sher, Dr Olga Taxidou, and, especially, Trish Todd, who made everything happen.

Virginia Nicholson for her invaluable help and kindness. For taking me to Charleston and sharing her Bloomsbury memories. For being so gracious, supportive, and lovely.

My extraordinary agent, Stephanie Cabot, who has made this book so happy. Rebecca Gardner, Anna Worrall, Ellen Goodson, and everyone at the Gernert Company.

Susanna Porter, my magical editor who, with huge perception and unfailing sensitivity, found the story inside the manuscript. And Priyanka Krishnan for helping me at every turn.

Barbara Bachman, Gina Centrello, Susan Corcoran, Kristin Fassler, Jennifer Garza, Jennifer Hershey, Kim Hovey, Vincent La Scala, Libby Maguire, Nicole Morano, Quinne Rogers, Robbin Schiff, and everyone at Ballantine/Random House who have taken such beautiful care of this book.

Helen Garnons Williams for her deft, kind wisdom and humour, Ros Ellis, Elizabeth Woabank, Lynsey Sutherland, Oliver Holden-Rea, and everyone at Bloomsbury UK for their wonderful care.

Kristin Cochrane for her brilliant notes and fantastic support, Adria Iwasutiak, Zoe Maslow, Louise Dennys, Brad Martin, and everyone at Random House Canada who have given this book such a happy home there.

The staffs of Charleston, British Museum, National Portrait Gallery, University of Sussex Library and Tate Britain who have been so helpful and kind.

And thank you to my dear friends who have rooted for me all along.

In London: Dan, Ewen, Jamie, Burt, Harriet, Charlotte, Alec, Ben, Sophie, Max, Minnie, Alex, Katie, Oliver, Kate, Tim, and Sam. And especially Sadie, Katy, Adriana, Simon, Felix, Jack, Jessica, Poppy, and my godchildren, Louis and Logan. You make London home.

In Hawaii: the beloved Smarts, Tora and Kirk; Denise, Ash, and Cliff; Lisa and David; Rebeckah, Sally, Carolyn and David Moore; Melissa and Neal; Denise T., David, Jane, Michelle, and Megan; Chris and Koah; Matt and Naomi; the dearest Garfinkles: Terri and Benjy; and Matt and Angela for thirty years of friendship. Wendy and Chad for being my family.

And the kids who are no longer kids. For the years and the flowers and the song and for making everything mean more. Amber, Chloe, Eli, Koa, Leila, Max, and Wyatt.

Philippa Gregory. For her astonishing, unwavering kindness and bolstering wisdom. For her rare, true friendship.

And to my family: my stepdaughters, Madison and Ava, my nephew Wyatt, my new siblings, Meredith and J.D., and to my brother and sister, Nicky and Tina, who are my watermarks—for a million things every day, thank you.

To my mother, who read every draft, and my father, who believed in me. You both are woven into every word I will ever write. I love you.

And with all my love to Brennon. For being my home.

CREDITS

The author and the publishers acknowledge the following permissions to reprint copyright material:

Extract appearing on page 1 from *Selected Letters of Vanessa Bell* edited by Regina Marler, Copyright © Regina Marler, 1993. Reprinted by permission of the author

Extract appearing on page 81 from *Virginia Woolf Vol. I* by Virginia Woolf. Published by The Hogarth Press. Reprinted by permission of The Random House Group Ltd. Extract reproduced in the eBook courtesy of The Society of Authors as the Literary Representative of the Estate of Virginia Woolf

Artwork appearing on page 83 based on the original letterhead of the New Willard Hotel. Reprinted by permission of the Willard Hotel

Artwork appearing on pages 88 and 212 based on original invoices from Winsor and Newton Ltd. Reprinted by permission of Winsor and Newton

Extract appearing on page 159 from *A Room With a View* by E. M. Forster. Reprinted by permission of The Provost and Scholars of King's College, Cambridge and The Society of Authors as the E. M. Forster Estate

Extract appearing on page 249 from *The Letters of Lytton Strachey* edited by Paul Levy, assisted by Penelope Marcus, Copyright © The

A NOTE ON THE AUTHOR

Priya Parmar is the author of one previous novel, *Exit the Actress*.
She lives in London and Hawaii.

priyaparmar.blogspot.co.uk

A NOTE ON THE TYPE

This book was set in Sabon, a typeface designed by the well-known German typographer Jan Tschichold (1902–74). Sabon's design is based upon the original letterforms of the sixteenth-century French type designer Claude Garamond and was created specifically to be used for three sources: foundry type for hand composition, Linotype and Monotype. Tschichold named his typeface for the famous Frankfurt typefounder Jacques Sabon (c. 1520–80).